CHAPTER ONE

The Ladies Get an Idea

"*I* think we might do it."

Those ringing words launched what the world now knows as the Larksdale Ladies. Granted, they may not have the deathless beauty of "Give me liberty, or give me death," or "Remember Pearl Harbor," or even "I Want My MTV!" They may not make you want to jump atop a pileup in the middle of a Broadway stage, wave a twelve-foot-tall French flag, and sing "La Marseillaise" at the top of your lungs. They may not even make you want to finish this chapter.

But consider the context.

The Larksdale Ladies Independence Club—formerly the Mostly Methodist Club—was the product of a group of ladies who (except for Deborah, the ex-marine) had never done a *single* adventurous thing.

My mother, I suppose, was typical. The most romantic thing she ever accomplished in her life was to name me Sophia, with a long "i," like a heroine in an old novel. After doing that (at age nineteen), she dropped out of college and spent the next twenty-four years as a housewife. Before that? *Nada*. Not even marrying my dad. *Especially* not marrying my dad. That was another gesture for me—or rather, for the me shortly to arrive, the unfortunate result of a tussle with my (future) father in the backseat of a '61 Chevy Malibu. If you call that a romantic setting, you probably don't know much about Chevys.

But I'm getting off the subject.

$\mathcal{I}$ wasn't actually there for the first weeks of the Larksdale Ladies' Club, the weeks my mother always referred to as "the time we spent finding our way," and which Skye Terrell far more frankly called, "Six weeks of listening to know-nothing men shoot their mouths off."

But my mom, bless her, was always a faithful letter writer, who sent me summaries of every meeting. Besides, I was only in Chicago (for my second year of law school), and my social life wasn't so exciting that I didn't find time to spend most holidays in Larksdale. I kept up with things. Trust me. This is how it happened.

$\mathcal{G}$ladys was late.

Within a few minutes of nine o'clock that Saturday morning, six of the other members of the Mostly Methodist Club had stepped across the threshold and into Martha Crittenden's elegant-but-fading foyer. Then they had stamped their feet against the outdoor cold, shown Martha their snack offerings, and hung their coats (which still smelled of summer mothballs) in the foyer closet.

It was mid-October, maybe the loveliest time of the year in Minnesota, when the apples hang sweet and crisp on the trees, and the air is cool, clean, and invigorating—it turns cheeks red, not purplish blue. Halloween decorations appear, monster amusements in black and orange, except in those houses where Halloween is shunned as Satan's own holiday. Even in the most spiritually firm households, the mood is growing festive and fragrant after a humid summer of mosquitoes, heat, and television reruns.

The Mostly Methodist Club met Saturday morning year-round,

Ladies with Options

CYNTHIA HARTWICK

BERKLEY BOOKS, NEW YORK

A Berkley Book
Published by The Berkley Publishing Group
A division of Penguin Putnam Inc.
375 Hudson Street
New York, New York 10014

This is an original publication of The Berkley Publishing Group.

PRINTING HISTORY
Berkley trade paperback edition / February 2001

The Penguin Putnam Inc. World Wide Web site address is
http://www.penguinputnam.com

Library of Congress Cataloging-in-Publication Data

Hartwick, Cynthia.
Ladies with options / Cynthia Hartwick.
p. cm
ISBN 0-425-17823-4
1. Women—Societies and clubs—Fiction.   2. Women—Finance,
Personal—Fiction.   3. Investment clubs—Fiction.   4. Investments—
Fiction.   5. Minnesota—Fiction.   I. Title.

PS3558.A71555 L33 2001
813'.6—dc21
00-050732

PRINTED IN THE UNITED STATES OF AMERICA

10   9   8   7   6

For DAN, whose idea it was in the first place

Ladies with Options

Cynthia Hartwick

INTRODUCTION

Fair Warning

by Sophia Peters, J.D.

Dear Reader:

If you picked up this book looking for one of those bikini-ripping sagas about jet-setting beauties whose lean, tanned, half-naked bodies quiver with desire as they plunge into affair after affair the way Esther Williams used to plunge into swimming pools—forget it. Except for the gorgeous Heidi, whose smallest gesture had grown men biting their palms and howling at the moon, the Larksdale Ladies were mostly a bunch of decent, ordinary women of various ages and middle-class backgrounds.

On the other hand . . .

By the end of the day, the ladies could certainly afford the jets, and as for affairs—well, you'll see. And while there isn't *much* gunplay, guns certainly *did* get pulled, both literally and figuratively. Scandal, we had—and hid. Suntans? Get real. This was Minnesota.

Nor is this, mainly, a racing tale of financial skulduggery. The ladies mostly made their money the old-fashioned way: they found new companies run by brilliant, hardworking people and bought their stock cheap—then quickly sold most of it to other people for a lot more money, and went out looking for *more* great ideas to buy into. Do that over and over, without getting too fancy, and pretty soon you'll have more money than Scrooge McDuck. Which was basically what happened, although I admit the Ladies were often—ahem!—quite *inventive* in the ways they came by their information.

Lastly, this isn't a book of financial tips. For those you can get yourself *The Larksdale Ladies' Independence Secrets, Business the Larksdale Way,* or any of the other tomes that Deborah and Martha are cranking out in yet another moneymaking sideline.

This is just a story about the Ladies themselves.

They could be annoying, wacko, devious, and frustrating. Often I kept them out of jail, and once I kept one of them out of the loony bin. Still, they were my friends and family.

I liked them, I respected them, and—nine days out of ten—I was very proud of them.

So hang on to your hat. Here we go.

but was at its best in autumn and winter, when it helped steel the ladies for the Sundays their men spent watching TV sports with eyes glazed like so many holiday hams.

This Saturday morning—the first in months when thin ice covered car windows—the ladies bore plump droplets of what would become, over the next ten weeks, a deluge of holiday baking.

Just at the stroke of nine, my mom, Lizzy Peters, arrived, prompt as always and carrying a very healthy and sensible pumpkin loaf. Mom and Martha were polite with each other, not warm, and conversation might have lagged. After all, Martha, at sixty-two, was a full generation older than my mother. Moreover, she came from a much wealthier, more upper-class background. Martha was Brooke Astor and the Ritz; my mom was strictly Betty Crocker.

But Mom had no sooner hung up her coat than the doorbell rang, and three coffee cakes appeared on the doorstep. That is, three members *bearing* coffee cakes—one cinnamon, one lemon, and one pecan crunch.

Dolly Suckling bore the largest cake. Blond, tall, and solid, Dolly had gone to high school with my mom, but then had made what everyone called an unfortunate marriage. Now she was a housewife living in the bad part of town and a part-time shopper for Dayton's in what she called the "portly porkers" division. Ever since I was a little girl, though, I'd imagined her singing opera with one of those hats-with-horns on her head and a spear in her hand. She was Valkyrie large and impressive. Just stepping inside and handing Martha the overflowing pecan-crunch platter, Dolly filled the foyer.

After her came Deborah Cohen, who was the "mostly" in the Mostly Methodist Club. Deborah was also the lone exception to what I said about none of the ladies ever having had an adventure. At twenty-two, Deborah had joined the marines, just after they had declared they wanted women, but well before they had figured out what to do with them.

In boot camp in some Carolina swamp, Deborah won two medals for marksmanship and the company championship for pugilstick fighting. As a reward, they made her a clerk at headquarters. As she put it, "For me, the chorus to the corps' *Hymn* began, 'First to *type* for right and freedom.' "

After three years defending the Republic with Wite-Out and carbon paper, Deborah came home and opened Larksdale's third beauty parlor. Over the next few years, it had never exactly prospered but had held its own, and Deborah was the MMC's only entrepreneur, as well as by far its most outspoken member. The cinnamon coffee cake she brought dripped gooey chocolate from its edges. Everything Deborah made had chocolate in it. She was hyperkinetic and could eat whatever she wanted—my worst nightmare.

Behind Dolly and Deborah, and a step below them, stood Agnes Jane Brinkley, as ever shy, heavy-footed, and reluctant. In her flower-print dresses and round glasses, Agnes reminded me of the comic strip "Cathy"—except that Agnes's concerns never seemed quite so adult.

Agnes was Larksdale's children's librarian, a job that suited her almost too well. Something about Agnes seemed never to have grown up. More exactly, she was one of those women who look at once younger and older than they are: she dressed very young, almost girlishly; but she had the timidity of a very shy sixty-year-old. She had youth's imagination without its energy.

It wasn't physical. Agnes was at least five-foot-eight and slightly plump. Nor was it intellectual. She was bright and good at her job. It was emotional. An adult who works eight hours a day with children ought to find it annoying sometimes; but Agnes never did. Adults more often seemed to annoy her. That was it. Agnes liked her job too much and carried it with her. She was like a human LEGO display—lovable but provoking.

When she was sure she would be in no one else's way, Agnes stepped inside and handed Martha a small, neat lemon coffee cake with white frosting curlicues. Then she bent down and picked up a medium-sized, smooth-skinned pumpkin. "For you to carve later," she said sweetly as she offered it to Martha.

Martha thanked her, almost as sweetly—though we may safely assume that Martha Crittenden would carve a pumpkin about the time Barbara Bush dyed her hair pink and took up bungee jumping. Martha was strictly old money (most of it, admittedly, long gone). She was all good manners and chilly reserve; pastel sweaters and neat strands of pearls.

But speaking of pink hair . . .

These five friends were all clustered together like grapes in Martha's foyer because Mary Maitland had warned them she was bringing a guest, a young woman who had been in trouble with the law.

This very interesting young creature had, it seemed, been arrested at the University of Minnesota for reducing her ex-boyfriend's dorm room to a pile of rubbish, and then scrawling DEATH TO PIGS on his windows. Now, as part of an experimental program, she had been released on probation to the care of the ladies of the First Methodist Church—which meant, as a practical matter, to the MMC.

Mary had specifically warned them that this young creature was sensitive and delicate, and that they must not, by word or deed, make her feel uneasy. Of course, trashing a dorm room (or, for that matter, in any way standing up to men) was hot stuff for the Larksdale Ladies—but they were at least as decent as they were curious, and they were determined to treat their young guest with just exactly ordinary courtesy. No more—no less. They could hardly wait to start.

And there in the foyer they stood energetically *not* talking about the young creature, until after two or three minutes they began to feel ridiculous, and were just turning toward the living room when the doorbell rang again.

A stir of excitement overwhelmed them; this was the reason

they had forgotten poor Gladys, who was already half an hour late.

They exchanged wild looks, then Martha threw open the door, and Mary led in her young ward, whose name was Skye Terrell, and who was small, pale, and extremely pretty. Indeed, she was just as Mary had described her, except for small details.

Like her wearing black jeans, a black turtleneck, and an army jacket three sizes too big for her.

Mary had also forgotten to mention Skye's delicate pink hair—which was not something generally overlooked in Minnesota in 1983. In fact, Skye's hair, and Martha's sweater, were a perfect match.

Still, Martha—who really did have fine manners and good values, for all that she scared the hell out of people like me—ushered them in politely, while the rest of the ladies reacted with not quite that high level of Minnesotan sang froid they might have wished. Dolly's jaw dropped; Agnes covered her mouth with her flattened hand; my mother gasped—and all this before Martha had the door closed behind Mary and the interesting young woman.

The ladies, though, were rallying, and likely would have managed the necessary number of polite, empty remarks, had not Deborah, arriving late from the living room, stolen a march on them by asking, very loudly, "Holy Cripes! What's with the hair!?" When everyone had turned to her, Deborah added, directly to Skye, "I mean, what's the plan, kid? You gonna sneak into the state fair disguised as cotton candy?" And then, to her outraged fellow members, she added, "*What?* You didn't notice?"

Somehow they made it into the living room.

Skye dragged behind, moving only reluctantly. Mary kept her company; given their identical pale blue eyes, and how fine Skye's hair was, it might have been possible to imagine Skye was Mary's daughter. Probably Mary didn't mind the illusion, since she and Mike were, unwillingly, childless.

Once they reached the living room, the ladies crowded about Skye, talking pointedly about everything in the world. Rapidly, awkwardly, they covered all the great safe subjects—the weather, the new café in town, the latest movies (except for Clint Eastwood and other crime stories).

It was a display of almost maternal affection, and Skye in return treated them as if she was their own daughter. That is, she absolutely ignored them, except for a variety of facial expressions which seemed to say she'd rather be dead than be seen in public with them.

After about two minutes of trying, the ladies gave up. Leaving Martha and my mom to try to talk with her, they drifted across the room to arrange their plastic-wrapped offerings artistically around the big silver coffee urn on Martha's fine old cherrywood side table.

That done, they eyed each other in hungry uncertainty. Traditionally the food was not served until everyone arrived. The pastries would have to sit there, wrapped and awaiting Gladys. Or so it seemed until about ten seconds later.

Deborah said, "Oh, good. Coffee and plastic wrap. My favorites," and without further ceremony pulled off all the wrappings, dumped them in the wastepaper basket, and loaded her plate with pumpkin bread, coffee cake, and the rest. Then, before starting to eat, she was suddenly moved by some impulse of compassion, and called loudly across the room—

"Hey, *stick girl*! Come eat something. You look like hell."

This was unfair. Out of her Russian paratrooper's winter coat, Skye was lithe and fit, but not scrawny.

And yet, oddly, Skye went to join Deborah at the side table. Deborah watched her silently until she had put cake on her plate. Then, nodding, and taking her own plate, she went to stand by the window to look for Gladys.

That left the strange little creature turning about uncertainly, and then, finally, slipping away from the others, heading toward the dimmest corner of the room—where, as it happened, my mom was sitting, trying to figure her out. She approached quite close before she noticed Mom seated in a corner chair, half-hidden by a dark green plant of Martha's which was the size of a young tree.

Skye was startled, and her expression, Mom told me later, seemed "both scowling and timid, like an angry sea otter."

Like most mothers, mine had dealt with her share of unhappy young people. With her usual practical sympathy, she said simply, "I bet it's really terrible having us all stare at you."

Whether or not this would have made any significant impression would be hard to say. Before Skye could answer, Deborah, who was still at the window, noticed motion outside.

It was Gladys Vaniman, sprinting from the bus stop to the middle of the block, and up the steps of Martha's big, slightly tattered home. Deborah set down her plate and hurried around to let her in.

The two women returned in a few seconds. Gladys, who at fifty-seven normally had something of the energetic frailness of, say, Miss Marple, now looked truly weak and badly flustered; solid Deborah was hovering, stutter-stepping to stay behind her, and looking uncertain whether she should offer a hand for support.

"Where were you?" Martha asked.

But Agnes studied her friend more closely and said decisively, "You look sick."

"I need to sit down," Gladys replied. And, gulping a big breath, she plopped herself into a chair.

CHAPTER TWO

The Bad News from Gladys

Gladys eyed them uneasily for a moment, looked down at her coffee, and began. "I read in last week's *Forbes*"—Gladys in those days always gave a reference for whatever she said, as if nobody would value her opinions otherwise—"that most Americans are setting themselves up for an impoverished retirement. So I checked. And I found out that if I work another eight years and retire, I'll have to get by on my pension and savings. Do you know how much? I would have one hundred and eighty-two dollars a month from the Minnesota Librarians' Pension Fund and two hundred and forty-one dollars a month from Social Security."

She paused to catch her breath, and then concluded, "So I'm supposed to live all through my retirement years on eight thousand in savings and four hundred twenty-three dollars a month in income. And that's assuming that nobody decides we're overstaffed and fires me beforehand. Yes, I feel sick."

It was as if a chill wind had somehow swept down from Canada and swirled through the room. This sense of their own financial mortality hit the Ladies hard—they didn't need any newspapers to understand the realities of the world economy. Not, heaven knows, that they were very savvy about economics or business.

In the Midwest in 1983, you couldn't turn on a TV without

hearing about another big plant shutting down, locking out, or moving overseas. America was discovering a world economy that bore a strange resemblance to King Kong. The whole country had figured out we weren't in Kansas anymore.

Pundits said the country was going through a healthy restructuring, that tearing down old plants and industries was the first step to building new ones. Maybe it really looked that way to them, sitting in good restaurants in New York or D.C. To us in small towns it looked like padlocked plants and unemployment lines, and in Larksdale in 1983 it felt like sitting in some medieval town, waiting for the Black Plague to strike.

"*A*re you sure that's right?" asked Mary. Forty and attractive in a used-to-be-a-cheerleader way, Mary wasn't so much an optimist as someone inclined to look away from bad news.

"If Gladys checked it, it's right," Agnes asserted, with both friendship and stalwart librarian solidarity.

"Well, even if the numbers are right, the principle of it is *terrible*. How can something like that happen?" Dolly Suckling, who looked so big and powerful, was actually the tenderest—and nearly the most timid—soul in the bunch.

"Hey!" Deborah demanded with her usual bluntness. "Look around you. You see any sign of anybody looking out for anybody else—especially those clowns in Washington?"

This kind of talk went on for about twenty minutes, before trailing away into a short, discouraged silence. Before the silence grew hopeless, though, Mary suddenly said, very firmly, "We really should do something about it."

For Mary, with her fresh-scrubbed perkiness, to say something this definite was utterly unexpected—as if Mary Poppins had stood up and yelled, "Somebody get a rope!" Mary's voice had so much authority that the cries of surprise were choked off before they began, so that everyone heard clearly when my mother asked, "Like what?"

"Like, well . . . like taking charge of things."

Nobody replied to this—and Mary, as if a door had suddenly given way, fell forward.

"I mean," she went on, stumblingly, "we all have at least a little money saved up. Mine's just sitting in the bank, and after taxes it's not doing any better than inflation. Can't we find some—you know—investments? Stocks or something? I mean, if men can do it, we can do it." She paused. "After all, it's not magic. All we need is information."

Mary had invented the project, and she intended to look after it. "I mean, suppose we each agreed to put up, say, fifteen hundred dollars, to create an investment fund? Eight"—with automatic courtesy, she included Skye in the calculation—"times fifteen hundred is, um, twelve thousand dollars. Wouldn't people come talk to us if we had that much to invest? Especially if they knew we were going to be saving for the long term?"

Mary's voice had a hint of pleading, but not much. Her willpower had not yet quite hardened like cement, but it was making progress. She eyed the others challengingly.

Dolly asked nervously, "What about those of us who are married?"

"What *about* you?"

"Well, what if our husbands don't like the idea?" Dolly was still big and blond and solid—I still could imagine her belting out Wagner. But the truth was that she became very small and timid when anything involving her husband arose. Buzz was huge and rough, with a reputation for drinking—it was easy to see how he could frighten someone.

But no one frightened Deborah.

"Oh, just put dinner on the table and beer in the fridge, and they'll never think to ask." Deborah said this rather cavalierly—

she'd never been married—but it seemed to strike a chord. Everyone nodded, though Gladys and Agnes both looked rather pale.

Mary turned to Martha and asked, "You know a lot about investing, Martha. Couldn't you organize us?"

This was overstating things just a little. To be blunt, Martha was the only one of them who'd ever had an investment more sophisticated than a Christmas Club savings account. Her ex-husband, the unlamented Doc Crittenden, had left her the home, plus some annuities, when he ran off with his nurse, the blond and curvaceous former Miss Minnesota Dilled Herring of 1978.

Everyone looked to Martha. "Yes," she said pretty confidently, "I think I could do that." Uncharacteristically she looked back to the others inquiringly. Usually Martha considered herself a majority of one; but somehow they all knew this was a very big decision. "Are we all agreed to risk it, then?"

Ideas have momentum, and every objection, even if it's overcome, soaks up a little of the energy. Something had gone out of the room; and without saying a word, they all knew it. Women who had spent their lives keeping things smooth were not quite ready to rock the boat. Nobody jumped up, guy-fashion, to pound the table and yell, "Yeah! Let's do it!"

Instead, there was silence, and the idea seemed to be dying, until Deborah said, quite loudly, "I know a joke."

They turned to look at her. She tried to look like she was telling a funny story.

"Guy goes into an empty syna . . . a church, and he's desperate. He throws himself down on the ground and he cries out, 'Oh, God! My business is in trouble, my kid's sick, my wife's upset! Help me out! Let me win the Lotto!' Week goes by, and the guy's back. Throws himself down, yells, 'Oh, God! I'm a good man. I begged you! Now my kid's worse, my business is broke, and my wife's threatening to leave me! *Please!* Let me win the Lotto!' Another week. Guy shows up in torn clothes, throws himself down, cries out, 'Oh, *God*! My kid's dying, my creditors are suing me, and my wife's left. Why have you forsaken me? Why won't you let me win the Lotto!?' Suddenly the heavens open up, there's a blinding flash of light and the smell of incense, and he hears God's voice. And God says, 'Maury! Meet me halfway. Buy a ticket!' "

Deborah stopped talking like a God from Brooklyn. In her own voice, she finished up with, "What do you say? Let's buy that ticket."

She eyed them levelly, and only a few seconds passed before Gladys said, "Absolutely."

Dolly drew a deep breath and said, "I'll get the money."

Lizzy seconded it. "Me, too."

And all the others, one after another, nodded. When the last, who was Agnes, had finished nodding, Martha put her hands on her knees, almost guylike, and said, "Good. I think we can do it."

With that settled, she rose, stepped to the cherrywood side table, turned back, and asked them, "Well, now. Who wants a pumpkin cupcake?"

CHAPTER THREE

While I Was Out: All the Good Advice in the World

I was still away at school over the next six weeks. The University of Chicago Law School is extremely tough, and nobody has ever called me brilliant. I'd gotten in by extreme hard work and was hanging in the same way; but having survived my first year, I now had greed added to my previous fear as a motivator. The mid-eighties were for lawyers what the sixteenth century was for the Spanish conquistadors—an age of unimaginable wealth and opportunity. My plan was simple: keep the hatches battened down and work hard for another twenty-one months, then set sail for New York and 100K a year. Juan Cabrillo de Peters y Dinero Grande, that was me.

Meanwhile, Martha Crittenden took the lead in organizing the first six meetings of the Larksdale Ladies Independence Club. Martha was the only choice. Not only because she had once actually been inside the Merrill Lynch office in St. Paul. Not only because she had once belonged to the Larksdale Country Club. No, it was more profound, more spiritual, than that. Martha Crittenden was patrician. She had that strand-of-pearls-and-pastel-cashmere, best-cliques-at-the-private-school kind of competence.

You know. The sort of person you automatically hate.

Now, Martha isn't a mean person—I doubt she's ever done an intentionally hurtful thing in her life. But she always displayed a sort of natural superiority that comes of having money. True, her grandfather had more money than her father, and her father had more money than she did—but still, Martha had been married to a successful doctor for nearly twenty years, until he actually started earning a lot of money. At that point, following the honored traditions of American medicine, he had divorced Martha and moved to Chicago with his twenty-six-year-old blond tootsie.

Anyway, Martha had a certain air of lonely aristocracy about her—a something that grew more admirable even as her money began running out. Even when that meant she was being a pain in the butt, most of us remembered Miss Dilled Herring and forgave her.

As nearly as I can tell, it was on Friday afternoon, November 2, that Martha stood before the group, briefly adjusted the silk kerchief at her neck, and announced that for the next five weeks the Larksdale Ladies Independence Club would hear from speakers on the following schedule:

November 9th	Mr. Otto Scwenkling, Difflinger State Bank (followed by a collection for the Methodist Church bake sale)
November 16th	Mr. Wilbur Pratt, Minnesota Grain Savings & Loan (followed by a collection for the Christmas Relief Fund)
November 23rd	Mr. Richard "Whizzer" Cantrell, Great North American Insurance, discussing annuities (followed by exchange of Thanksgiving recipes)
November 30th	Mr. Orville DuBonnet, Ripley & Co., Stockbrokers (followed by exchange of Thanksgiving leftovers)

December 7th	Mr. James Butterworth, Sunrise Mutual Funds (followed by Christmas-tree-decoration swap)

I'm much too considerate of your feelings, reader, to describe what went on at each of these private lectures; but after the third one, my mother sent me the following letter:

My Dear Sophia:

We are now halfway through our set of lectures on investing, and while I am sure it was very good of Martha to arrange it all, I cannot for the life of me see what it is going to be good <u>for</u>. First, we had a fat little man from the bank, telling us we should all leave our money right where it is (in his bank, of course, earning about 6 percent a year), and not worry our pretty heads about doing better. Next, we had a fat <u>big</u> man from the savings and loan, who told us we should deposit our money with him, and not worry our pretty little heads about all those nasty stories about savings and loans going bankrupt and being seized by the government.

This afternoon, we hit a new low, with a burly, bald man named, or nicknamed, "The Whizzer", something or the other, who, about thirty years ago, apparently played the greatest football game in the history of the University of Minnesota and became a hero to Gopher fans everywhere, and then lasted almost half a season for the Vikings. His idea (after telling thirty minutes of extremely dull football stories) was that we should give him all our money, and not worry about anything except making our husbands really good weekend buffets so they can watch the games in states of delirious happiness. If I ever need some advice on how to run the halfback option, I will cer-

*tainly call Mr. Whizzer (as in, "Gee, Mr. Whizzer"?); but
for investment advice, I would sooner ask Dolly's dog, Tahiti. (Maybe we should invite Tahiti to speak. No doubt
he'll tell us to put our money in dog biscuits, give the biscuits to him, and not worry our pretty heads about anything.)*

Your father, *who remembers the game, thinks we should
definitely invest with the Whizzer—or Wheezer, or What-
eezer. But that's just part and parcel of his thinking our
whole idea is silly, so I don't mind.*

*The only thing I can think of is that poor Martha acci-
dentally sent out the invitations on the letterhead of the Association of American Female Idiots, and the lecturers
designed their talks accordingly.*

*So it may be that by the time you get home for the holi-
days, this will be but an amusing memory for us all, including,*

Your Loving Mother,
Lizzy

CHAPTER FOUR

I Enter the Story

Not much had changed by the time I arrived back in Larksdale. In six weeks of weekly meetings, the Ladies had heard six variations on a single theme: "Give me all your money, and every six months or so, I will send you a piece of paper telling you how it's been doing—minus my expenses." No doubt, most of those experts were honest men (for men they all were), and perhaps some of them were even good at their jobs.

But it wasn't what the Ladies wanted. It wasn't hands-on. It wasn't a test of their brains, initiative, or creativity. It was passive and submissive. It was all a matter of trusting someone else to do the thinking for you.

In short, it was a lot like being married.

That was how things stood, in fact, when, around the fifteenth of December, I came home for the Christmas break. I arrived with my clothes in a backpack and my two suitcases crammed with books. My plan was simple: I was going to lock myself in my room and study until my eyes crossed. Christmas was going to be from six A.M. until noon on the twenty-fifth. God would understand.

And so would my mom. That was around the time I realized how special my mom really was. Deborah once told me that Judaism says there are ten righteous people alive at any given time, for whose sake God spares the world—the trick is, you never know who the ten are, so you have to be nice to everyone. Increasingly I often suspected my mom was a candidate for one of the ten.

But now I get to tell you how, for once in my life, I was accidentally clever.

After a week locked in my room twelve hours a day, with sandwiches brought up by Mom every day at noon, I was down to take tea with the Ladies. I had a head whirling with torts and constitutional law and was annoyed with myself for being so generally dull-witted. In fact, I paid only the slightest attention to what they were saying.

Finally some of it soaked through. Martha Crittenden, with her silver hair perfect and her tea napkin geometrically arranged on her knee, was saying decisively, "Well, they *are* the experts, and they *have* given us very sensible advice. I don't see why we can't take it."

Skye, of the pink hair and the bike racer's body, came perilously close to interrupting, and declared, "We've been taking it long enough, that's why. They're just another bunch of men telling us to rest our little heads and let *them* do all the thinking, and I for one am sick of it."

That got my attention. In the first place, nobody interrupted, or even *nearly* interrupted, Martha Crittenden. Especially someone who was really just Mary's pet project and a virtual stranger.

Maybe Skye's boldness would have annoyed me; but then again, I happened to be going to a very prestigious law school, where in a year and a half I'd had exactly *one* woman professor—who was nontenured and taught (big surprise) family law.

So I cleared my throat—which nobody noticed except Mom, who asked, "Yes, honey?" By then, everyone was looking at me, and it was too late to pretend I was choking on Agnes's carrot cake (though anyone would have believed choking on her cake, that's for sure).

So I said, trying to be offhand, "Well, it's just that I read in the *Times* last week about some legendary stockpicker, who runs, I think, a ten-billion-dollar mutual fund"—I didn't exactly know what a mutual fund was—"and he said the secret is just to invest in what you know. One of his examples was how he goes to shopping malls and looks for new stores he thinks would be fun to shop in. If they're well run, and other people are shopping in them, too, then he runs out and buys their stocks. And that's made his mutual fund the most successful one in the country."

They were all staring at me with a fierce, unsettling intensity. I figured I'd been even dumber than usual.

"Well," I wound up lamely, "no man alive knows as much about shopping malls as you all do."

There was a deathly silence. I felt that particular sinking ache you get when what you intended as a compliment comes out as an insult. *Sophia,* I told myself, *You've put your foot in it yet again. I wonder what the world record is for stupid remarks.*

"Anyway," I said aloud, trying desperately to reach shore, but feeling the waves closing over me, "don't you think you might be able to find some stocks on your own?"

About two minutes later, in a lull in the conversation which seemed certain to stretch forever, I stood up and said apologetically that I ought to be getting back to work.

The room remained quiet as I went up the stairs. My ears were burning; I was sure I'd offended them.

But it was much worse than that.

They were thinking.

CHAPTER FIVE

The Ladies Go Shopping

Minneapolis, in case you'd like a piece of extremely dull economic history, is generally considered the home of the shopping mall. That's not really too surprising when you think about Minnesota winters, since indoor shopping malls are a lot like caves where ten thousand or so people can keep warm by burning up their savings.

By 1983, there were more than a dozen major malls within a three-hour drive of South Larksdale—not counting the large section of downtown Minneapolis which, covered by linked skywalks, is almost its own special kind of mall.

None of this—indeed, nothing but coffee and toast—was on my mind the next morning when I stumbled downstairs, to find that:

At seven-twenty that morning, which was Saturday (and dark, and cold, but not snowing), the Larksdale Ladies, with their puffy parkas of varying degrees and grades of down and fabric hung on the hallway pegs, were assembled around the dining-room table planning their first campaign.

Okay—campaign is too strong. But there were maps (AAA, not terrain-and-artillery, admittedly) covering the table, nodding heads with narrowed eyes, and steaming coffee cups being brought thoughtfully to lips. My imagination tends to run away with me—

Mom, I was discovering, had a style of her own. She wouldn't ever try to wrestle the microphone from anyone (so to speak); she wouldn't make speeches or stand on ceremony. Her style was more to make the coffee; put out the snacks; smooth ruffled feathers. When—as now—somebody needed to look at a map to figure out the best route to the malls, Mom would happen to have one—and the route would happen to be sketched in. She was a mom to her toes: people looked to her for small things and gradually trusted her in large. Maybe "leadership by doughnuts" would be the right term.

$\mathcal{T}$hey were out the door a little before eight; I heard them milling around in the hallway and making a noise like what you might expect from a hive of middle-aged bees before they swarmed from the nest. I found myself standing at the upstairs window and watching as they marched out to their vehicles: Mom's van and Martha's Chrysler Imperial. Martha's old Imperial had to be twenty years old. Twenty Minnesota winters, and not a spot of rust. Rust wouldn't dare mess with Martha.

Neither Agnes nor Gladys owned cars. In fact, I doubt they even remembered how to drive. But they were always sure of a ride with somebody, and both were very good passengers, appreciative—and quiet.

Anyway, they marched out like a line of ducks, boarded their two vehicles—with an exchange of honks which I'm sure meant something important—and disappeared down the road.

I marched myself back to *Brimsley on Torts* and resolutely shut out the real world for the next twelve hours.

$\mathcal{D}$ad and the boys (my brothers Arthur, Daniel, and William) had driven into Minneapolis for the day to buy Christmas presents and then to see Minnesota play Ohio. After that they were going to go out to dinner with all the male members of the extended family and probably do something really rowdy, like catch the new Sylvester Stallone movie. It was a big, annual guy thing, and it meant I had a quiet house until Mom came home a little after eight.

By the time I heard her key in the lock, I had eyestrain, potato-chip poisoning, and another few hundred pages of legal wisdom sloshing around in my brain. Desperate for amusement, I had the book closed and my desk lamp out before Mom had the front door open; and I was down the stairs about the time she reached the living room. I'd decided she must be feeling as frazzled as I was.

But she didn't look harried—she looked flushed. Her eyes were bright, and her face was red. So my first words were, of course, "Mom, do you feel okay?"

She came into the living room pulling off her coat, and stopping, looked me in the eyes and said wonderingly, "Honey, I feel wonderful."

We both glanced at the clock on the fireplace mantel at the same instant—and I knew we were thinking exactly the same thing: Dad and my brothers would not possibly be home for at least three hours. It was wonderful.

"I'll put the kettle on," I said.

I'd been back in my room about half an hour when Mom knocked softly and entered. I closed the book; it was after eleven, and I was finished.

While I blinked and rubbed my eyes, she walked all the way up to the desk before asking softly, "Honey . . . let's not tell your father about this for a while, okay?"

I liked the hint of conspiracy. "Sure, Mom. If it doesn't work out, he doesn't have to get the chance to laugh at us."

"No, dear," she said, "it isn't that. We're all going to be very rich. But I want to . . . surprise him."

After she left, I couldn't get to sleep.

Mom never got excited about anything.

CHAPTER SIX

The Outing

My mother was excited because the Ladies, on their first outing, had discovered two companies to buy. That would have been, of course, a highly creditable performance for a professional investment group. For the Ladies to accomplish it fell somewhere between amazing luck and a miracle.

Certainly the week before Christmas, every store owner in America looks like a retailing genius. Especially in the malls, the crowds press in on each other like reindeer herds, shoving and bellowing—and waving their credit cards. That's not only exhausting, it makes it nearly impossible to discover which stores have real investment potential.

The Ladies had already spent more than five unsuccessful hours walking the smaller malls when, shortly after two, they arrived at the Grand Mall of Minnesota.

Until the Mall of America opened, the GMoM was the world's biggest shopping arena. GMoM was a mall like the Grand Canyon is a hole in the ground: the description's correct, but not exactly informative. This three-story behemoth contained, for example, an entire indoor ride zone/amusement park, complete with Ferris wheel and carousel, as just one part of its strategy to keep visitors dazzled.

For the weary Ladies, who stood looking up at the multiple levels of shops stretching in every direction, while a nearby twenty-two-piece orchestra played "It's Beginning to Look a Lot Like Christmas" and half a dozen of Santa's elves raced by, smoking, on their lunch hour, it was daunting indeed.

Except for Deb, who could have done the hike wearing a fifty-pound backpack and whistling "The Halls of Montezuma," they ached from feet to shoulders and were almost doubled up with hunger. Trying to avoid a Grand Mall seizure, they stood wearily in the food-court line for almost an hour, then wound up eating Sbarro's pizza and drinking watery coffee from Styrofoam cups before feeling strong enough to set off again.

The Grand Mall was so big they decided to break into teams, each heading in a different direction. They had already learned that the kinds of stores that interested them—the ones not part of major chains—were likely to be hidden in the mall's backwaters, the dim stretches farthest from the amusement rides and tinsely holiday displays.

They finally split into just two groups. Because those groups would be separated by considerable distances, they arranged a rendezvous point, as if they were visiting the state fair.

Dolly and Gladys, bound for the eastern wing, had walked a good fifteen minutes before they began to leave the "anchor" stores behind. Gladys, who was literary, amused herself by mentally composing a mock explorer's journal: "20 December: Ammunition gone, water getting low. Nothing to eat for three days but LEGOs and Mrs. Fields cookies. I fear none of us shall see England again." It kept her going until she and Dolly had reached the farthest unexplored branches of the mall, where the decorations were few and dull and the lighting somehow dimmer. There they agreed to split up, each taking one side of the corridor.

.   .   .

*D*olly had swept through four women's clothing stores, two men's clothing boutiques, a card shop, and a rather hopeless-looking place called PuzzleLand when she finally noticed a knot of shoppers trying to squeeze their way into a store at the very end of the mall.

Curiously excited, she pushed forward and, after several minutes' good-natured jostling, found herself just inside the door of Earth&Nature.

It was unlike any store in her experience. For one thing, there were virtually no shelves. Instead there were plants—mostly green ferns, but a few small, orchidlike plants, with tiny purple-and-yellow flowers. There were also half a dozen little self-contained fountains, with water splashing caressingly over small arrays of stones; behind that, some strange but soothing flute music. Music from a South American wooden flute, it seemed, was following its own plaintive course over the stones.

The place really was melodious; despite the crowd of shoppers deeper back in the store, Dolly felt herself relaxing. Having momentarily forgotten her mission, she lingered, absorbing the music, the sense of the green calm all around her. Then, unthinking, she felt herself being drawn farther back into the store, toward the wooden shelves packed with wooden merchandise, toward bins of polished stones and small toys, toward video screens showing even more soothing nature videos.

Then another sound began to rise above the flutes. It was also melodious, but quite different.

It was the sound of cash registers ringing, and it snapped Dolly out of her reverie. As she got nearer to the line of shoppers, she found them holding stacks of pending purchases: board games, videos, handicrafts with extraordinarily high prices.

Almost nobody was buying plants—but the cash registers kept humming.

She moved around the store until she spotted a fresh-faced,

somewhat beefy young man wearing white cotton slacks and a blue work shirt that bore a tag reading, *Walt—Manager*.

Dolly stepped up to him, gave a smile that was winning because it was very slightly embarrassed, and asked, "Excuse me. This might sound a little odd—but could you tell me what exactly it is you sell here?"

He was a nice young fellow, and—except for a few darting glances around the store—answered as if this weren't one of the busiest days of the year.

"We specialize in nature products, to help people rebuild their connection to the natural world. That's the whole idea." It sounded like a corporate mission statement—and to someone who'd grown up about half a mile from farmland, it wasn't entirely understandable. But Dolly knew shoppers when she saw them, and shoppers were all around them.

Just to make sure she understood, she asked, "You mean you sell rocks?"

"Oh, rocks and wood carvings, and these little electrically powered fountains, and leather goods in Indian styles, and nature games and—" He waved all around him.

"So, it's sort of like a really fancy crafts show?"

He smiled broadly. "Exactly!"

Dolly felt both relieved—she understood crafts shows—and mystified. This was seeming too easy to be trustworthy.

"Are you a chain?"

"Yes, ma'am." He was beginning to glance about the store more anxiously, and Dolly knew her time was short.

"How many stores?"

"Three. We started in San Francisco—"

Dolly grew excited. San Francisco sounded very hip.

"Our next one was in Los Angeles."

Even hipper.

The young man swung his arms to indicate the store. He was

getting ready to take off like a helicopter. "And this one is because our founder grew up in Red Wing."

All that, and good values, too.

"But if you'll excuse me—"

He was starting away, but surprising herself, Dolly took his arm. If "WWF" ever comes to stand for "Women's Wrestling Federation," Dolly could make a nice living. He stopped in his tracks, as she said, "Last question, I promise."

"Yes, ma'am."

"Are you selling stock in this place?"

"Yes, ma'am—since last week. We all got shares."

After that, Dolly did indeed excuse him. In fact, she squeezed his arm gratefully and smiled as if he'd given her the nicest of Christmas presents.

Dolly walked thoughtfully out of the store; but back on the dim and largely deserted internal street, she unaccountably found herself hurrying. She was almost in a lumbering run by the time she'd crossed to the other side and began to search the shops for Gladys.

She found her studying the menu of a deserted pretzel stand. Stepping up to her, she whispered, "I think I've found something."

Gladys, seeing her excitement, felt a little excited herself. "What?"

"It's a nature shop."

Gladys, not certain how nature could be sold, simply looked at her, and waited for more.

But Dolly, suddenly conspiratorial, took Gladys aside and whispered, with something between excitement and confusion, "They're selling rocks for twelve dollars each."

Gladys looked back sharply, like a prairie dog on guard. "Where!?"

"Come on."

As they hurried away, Dolly, in the lead, looked backed and asked, "You have the book?"

Dolly was referring to a small paperback, *Understanding Stocks in Fifty Questions,* which Gladys had decided was the most useful handbook available, and from which she had been answering the others' questions for the last week and a half.

Gladys tapped her handbag and answered, "Right here!" But the truth was that, like a good librarian, she'd long before committed the key facts to memory.

Besides, they were moving too fast for her to pull the book from her purse.

*T*he other two teams of Ladies, meanwhile, had converged at another store, a good half a mile away, at the far end of the mall. Like Earth&Nature, RipStop was drawing crowds—in fact, the two teams met at its door by following separate streams of shoppers.

The Ladies had all seen camping gear—Deborah, probably, more of it than she had ever wanted to—but it had all been the army-surplus sort. Heavy, inelegant, and in the dullest, darkest colors—often some variation of green camouflage mottling. This looked more like an explosion in a paint factory—like expedition wear for California surfers—like it was going to give a lot of woodland creatures splitting headaches.

"What on earth . . . ?" Agnes let the question hang in hopes one of the others could make sense of it.

"It sure as heck isn't for hunting—unless you're out after the rare color-blind elk," Deb answered decisively, lifting off a rack a tangerine-and-puce vest.

Mary, who had fairly often gone camping with her husband, Mike, gathered her nerve and approached one of the young people who were stripping the shelves like a cloud of shopping locusts.

Pointing at the white-and-lavender down jacket the young woman held, she asked, "Is it good for camping?"

"Camping? I don't camp."

"But, then . . . ?"

"I just like the look. It's hip."

Mary checked the price tag: $49. She'd paid about that for her good winter coat, on sale postseason. She'd been wearing it for three years. It had never gone out of fashion. Of course, it had never been in fashion—but that was another issue. Focusing her mind, she asked the young woman, "How long do you wear something like that? If you don't mind my asking?"

"How *long*? Maybe twice. A couple of outdoor parties."

Mary looked dazed.

"And then," the young woman continued, realizing she was dealing with an older and uninteresting generation, "you give it to your little sister and buy something different."

The ladies stepped to the quietest corner of the store. Their ingrained frugality was struggling against their sense that this was the retail equivalent of the Gold Rush.

It was hard for them to talk. From the sales station about ten feet away came the steady whir of electronic cash registers. The Ladies studied the crush all around them. They were feeling an unexpected electricity. After decades of being buyers-as-victims, they were becoming buyers-in-charge.

"I don't know," Mary said finally. "It seems to be encouraging young people to be awfully frivolous."

"So?" Agnes asked with surprising bluntness. They turned toward her.

"I mean," Agnes went on, "what's the point of being young?" It was a question that had long interested her, but here it was purely rhetorical. "Just because we never had any fun doesn't mean they shouldn't."

This was putting it harshly, but it still made sense. They looked at her and, one after another, nodded.

Then they froze up. They were gazing at each other—down at the clothes—and again at each other, uncertain what to do next, when Mom spotted the manager across the store.

He was about fifty, slight, with thinning gray hair combed straight over, and steel-rimmed glasses covering worried eyes.

"Can I help you find anything?" he asked Mom coolly when she, trailed slightly by Skye, reached him.

"Actually," Mom said, stammering only a little, "I'm interested in buying your stock. Is it publicly traded?" She liked saying this. It made her feel rather important. The other Ladies were crowding in around her, which made the poor manager rather nervous.

"I think so," he muttered, looking for an escape route. "On something called the OBC market."

"You mean OTC. It stands for—" Skye started to correct him; but the others hustled her to the back of the crowd, with only my mom left to ask politely, "I hope I don't sound stupid, but . . . where would I find that?"

The manager looked annoyed—frustrated—perhaps, Mom thought, even angry. He turned on his heel and strode back to the main sales counter. There, with rough gestures, he yanked open a drawer, searched hastily, found a piece of paper, shoved more items aside until he found a pen, scrawled something on the paper, and slammed the door shut again.

He strode quickly, twisting to avoid other shoppers, back to my mom.

"Here," he said brusquely, thrusting the paper into her hand. "This is the broker's name." That was all—swept away by a paying customer, he was gone in a rush.

Clutching the slip of paper, Mom dashed for the front of the store. She had not felt this intense, alarmed excitement since she'd stolen a pack of Reese's Peanut Butter Cups from the five-and-dime when she was about six years old. Reaching the other Ladies, she emitted a sigh of relief that was almost a yelp. Only then did she realize how absolutely frightened she'd been. She wouldn't let them see the slip of paper until they were out of the store.

She knew she'd behaved like a six-year-old snatching candy from a store.

And frankly, she didn't mind.

.   .   .

*A*t the reunion spot, near the Camp Snoopy play area, it would have been hard to say which of the two groups of Ladies was the more excited; in fact, it was like bringing two subcritical masses into close contact, which is, of course, the basic principle of the atomic bomb.

In another hour, they had seen each other's sites and adjourned to the food court to reach their decision. The vote took less than a minute.

"I move we split our investment between the two stocks—I mean, assuming we can figure out how to do it," Mary said firmly.

"I second it," Agnes added immediately.

Martha looked at the semicircle of faces. "It's been moved and seconded," she said calmly. "All in favor?"

"Aye," the Ladies all answered.

Two minutes later they were out in the parking lot and starting for their cars. The late-day sky was bright blue and frosty, with not a cloud in sight. As they walked, an amusing notion struck my mother.

" 'Minnesota,' " she said. "An old Chippewa word meaning 'land of the deals.' "

It was the universal opinion. They had struck gold.

CHAPTER SEVEN

A Very Small Miracle

The Ladies decided to rush into the business, for one very simple, practical reason: if they held on to the money any longer, they'd feel pressured into spending it on Christmas presents.

But they still needed a broker. Embarrassing as it was to have to talk someone into taking their money, that was their problem, until someone mentioned Axel Langsgaard.

Axel Langsgaard was about as bland as Midwesterners get. He was as pale as bleached white bread. He had a bald dome of a head, with just a fringe of polar-bear-blond hair turning white; pale blue eyes behind silver wire-frames; and a smile he tried out about twice a year, just to make sure it still worked. But the eyes and the smile were honest—and so was he. However the ladies found him, they found the right man. Martha, Mary, and my mom landed the job of interviewing him, and it all came down to just a pair of questions.

"Are you going to try to sell us things?" Martha asked him.

"It doesn't sound like that's what you're hiring me for."

"What if we want you to do something really stupid?"

"I'll give you Merrill Lynch's phone number and wish you luck."

He got the job.

. . .

$\mathcal{B}$oth Earth&Nature and RipStop were publicly traded in the smallest Over the Counter market. The Ladies, through Axel, bought shares of Earth&Nature at $3.22 a share and RipStop at $2.58, two days before Christmas.

Three weeks later, Earth&Nature reported excellent year-end results. Small-stock and retail analysts took note, and the shares rose rapidly, climbing three dollars a share over the next ten days. That thrilled the Ladies—who called the good-natured Axel every business day at a quarter to five for the latest numbers—but it was only the beginning.

On January 28, the day before the Super Bowl, there came electrifying news. A Massachusetts conglomerate, which specialized in buying up promising leisure-related companies, had made a bid to buy RipStop at eleven dollars a share.

The Ladies had tripled their money in a month—and more importantly, they were in the game.

$\mathcal{A}$s we reach the point where the Ladies began making money, I wish I could record (with all due modesty) how they owed all their subsequent, much greater success to me.

Well, I could record it, but it wouldn't be true. In fact, it wouldn't even be a first-class lie, since anybody who cared to check would easily discover that I was still camped out in the law library at the University of Chicago. There I sat trying to memorize every law book since Blackstone's *Commentaries* in preparation for finals and then (the brick wall at the end of the tunnel) the bar exams.

So, no credit to Sophia as an investing genius.

The truth—so strange as to seem almost a mundane miracle— is that it took Skye Terrell, pink hair and all, to start them on the road to legend.

CHAPTER EIGHT

Martha and Skye, Part One

To go forward, I first need to back up a little.

All through November, the Ladies had tried their best to make pink-haired Skye feel like a member of the group. True, she had shown a few small signs of reluctance—like scowling, grunting, and folding her arms in front of her and staring at the floor—but still, they tried.

And gradually they seemed to be succeeding.

For the first two weeks, Skye had trailed behind Mary to the meetings only to sit like a glowering storm cloud blown up against the darkest corner of the room. Then, when the first guest speakers appeared, she seemed to take an interest in the discussions. And when the Ladies had made their field trip to seek investments, she had barely been able to hide her enthusiasm.

But after the Ladies decided to buy into the two companies, it became clear that while Skye might be welcome to attend the Mostly Methodist Club, she lacked the cash to become a full member of what they decided to call the Larksdale Ladies Independence Club.

At the very next full meeting, when Martha announced that Axel Langsgaard had passed inspection and would be expecting their check on Monday, the Ladies realized that Skye, who was penniless, was now automatically a second-class member of the MMC. Certainly Mary, Martha, and my mom noticed Skye deflating with this news; but nobody had a spare fifteen hundred dollars to lend such a silent, troublesome creature as she had been.

Or so it seemed.

A few minutes later, as the Ladies were munching through the usual postbusiness snacks and chat, Martha drew Mary aside for a whispered conversation. This conversation, which involved many glances in Skye's direction, ended with one long, final nod by Mary.

The other Ladies, meanwhile—perhaps embarrassed at the limits of their goodwill—did their awkward best to pay extra attention to Skye. She, for her part, withdrew into a silence even darker than usual.

But as the meeting ended, and Skye was trailing the others in her skulk for the door, she was brought up short by Martha's best command tones.

"Young lady, come over here."

Skye turned reluctantly. Martha, seated regally upon the room's best sofa, was eyeing her coldly.

Skye approached, closing the gap between them from about twenty feet to about eighteen.

Martha stamped her Ferragamo-clad foot. "I'm not contagious and I'm assuming you're not. Over here. Now."

Skye did it, though her style of walking had in it much of the old mime-walking-against-a-wind routine.

"I have a deal for you," Martha continued when Skye had closed to about five feet and was clearly incapable of coming closer. "I'll put up your fifteen hundred dollars. You pay me back with housework for—"

"*What!?*"

"Don't interrupt. It's rude. With housework for ninety days. You'll get room and board, of course."

Skye, in those days, had many of the mannerisms of a trapped badger. Backing quickly away, she hissed, "I think you're disgusting."

"I'm not looking for love. I'm offering you a deal. Do you want it or not?"

Skye said nothing.

"It's a chance," Martha elaborated—and by her standards, that was a major concession. Martha may have looked like Brooke Astor, but her code was pure Disraeli: "Never complain, never explain." Having gone so far beyond her usual bounds, she quickly lost patience. "I guess not. Well, go away." And, quite calmly, she reached over and took a copy of *Town & Country* off the nearest end table. She was well into an article on English hedgehogs, when Skye responded.

"Okay."

Martha looked up. "Excuse me?"

"Okay. I don't like the deal but I'll take it."

"I refuse to force you," Martha said briefly, and went back to reading the article.

A brief hesitation, a bowed head. "I like it."

"There's an apron on a peg in the kitchen. You can start by cleaning up in here," said Martha, not looking up. A good hedgehog story is hard to top.

CHAPTER NINE

Martha and Skye, Part Two

The Ladies' rise to fortune actually grew from the amicable feud or angry friendship—call it what you will—between Skye and Martha. Perhaps their edgy friendship was inevitable, since they had bonds of mutual loneliness and mutual stubbornness, after all, and were in each other's company almost all of every day.

At first there was far more feud than friendship, a cycle of angry words, angrier silences, and peremptory sendings-to-rooms. Still, when you consider how much time they were inside together during the January blizzards, I suppose we're lucky they did not turn into the Larksdale version of *Fargo*.

But early in February the Ladies began to notice a change. It was mostly small things. After one meeting, held at my parents' house for variety, Skye didn't dash directly to Martha's car the moment the meeting ended; she actually stood waiting in the foyer while Martha put on her coat. True, she had her arms crossed and tapped her foot the whole time; but still, she waited, and the Ladies were touched.

About two weeks later, when they were alone at Martha's house, the change in Skye took on specific form. The signs were nothing so immediately hopeful as washing out the pink dye or asking for a shopping trip to Banana Republic; but they were interesting.

Martha had the catalogs from Burpee's and a pair of tulip specialty houses spread out on the kitchen table and was studying them avidly when Skye, standing beside her, began clearing her throat, commencing softly, and then rising to a gasping that sounded like the last act of *Camille*.

"Yes?" Martha finally asked, carefully marking her page in the Burpee catalog and closing it.

"I want to go back to school."

"To the U?"

Skye nodded.

"Impossible. You know you're on probation for the whole year." Martha unbent as much as her hardwood nature allowed. "Maybe, if you're good, we can try to change their minds for summer term."

"I didn't say I wanted to take classes."

"What, then?"

Skye was something of a maple sapling herself. She hesitated—calculated—looked away—for half a minute before grudgingly admitting, "There's a CUG."

To Martha "CUG" sounded like the last utterance of someone dying of apoplexy. She said it back to Skye as intelligently as she could: "CUG?"

Skye rolled her eyes. "It means Computer User Group. People sit around in a big room and ask questions like, 'In CP/M compilers, how do you get the system to read Boolean—' "

"Do they use drugs?" Martha had the older person's annoying habit of abbreviating uninteresting conversations.

"Yeah. Coke." Skye rolled her eyes as she said it.

Martha, missing all the signals of being treated like an annoying parent, rose from her chair and said in her best Margaret Thatcher tones, "You will not go anywhere near cocaine."

"Coca-Cola! Coca-Cola! Everybody knows hackers just sit in

front of terminals and suck Cokes and eat Fritos! They even put Cokes and Fritos at the front of the checkout aisle at the U Radio Shack. Hackers never do drugs."

Martha remained stonily unconvinced. Skye escalated the attack.

"Don't you know how they test keyboards in Silicon Valley? They pour a slurry of Coke and Fritos over them. If they don't jam up, they're good enough to be sold." To Skye this prospect— indeed the whole idea of Silicon Valley—was strangely exciting. Once, perhaps, young people had dreamed of going to India for adventure, or the New World. Skye's was the first generation to dream of going where computers were made.

But that was incomprehensible to Martha. In 1984, after all, most people still thought Silicon Valley was where they'd filmed all those John Wayne movies.

"So you want to go so you can pour Coca-Cola over computer keyboards?"

"*No!*" Skye was beside herself with frustration.

And it was about to get worse.

"What, then?"

"I don't have to tell you."

"Absolutely not. You can stay home, or I can go along with you."

Skye cried to some celestial audience, "Oh, great. I have to bring my mom." Then she added to Martha, "I'd rather die."

"That's always an option, of course," Martha answered agreeably. She was flustered, though: the notion of being Skye's mother had pleased her oddly.

"Oh, just forget it," Skye said, not at all agreeably; but she did not storm away.

Martha, following her standard modus, was reaching for the seed catalog, when Skye continued.

"If I tell you, can I go?"

"I don't know. What if you tell me you want to go hold the

place up at gunpoint?" The catalog was open again. Martha saw from the corner of her eye that Skye was walking away. She picked up her pen and turned to the Burpee order form.

"What if I find something for us to invest in?"

Skye had returned. Martha threw the pen onto the catalog.

"Come into the living room," she said, rising, "and tell me about it."

CHAPTER TEN

Skye Breaks Loose

What Skye told Martha seems absurdly obvious today but seemed simply absurd when she said it. This was six months before the first Apple Macintoshes and IBM PCs appeared—and an age when people thought of computers strictly as huge gadgets with whirling tape drives that cost millions of dollars and sat in air-conditioned rooms on elevated floors with built-in fire suppression systems. Skye sat primly on Martha's flower-print sofa and insisted categorically that within ten years computers would be as common as televisions.

Martha, to her credit, restrained herself from laughing.

Who knows why she kept a straight face. Perhaps it was the lingering effect of Skye's reference to her as "Mom." If there was one thing Martha would have liked a second chance at, it was motherhood.

Then there was Skye's odd talent for making sense. Martha had a good ear for lying and nonsense—after all, she'd been married to Old Doc Crittenden for two decades before he roared out of town with his latest nurse/girlfriend and most of their liquid community property. Skye's ten-minute summary of the future of the computer industry might have been strung together with youthful enthusiasm—but beads of what sounded suspiciously like hard facts shone upon the string.

And yet Martha had facts of her own to consider.

Her first act after rashly offering Skye employment, all those months ago, had been to collect—from Skye's probation officer and psychiatric social worker—the details of Skye's case.

They were not exactly lurid, but neither were they exactly inspiring.

It seemed that Skye had been recruited to the university as a mathematics student and had shown something close to genius— but had also appeared lost in the big city. Then, late in her first year, she had discovered computer programming and had seemed to find her calling.

But in the fall of her second year, Skye had found a boyfriend. As nearly as the probation officer could tell, he had been Skye's first serious boyfriend. He also was—in that old-fashioned but still useful phrase—bad news. "Bad news" is often just a code phrase for "outsider," but Randy Corbin was just the opposite, an insider from an old-money Midwestern family.

Randy was good-looking, in a clean-cut, boyish way, with a sort of perpetual tan, which in Minnesota meant tanning salons, frequent vacations in Mexico and the Caribbean, or—as in Randy's case—all of the above. Despite being an avid tennis player, he was actually, if you studied him, rather frail looking; but he knew how to wear clothes (especially the casually expensive Polo look) so as to seem quite the upper-class jock. He was just the guy you'd choose to photograph modeling blue blazers amid the turning autumn leaves on a college campus.

He was also one of those old-style frat brothers who rated their lives upon their ability to seduce as many women as possible. Yes, that's a curiously old-fashioned and melodramatic phrase; but if modern times had made seduction sound rather silly, betrayal is about as rotten as it ever was—and the whole point about seduction (as opposed to, say, sport sex) is that it involves winning and betraying the trust of people who are, by reason of innocence or neediness, somehow vulnerable.

Skye was almost too easy a target. At eighteen she was desperately shy, badly dressed, awkward as only a young woman from a struggling upstate dairy farm could be, and utterly mystified at her own ability to understand all the computer-science course work at a single glance.

Only in the classroom did she feel confident. And that was where she met him.

She had just raised her hand and answered what she considered a comically easy question: the exact difference between a programming language and an operating system. When she finished, there was a brief, half-admiring, half-envious silence, which she savored. She looked over and saw the handsome young man in the blue blazer looking at her. No, he was studying her. And he kept studying her—as she noted in frequent, brief glances—for the remainder of the class. Then, amid the rumble and stomping of the class changeover, he pushed his way through the crowd to talk with her while she stared at the floor.

After he'd told her how brilliant she was, and how he struggled to understand computers, he asked, "Say, would you do me a huge favor?"

"You want me to help you study?"

He grinned, showing perfect teeth. "Oh, no thanks. I'll get the final from the frat files." He looked at her with a precise earnestness. "I just wanted to meet you. Do you ever drink wine in the afternoon?"

Oddly, given his good looks—he had neat features, bright blue eyes, and black hair—she did not find him very attractive. In fact, his soft dark blue flannel blazer was probably more attractive than he was; but his attentions were dazzling. He was much too subtle to try to get her drunk at a frat party; in fact, he soon made a great point of saying she was too important in his life for him even to think of dragging her to one of those affairs.

He seemed, indeed, to treat her as very special. The few times she called for him at his frat house, his brothers all remarked that he was a changed man. What he seemed to want to do above all else was to go off with her for quiet walks.

These walks led finally to a car, an airport, and a January weekend in an Idaho ski lodge. Except for the lodge itself, which reminded Skye of some movie setting, with its huge stone fireplace and rugged beamed ceiling, the weekend was devoid of romance. Still, there was one brief stretch, late on their first afternoon, when they sat on the ledge before the great fireplace and drank some curious drink made with peppermint schnapps set ablaze, which seemed quite wonderful. For those few hours Randy had acted endlessly tender and affectionate.

The rest of that evening she remembered only a lot of trembling, a little pain, and a considerable disappointment.

Everything thereafter was much worse.

A lot of Randy's friends were casual about conquests; he was probably a little unusual in being positively cruel about them.

A few days after they returned from Idaho, he called her to say he had the pictures from their trip.

When she arrived, he was sitting on the bed just pulling a pair of pictures from the photo-shop envelope. On the bed beside him was a photo album. He looked up and smiled.

"This one's for you," he said, handing her one of the pictures. "And *this* one is for me."

Saying that, he picked up the photo album. Skye, meanwhile, sat beside him and studied the photo he'd handed her. It showed them perched together in front of the ski lodge's big stone fireplace, and she was surprised to discover she looked bright-eyed and excited and pretty.

Randy was opening the photo album.

Medium-sized, dark-green loose-leaf, it seemed to hold only

about a dozen of those thick, plastic-covered pages. The first was a title page, which read, *The Stud Book*. The other pages were filled with snapshots of various attractive and very young-looking women. They were all seated beside Randy and all posed in front of the very same fireplace at the ski lodge.

Skye glanced back up at Randy and saw he was eyeing her with triumph in his eyes, and a taunting grin stretched across his face.

Skye knew instantly that what he wanted was a scene, at least with screaming and preferably with a lot of crying. She also knew she would rather die than give him that satisfaction. It cost her a great deal, but she kept her lips pressed together and managed to bend them barely up into a smile.

He still had the shit-eating grin on his face, but his eyes were less triumphant. She took her coat off the bed and left.

Since she knew she wanted to pay Randy one last visit, she made a point of nodding and smiling at his frat brothers down in the lounge on her way out of the house.

That was why nobody cared when she returned two days later, while Randy was in his poli-sci class, and let herself into his room.

Skye, even furious, had a very logical mind. She knew noise would bring attention, so she started by using her pocketknife to slash his clothes, then the strings of his beloved tennis rackets. Then she had pulled the Stud Book from under his bed and methodically torn up each of the photos.

Only then did she grab Randy's favorite racket (now stringless) and begin smashing mirrors and ornaments as thoroughly and as noisily as she could.

When Randy's frat brothers, having heard the commotion, finally broke down the door, they found Skye standing amid the ruins, holding a pack of matches and apparently trying to decide whether to strike one.

.   .   .

*T*he court had required her to have four presentencing meetings with a psychiatric social worker, a stocky, fortyish woman whose directness was somehow very sympathetic.

"Can you tell me why you wrecked the boy's room?"

" 'Boy'?"

"Young man's?"

"I wanted to teach him a lesson, first of all; and to make a statement secondly." When the woman looked at her intently, Skye elaborated, "That his family money couldn't keep him from feeling some consequences to his actions."

"You really think that will make a difference?"

"Practically? No," Skye had answered immediately. "His parents will replace everything his insurance doesn't cover."

"Why, then?"

"In the first place, because I hated his guts. When guys get mad at each other, they knock each other on their butts. I'm too small to knock anybody down. This was the best I could do."

"Was that very mature?"

"In 1941, the Japanese bombed our fleet at Pearl Harbor and killed two thousand of our soldiers. By the time we'd gotten over our irritation, we'd firebombed Tokyo, atom-bombed Hiroshima and Nagasaki, and killed eight hundred thousand of their civilians. Was that very mature?"

"Do you expect me to answer that?"

Skye shook her head. "Frankly, when I saw his album, I decided he was an emotional serial killer. He was knocking off as many women as he could. Maybe that didn't deserve the death penalty, but he sure deserved to have someone bring it to his attention."

After three more chats with Skye—including one about farming and one about computers (in which Skye finally showed a spark of enthusiasm)—the psychiatric social worker wrote a brief report, remarkably free of jargon:

Ms. Terrell made a considerable error of judgment under the general pressure of a new and rigorous academic life, plus the specific pressure of a first, unhappy love affair with a young man who behaved badly. If we teach her a lesson, she'll learn it—whether the lesson is one of harshness, or of kindness.

Recommendation: Restitution, one hundred hours of community service, and one year's probation in the Community Guidance Program.

Talking with Martha, the social worker had concluded very simply, "If Skye Terrell's crazy, so am I. But, given the way the system works, if I'd said that, they would just have given her case to someone else. So I recommended the mildest punishment I knew they'd accept. Personally, I'd have given her a medal. That boy was a pig."

The social worker stood and offered Martha her hand across the desk. "If you see her, will you tell her I said hi?"

*I*f she had actually lit a match, Skye would have certainly done time—in a mental hospital, if not a jail. As it was, there was room for leeway.

Randy did his civic duty. He went down to the courthouse and told the hearing judge that Skye was, in his opinion, dangerous, emotionally unstable, and probably a pathological liar who could convince nearly anyone that she was a victim. That was a great sacrifice of language in honor of the dignity of the court. The nicest phrase Randy used with his fraternity friends to describe Skye was "sick bitch and a lousy lay."

*M*artha, having heard all this, was very much inclined to give Skye another chance—indeed, as many chances as she needed.

Still, Martha understood she was taking a risk—perhaps even breaking a promise to the rest of the Ladies.

And a rigid prudence was the core of Martha's character. She had not navigated the dangerous waters of divorced life by letting the ship run free while she stood on the bow whistling. She steered close, did Martha, with a hand on the tiller as hard as the tiller's wood. She didn't take chances.

Accordingly, she knew before she opened her mouth exactly what she was going to say.

Then she opened her mouth and said exactly the opposite.

Martha said, "You give me your word you'll stick to business?"

Skye felt instantly what a broad, cheery word "business" was. Almost anything could be considered business.

"Absolutely," she promised, while thinking she was entirely free.

CHAPTER ELEVEN

The CUG

Odd as it seems today, in 1984 Minnesota was a world center for computer research and development. From Cray Supercomputers to Control Data, we were the hottest spot between Boston's Route 128 and Silicon Valley.

The fact of that made Skye's adolescent heart beat faster as she cycled onto the campus of the university one late-February night.

Nearly every adolescent, I think, has at least one place with electric associations, one spot that brings up instantly those brightened eyes and heart thumpings. It might be the beach with the towering surf or the sports arena with the thundering concerts. For Skye, it was the four-hundred-seat main auditorium of the computer-science building, where the Minnesota Students Computer Users Group met every Thursday.

Crossing the campus, she felt like a cowboy back in the saddle again. She was on top of the world and ready to ride.

That lasted all the way until she saw the classroom lights, bright against the night's darkness; for the truth was, Skye was almost morbidly shy—a trait that her time with Randy and his friends had done nothing to cure.

She locked her bike to a rack, then drifted from the main path, into the shadows of the trees. The prospect of running away seemed absolutely irresistible. Then the thought struck her that poor as she was, she still had courage—or she had nothing.

She straightened her jacket and stepped back onto the path.

From the very start of the meeting, Skye had been distracted by a big, blond-haired young man seated across the aisle and one row ahead of her. His army jacket might have been a twin of hers; he had ruddy cheeks and big blue eyes, and his lank hair was cut in what could charitably be called sheepdog fashion. He was a farm boy, Skye knew absolutely. She didn't mind that; indeed, for most of her life, farm boys were all she had known.

He had any number of odd quirks, from giggling at remarks made by the dark, smallish woman sitting next to him to tossing his hair back out of his eyes by throwing back his head as he looked about the room. His restlessness came out in drumming his fingers, whispering to the small woman—even in stretching rubber bands back from his index fingertip and aiming them at targets around the room. Skye had almost, but not quite, decided he was an idiot.

He did not make a target of Skye, but he did make an annoying habit of turning to look at her. Once their eyes locked, until Skye looked away, embarrassed. After that she kept her gaze focused on her notebook until the meeting ended a few minutes later.

She ought to have gotten to her feet at once, but she hesitated, so she had to continue looking down as the farm boy climbed the aisle steps past her. He was talking to his companion as he passed, in a speech peppered with unnecessary question marks.

"My computer-science professor? Mr. Andreesen? He says that, like, by this time next year you'll be able to buy a desktop computer with a *megabyte* of memory."

Farm Boy's dark companion had answered this with a snort and a quiet, "Yeah—right." Then they were out of hearing, while

Skye, curiously disappointed, pushed her notebook and pens back into her pack.

And then, to Skye's quiet satisfaction and slight alarm, Farm Boy loomed over her. He was so large, he blocked out the room light.

"New here?" His voice was soft and his diction rural, slightly slurred and shy.

She nodded, not looking up.

"Want to get coffee?"

She shook her head. "No."

A silence, then—

"Wanna go tip over a cow?"

She burst out laughing.

Pleased, he said, "I knew it! A farm girl."

"Even with pink hair?"

"Pink hair!?" he cried in mock surprise, while swiveling his head. "Where?"

She laughed a little more. He turned serious, even hesitant, and said, "Carter Armstrong." He stuck out his hand. It was detectably smaller than an Easter ham; Skye put her small hand gingerly against it, and he shook it by folding his thumb over it with almost undetectable pressure.

"Skye Terrell," she answered, reclaiming her hand.

He grinned. "Carter Armstrong and Skye Terrell? We sound like a forties radio serial." He dropped his voice two octaves. "Tune in next week when Carter and Skye . . ." In his normal tones, he added, "My mom figured a guy named Carter'd have a better chance of getting off the farm than one named Jim-Bob or Buzz. What about yours?"

"I named myself. I couldn't stand Betty."

He raised his eyebrows and nodded. "Good call."

Skye liked him at once. It wasn't a physical attraction: under the army jacket, he had remarkably broad shoulders and thick arms, and his shambling walk suggested immense, clumsy strength.

The few men Skye had ever found attractive had all been slightly built, elegant, even rather feminine in their graces.

Still, one part of his charm was easy to understand. He felt like home.

She wasn't, especially at that time of her life, a great advocate of smiling at men, but she smiled at him—and he certainly seemed to like the idea. In fact, flushing bright red, he asked, "What about that coffee?" then added, "A bunch of us are going," so she wouldn't get the wrong idea.

The tyranny of the Marthas began to seem unbearably cruel. Skye's first thought was to hang out until dawn and let Martha call out the National Guard. But she quickly shook her head. "I have to get home right after the meeting."

His face fell; so on some mad impulse, she added, "I'm on probation."

"Really? You mean, like, probation with your parents, or probation with the cops?"

"Like, probation with the cops."

"Wow."

She nodded, already furious with herself for having spoken.

He studied her with extreme curiosity, and then asked, "You gonna rob any banks this week?"

"No!"

"So you'll be here next week, for sure?" he summarized with relief.

Skye, thinking she'd done enough laughing for one night, nodded shortly, turned, and headed for the door. She was feeling happy, but she'd be damned if she'd admit it.

CHAPTER TWELVE

Carter

Despite herself, Skye began keeping company with Carter, even though it required a whole awkward process of bringing him home to dinner to meet Martha.

Nominally the main course was lamb chops; but Martha gave Carter the more thorough grilling, flipping him after he was half-done. She not only pried into his family, his schoolwork, his hobbies, and his future plans; she rayed him with an unrelenting stare which seemed to check everything from his haircut to the cash in his wallet. But after it was over, and a shaken Carter had taken his leave, Martha granted Skye permission to spend time with him at places other than the weekly CUG meeting.

On their budgets, and at the end of a Minnesota winter, that meant little more than library time, well-bundled walks, and the occasional cup of coffee off campus. Still, that suited Skye, because what most excited her was Carter's nascent career. He was a graduating senior, double-majoring in computer science and engineering, with the top grades in his class. Job offers were coming in from everywhere. Carter, in his shambling way, was exuberant. Skye wasn't envious—he'd paid the price in four years of unheated apartments, bad food, and late hours. Besides, she'd decided to follow the same path: what he was enjoying now was a reward she wanted for herself.

Carter was endlessly encouraging, and in his own countrified way he got across his one big lesson: if you want it badly enough, go after it unrelentingly. There was an immense drive for success hidden within that shambling body and quiet, joking style.

It was in the midst of one of these oddly exciting conversations, in a coffeehouse much like a wood-paneled Starbucks, that Skye unexpectedly heard the last voice she ever wanted to hear again.

"Hey! It's psycho-bitch," the voice said in a stage whisper.

She'd read somewhere that sharks never bite a victim directly. Instead they brush past, scraping with their rough skin. After you start bleeding, they really attack.

Whether Randy intended to attack Skye in earnest must remain unknown. Carter, who'd ignored the remark, saw Skye turn red—studied her briefly—glanced toward Randy—and was suddenly on his feet and crossing swiftly to Randy's table.

It was funny: she'd thought of Randy and his friends as big; but next to Carter, they looked like scale models. Approaching Randy, Carter threw him entirely into shadow.

Carter had an arm over Randy's shoulder and, after leading him away a few feet, was leaning down to whisper in his ear. She couldn't hear what they were saying, but the color drained swiftly from Randy's face. Then Carter patted Randy's shoulder, grinned at him, and returned to Skye's table.

Even before Carter was seated again, she heard Randy tell his friends urgently, "Let's go."

"Aw, man."

"I said, let's *go!*" Randy was already hurrying for the front door; his two friends, exchanging annoyed looks, put money on the counter and followed.

Carter was slipping back into the chair beside her. He'd begun shambling again. She realized, with some alarm, that he moved slowly only when, like an elephant, he feared crushing someone.

She looked toward the front windows. Randy, after glaring in her direction, disappeared into the night.

"What happened to him?"

"I told him if he laughed at you again, I was going to drag him to the bathroom, turn him upside down, and shove him down a toilet till all I could see was the waffle souls of his goddamn Nikes, and then I was going to flush."

He said this in such a quiet way it took care to see he was pleased with himself, and Skye felt her face beginning to burn with anger.

"Go away."

His smile vanished. He turned quite pale. "What?"

"Go away."

He still sat there, shocked. Afraid she would relent out of pity, she stood quickly, almost knocking over the chair, and hurried for the street.

He caught her as she stepped onto the sidewalk.

"Wait a minute. You can be mad at me, but you wouldn't want to be mad over a misunderstanding, would you?"

Skye nodded stiffly. Her temper wasn't easy to control.

"I know you're burned. But I was trying to help."

"Men always try to help women. Then they send you the bill—and it's always worse than the trouble they saved you."

She started away, but he skipped around in front of her. It was startling how quickly he could move.

"What?" She tried to keep her voice steady.

"You're all wrong."

She didn't answer. He took a deep breath and plunged ahead. "Where I come from, anybody in school who liked books, or art, or even science was counted a freak and expected to get the cr— the stuffing beat out of them all the time. That's just how people are.

"People left me alone because I played a lot of football and was—well, sort of state heavyweight wrestling champion my senior year. And I kind of took on the job of protecting the smart kids at school. Somebody had to. Anyway, it's a habit with me, and that's why I jumped in— It's not 'cause you're a girl. It's 'cause you're a nerd."

He had said this with a most heartfelt sincerity and then, a second later, realized how absurd it sounded. It would be hard to say which of them burst out laughing first.

"Besides," he added when they were calmer, "I tried it one time. Jimmy Beckett called the president of the drama club a fag and stuffed him in a locker. So I dragged Jimmy to the bathroom and tried stuffing him down a toilet—but all he did was burble in the water and then fold up when I tried pushing him." He stopped and raised his eyebrows. "So it's really just a bluff." He paused, then added meditatively, "But it sure did get his attention."

Skye had stopped laughing, though she was still wondering at how good laughter felt, and how long it had been since she'd had anything to laugh about or anyone to laugh with.

CHAPTER THIRTEEN

A Funny Little Company

Of course, Skye had realized Carter wasn't going to be willing to stay just her friend for long. She'd guessed it from the first night at the CUG, and known it from the night he'd offered to stuff Randy down a toilet. On that almost violent night, she'd told him the whole story of herself and Randy; and as Carter really was a kind soul, it made him even more patient and circumspect.

Still, she hardly could expect him to wait forever before raising the topic of romance.

In fact, he waited another four weeks. By that time they had become very good friends indeed, and Carter was in a position to think well of his claims. His senior thesis, *Resource Conservation and Speed Optimization in Instruction-Set Design*, had been accepted for publication two weeks after it was approved by his committee. Every day his mail brought another grad-school acceptance or job-interview offer.

At the end of March Carter flew to Texas and came back saying he had taken a job with a company called Dell, which a U. of Texas student had started in his dorm room the year before.

"I'll be running manufacturing and design," he half shouted, waving his arms.

"Do you know enough?"

"We'll figure it out as we go. That'll be fun. We'll—"

"What about money?" Skye interrupted. She'd grown practical of late.

"Mostly stock options. Those are, like, notes to buy their stock dirt cheap. If the stock soars, I take a one-day loan from a bank, buy the stock for pennies, turn around and sell it for megabucks, then repay the loan. I make a fortune—and the tax rate's only half what it would be on salary. People have become millionaires in less than a year."

She had never seen him nearly so excited. It wasn't greed exactly; it was vindication. He'd gambled and won, and finally made it off the farm.

They agreed to celebrate. Dell had sent him three hundred dollars in incidental expense money for the trip; he'd hitchhiked from Dallas to the offices in Austin, and generally economized, and pocketed nearly two hundred bucks.

"Let's spend it," he concluded. "A really fancy night out. Champagne and stuff."

She was happy for Carter at least as much as she was envious, and worried about what else he might have on the program for the evening.

The restaurant was quiet and elegant, and the waiter was quite gracious about asking to see Skye's ID before serving them the wine. They laughed over not knowing half the things on the menu and made up silly explanations for what they might be.

In fact, everything went beautifully until the waiter ladled the brandy over the dessert crêpes and set them ablaze; then, as the waiter departed, Carter had leaned toward her earnestly.

"You know," he said, "I've been thinking a lot about us, and . . ."

She could already hear the speech coming; and very quickly she tried to avoid it. She shook her head almost violently.

"What?"

"I know what you're going to say, and . . . don't."

He waited, fiddled with his wineglass to give himself something to do, and then said—or perhaps, asked, "Maybe you're just not ready to be serious about another guy." He could have been trying to convince one or both of them.

She shook her head. "It's not that." Her voice had become almost inaudible. "I don't feel that way about guys. I don't think I ever have."

Suddenly *she* felt like crying.

Carter studied her intently. He seemed about to speak, but stopped. He wasn't only intelligent; he had the disconcerting habit of taking her seriously. He looked down at the cooling crêpes and nodded. His massive forearms were crossed, flat, on the white tablecloth, and leaning forward, he had something of the aspect of a St. Bernard—but it wasn't comical. More like endearing.

"Hey."

"What?" He didn't look up.

"Look at me."

"What?" He still didn't look up.

"Carter!" She put her hand on his forearm. She wasn't eager to do it, but he looked up.

"You're my best friend in the world. We just have to think of something other than boyfriend or girlfriend."

"Like what?" He wasn't very interested but he'd regained enough self-respect to straighten in his seat.

"Well, maybe we could work together on something."

"It'd better be something small. I leave for Texas in three weeks."

"Don't sulk."

"I'm not sulking."

"Okay, you're not. Do you want us to work together or don't you?"

He eyed her sulkily and decided to make the effort to pull himself together. This he accomplished with one deep breath and exhalation: it would have blown papers off the table if there'd been any. With the end of that epic breath, he asked, "On what?"

She started talking in a rush, explaining about the Ladies. Persuading him seemed desperately important. She finished up by saying, "So if we can come up with some good companies, I'll share the money with you. What do you think?"

Skye didn't know whether she was using him or really trying to save a friendship. Probably both.

Carter had entirely reversed his stance. Now he was leaning far back in his chair, with his arms folded across his chest and his chin dropped down low. He was thinking hard, exhaling slowly, in a way that blew his lower lip out, and only occasionally taking little glances up at Skye. She couldn't tell whether he was considering business possibilities or trying to decide if he was annoyed enough to tell her to get lost. Probably both.

"Well," he said finally, "there's a little company up in Seattle . . ."

"Wait!" Skye searched her purse for a pen; then, finding no paper, took the napkin from her lap. "Go ahead."

". . . called Microsoft," Carter concluded.

"Is that one word or two?" she asked, the pen halted above the napkin.

The corners of Carter's mouth turned up shakily. It was a weak smile, but a smile. He answered—

"I interviewed with eighteen companies. You'd better get a bigger napkin."

So, near the end of the next meeting of the Ladies' Club, Skye stood up, stared boldly at the floor, and mumbled something which, when repeated at Martha's insistence, turned out to be, "I think we should invest in a company called Microsoft. They make software."

Dolly raised her hand and, intending to be encouraging, asked, "You mean like fluffy coats and things?"

Skye's mouth twitched—and not with amusement. She still lived in that adolescent world of sudden, terrible shames and annoyances. At any moment the sense of being laughed at, or of being surrounded by idiots, enemies, or worthless allies, was likely to overwhelm her.

But she rallied: she raised her head, squared her shoulders, and looked Dolly in the eye. Very calmly she shook her head from side to side, then explained, "No—software is the instructions that tell a computer how to work. Microsoft is building the software for what's called a personal computer."

Agnes laughed merrily. "Personal computer? That sounds like a contradiction in terms!"

Skye swallowed hard. "They're new. Small computers that sit on your desk. In a few years they'll be on every desktop in the country. And they'll all run on Microsoft software . . ."

"Why Microsoft?"

Skye gave a slight smile. "Nobody's supposed to know this yet, but in ten days, IBM's going to announce they're getting into the personal-computer business, and all their software's going to come from Microsoft. And if we buy Microsoft stock now, we'll get unbelievably rich."

For an unbearable time they simply stared at her—breaking off only to shoot occasional little glances at each other.

Skye ran back to her chair, opened a manila folder she'd left there, and took out a handful of photocopies of a short article in the San Jose *Mercury News* entitled, "Enthusiasts Gather for Small Computer Show."

The Ladies had a long way to go. But Skye was going to help.

CHAPTER FOURTEEN

I Pick a Job

Take the purchase of $20,000's worth of Microsoft stock the day it went public, add in a few smaller coups like RipStop and Earth&Nature, and combine them with some steady and patient minor investments, and what do you have? You have the explanation for the short but (to my mind, at least) memorable conversation I had with my mom over the phone later that year.

It was the following autumn, and I was in the midst of what may be the only completely pleasurable stretch of a young lawyer's career: deciding which job to accept.

I had ended my second year standing far higher in the class than I'd expected. That was probably due mostly to the benign influence of my study partner, Milton Green (much more about him, later); but whoever deserved the credit, it meant I had more job opportunities than I had expected.

In 1984, the Reagan era was just getting under way. The Apple Macintosh and the IBM PC appeared that year, and the tech boom (and the Great Eighties Lawyer Boom) were both beginning to rattle dishes. As a result—and because firms were starting to mumble faintly about hiring women—I had five and a half job offers: three in Chicago, two in Minneapolis, and one half in New York. The half was a prestigious firm that, on my friend Milt's recommendation, had said they might find work for me if I'd get myself to the big city. It was a real opportunity—if I hung on, I'd be in with one of the country's highest-paying firms. But there were, well, *issues* involved in being at Milton's firm (more about *those* later, too).

Besides, after three years of law school, I'd had enough groveling to hold me for a while. I decided to pick a firm where I'd rank at least a little higher than a tadpole in Lake Michigan.

In the meantime, I'd had so much nonstop work that I'd largely lost touch with events in Larksdale. Sure, I'd get and (usually) read Mom's weekly letters, but none of it penetrated very far into a skull stuffed with torts and briefs and subtle legal arguments.

But that autumn I was in for the shock of my life.

In fact, I had called home to tell Mom I was taking one of the Chicago offers. Inevitably she tried to talk me into taking a Minneapolis job instead.

I thought I was ready for all her objections, but just at the end (after she'd exhausted such zingers as, "How will you stand the Chicago winters?"), she finally caught me off guard.

"But, honey, aren't clients important? I mean, aren't you in stronger shape at a firm if you bring in some clients of your own?"

This seemed so far off-point that I relaxed. The only possible client my parents might be able to *mention* was the town's main employer, Prairie Machine Tool. My dad was a fairly senior middle manager there—but Prairie Machine's legal work had long been done by a firm with decades-old connections to the company's founders.

"Gee, Mom," I said with intense mock gratitude, "that's a brilliant idea. Who in Minnesota do you see as running to sign with me?"

Snottiness goeth before a fall.

"Well, I think we might be your clients."

"You and Dad?"

"The Independence Club."

"Oh, sure. Terrific. And I'd do exactly what for you? Represent you against ValuShop if they sell you stale cookies?"

"We're starting to have some really solid holdings, honey. We've got some real money now."

"Oh, I bet, Mom," I answered, as tactless as only a newly minted lawyer can be. "And how much might that be?"

"Well, I'm not exactly certain, but according to our last quarterly summary, we had about ninety thousand in cash waiting to invest and about eight hundred and sixty-some thousand in our portfolio."

The hair stood up on the back of my neck, and there was a dull *thunk* as the phone hit the floor.

There was just a brief pause, and I think she added in a tinny voice coming from the phone on the floor, "That Intel sure is a marvelous stock."

CHAPTER FIFTEEN

My Brilliant Career

So, to be brief, I took the best of the three Minneapolis jobs and returned to Larksdale. With the help of my friend Marcy Ansdahl—who, against all predictions, had refused a lapful of prestigious New York jobs and was starting with the Twin Cities' top firm—I found an apartment, bought a used Chevy Corsica, and began the life of a rookie lawyer.

My apartment was suitable for a movie star—specifically, one of the stars of *Das Boot* or any other submarine film. I could stretch out my arms and touch both walls of my bedroom at once. But who cared? I practically lived at the office.

My mother had arranged for me to be a minority investor in the club. This had two immediate effects. After making payments on my student loans and covering such extravagances as food and rent, I had almost no spending money. Also, I earned the considerable anger of Veronica Harris, who could not understand why I could invest in the Club and she could not.

Veronica Harris had been my nemesis since I was eight, when she had taught my Sunday-school class. She'd been quite a beauty then, but now, with dyed red hair and baggy pale blue eyes, she looked (I would say, if I were mean) like Maureen O'Hara after a six-day drunk. She was, moreover, a person I always suspected of being "righteous overmuch," expecting perfection from eight-year-old girls who already qualified for sainthood merely by sitting quietly while their precious weekend days were stolen from them. Accordingly, though I tried many times to like her better, Veronica and I lived the Minnesota version of a blood feud—meaning we rarely chatted for more than five minutes when we saw each other and never sent each other the really good Hallmark cards at Christmas.

Veronica was, however, a very competent CPA; and since she had always held observer status with the Mostly Methodist Club, she had been a reasonable choice when the Ladies began to need an accountant several months before I returned to Larksdale.

So she was understandably galled to hear I could invest and she could not. Being Veronica, she found subtle (and not so subtle) ways to tell the Ladies how she felt. But being Veronica, she never went so far as to offer to resign as their accountant.

Mostly I ignored Veronica. I ignored a lot that year. It was easy to do, since my job required roughly one hundred hours a week—divided roughly into ninety hours of legal work and ten hours of being yelled at by my supervising partner, who apparently thought that "mentor" was from the Greek meaning "to kick in the butt."

Still, I enjoyed myself. My boss may have growled and roared, but when annual reviews appeared, he was generous. Unlike some partners, he wasn't a backstabber, merely overstressed and de-manding—and convinced endless work was the way to train young lawyers. The time flew by: nothing tops the panic and ex-haustion of the first years of legal practice for making the hours get up and dance.

So, my role in the Club's early days was part-time and small, confined to legal gruntwork.

The creative stuff the Ladies handled themselves.

Except when things got out of control.

CHAPTER SIXTEEN

Gladys Makes a Score

Skye's adventures—and Microsoft and Dell's rocketlike ascent—had inspired all the Ladies.

But no one took it more to heart than Gladys, who had an explorer's soul within the frame of an aging librarian.

To look at, Gladys Vaniman was by far the least impressive of the Ladies. Pushing sixty, small and slender, she was beginning to seem frail. Decades of gardening under broad sunbonnets had not harmed her milky-white skin or large, innocent blue eyes. She was a stealth person: so much the quiet country lady that you only later realized how brisk and incisive her mind was.

Her mind became particularly active after Skye's Great Microsoft Caper. Like a great many women of a certain age, who gave up hoping the world would allow an outlet for their talents and energies, Gladys had reconciled herself to her situation but never lost her regrets for what might have been, or her kindly envy of young women with so many more choices.

And when the Club began working so brilliantly, Gladys saw it as a long-awaited chance for her own personal springtime. If a pink-haired teenager could do brilliant research, Gladys decided, so could she.

She set to work using the resources of the Larksdale Public Library.

Now, if "Larksdale Public Library" brings to mind images of a pathetic little sixties-style concrete bungalow, or a set of tin Quonset huts, let me clarify.

The first Larksdale Public Library, funded by Andrew Carnegie in 1906, was a really imposing granite building, fronted by green lawns and shaded by a set of noble elms. But on two large lots behind it, donated by Prairie Machine in its brief salad days after WWII, was an annex, connected to the main building by a brick, Italian Renaissance enclosed walkway. This annex, also grandly Italianate, held the large children's and business rooms, as well as the library's administrative offices.

Larksdale Public Library was, in short, the town's glory, backed (as success always breeds success) by an active Friends of the Library group and generally rated one of the top five small public libraries in the Midwest. It was, like every small-town library, the source and repository of dreams for summer-reading children; but it was also a passable research facility for smart investors.

Accordingly, as spring drifted toward summer, Gladys drafted her fellow librarian, poor, kindly Agnes, into a campaign to dig out some hidden gem of a local investment target.

Agnes, unfortunately, lived in absolute terror of their supervisor. He was a short, dark-red-faced man with the preposterous name of Inigo Stout, who ran the library like a prison camp with books.

Agnes found the prospect of undertaking a secret project on library time far more frightening than amusing. Of course, she was also handicapped by the fact that she was only a children's librarian. Still, to her credit, she did her best. On those rare days when Inigo Stout was away, she searched everywhere for leads on toy makers, day care providers, and anyone else who might need an investment from the Larksdale Ladies Club.

There certainly were business opportunities to be found in the children's reading room; but by the end of May, when she had to cease her searching to begin preparing for the summer rush of children on vacation, Agnes had not yet found them. What she *had* done (though she didn't realize it until months later) was to bring herself to the attention of Inigo Stout. He had previously tagged her as one of the "safe" (read "mentally dead") ones—but from then on, he had his eye on her. It was that evil eye which, several years later, finally woke Agnes up.

Meanwhile, though . . .

It was Gladys who put two clippings together and made us one small fortune.

As an avid gardener, Gladys paid more attention than even Martha to the agricultural news. In particular, she discovered something interesting.

For all the excitement about biotech, by 1986 only one biotech company in the world was solidly profitable—and that on the basis of a single product. The rest were losing money hand over fist as they invested in medicines still years from market.

The sole important exception to this was in agronomics—specifically, the biotech-based creation of new kinds of seeds.

And so the two clippings.

The first, dated six months previously, was an interview in *Business Southwest Minnesota* with the CEO of a seed company called Greensland. This CEO, a pleasant-looking middle-aged man named Jaworski, told the magazine he believed the company's ten-year effort to isolate the frost-resistance gene in a rare species of rapeseed was very close to paying off.

Gladys hadn't the dimmest idea there even was a frost-resistance gene—until she sat down to teach herself the basics of genetic engineering. For that, of course, even Larksdale's splendid little library was too small; over the next six weeks she spent every weekend at the University of Minnesota's Biomedical Library. When she was done, she understood as much about biotech as most second-year medical students.

She also thought she understood what the rapeseed antifrost gene meant.

There were two possibilities:

Either Gladys was bonkers, or Greensland had found a way to grow oranges in the snowbelt.

So, when she learned from the business section of the *New York Times* that the CEO of America's second-largest chemical company, which had a huge agribiz subsidiary, planned to spend three days "vacationing and fishing" at Lake Manawheeni (six miles from Hastings, the hometown of Greensland), Gladys put two and two together—and came up with an idea.

It was a warm spring morning. Soft breezes blew in through the open windows. And Inigo Stout was nowhere in sight.

Gladys gave everyone a big, librarianly "shhh!" with fingers to lips, then slipped into her glass-walled cubicle behind the reference desk, took a deep breath, and called the corporate headquarters of Greensland.

It's remarkable how much authority librarians can put into their voices.

Gladys worked her way through the switchboard, until a cool voice said, "Office of the president."

"Yes, I'm calling on behalf of G. J. Vaniman, of LLIC, Inc."

"LLIC, Inc.?"

"We're an investment group, specializing in growth companies." Gladys got good wood on that one, making it sound first, like anyone with a brain would know LLIC, and second, like she was such a broad soul that she could pardon even an idiot. "G. J. Vaniman heads our Life Sciences Analysis Group and would like to meet with Mr. Jaworski—tomorrow, if possible." Gladys was grinning uncontrollably out through the glass office walls. She was having fun.

"Could you tell me the purpose of the meeting?" the cool voice asked.

"I'm afraid not."

A silence. Then, "Mr. Jaworski has fifteen minutes tomorrow at one-thirty. Will that work?"

"Very nicely. Thank you."

That afternoon, Gladys left early. Walking down the library steps, she thought briefly about buying a new dress for the meeting, but her confidence had not yet soared that high. She turned instead to figuring out in her mind the buses she would take to get to Hastings the next day. As nearly as she could tell, the Greyhound trip would last about three hours each way.

She would have to pack a sandwich and some fruit to fit into her purse.

The headquarters of Greensland actually lay about halfway between Hastings and Lake Manawheeni, on what in central Minnesota passes for a hilltop. It was a gorgeous spring day, when the young cornstalks waved mint green under blue skies, and Gladys was happy to walk the three miles from the Greyhound station to the facility. She ate her sandwich on a bench at the station, then brushed her teeth in the station rest room and struck out for the open country.

Most of Greensland resembled a farm that had mutated, like a bug in a fifties horror movie. It consisted of a wide scattering of buildings built in what might be called "grain-silo modern"—a very industrial construct in the midst of pretty farm country. Central to it all was the main corporate building, squat, serious, and beige; four stories tall and fronted by a very large parking lot.

Gladys took the main building's slightly rickety elevator. On the fourth floor half a dozen polite gentlemen waited for her to exit first. She turned left, walked a few paces, and sat on the nearest padded bench to let them rush about their business. Because people will always ask an unoccupied older lady whether they can help her, she studied her watch and discovered she was ten minutes early.

For lack of anything better to do, she decided to stroll around the top floor. She told herself she could at least get a sense of the company's physical plant and capital expenditures—terms she would not have known, six months earlier—and reminded herself to keep moving forcefully, lest someone ask what she was doing there.

The walk was informative. She decided Greensland, in true Midwestern fashion, had wasted little of its money. The offices she saw through open doors were decorated with industrial-gray-metal furniture probably dating from World War II.

But then she found the most unexpected thing: a metal door, which somehow proclaimed "laboratory," was labeled AUTHORIZED PERSONNEL ONLY. Gladys authorized herself, turned the doorknob, stepped in, and peeked.

Inside, on benches, sat row upon row of small, neat green bushes, as mysterious and out of place as something from *Day of the Triffids* or *Invasion of the Body Snatchers*.

It was of automatic interest to any gardener: rows of midsized seedlings. Not everyone would have recognized them, but Gladys did.

They were orange trees.

Her pulse accelerating, Gladys retraced her steps. But she was too flustered by her discovery to enter Mr. Jaworski's office. She turned off into a darker pathway.

After two minutes' walking she found herself at the end of a small, dim corridor. Nothing unusual about it, except for a fire alarm, which struck her as oddly located and nearly impossible to find in an emergency. The curiosity of it helped Gladys get her mind off orange trees in Minnesota and contemplate more humorously the vagaries of architecture.

With that thought stuck in her mind, she started back the way she'd come.

*I*t was one-thirty precisely when Gladys strode through the door to Mr. Jaworski's outer office, and the prim blond secretary behind the desk glanced up and asked if she could help her.

"Yes!" answered Gladys briskly. "I have a one-thirty appointment with Mr. Jaworski. Gladys Vaniman."

"I'm sorry?"

"G. J. Vaniman? From Larksdale Ladies Independence Club? I spoke with you yesterday?"

It was just at this instant, I believe, that Mr. Jaworski's secretary finally realized that the G. J. Vaniman she'd expected to arrive from LLIC, rather than being a hale-and-hearty fifty-year-old ex-football player, or even a twenty-eight-year-old hotshot from Harvard Biz, was in fact a grandmotherly unknown-years-old *woman* in a rather frumpy flowered dress.

The prim blond secretary called an audible from the line of scrimmage—an instant after Gladys introduced herself, she blushed, looked toward the boss's august door, and said smoothly, "I'm terribly sorry. Mr. Jaworski's been called out of town suddenly," even while she was dropping back, scrambling for a file cabinet, and coming up with some photocopied PR materials. "Here," she continued with awkward cheer, while handing them off to Gladys, "I think these will answer your questions. I hope you ladies have a lot of fun with your club."

"But you don't understand," Gladys cried urgently. "We're very serious investors, and—"

"Oops!" interrupted the prim secretary. "That's my phone."

No doubt she knew her own phone; but if she had meant by

that that it was ringing, she was quite mistaken. However, she picked it up and said into the receiver, very distinctly, "Mr. Jaworski's office. May I help you?"

Gladys took this insult quietly, just as you'd expect of someone who'd worked so many years for Inigo Stout of the Larksdale Public Library. She smiled at the secretary, shook the brochures, and mouthed, "Thank you," and left the office quietly.

Then something very strange happened. First Gladys got angry. Nothing strange about that—she'd spent some part of nearly every working day of her life angry, or humiliated, or something similar. No—the strange thing was that Gladys did something about it.

On her way down in the elevator, Gladys considered her options and began to smile. When the elevator reached the ground floor, instead of walking straight out of the building, she made a right turn, and then another, and then a left—and then walked on until she was quite by herself in a darkened, windowless short corridor. Nothing marked the featureless walls except a dim stairwell at the end of it, and near it, the small-but-interesting red box of a fire alarm.

Gladys stopped beside the fire alarm. She reached inside her purse, drew out her pink gloves, and put them on carefully. Then she swung the alarm's miniature hinged hammer into position against the glass and banged it with her fist. The noise of breaking glass was a slight tinkle; but she turned swiftly and looked down the hallway while standing so she blocked the red box from view.

She counted five, saw she was still unobserved, and gave a hearty downward yank to the red handle of the fire alarm.

As bells clanged and yammered throughout the facility, she began to walk purposefully back down the corridor. She retraced her steps to the elevators, then continued out the glass front doors looking as prim and unflustered as Miss Marple.

She stopped as soon as she reached the company parking lot. Hundreds of startled employees—most of them bouncing with secret delight to be out in the fresh spring air while daylight remained—were streaming from the building. Gladys flipped hastily through the copy of the company's annual report the blond secretary had thrust upon her. She found the quarter-page black-and-white photo labeled, *Mark Jaworski, CEO*. In the picture he was hale and hearty, with a frank smile, a football player's neck, and a big, bald circle of a head, just fringed by close-cut black hair.

In real life he was one of the last ones out of the building, somewhat stouter and a good deal more harried looking than his photo. But he still looked likable, and Gladys knew her plan would work.

He was clearly heading toward the main parking-lot entrance, so Gladys, who could move quite smartly when she had to, rushed to get there first. She was ahead of the crowd; it was easy enough to beat him and then to crouch as if examining an injured ankle.

She stayed that way until a polite voice from above asked, "Are you all right, ma'am?"

"I believe I am. Thank you." She rose and pretended she needed to catch her breath. "I'm just not used to this much excitement."

Jaworski, distracted, nodded, then surveyed the parking lot intently, a responsible executive. The crowding workers appeared about as panic-stricken as if they were waiting for the company picnic to start. His brow furrowed. He wanted to do something executive, but nothing came to mind.

Following the spirit of this, Gladys grew more serious, scanned the main building for signs of smoke, then looked back to Mr. Jaworski. "It really doesn't look much like there's going to be a gigantic fireball, does it? What a shame to take so many busy people away from their work."

This had the right effect. After hesitating a moment, Mr. Jaworski shrugged off his concerns and smiled at her.

Gladys smiled back. "What a scene. I don't suppose you work in this madhouse?" she asked with great good humor.

"Afraid I'm the head lunatic." He bowed his head momentarily, then grinned even wider and offered his hand. "Mark Jaworski, CEO."

Gladys jumped in surprise. "No! I don't believe it. You don't mean such a young man as you is running this entire huge company!"

Mr. Jaworski, who really was a nice fellow, blushed slightly and made another nodlike bow of his head.

Gladys beamed at him. Then her eyes narrowed, and she said while studying him with respectful sympathy, "Of course, I can see you must have an important job. My stars, for such a young fellow, you look *very* weary. They work you too hard, and you need a vacation!"

"Why, bless your heart for saying so!" He smiled at her with genuine gratitude. When she still looked worried, he leaned closer, lowered his voice, and went on confidentially. "Now, I can't really tell you why, but I'm expecting to come into a whole bunch of money within a few days—and I can just about promise you I'll be taking one heck of a vacation."

Somehow that made Gladys feel a whole lot better. She positively glowed as she patted his shoulder and told him, "You can't imagine how happy that makes me. I hope you get *lots* of money and a really fine vacation."

She offered her hand, and Mr. Jaworski, startled but pleased, shook it.

With that, she turned quickly and started for the main road. She moved fast, because from the corner of her eye, she'd seen Mr. Jaworski's prim blond secretary moving toward her with a curious expression on her face.

Gladys was pretty sure she hadn't been spotted, but she scrunched down a bit as she exited the parking lot and banked around the decorative stone wall that surrounded corporate headquarters.

Her timing was good.

The fire trucks were just roaring into the lot as she left. They covered her escape, and before the sirens had been shut off, she was in the clear, walking alone down the country road back to Hastings.

A wondrous exuberance had overtaken Gladys. To her surprise, she found herself hearing—and then, egad, *singing*—"I Sleep Easier Now," Cole Porter's zippy little ditty about youthful lust and old age's contentments.

It was a perfect spring day, and her voice sounded just fine.

CHAPTER SEVENTEEN

Aiding and Abetting

By the time Gladys reached my office, some three hours later, her exuberance had crossed the border into panic. This, after all, was a woman who would stand for five minutes on a deserted street waiting for a broken light signal to turn green—and then walk a block to try another signal.

"Am I in a lot of trouble?" she asked with a little tremble in her voice.

"I don't think so," I answered. "Just pull your car into the back alley so I can change the plates." I was going to buzz Krista, my moonlighting secretary from Senior, Winters and Willow, and ask her to bring me one of the fake Czech passports and a couple of Glock 9mms when I realized Gladys was serious: that is to say, she was almost as frightened as she was excited.

"I'm *kidding*!" I added hastily, forgetting my fantasy of Gladys shooting her way across the Canadian border—if only because it's so hard to shoot at border guards who are waving and yelling, "Have a nice day!"

I had assumed it could all be laughed off. Now, somehow, I knew Gladys needed to hear that the moral order of the universe had not been suspended. I leaned forward and tried to look serious.

"In the first place, nobody saw you. In the second, even if they suspect you—and frankly, you don't exactly look like Public Enemy Number 2000, let alone Public Enemy Number One—they'd be nuts to pursue it because all they'd wind up with is a story on the six o'clock news showing they were outsmarted by a sixty-year-old librarian, while you'd be at least halfway to folk-hero status." She smiled at that; the crisis was passing. But I knew the standards of the Mostly Methodist Club—especially our proud tradition of pointless moralizing—had to be upheld.

"Of course," I said sternly, "as your attorney, I certainly can't advise you to make a habit of this sort of thing. It's certainly morally suspect. If nothing else, it will raise the bar for the other ladies—and I'm not sure they can match your creativity. Shall we agree this will be your last adventure of this sort?"

"Oh, yes. Absolutely," she answered, primly apologetic—and I had, not for the first time, the unsettling feeling that Gladys and I shared a secret pact of laughing quietly at the rest of the world.

We chatted a few more minutes, and then Gladys left.

*O*f course, there's moral—and then there's crazy. The next morning, which was Saturday, Gladys gave the Ladies a full and detailed summary of her first adventure as a stockmarket analyst, after which the following brief conversation took place:

AGNES: You told him he looked peaked?
GLADYS: Yes, dear.
AGNES: And he said he was about to come into money and take a long vacation?
GLADYS: Yes, dear.
AGNES: (pause) Move we buy two thousand shares.
MOM: All in favor?
ALL: Aye.

Four days later, on Wednesday morning, the *Wall Street Journal* announced that a tender offer had put Greensland Seed in play, and in another three weeks the Ladies had once again doubled their money.

It was certainly a brilliant investment move; but to be honest, by 1986, I was getting used to brilliant moves from the Ladies. What pleased me most was that Gladys's adventure was going to give a funny anecdote to use that night, when I sat down to write my monthly letter to my faraway friend, Milt.

CHAPTER EIGHTEEN

My So-called Social Life

The fact that I was planning my Saturday evening around writing a letter to a law-school studymate ought to tell you nearly everything about the blazing success that was my social life.

My mother, of course, put it all down to my being too "choosy." I in turn was convinced she applied the Breathalyzer test to any prospective companion for me: if he was breathing, he was a candidate. I—no matter what she thought—was hardly rigid on the matter.

Still, things never seemed to work out.

For one thing, I was chronically short on cash. I was taking more than half of my salary—which was modest to begin with—as shares in the investment club. Of course, that was rapidly turning into a tidy sum; but none of it was in my greedy little hand to spend.

For another, I don't drink. That's not a moral decision, exactly—more like a civic choice for the good of all Minneapolis. Two glasses of red wine, and I'm ready to stand on the balcony, throw out my arms, and sing "Don't Cry for Me, Minnesota" at the top of my lungs. That's probably fine if you have a voice like Kathleen Battle, but less socially acceptable if you sound like a professional beagle imitator. Not even downtown St. Paul deserves that. Hence, Sophia the Sober (and the Badly Dressed)—not exactly the life of every party.

I'm not sure I'd have gone out at all, except for my friend Marcy.

Marcy and I had been friends since we were eight—specifically, since the day she had nailed our overbearing Sunday-school teacher with a magnificent spit wad. This teacher, whose name happened to be Veronica Harris, I also found annoying beyond bearing. My solution had been to write a really cutting limerick rhyming "Harris" with "Grizzly Bearis"—and then being too embarrassed to recite it. That pretty much epitomized the difference between Marcy and me.

We had stayed friends through law-school days (she went east to Yale: Marcy was as smart as she was tough), and when, to my considerable surprise, she took a job back in Minneapolis, we liked each other just as well. That was in spite of the fact that she had, on launching her career, embraced the eighties as if they were the greatest weekend lover in history. From Armani suits and Ralph Lauren glasses (she had twenty-twenty vision) to spiffy German sports sedans, Marcy was like a cover girl for *Yuppie Quarterly*. She was also blond, green-eyed, fit, and shapely, with cleanly cut features that blended sex and business in a perfect way for the times. She could get a date in the Vatican.

Despite being a litigator with a downtown law firm, Marcy had a kind heart and had decided she would rescue me from loneliness. I asked her one day when she was going to paste a "Save the Sophias" bumper sticker on her BMW; but nothing deterred her. Her view on relationships was that if you had to be miserable, it was better to do it while some guy was buying you Peking duck. Roughly every other Thursday, I'd get a call along these lines:

"Listen: Tomorrow night, Brigham's, you and me. Drinks."

"I don't drink."

"7UP's a drink. Don't make me get rough with you."

"I don't know."

"It'll be fun. Six o'clock." And she'd clinch the argument by hanging up.

On those occasions—about twice a month—when Marcy would drag me to a yuppie singles bar, I'd generally endure the torments of the socially damned. Usually I'd wind up sitting at some back table so small the 7UP glass would hang over the edges, and watching through the smoke as Marcy stood at the center of some group of well-dressed young professionals, all baring their teeth in laughter and slapping each other on the back. Regularly I'd try to get up and join them; but there was something wrong with the gravitational field, and I could never manage to rise.

Those were always the most miserable moments, as I sat there convincing myself the reason I fit in so well with a bunch of aging stay-at-homes was that I was really an aging-stay-at-home in training.

About this time, across the room, Marcy would get a more serious look, lean forward, and whisper to one of the better-looking guys in the circle, who almost at once would start shooting appraising glances in my direction, and then, likely as not, detach himself from the group and start toward me.

Watching one of these guys, wearing a Versace suit and holding a double Stoli, lumber across the room toward me was always inspiring. Sort of like being a baby seal during the Canadian hunting season. I was generally tempted to scurry across the floor yelling, "Ar! Ar! Ar!" while a voice intoned, "This month on *National Geographic* . . . hunting the wild Sophia."

But keeping my seat always guaranteed me the fun of hearing some good-looking guy with a voice like a radio DJ introduce himself as Brent Rickly or Rick Brently or something, and then, a sentence or two later, move onto the ever popular, "So, Sophe— can I call you Sophe?—Marcy tells me you two have been friends since way before law school."

"Absolutely. Me and old Marce." That's me at parties. A dazzling conversationalist. It's like talking to one of the ice sculptures.

"Great, great. You must have a really cool job—lawyer's what you want to be these days. I'm with Merrill Lynch in St. Paul. Broker. Retail accounts." He makes a quick survey of the room, to see if anyone better looking was available. "How would you like to go grab a bite to eat?"

Instead of answering, "Love to. See you later," I inevitably nod and smile agreeably, and we head off to some restaurant a block or two away which always manages to look exactly like the bar we just left, except that the tables are different. Sometimes I think they just drive me around the block while the set's being rearranged.

Once we're seated, the conversation nearly always takes exactly the same course:

"So, Sophe. Who do you work for? One of the big firms down-town?"

"Just a small investment club."

A silence, then, "You mean a bunch of doctors or something?"

"Actually, they're about four housewives, a hairdresser, and a couple of librarians."

A *long* silence.

"Seven little old ladies, huh? Great. Great. Hey, listen: I have to go make a quick phone call. Stay here—I'll be right back." A short wave of the hand. "Waiter, another iced tea for my friend." Terrific. Fifteen minutes into our eight o'clock date, and he's already running to line up something for later. Like, about eight-thirty.

Once every six months or so, I'd get desperate enough to tell them what they wanted to hear:

"So, Peters, enough about me—tell me about *your* work."

"I handle just a small group of private investors." It all depends on how you read the line. Lean forward confidentially and say it with the right air of amused, awed mysteriousness, and they'll be sure it's just you, the Rockefellers, and Bill Gates.

"Sounds pretty exciting."

"Oh, I don't know. Mostly old money." That was true in a sense: they had money, and most of them were old as hell.

"Pretty lucrative work, eh?"

"You wouldn't believe it." Neither would anyone who'd ever seen my bank balance.

"Wow. Say—after dinner, how'd you like to swing by my condo? I just got this killer stereo. CDs—everything."

"That sounds great."

So sometimes I would go. Sometimes it was exciting. Once I even met a guy I liked a lot. We were still dating six weeks later when he decided to move back to Los Angeles to be closer to his ex-fiancée.

Most often it was slightly less satisfying than staying home and writing letters. But sometimes the Breathalyzer test is the best you can do.

CHAPTER NINETEEN

Father O'Sophia, or the Good Times Start to Roll

*I*f you can't have a social life of your own, I suppose the next best thing is to have access to everybody else's. This is the propelling force behind romance novels, talk shows, and on-line chat sites— and it was also probably what kept me from going totally bonkers and joining a cult.

My own private version of Oprah, of course, was the Club. With the passing years, the Ladies began to talk ever more freely among themselves at weekly meetings. As their holdings grew, the business part of those meetings grew steadily more efficient—with the primary purpose, I think, of clearing the business away so they could get on to what they most enjoyed, the chatting.

By 1986, meetings began promptly at nine A.M., with a review of news that might affect their holdings, then a call for any special issues needing attention—which included any related to the Mostly Methodist Club's original charitable purposes. Then a short break, and at ten exactly, an hour devoted to three twenty-minute pitches for possible new investments. In theory, each Lady was supposed to pitch one new idea every other week, but in practice we heard from Deborah and Skye often, from Gladys and my mom occasionally, and from the others only rarely.

Skye had long since come off probation; she was back in school and doing brilliantly, and undoubtedly the most dignified pink-haired person in any investment club anywhere. It didn't hurt, of course, that she had a pipeline into the hottest tips from Silicon Valley.

The only awkwardness in these meetings came during Veronica Harris's monthly appearances to summarize the Club's holdings. For Veronica I was a sore spot—one which, rather than healing, seemed to grow worse with passing time. By common, unspoken agreement, I began skipping about half of her presentations. That way, I saw her only every two months and spoke with her only when absolutely necessary on business, and so we kept our animosity under control. I understood why she disliked me; but that didn't make me any more eager to endure her scowling, muttered sarcasm. I could get enough muttered sarcasm any day at work.

*A*voiding Veronica was all made easier when, early in '86, we decided I had enough Club legal work to fill one day a week. The Ladies by that time were buying a small office building on Elm Street in Larksdale; I received a tiny office, with a tinier reception area, rent-free, and was available to them there Saturdays after meetings and every Thursday evening. Krista, my secretary, moonlighted in order to help me out, and because, newly married at twenty-one, she needed the money.

Perhaps some of the Ladies began visiting my office just to be polite, others because they were fascinated by the idea of having their own private attorney. Inevitably, though, their legal problems were simple; and just to pass the time, we'd begin talking about our personal lives. Since I barely *had* a personal life, that meant we'd soon be talking about *their* lives.

Moreover, I was always a sort of mother-confessor type. People who had done things—good, bad, or simply dull—could rarely ever wait to come and tell me. Probably because I was never competition for anyone.

Naturally enough, I suppose, I had become the most frequent confidante of Skye, who was, by a good margin, the nearest to my own age. I had not left college so long before as to have gotten sentimental about it, and we had fairly frequent chats about idiot professors, dumb requirements, and pointless assignments.

Sometime in early July of '86, though, Skye disappeared.

That is, she missed the Club's legendary Fourth of July barbecue (complete with Dolly's blueberry, strawberry, and banana American-flag cake) and then failed to show for the next four weeks' regular meetings.

Of course, Skye was long since an independent agent and not obliged to show up if she didn't feel like it. Still, we couldn't help worrying—especially Martha, who, I suspected, had probably taken to trying to phone her almost daily.

So it was a mild surprise, the first Thursday in August, as thunder from an approaching storm rattled the office windows, when Krista stuck her head in my door and announced, with raised eyebrows, that Skye had come to visit.

I had switched off my computer (we had two of them in the office by then) with the first hint of lightning and was reading a forty-page commercial lease. If someone ever offers you the chance to read one of these, take my advice and wait for the movie. I was delighted to see Skye for more than one reason.

Out of respect for her privacy, I acted as if I had seen Skye only days before, and we began chatting as if no absence had intervened. For about twenty minutes, over lemonade, we covered the usual topics: summer vacation, her fall class schedule, the news from Carter.

Then Skye, having exhausted the topic of research grants, began rather diffidently discussing a "someone" she'd met. She kept her head down and talked in the half-mumbled style I hadn't heard from her in more than a year. Moreover, from her occasional blushes of apparent pleasure, it was soon clear she had fallen hard for this unnamed someone. She looked about sixteen and flustered with delight. The lease forgotten, I found myself suppressing a smile of genuine, if envy-tinged, pleasure at her happiness.

Finally, sounding only a little teasing, I asked, "So, what's his name?"

There was the longest imaginable pause. I was about to speak again when Skye finally answered, "Actually he's a she."

Larksdale in 1986 was not exactly in the Dark Ages; yet Skye's response was both exotic and a little alarming. The sharp cracks of the thunderstorm sounded just a bit louder. For the sake of our common humanity, however, I am happy to say I responded kindly—even if not very elegantly.

"Oh," I said, "that's interesting."

She looked up with such a pitiable defensiveness that I revised. "That's great, I mean."

She eyed me levelly. "Well, maybe. Except that I can't tell my parents, and she can't tell hers, and everybody—" She stopped, swallowed hard, and pressed her fingertips hard against her lips.

"And besides," she finally continued, having regained her self-control, "those rotten frat boys—that jerk Randy—will be right."

With that, she began crying.

It was not precisely what I'd expected.

Indeed, it was at this exact moment that I discovered the difference between me and Oprah Winfrey. I'm fine with expressions of strong emotion—just as long as they don't involve anyone I know. As soon as Skye began weeping, I took the most direct action possible.

I panicked.

I was tossing tissues at her as fast as I could pluck them from the box. They were landing on her shoulders, piling up on her lap. It looked as if she'd been overflown by a diarrhetic paper seagull.

She was still crying and ignoring the tissues. Some people you just can't help—but more panicked than ever, I kept trying.

I dashed around the desk and, not knowing what else to do, endeavored to pat her comfortingly on the back. I used about the right force for someone with a chicken bone stuck in her throat. She pitched forward and banged her head against the desk. So much for all women being born nurturers. I was about two inches from an assault charge.

"Ow!" she said, sounding (oddly enough) somewhat better.

"Sorry," I offered. I, too, felt calmer. She wasn't bleeding. "I was upset. You okay now?"

She nodded—thought—nodded again. "I'm just not ready for my parents to know." The idea of her having a family up-country somewhere was vaguely startling; I'd somehow thought of Skye as being either Martha's granddaughter or else the common foundling of the entire Club.

"Don't worry. I won't tell anybody."

"Oh, but I want you to." She had abandoned nearly every thought of crying, and was answering with almost her old level calm.

"Eh?"

"I'm not ashamed. I'm just shy. And I'm just afraid my parents couldn't stand it." She paused and eyed me closely. "I mean, I *know* they couldn't stand it."

Having no reply to that, I waited until she went on. "But I certainly don't mind if the Ladies know." Her tone was more like an announcement that she *wanted* the Ladies to know.

"So you *want* me to tell them?" I asked uncertainly. "I'm authorized to gossip?"

She had finally brightened. "Would you, please?"

I was left (as perhaps always happens when another person finishes crying) with a faint suspicion that I had been manipulated; but considering Skye's situation, I decided the case was otherwise.

"Sure," I said, thinking I was being way too quick to answer.

.   .   .

That night at home, I kicked myself for having taken a job Skye ought to have undertaken herself. Still, I had given my word, and the next morning, at the weekly meeting, I began circulating the news. I started with Martha, both because she deserved first notice, and because I figured I might as well get the toughest part over first.

By ten-fifteen, Skye had not arrived, and the meeting hadn't started. But I'd told everyone; so when Skye finally appeared, they let her slip into the room studiously unnoticed.

I had grown pretty good at guessing Skye's mood. Somehow, it seemed, my panic attack had set exactly the right tone. Once Skye realized her situation was not *that* serious, she began to think more reasonably. At least, she saw no further need to hide from her friends.

She was waiting awkwardly by the snack table when Martha approached her and said sociably, "Sophia says you've met someone special."

Skye couldn't quite face her. "You aren't mad?"

"My dear. We're religious, and I'd like to think we're often right—but that hardly makes us the religious right."

Skye looked up gratefully—and seeing her expression, the other Ladies rushed to join her. From private, the discussion had turned general.

Not that Skye was making easy or casual conversation. She realized she was going to have to test every single relationship she had—every person who knew her was going to be given the chance to review his or her acceptance of her. Even those who liked her were going to be liking a different person. Over the next quarter hour her looks changed from hopeful to discouraged many times.

Nor was all the advice comforting. When Skye said her parents would never welcome her back, Dolly told her bluntly, "Honey, some things we can't fix. Some things we just suffer through."

When Skye had finally gathered the nerve to voice her biggest concern—that Randy and his obnoxious friends would feel vin-

dicated in despising her—nobody answered, until Gladys cleared
her throat, and said, "My grandfather was born in 1871, when
times were simpler. He once told me, 'Whenever people decide
you're not good enough for them, stand up straight, put back your
shoulders, and spit in their eye.' Not very sanitary—and maybe
not very Christian—but I think it's a fine starting point."

"Yeah," Deborah seconded, "like Aristotle said: 'If they can't
take a joke, then f—"

"Ahem!" Gladys interrupted, clearing her throat sharply. She
glanced down at her watch and exclaimed with sweet surprise,
"Goodness! Ten-thirty. Shouldn't we start the meeting?"

Deborah shrugged; Skye nodded, and that was that. The Ladies
had, not quite expecting it, become her family.

And there were other unexpected effects. The Ladies discovered
that for all their friendship, there had been a vast and important
array of topics they had not been willing to share with each other.
Gradually that began to change.

In all of this, of course, my part had been ridiculously small.
Still, panic attacks and all, I had become the Club's recognized
informal advisor on matters of the heart.

I thought of Skye, who seemed so happy and secure, and decided I must indeed have been preordained for the job of local
Oprah—over a wider range of topics than I had ever imagined
would be possible.

It was a dirty job, but someone had to do it. As long as I could
learn not to bang people's heads against desks.

CHAPTER TWENTY

Love, Waffles — and Zorro

Skye's new friend, Lynne, finally appeared a few weeks later. She was an anthropology student, squarely built, serious, and a heavy smoker. I thought she looked more like Skye's past than her future; but when I said that to Dolly, she nearly bit my head off before telling me to mind my own business. Oprah Winfrey never had days like that.

On the other hand, beginning that summer of '86, the Ladies rarely let me go long without another chance to polish my meddling skills.

I think I'm as willing as the next person to take credit for talents I don't really have; but the problem with being known as the Club's resident sage was that I was a sitting duck.

Even worse, because the Ladies most often simply had straightforward business or legal questions, I began to get a very inflated idea of my own wisdom. Sophia the Clever. In short, I was starting to believe my own propaganda.

By late that summer, in fact, I thought I was ready for anything—personal, legal, or financial.

But I never expected the visit from Mary Maitland.

Mary, at forty-three, was still cheerleader pretty. The small lines at the corners of her mouth and eyes merely gave her depth and character: as if she knew exactly what she was cheering for. But her face also held some of the toughness of our great-great-grandmothers in sepia prints. Women who'd held down plains farms while their husbands fought the Civil War, they stared back at you with eyes and lips compressed, and mouths widened by determination.

If you looked too quickly, you thought they were smiling.

From such a woman, I expected nothing but business questions.

Which was why I was so startled when Mary—whose life had seemed a four-decade version of a Mormon-church "families' values" commercial, leaned toward me with her hands held primly on her lap, and asked, "Why do men lose interest in sex?"

I had, as usual, a ready and brilliant reply. I looked right at her and answered, "Excuse me?"

That should have killed discussion. But Mary was determined to explain.

Mike, she said, was a model husband. Once they'd lost the hope of having children, and she wanted to work part-time and finish her college degree, Mike's only response was, "Okay. I'll learn to cook." Mary awoke the next morning to the smell of bacon and waffles and fresh coffee perking. Mike might have been a trifle dull, with an engineer's vague grayness and lack of sparkling conversation, but he was kind and trustworthy. A slender ex-soldier who never told war stories, he was a good fellow, plain and simple. My mom had once or twice made veiled references to him as a class clown and brilliant math student in college, who had "come back different" from Vietnam. Now he ran a very small, very clever research team at Prairie Machine—a bunch called the Hog Farm. They had the unhappy job of devising breakthroughs that somehow were never green-lighted as products.

The rest of the time Mike taught karate for kids and self-defense for women down at the Y, and was respected by all. He was the perfect husband—kindly, decent, and dull.

That was what Mary told me (though not in exactly those words). Then she paused for my reply.

Alas, my imagination, as usual, took off like a barnstorming pilot.

It developed the instant theory that all men, at some advanced age like fifty, reach a point where food interests them more than sex. You could graph it like a biz-school chart: over time the "sex interest" line plunges while the "food interest" line rises. Where the lines cross is the technical onset of middle age: if men were stocks, that's when you'd sell them. It has something to do with their prostates, I was pretty sure.

Not for a million dollars could I have brought myself to share this with Mary. Instead, I scrambled to think of something helpful to say.

Alas, while my brain was trying to think of something kind and sensible to offer, my mouth got bored and started in on its own.

To my appalled amazement, I began talking about the rare and special magic of a long-lasting love. I sounded like Shakespeare on a skip loader: it was like the ABC Wide World of Poop. I even heard myself reminding her that the Bible put no limits on relations of married couples.

It got worse. All of a sudden I felt like Barry Fitzgerald playing the kindly Irish priest in a Leo McCarey film. Slap enough of a brogue on your advice and you can make anything sound good. "Faith, lass, we'll be sellin' ye down the river to Rio." "Oh, thank you, Father. That's just what I need." That was me. Father O'Sophia.

About this time my brain fought its way back to the controls: the thrill ride was over. So I wound up lamely giving Mary advice I must have cribbed from a *Cosmopolitan* in some forgotten doctor's office about "Making Him Burn for You." The tactics that occurred to me were too astounding to share with my best friend (let alone Mary), so I ended lamely by telling her to ease her way into it, that husbands, like small animals, were easily frightened.

I was twenty-seven and never married. *Married?* I hadn't had a *date* in two months. Where did I get off advising her? I don't know. My mouth is an independent creature, with which I share a sometimes symbiotic relationship. Still, Mary took no offense. In fact, I can't remember ever seeing her overtly angry—until one later event, which I'll get to in a while.

*B*ut the most bizarre thing was that Mary took my advice to heart—or at least adapted it. From then on I was her confidante in a project that took her down the broad path to cellophane sundresses.

The only problem was that her growing enthusiasm for the project collided wildly with her husband's loving, but laconic resistance.

She started small. The day after our conversation, she gathered her nerve for a trip to Victoria's Secret. There, blushing furiously, she managed to purchase a moderately sexy nightgown. It would have been hot stuff in Carole Lombard's day. But it took all her nerve to manage it, and she was trembling with excitement when she donned it that night.

Mike eyed it with warm approval.

"Hey, nice," he exclaimed. "Sears?"

Thus began a comic chain of trial and failure. "Comic" because none of Mary's costumes exactly failed. Mike was nearly always precisely the same. He was a considerate lover, who somehow never displayed that wild enthusiasm Mary would take as speaking of true love.

Technically speaking, there was nothing to complain about. He was always tender, always thoughtful. The soldiering, the years of martial arts, and a life naturally abstemious had left his body taut and capable. He paid attention to her wishes and never seemed to be bored or disappointed with her.

But Mary wanted that inexpressible magic—the romance which

almost always arrives in images. She wanted a last waltz, with tiaras glittering and a regiment that rode at dawn . . . she wanted a fiery kiss from a chevalier mounted on a dappled charger, who had to bend down to reach her ruby lips. She wanted the night we missed the boat at Algeciras, and those handsome Moors all in white and turbans like kings, and the sea crimson like fire . . . and her heart was going like mad, and yes she'd read James Joyce, yes, and—

And what she got was good, old, reliably male Mike, steady as a field gun and about as imaginative; uncomplaining, loyal, and handy. He was the Chevy Malibu, the Zippo lighter of love. She wanted a Ferrari. She wanted to play with matches.

For many another sort of woman, this would have been act one of an affair. Where Mary differed, I suppose, was in the intensity of her love. She sensed in Mike some buried sadness, some stubborn resignation to life's unfairness. Staying the course was destroying him slowly. Whatever was most valuable in him, whatever she loved, was suffocating, and she wouldn't give up on it.

*A*nd somewhere in the process of trying to light Mike's fire, Mary discovered a stubbornly inventive erotic side of herself. It was the challenge she loved. Her clothes, her costumes, and her settings grew steadily more imaginative—she went, over the course of that fall and winter, from Carole Lombard modern, through Saran Wrap, to cowgirl and harem outfits.

Finally she found the one that did it—and she succeeded because she made Mike part of the fantasy. More than that, she rediscovered part of her own past, remembering exactly the day in high-school Spanish club when she fell in love with the gawky basketball star and math wiz, who'd starred in a self-written play about the hilariously inept, but basically charming Don Pedro, "the greatest swordsman in all *vieja California*"—who somehow couldn't keep from crashing backward over the scenery. He'd been fun, and humorous, and dashingly theatrical then. Vietnam had changed all that—Vietnam and marriage, and twenty years of bills and work and just showing up.

Well, Mary would change it back.

She took the day off work, and as soon as Mike had left the house, she drove to the Twin Cities to visit, in the course of a long morning, costume, fabric, theatrical-supply, costume-jewelry, music, and electronics stores. She even found a shop specializing in antique weapons.

By the time she left St. Paul, the car's trunk and backseat were both jammed with packages.

Mike came home that night to find a note in high-school Spanish telling Don Pedro his new clothes awaited him in the bathroom—and that when he put them on, he'd know what to do.

Mary had spent a bit of her dough to costume herself as a nineteenth-century Spanish señorita, complete with crinoline and hoops and combs in her straw-blond hair. She'd bought satin sheets for the bed and changed the lighting. And she'd hooked up a fancy new stereo.

The front door opened. Footsteps—then silence. Then slower, more deliberate footsteps toward the bathroom. She waited another minute, hardly breathing, then used the remote to start the CD player: Rodrigo's Concierto de Aranjuez began its gorgeous first notes. Yes, señorita, it *was* the theme music for Ricardo Montalban and Chrysler's fine Corinthian leather—but it was also swellingly romantic, all the sexiness of the Mediterranean pouring through new $500 speakers.

She waited on the bed in utter trepidation. Would he be angry? Or worse, would he sneer with indifference? Was this the single worst idea in the history of male/female relations?

The door flew open—there stood Mike, the stick-on curling black mustachios gleaming in the lamplight, his silk shirt open down to his belly button, the flat black hat with the fringe of Zorro

balls; a fat bulge in his silk breeches, the fake eye patch giving him
a rake-hell look.

He squinted at her appraisingly.

"*Ai, señorita.*" Douglas Fairbanks had never looked bolder or
more dashing. He started toward her—did a perfect pratfall over
the daybed, drew his sword, turned, and flung it skillfully at the
door. Its point plunged into the lintel with a resounding *thunk* and
wanged there, slender until the bulge of the hilt, waggling back
and forth. It was the greatest personal advertisement since the
Marlboro Man. He spun his fringed hat away like a Zorro-balled
Frisbee and hand-sprung onto the bed beside her.

"*Venga aquí, querida!*"

"Oh, Don *Pedro*!"

They had a night of absolutely spectacular sex—they left their
brains on the bedsheets, Mary told herself with satisfaction—and
then, at dawn, as the birds sang and Mary snuggled close, he
turned to her lovingly, and said—

"You know? I could make waffles."

Same old line but spoken a whole new way.

CHAPTER TWENTY-ONE

Breaking Out

$\mathcal{M}$ ost of the time work provided most of my fun. I found I liked business, and the more money the Ladies made, the more fun I had.

We started paying out smallish quarterly checks in the summer of 1986; but except for Mary's romantic endeavor, most of the Ladies seemed just to be putting most of what they received right in the bank.

The first of them to get over the psychic embargo on spending any of their money was Deborah. Near the end of February 1987—as what had been a very mild winter seemed about to give up its seat for the young spring—she came to me and said she wanted to draw $5,000 against the coming year's quarterly cash payments.

That was certainly easy enough to arrange; even by early '87, $5,000 was beginning to look surprisingly like chicken feed compared with the Club's portfolio. Still, it was the first real withdrawal since we'd started, so I let my curiosity get the better of my tact and I asked why she wanted it.

"I'm going to overhaul the Snippers," she answered without much enthusiasm. "I'll let you know how it goes."

.   .   .

*D*eborah had bought the Golden Snippers some six years earlier, when she'd gotten out of the Marine Corps. It was a small, undistinguished salon just off Main Street: four stations, of which Deborah had one and one was rented out to a succession of marginally talented journeywoman hairdressers.

The other two stations belonged to Deborah's two remarkably gifted employees. Maggie was a jowly, taciturn woman of about fifty, whose only excuse for being in the business was that she had the eye of an architect and the hands of a surgeon: if Euclid had cut hair in ancient Athens, he would have given the *hetaerae* cuts as sharp as Maggie's. Tamara, Maggie's twenty-two-year-old colleague, was not *quite* as good with scissors, but she had additional attributes. In the first place, she seemed almost telegraphically wired in to the latest salon fashions from all over the world. In the second, she was shockingly beautiful—with "shockingly" being the exactly right word. She was tall, rail-thin, with absolutely pale skin, perfect, small features, and luminous black eyes. Sixteen-year-old girls who wanted to go to Paris and be poets wanted to look like her. She was like the Julia Roberts of the Bizarro Universe.

Being a gorgeous woman is not an automatic advantage to a hairdresser, but—as you'll see shortly—it came in extremely handy before the year was out.

In March, though, a $5,000 improvement loan for the Golden Snippers was not exactly the kind of news to make the *Wall Street Journal*. Across America, there must be fifty or a hundred thousand similar beauty shops: dull, struggling, and uninspiring. Of course, Deborah ran it well. In fact, she had always had more business skill than the place deserved. For the last three years she'd been driving into Minneapolis three nights a week to take business courses at the university. She had also tried a great many minor innovations—from two-for-one mother-and-daughter coupons to joint promotions with Brinkmeyer's Bowling Alley's Ladies' Night. None of these had been clever enough to overcome the shop's basic lack of funding; but at least they'd kept Deborah from dying of boredom.

In short, Deborah had made the Golden Snippers, if still nothing spectacular, into a going business. Yes, the talents of Maggie and Tamara were probably wasted in a town where the hair-fashion ideal was Barbara Bush; but the salon, though slightly dingy and off the main drag, still paid its way.

By 1987, though, I was beginning to get the dim idea that the Ladies might be on the verge of getting really rich off their investments. It wasn't really my place, but I tried, by indirection, to talk Deborah out of withdrawing money from the fund.

"Five thousand dollars. I guess you really love that place, huh?"

"What're you nuts? It bores the living shit out of me."

"Then—?"

"I just hate to admit I blew it, that's why." She paused, then added, "Besides, if I can get it up to a reasonable level, I can sell it to Maggie and Tamara. They've got talent to burn—which nobody would ever say about me. But I won't do it while it's so rickety."

I figured that was as good a cause as any, so I called in Krista, and we drew up an amendment to the Club's rules, to allow small loans to members out of our cash reserves.

The Ladies passed the loan amendment without protest and with a lot of words of encouragement for Deborah's new investment. I put the issue mostly out of mind, as a matter of no importance.

But something curious happened.

About two months after I'd written Deborah the first check, I happened to ask her how business was going.

"Funny you should mention that," she said. "I was going to call you for an appointment."

"Yes?"

She nodded. "I want to borrow another thirty thousand."

My stomach knotted. "Are you in trouble?"

"You kidding? Any more customers, and I'm going to have to call out the riot squad."

Deborah was kidding, of course, but this was what had happened:

Her first plan had been to bring in the linoleum guy, the curtains guy, and the painter and see what spiffing up she could get for her five grand. After a day of being high-pressured by those rough customers, she'd pretty nearly decided to follow their advice for a low-cost overhaul.

But when the last of them, the painter, had left, and Deborah was standing in the doorway with his estimate still in her hand, she was startled to have Tamara tap her on the shoulder. By the time she turned around, Tamara was standing over her with her hands on her hips.

"Look," Tamara said, not taking her hands off her hips, "I've got a much better idea."

Deborah, feeling extremely low and somewhat bullied by a succession of men who all managed to smell sweaty in Minnesota in March, was ready for help. She waved her hand with a "gimme" gesture.

"Paint it all gold."

" 'Gold?' " Deb was uncertain. "Is that, like, in good taste?"

"Hell, no," Tamara answered, "it's tasteless as hell. But in this town it'll go over gangbusters. In the first place, it matches our name, and in the second, it'll look like we're puking money. Especially if we can get gold curtains and—wow, this is perfect— like, fake gold-plated scissors and stuff."

Deborah closed her eyes, trying to picture the place all in gold. The best image she could conjure up looked like a bad outtake from *The Wizard of Oz*. She opened her eyes again to study Tamara's face for signs that she was joking. Finally she reached a design decision worthy of one of the Italian Renaissance merchant princes. "Yeah," she said. "Sure. What the hell. You gotta know as much as those sweaty jerks. Let's paint it all gold."

*T*amara, it turned out, was a design genius.

Just as she had predicted, the freshening of its interior had led to a rumor that the Golden Snippers was doing very well. That in turn had led to a rumor that it was *the* place in Larksdale to get one's hair dressed. And *that* in turn had led to the long-overdue discovery that Maggie and Tamara were absolutely brilliant stylists. They could do Barbara Bush and make it look good.

Before the end of April, the Golden Snippers, despite having raised its prices, was booked solidly a week ahead. The reservations were coming from as far away as South Minoga—and most were for expensive items, like perms.

And so, at the end of the second week in May, Deborah was answering my casual question with a request for expansion capital.

"In fact, I may want forty thousand. I'm moving to a bigger location."

"That's wonderful," I said with as much enthusiasm as I could muster. Truth was, I'd always wondered why Deborah had been involved with something so far from her character and so cutesy as hairdressing. In fact, in visiting the unbearably golden Golden Snippers, I'd seen only one thing that struck me as even vaguely representing Deborah's character: on the work shelf behind her barber's chair, cheaply framed, sat a very grainy eight-by-ten black-and-white blowup of a snapshot a friend of hers had taken of Deborah at boot camp in North Carolina. Deborah was whacking some other poor schlub of a recruit with a pugil stick. The poor schlub's face was contorted with the impact of the stick, and Deborah's face was contorted with the force of her effort—and both of them looked hot, dirty, and wonderfully alive.

It was a long way from gold-plated combs.

"I guess so," Deborah answered, obviously thinking of those combs with less than wild entrepreneurial enthusiasm.

We both thought hairdressing was boring as milk soup.

But all that was about to change.

CHAPTER TWENTY-TWO

Combat!

It all changed when luck and genius shook hands. Or, in plain English—

Deborah figured out what she was doing.

It happened mostly by accident. Deb's most recent tenant hairdresser—a steel-gray, blunt woman named Hannah, who'd moved down from Duluth—made her a cash offer for the touched-up Golden Snippers. Deborah, who disliked Hannah intensely, grabbed it, and then decided she was ready to take her own business to the big city.

She found a location on Hennepin, not far from the financial center of Minneapolis. It had room for sixteen booths, plus office space in the back and a large front reception area. That was more than Deb wanted, but it was available dirt cheap after the previous tenant went bankrupt. Deborah held her breath and signed the lease. Then she brought Tamara and Maggie up with her to meet with a woman from Chicago, who specialized in designing topnotch hair salons.

This woman, whose business card read promisingly, *Ms. Kennedy, Salon Designer,* impressed them mightily when she first walked onto the bare floor of their salon-to-be. Her posture, her hair, and her tailoring were all impeccable.

Her presentation went great, until she started talking.

Then for nearly an hour she tried to persuade them the look they wanted was "hip pink, the perfect color for your target market—all the Mary Richardses of the late eighties." Ms. Kennedy apparently thought that aiming at the perky and imaginary young woman of the only old TV show ever set in Minneapolis was a brilliant strategy.

After she left—promising over her shoulder that she would bill them promptly for her time—they walked to Starbucks for coffees, brought them back, and sat on the only three chairs in the soon-to-be salon to drink and think.

The drinking went fine; the talking started slow. For a full three minutes none of them could think of a word to break the gloomy silence.

Finally Deborah set down her coffee, jumped to her feet, and nearly yelled, "Listen. We're crazy. I mean, look out that window!" She pointed out the front window. Beyond it, out on the sidewalk, in the next thirty seconds, probably fifty people rushed past. Maybe it was luck, but nearly half of them were young career women, all wearing the mock-guy suits popular for women in those days.

More importantly, in those thirty seconds they saw perhaps a third of those young women shoved aside by more aggressive—usually, much bigger—men. Some looked startled, some upset; but most pushed on (though not back) resolutely.

Deborah turned to face her two colleagues.

"You get it? Old Rose Kennedy there thinks we're here to do hair for, like, Mary Tyler Moore. It's 1987, and she wants us to recreate *Little House on the* Fuckin' *Prairie*. Those women need hand-to-hand training, and we're supposed to hand out lollipops!"

It had just been a burst of frustration; but now suddenly Deborah realized they—especially Tamara—were staring at her fixedly.

"What? What're you looking at?"

Tamara took her hands off her hips. "You. You're a genius." She was looking past Deborah to the only decoration on the counter: the grainy, black-and-white picture of Deb in the marines. Stepping up to it, she asked, "How many of these do you have?"

Now it was Deborah's turn to stare then shrug. "I don't know. Maybe a dozen. A buddy took 'em during boot camp. You want to burn 'em or what?"

Tamara shook her head and uttered a barely articulate, "Uh-uh." She walked resolutely to the counter, picked up the photo as if it were an heirloom, and carried it gently to deposit it in her own oversized purse.

*L*ate that afternoon, Tamara showed up at Deborah's apartment to collect all the dozen pictures. She told Deborah she had important errands to run, and the next day she wasn't in to help with the turnover of the Golden Snippers to its new owner.

But the day after that, Deborah got a call at home: Tamara wanted Deborah and Maggie to meet her at the Minneapolis shop at six that evening.

*W*hen they arrived, Tamara had a certain bored, sleepy look which Deborah had not yet realized meant concealed excitement. Seeing that mysterious look, and nothing new in the shop except for a row of large, thin packages, each about five feet high and seven feet long, propped up against the long side shelf that ran the length of the main salon, Deborah asked, with slight irritation, "So what's up?"

"You owe me nine hundred and eighteen dollars and forty-five cents."

"For what?"

"Come here."

She stepped to the nearest propped package and tore off its

wrapping in long, wide strips. Underneath the brown paper she'd had the photo of Deborah fighting with pugil sticks blown up to life size. Before Deborah could react, she stepped to the next package and tore it open, too. She kept moving until all six packages were open.

She'd had, in total, six of Deborah's photos—of boxing and running the obstacle course and firing an M-16 on the target range—blown up to epic size. On that scale, they were startling: grainy, tough, and arresting.

Maggie, fascinated, and Deborah, annoyed, studied the pictures like a couple of critics at a Manhattan gallery. Then, after about fifteen seconds' worth of tense silence, Deborah responded with a reply probably rarely heard in New York art circles—

"Are you fucking crazy? What are these butt-ugly things for? You want to do sets for *Nightmare on Elm Street 2*?"

Tamara gave another barely audible "uh-uh." Then, for the first time since Deborah had hired her, she spoke up clearly. "They're artwork for the hippest hair salon in America. Come on."

She walked them to the back of the salon, where a cloth covered a thin rectangular object about six feet by twelve. Tamara grasped one edge of the cloth, paused dramatically, and then whisked away the cloth. It revealed a large, professional sign that read:

COMBAT!
LIFE'S A BATTLE. BE PREPARED.

Deborah, stunned—and, I suspect, too excited to admit how pleased she was—fell back upon her favorite part of her personal catechism:

"What're you—nuts?"

"It's perfect," Tamara answered, "and you know it. Everybody's sick of cutesy-poo hair salons. It's time for women to get serious. This is hip—but it's serious."

Warming to her topic, she went on. "A girlfriend of mine blew up the photos and designed the logo. She's an architecture student at the U. She wants to design the whole place—she'll work for, like, nothing, for the experience."

Deborah hadn't taken her eyes off the stretched canvas. Now, almost dreamily, she asked, "You think she can pull it off?"

"Hey. A woman did the Vietnam Memorial. A woman can do this."

Deborah rubbed her temples with her fingertips. The excitement—the prospect of doing something truly interesting—had given her a headache the size of an M-1 tank.

She looked to Maggie. "What do you think?"

Maggie shook dewlaps suitable for a shar-pei puppy and growled, "Yeah."

Deborah turned to stare out the window. It was the famous "Thousand Yard Stare" of the fabled U.S. Marines. Not taking her eyes from whatever vision she was seeing, she told Tamara, "Tell her to bring me the sketches. I'll try to sell them to my friends."

So Deborah needed all the forty thousand, plus what she got for Golden Snippers, just to get the door open. Actually she ultimately took closer to $100,000 from the Club—but she didn't have to draw down her own account. The Ladies took three minutes to look at her artwork, and five minutes to deliberate, and then voted to invest the $100,000, in return for 20 percent of the salon.

It wasn't as good a move as our buying Microsoft on its first trading day—but it wasn't too shabby at that.

CHAPTER TWENTY-THREE

Deborah Builds an Empire

Combat! was a direct hit. The salon, from its flat, olive-green paint, to its "neoindustrial" fixtures, to its pictures of mud-splattered women in action, hit a nerve. It played to (and with) the rough realities of women breaking into professional careers in those go-go years.

Two weeks before the salon opened, a curious reporter from the *Star Tribune* happened to walk by and see the giant photos going up on the wall behind the counter. She tapped on the glass and talked her way into an interview, which ultimately stretched to an hour and a half, then came back later with a photographer.

The story, with three color photos, appeared in the Sunday magazine the day before the salon was due to open.

When Deborah checked the salon's voice mail Sunday night, there were seventy-seven requests for callbacks for appointments.

Still, Combat! might have been a one-trick pony, a business that got lots of press then disappeared, except for one thing—or rather, two people: Maggie and Tamara.

They knew the haircutting business cold. More precisely, Tamara knew every hot fashion two seconds after it appeared in Milan or Tokyo. It was as if she had her own personal fashion Internet wired into her skull.

Maggie, meanwhile, knew instinctively how to adapt each fresh fashion twist to the Combat! style—and, just as importantly, how to teach it, quickly and accurately, to the dozen new stylists Deborah had to hire and train in the weeks before they opened.

I was one of the volunteers for the preopening tryout—but, unwilling to risk much, had my hair cut by Maggie herself. To my untutored eye, the cut seemed just a snazzy variation on the chic, short cuts of Vidal Sassoon.

It wasn't until next morning, when, running late, I discovered that the blow-dried cut looked perfect after two minutes' attention instead of the usual twelve. Somebody had just handed me an extra week every year—and, moreover, I was spending no longer on my hair than the average man.

Suddenly I had an image of women all over the Twin Cities rushing for their cars through the morning mists crouched down and yelling things like "Geronimo!" and "Go for Broke!"

It wasn't a bad feeling at all. And when I got to the office, and Krista, my usually subdued secretary (looking much better than I in the identical cut), jumped to her feet and yelled, "Captain's on the bridge!" I felt better still.

$\mathcal{T}$hey worked every detail. Some were obvious—like the Combat! Haircare Kits in drab olive rip-stop nylon, with the small Swiss Army knife fitted in between the comb and the brush. Some were subtle but practical: the salon dumped those idiotic oversized magazines full of overdressed Eurotrash but had three copies of the *Wall Street Journal,* plus *Business Week, Forbes, Fortune,* and the rest available each day. Women knew what Combat! was really about—how much of it was a joke and how much of it wasn't.

For Deborah, finally getting into Combat! meant a real liberation. She made Tamara head stylist and general manager, and Maggie director of training—and gave up cutting hair forever. She planned to remove herself to the back room and just handle the numbers, but it turned out the posters had made her a local celebrity, and women expected to see her either up at the front counter, or at least walking about, shaking hands. As she said, with her usual gruff practicality, "We're making seven hundred and fifty bucks an hour, six days a week. If they want me to stand on the counter with a bucket on my head and sing the 'Marine Corps Hymn,' I'll do it. Why not? They made me do it in boot camp."

Truth was, after a month the place was so busy, they couldn't have spared the floor space for Deborah's Marine Corps medley. Besides, Tamara had gradually created a whole illusion, from receptionists to stylists, of a military organization. Deborah became secondary and was able to retreat to the back office and cook up ways to turn Combat! into a big business.

So that was that. It was bye-bye Barbie, hello *G.I. Jane*.

CHAPTER TWENTY-FOUR

Vic, Part One

And hello, big money.

You see, hair salons have what the MBAs call "low variable costs." In other words, if you're making cars, every time demand picks up, you have to buy more wheels, spark plugs, steel—whatever. Those are high variable costs. But with a hair salon, if demand picks up, you just keep the scissors sharp, stay open later, and put the extra dough in your pocket.

(Plus, of course, in such a nice, simple, no-paper-trail business, it's shamefully easy for the unscrupulous to hold down other expenses—like paying their taxes. This is why the owner of any city's most successful hair salon generally drives around in a cream-colored Rolls-Royce with lambskin seats.)

Deb, as it happens, was extremely scrupulous; but money still poured in. Her estimate of $750 an hour was low: it didn't include sales of Combat! merchandise, from those olive-green makeup kits to the "Camouflage" hair tints in colors like Libyan Desert. At the last LLIC meeting in August, Deb stood up sheepishly and gave the following report:

"Ladies, this month we closed for a week for vacation, and I gave everybody a bonus for their hard work. And we still made a net profit of thirty-four thousand dollars. So, like, I dunno—either we gotta expand, or we better go out in Martha's backyard, here, and dig a big hole where we can start burying the money."

Knowing that you only messed around in Martha's garden at your peril, they voted to consider expansion—and Deborah pitched them two ideas. The first—which she pitched publicly— was for a day spa called "Boot Camp," which turned out not to be silly at all, since it was divided into a four-hour morning course in self-defense, followed by lunch and four hours of pampering. Beat the stuffing out of some guy in a big, padded suit—then a massage and your nails done. It was irresistible.

*A*fter the meeting, Deborah pitched the second idea. She took me aside and whispered, "I couldn't tell them the whole story. Tamara's got all the haircutters running around in these tight khaki shorts for summer—and now I've got, like, twenty guys at a time in the place, saying they're keeping their girlfriends company, but mostly just drooling over the stylists. It's embarrassing."

I said I could see that.

"So, anyway, I figure if these schmucks are going to stand around drooling, they might as well cough up some dough."

I just looked back at her and nodded.

"*C*ombat for Men" ("Because Guys Fight, Too") opened on a blazing day in the middle of August, with a big party and a line down the block. Tamara had an instinct for making it hip—and for knowing how to stop just short of kitsch.

And, amazingly, Deb had begun to enjoy her celebrity. When I got there, she was walking up and down the line of stylists' chairs conducting a mock inspection.

"Hey, Deb! How do I look?" A good-natured and slightly pot-bellied young investment banker yelled from chair number eight.

She grinned at him. "Like hell. Drop and give me twenty."

And the poor guy actually did—to a chant of "go-go-go!"

That was the summer half the yuppie guys in the Twin Cities showed up at the lakes wearing "high-and-tight" haircuts. And when the guys were hanging out at Lake Larksdale, the beach looked like a Club Med in the Balkans—while the Ladies' cash reserve account was starting to look like a bank in Zurich.

*I*t was just too hot an idea to go unchallenged.

We all told Deb to brace herself for competition—but what walked into her life was something quite different from that.

She was in the back room, totaling the day's receipts, when Tamara buzzed her and said in a voice suitable for announcing a surprise visit by Sean Connery, "Deb? Vic Carter's here to see you!"

Victor Carter wasn't a movie star—but he could have played one on TV. He was six-two, a dark-haired, blue-eyed former college swimming champ, and owner of what had been, before Combat!, the three most successful high-fashion salons in the Twin Cities.

Deborah stepped from the office, saw Vic Carter, and froze. It was a moment romantic beyond her wildest hopes, and she felt an orchestra ought to have begun playing "Ah, Sweet Mystery of Life at Last I've Found You."

Instead Belinda Kenney, the shop's youngest and cutest blond receptionist, had drifted mothlike from the front counter toward Vic. She was already opening her mouth to speak to him. Deborah thought her chance was blown, but Tamara looked at Deb looking at Vic and instantly spun and grabbed Belinda by the arm. Dragging her toward the front door, she whispered, "Come on—we're closed!"

"Ow! Let go—you're hurting!" Belinda whined, just before Tamara dragged her through the door and out onto the street.

It was embarrassing, but Vic seemed not even to have noticed it. He wasn't taking his eyes off Deb, who suddenly felt the room was extremely warm.

Feeling stranger and stranger every instant, Deb finally rallied and asked him, "You want a Coke or something?"

He nodded, very slowly, and Deb, feeling like a mouse paroled by a cat, turned gratefully toward the small staff refrigerator.

When Deborah turned away from the refrigerator, Vic Carter was staring at her—with the burning look in his eye she had heretofore considered merely a theoretical possibility, like black holes. She suddenly felt like the Wicked Witch of the West; she was rapidly melting from the ankles upward.

"What?" she demanded, stumbling forward onto a counter stool and handing him his Coke.

"Nothing."

"Come on—what?"

"It's just that you're so . . ." He let the phrase die away, then asked in roughly the reverent tone an Old Testament figure would have used to address an angel, "Would you possibly have dinner with me?"

"You mean, like—now?" The wicked-witch melting had apparently reached her brain.

"Absolutely."

*T*hey drove crosstown in Vic's cream-colored Rolls. It was probably just coincidence that their route took them past Vic's #1, the Gibraltar of his hairdressing empire. Until Combat!, Vic's had been the most successful chain in town; now the darkened building had the aura of a siege about it. Deb, feeling vaguely guilty, sank down in the lambskin bucket seat and closed her eyes.

She didn't open them until Vic had walked around the car to hold the door for her. She let him help her out and keep her arm as they walked toward the restaurant, which, on the dark street, seemed richly mysterious. Its front door was made of thick, rough planks bound with wrought iron, and through its inset diamonds of dimpled glass, only the faintest sparks of deep red light flickered.

Inside, the restaurant was pitch-black. There were better-illuminated bomb shelters during the London Blitz in 1942.

Deb saw dim shapes dangling near the rafter. Of the vague silhouette ahead of her, which she hoped was the maître d', she asked—

"Yo! Are those bats hanging there?"

"Cheeses, madam."

"Oh, yeah." She smiled at the looming shadow she hoped was Vic. "Very classy."

By the time they had stumbled to their table, Deb's eyesight had adjusted, and certainly she liked what she saw seated across from her. Vic was the essence of aquatic grace—*like a goy Mark Spitz,* she thought to herself.

Well, metaphors weren't Deborah's strong suit; but you get the idea: he was tall and lean, and the shadowy light sharpened his chiseled features. In fact, "chisel" was probably the key word in Vic's character—but Deborah didn't know that.

What she did know was that she liked the way he made her feel. To put it simply, she was in a desperate mood for a romantic dinner, a romantic drive, and a romantic everything else.

The dinner started perfectly. Vic was a great orderer. Some people really master the small things of life; and one thing Vic had mastered absolutely was ordering. The barest glance at the menu—the barest glance at Deborah. The menu shut and tossed to the waiter. The back of the hand studied as if it held a crib sheet.

"Prosciutto and melon. Antipasto grande. Braciola. Tiramisu." A glance to Deborah while the waiter kissed his fingertips in approval. "Okay?"

A nod from Deborah, who had clearly recognized the word "melon."

To waiter: "Okay. And a bottle of champagne. Your best."

"*Very* good, Signore Carter."

The prosciutto and melon arrived, and seemed wonderful to Deb. In the first place, most of her life the food had come either from a tin can or a chow line. Second, she had already passed that landmark in a working woman's life—the day she stopped cooking a chicken on Sundays so she'd have homemade leftovers for at least half the following work week.

"You don't mind my ordering?" Vic asked, after the waiter had long since disappeared.

"You kidding? For the last four months every weekday dinner I've eaten came packaged in either butcher's paper or those white deli cartons with the little wire handles. I'm eating twelve meals a week in the back of Combat! Any restaurant that smells of food instead of shampoo is fine with me."

"Good. I'm glad you're not too much into that, you know, that feminist thing." He said it with ever so slight distaste. "I mean, I'm all for women's rights, but I hate to see things get out of control."

Deb let the remark flutter, batlike, past her. It took a little of her self-respect with her as it went. But she had plenty to spare.

Besides, Vic soon found a more agreeable topic. He began telling Deb how wonderful she was.

He kept on that theme steadily for an hour, until they had finished dessert, gone back to the Rolls, and driven to his strikingly elegant penthouse apartment. There he turned the lights down low and put soft music on the stereo before inviting her to sit beside him on the couch. It was like a Dean Martin tribute night—a little laughable, but still romantic.

He almost spoiled it by returning briefly, and energetically, to the issue of women's rights.

But once he stopped talking, everything was great.

CHAPTER TWENTY-FIVE

The Summer of the Vics

Deborah wasn't silly or simpleminded. She knew something was very fishy about Vic Carter's sudden passion for her. So why did she give in?

You could probably pick your own reason: loneliness or the desire for excitement. She told herself she deserved some attention—which was certainly true. She told herself she was attractive, at least to any man not put off by a strong woman. And that was even truer.

Pretty early on, she convinced herself it wasn't even such a bad thing if Vic was drawn to her, at least partly, because of her success. Men had been attracting women that way forever; what was wrong with turnabout? In fact, Deb made a very elegant distinction:

She didn't mind if Vic loved her *for* her money—she'd earned it by her wits, and success was part of her. But if he loved *just* her money, there was going to be trouble.

Aren't principles wonderful? Deb had the faint, nagging feeling she was reasoning herself into being a fool. But she didn't feel like stopping. At heart she was a romantic, of a most poetic disposition.

Deb's affair with Vic peaked early in summer, the season when mosquito monitors take their posts in neighborhoods throughout the Twin Cities. These fearless volunteers bare their arms for

twenty minutes, four times a day, then report the number of mosquito bites they suffer. The program provides a crucial service for
those living in lake-rich Minnesota, and would have been good
implicit advice for Deborah:

Always keep an eye on the bloodsuckers.

Unfortunately very few of us take our romantic advice from
Minnesota Public Health—just as, alas, not all the world's bloodsuckers announce themselves by immediately dropping onto your
arm and jabbing you with their snouts.

In fact, most of them begin charmingly.

No sooner had their affair begun than Vic caught Deb off guard
by changing his style. The weather turned hot early that year—and
instead of the slick urban Romeo, Vic became the irresistible small-
town boy who made every weekend a rural adventure. Picnics,
swimming, boating—it was all warm and lazy and fun. Plus, of
course, it didn't hurt that Vic looked spectacular in swim trunks.

All through early June of that glorious summer, Vic pitched a
solid six innings of old-fashioned woo—and Deb was more than
willing to catch whatever he tossed. It began as a summer of ripe
watermelons split open on red-checkered picnic cloths, of fresh-
picked corn boiled in the field.

And maybe, from Deb's point of view, the sweetest part of it
was the poetry. Deb, who was secretly mad about books, loved
reading Shakespeare's sonnets under a parasol, while nearby scat-
tered ducks floated on the lakes. From there she moved on to
Petrarch, to Shakespeare's plays, to Boccaccio's naughty tales. She
wanted to spend every minute she could with Vic and books, on
boats or just lounging by the lakeshore.

It didn't go perfectly, of course—since the murmur of Deb's
quite excellent reading was almost always augmented, within a
few minutes, by the mellifluous sounds of Vic's snoring. But they
found other things to do together later.

For Deb that meant staying at Combat! until after midnight all week, just to have the weekends, but it was worth it. Vic was worth it. Enchantment was worth it.

She hardly knew when it began to change—or rather, when she began to realize what Vic had actually intended from the start. Her awareness grew in stages, like that unpleasant itch that starts well before the first red bumps appear.

Still, it wasn't long until Deb realized Vic was steering every conversation to business—her business. At first it was disguised in a kind of code, as lovers' talk. Phrases like "I can really see us building something together," "I want us to be partners for life," and the ever-popular "You can teach me so much" began to pepper his conversation. They seemed to suggest that within that gorgeous, tanned exterior, he was a solid, old-fashioned guy who wanted to settle down and build a solid life. A good, honorable, Presbyterian *mensch*.

It took Deb most of June to realize—or at least to admit to herself—that when Vic rhapsodized about partners for life, he was talking not marriage, but franchising.

At first Deb was oblivious. Then, briefly, she was flattered—it wasn't so bad, after all, to be admired for her business brains. Very quickly, though, she moved on to being bored, suspicious, and angry.

Vic, meanwhile, became impatient. He wanted the secret of Deb's success. He wanted the key to her genius. More precisely, as Deb would sometimes admit to herself in those brief interludes when she was ready to be honest, he wanted her to sell him the salons.

*A*s summer began in earnest, it seemed they spent all their time over Deb's kitchen table planning their *financial* future together. Deborah tried over and over to get him off the topic, but he stuck to it like a refrigerator magnet.

"Can't we talk about something other than business?"

"Gee, babe, I'm just trying to be practical."

It was around this time that Deb began to wonder why exactly she couldn't tell him good-bye. She had hit the terrible realization that she was sounding like a chapter of some book called *Smart Women, Total Boneheads*. But she just couldn't quit.

By the first of July, the weather had turned Midwestern-summer hot, and as the muggy days seemed to be steaming the passion from their time together, Deb launched a campaign to turn Vic toward more telling subjects. She hoped that by focusing his mind on deeper issues, she might get him to realize there were more important things in life than quarterly sales.

She had not the slightest success. Vic never met an issue he couldn't dodge.

Deborah might have been dazzled, but she was no fool. Something made her keep scratching at those bumps, whether or not she enjoyed the sensation. She needed to be sure. Finally she could think of nothing more clever than simply asking him, straight out, whether he loved her.

"You said it, babe," he replied, and kissed her.

The first time he responded this way, as they were sitting on the deck of Vic's elegant cabin, far out in the woods and under the moonlight, Deborah took it as conditional victory, and kissed him back. Moonlight works that way on romantics.

But over the next two weekends, "You said it, babe" began sounding suspiciously like a stale political slogan.

The next weekend was the Fourth of July, when the Ladies and their families all gathered for a gigantic picnic out at Lake Larksdale. The spread the Ladies provided—from fried chicken to double-frosted chocolate cakes—generally put the best efforts of the Heart Association back about six months. It was not to be missed—and when Vic resisted the idea of going, Deb for once dug in her heels.

Unfortunately, the picnic, which started splendidly with coffee and fresh-baked Danish around nine in the morning, was gradually damaged by two problems. First, Vic, claiming the sun was bothering him, insisted on staying hidden deep within the shade trees a hundred yards from the rest of the Ladies and their friends and wouldn't join them all until after dark. Deb, feeling abandoned, had to scuttle back and forth between the two sites all day.

The second problem was worse. Buzz Suckling, Dolly's husband, had a drinking problem, which in recent years had worsened. The Ladies weren't all teetotalers, by any means, and a cooler full of beer sat alongside all the soft drinks. But Buzz had become a mean drinker, turning first sullen and then nasty.

It was one of those scenes small-town people are very good at ignoring, and probably nothing would have come of it except that, around sundown, Buzz began trying to argue with Dolly—and when she wouldn't argue, he became steadily louder and more abusive.

By full dark, the scene had become unignorable: Buzz was waving a beer can so wildly that the contents sloshed over his hand; his stride was wobbly; and I was vaguely afraid he might hurt Dolly just out of clumsiness.

By this time Vic had rejoined us. I heard—or rather, saw—Deb urging him to step in, and heard him answer peevishly, "It's their business. I'm not getting involved."

Before they could go any further, Mike Maitland rose to his feet, brushed the grass off his trousers, and strolled over to ask Buzz if he had a few minutes to talk about bass fishing. Buzz looked briefly eager to transfer the quarrel, but Mike kept the friendly look on his face and added he'd heard Buzz had lately bought some expensive new poles. That did the trick; they walked off together, with Mike boasting loudly and sloppily for as long as they were within hearing. The rescue left Dolly behind looking downcast and embarrassed, and us embarrassed for her.

It also left Deb severely annoyed with Vic, and wondering just what sort of a man he was, and what, if anything, mattered to him.

And so, half an hour later, when they were rowing on the lake and Vic's strong pulling had taken them all the way across and around into the quiet, weedy area they called Haskell's Cove (in classic Larksdale overstatement), she asked him a series of questions, which led once again to the question that had been bothering her for over a month.

Again he answered, "You said it, babe."

She responded, a little testily, "No; *you* say it."

"Say what?"

"Say you love me."

Something seemed to be stuck in his throat: he cleared it hoarsely—looked out over the water—looked down at the bottom of the boat—then said it.

It didn't sound as wonderful as Deb had thought it would. What with the fireworks exploding overhead, she felt more as if she'd extorted a confession from a POW under fire.

After a while, though, Vic got over his aversion; he'd say, "I love you, babe," with the same easy verbal snap he'd use to yell, "Waiter! Another pitcher!" And with nearly as much passion.

Somehow, though, Deb found it ever harder to believe he did love her—especially as he became ever more insistent about the idea of their running a business together. Unmistakably, even to the love-struck Deb, the business under discussion was Combat!—and she was already running that just fine without any help from Mr. Vic Carter.

Deb, lonely, biologically a-tick, had fallen hard for her good-looking suitor. Deep down, though, she knew too many notes were ringing false.

And the symphony had barely begun.

CHAPTER TWENTY-SIX

The Play's the Thing

*M*ost of us, if we can't have wonderful, will take mock-wonderful.

A month later Deb was still trying to convince herself that Vic loved her—and getting precious little help from Vic.

You must understand this was absolutely humiliating for Deb, who'd always been able to rely upon her willpower. To find herself using every trick she could invent to avoid facing the truth, on the one hand, and to force true love from her sow's ear of a boyfriend, on the other, was embarrassing beyond words. But of course her pride was working against her; she couldn't admit she'd been played for a fool.

In an odd way, Deb convinced herself Vic couldn't be lying to her on the grand premise that, as an honorable man, he couldn't lie to anyone. For proof of this neatly circular syllogism, she told herself she'd never heard him lie to anyone else.

The worst anyone could say about Vic Carter, Deb kept telling herself, was that he wasn't terribly bright. Ambitious and not very bright—but basically honorable.

That noble conviction lasted until late August, when, at the end of a blazing summer day, they went to the Guthrie to see Shakespeare's *Two Gentlemen of Verona*.

Deb had bought the tickets nominally as a present for Vic; but mostly, in fact, for herself. Going to see Shakespearean romantic comedy was just a way of trying to revive the dying feeling she'd had at the start of summer, when she'd been reading to Vic on warm afternoons.

Those days were long gone. They had reached the stage of their relationship marked most often by troubled, snarly silence; but she was certain, from a careful study of *Cosmo,* that things could still be saved, and was intent on trying. So she took Vic to dinner and then to the play, which she hoped he'd find funny.

Actually Vic didn't squirm at all during the play. The Guthrie troupe played it strictly for its *commedia dell'arte* laughs, with plenty of slapstick and juggling, acrobatics and music and bright costumes. The theater was literally rocking with laughter.

And then came the intermission.

The lobby opened onto a patio area, where the warm, dark, moist air, with the excitement of a happy crowd (relieved not to have been bored senseless by a classic), felt invigorating and romantic. String lights twinkled, and from somewhere came the scent of what Deborah was pretty sure were roses.

She was trying to spot an unoccupied dark corner, ideally behind a tree, where she could drag Vic for some good-natured smooching.

She tugged at his arm. "Come on," she insisted, "I want to show you the flowers." At first he seemed willing. But then—

Suddenly, and not at all subtly, Vic tensed and resisted the pressure of her arm.

He was staring, alert as a hunting dog, at a group of four well-dressed and well-groomed men exiting the theater.

Seeing them, Deb relaxed. She knew the men: they were her competitors, controlling a group of hair salons collectively bigger and better run than Vic's, though not so wildly successful as Combat!

As competitors, they were good: tough, creative, but never malicious. Deb never understood exactly why they took her success so graciously—Deb never really understood how rare, and appealing, a straightforward person can be. Plus, of course, they were old pros who likely knew that business fads rarely last.

Vic was already veering toward them. Deb wasn't much disappointed. Though she slightly regretted the loss of the smooching, she liked the men, and knew they'd have more to say about the play than Vic ever would. Besides, if he spent the intermission talking with them, he'd drink less.

But what happened next took her entirely off guard.

First, Vic slipped his arm free of hers. Then he accelerated toward the four men, leaving her well behind. Before she could catch him—before he could reach them—he called out in a strange, musical voice, "Edmund, Donald—Arthur and Dan!"

He had reached them, taken their hands, and given them little semihugs. It all looked very European and stylish, and Deborah was uncertain why it annoyed her so much.

Deb was not very subtle about social matters; it took her further study to realize what was happening.

Somehow Victor had turned and stepped away so that she couldn't take his hand. He actually waved toward her as he said, "Oh, you all know the loyal opposition. Deborah Cohen?" Those last two words were the first two unmusical ones he'd spoken to them.

And then she got it.

Vic was playing gay.

Deborah opened her mouth to reply; but from all the welter of thoughts, no words emerged.

"Well, so what do you think?" Arthur Bryant asked Vic suddenly. Arthur was Deborah's best friend among the four men, and he had seemed to catch something—some tension in the air. Whether he understood the issue or not, he was trying to help her out.

"The *play*? Oh, *please*." Vic was gushing sincerity. "I mean, 'two gentlemen'? Why don't they just come right out with it?"

Probably Victor was overdoing it—but since campiness is by definition parody, there are really no limits to it. He was being amusing, and that seemed to be enough.

It was a complete transformation. Deb thought she'd seen some good actors up on stage, but Vic was in a class by himself.

For Deborah, it was like partly losing consciousness. From then on she heard only snatches of the conversation. The voice in her head was much louder.

Just what, exactly, *was* the lie? That he was gay or that he wasn't?

Deborah felt a flash of absolute terror, since this was 1987, perhaps the bleakest year of the age of AIDS. Stories about a million infected Americans—about bisexual men giving the virus to straight women—were the everyday stuff of the news. The disease with no cure; the long, painful, ugly death.

Suddenly she had the choice of two horrors, and she kept rebounding between them: either Vic was bisexual and putting her at risk, or he was the biggest fraud and liar on the planet.

It was all she could do to keep from running into the night; but she managed, barely, to return to her seat and to remain there, trembling, until the play ended. But they had barely left the theater when she demanded, "What the hell *was* that?"

"Was what?"

"You know damn well. When you turned into Isaac Mizrahi in the lobby at intermission."

She could tell from his face that he considered playing dumb, then abandoned the idea.

"It's no big thing."

"Oh, yes, it is. Who the hell have you been lying to, Vic? Them or me?"

Somehow, from the slush of his brain, he dredged up the idea of going on the offensive.

"You don't like gay men?"

"I like gay men fine. It's liars who make me want to throw up."

"Hey, babe, fags run this business. You know that. So I play to them. So what? It's not lying, really; it's just business. Like . . . like they say in *The Godfather*. 'It was never personal. It was always business'?"

The answer was at once so cold and so offhand that it froze her. In the same instant that the AIDS issue disappeared, the bigger question of the vast lie of his character overwhelmed everything else. Suddenly a great many points—including the fact that they almost never dated in the city proper—fell into place. Whatever Vic was—if at heart he was anything at all—he was somehow maintaining two complete and distinct lives. She felt ashamed for herself, and for her friends. Vic as dope she'd accepted. Vic as master manipulator was unbearable.

In a fury so great it made her feel covered with ice, and far too angry to talk, she spun away from him and walked as fast as she could for the parking garage.

$\mathcal{L}$ater, in the car, Deborah sat paralyzed by anger for nearly the entire ride home. The evening was still sweltering; Vic had the windows up and the air conditioning on max, but suddenly Deborah, feeling she was suffocating, rolled down the window.

"Hey! You're letting in hot—"

"Shut up."

He looked briefly startled, then sullen—and then he shut up. There was nothing very tough about Vic.

CHAPTER TWENTY-SEVEN

The Great Vic
Hat Toss

That night at the theater was exactly the wake-up call Deborah needed. Not even love's old sweet song could drown out the alarm bells now.

But even with the unshakable and growing certainty that Vic was a skunk, Deborah couldn't quite persuade herself to give him up.

I'd like to believe we all make intelligent, reasoned choices, uninfluenced by our hormones and unshaped by folly. I'd also like to believe in Santa Claus.

Of course, Deb realized Vic was a jerk, a liar, and generally untrustworthy. The best lawyers in America couldn't get him off those charges. Still, it all came down (as it so often does) to whether she could convince herself he really loved her. If he did, she could fix those other little flaws.

Perhaps not surprisingly for someone who loved Renaissance literature, Deborah decided she'd subject him to a test.

And that was where I came in.

On a hot August morning three days after the play, Deborah appeared at my office with a sharp look in her eye which was really savagery, but which I mistook for amusement.

"Got a minute?" she asked from the doorway.

"For you? Absolutely."

I waved her to a seat, and when she was comfortable, I leaned back in my chair. Deborah with time on her hands was the most fun of any of the ladies.

"What's up?"

"I want bankruptcy papers."

I sat bolt upright. It was lucky I didn't pop a disk. I'd convinced myself instantly that Vic had gotten her into some kind of a horrid jam.

"What!? But I thought . . . how come you're . . . ?" When really excited, I can talk almost a whole minute without forming a full sentence. But Deb held up a hand.

"Hold on, will ya? I didn't say I'm broke; I said I wanted bankruptcy papers."

She leaned forward and explained what she had in mind. She needed only a couple of sentences; her plan had the elegant simplicity of a passage from *The Art of War*.

When she was done, I called in Krista and switched on my computer.

When Deb left an hour later, she had exactly what she wanted, slipped into a simple manila envelope.

*I*n those days Deb still had her ratty little house on Maple Street in Larksdale, as well as a much nicer apartment in the city for weekdays. From my office she went straight back to the house. From there she called Vic to tell him she was feeling a bit under the weather and was canceling for that evening, but would love to see him the next morning. She tried to put it so that any halfway-sensitive human being would suspect she was more depressed than sick; but of course that went right over Vic's head. Delighted she was still talking to him, he simply replied, "Fine, babe. I'm playing tennis at eight-thirty. I'll come over around ten, unless we decide to go to breakfast first."

Deb said that would be perfect and hung up. Outside, through the bow windows of the kitchen, she could see a Salvation Army truck and two neat, uniformed men—one large, one small—getting out. She had called the Army the day before, and they were right on time.

"Two large chairs, two end tables, and two lamps?" the bigger man asked when she met them at the door.

Deb turned and pointed toward the living room. "There they are. Need a hand?"

"We got it," he answered, shaking his head genially and already moving past her.

They were quick: two minutes, and she had the signed receipt, and a very abandoned-looking living room. Indeed, "derelict" might have been a better term, since the fading of the blue carpet had left dark silhouettes where the furniture had been, and the remaining old couch and coffee table were the two dingiest pieces she owned.

Deb studied the sad, empty scene contentedly for half a minute. She'd been thinking halfheartedly of redecorating for ages. Dumping the furniture now fit perfectly with the plan.

Then, realizing time was short, she returned quickly to the kitchen and moved all the food except for a can of really vile reducing drink from the refrigerator to boxes on the counter. She added most of the dry edibles from the cupboards, and then, on an impulse, unplugged the toaster and put it atop the boxed foodstuffs.

It took nearly two hours to load all the boxes into her car, then drive them to a women's shelter in Minneapolis. When she had finished, she felt restless, so she stopped at her favorite, rather literary bookstore to pick up a novel. Deborah read four books a week. That was one reason she and I always had something to talk about.

In the bookstore Deb suffered her usual pang of disappointment that Jane Austen had written nothing new of late and settled instead for the latest biography of that most elusive of authors. There she learned, with some envy, that Ms. Austen's life had apparently been one of complete domestic boredom. After reading about half the book, she turned out her light and went to bed, to stare at the ceiling, thinking restlessly about what the morning might bring, and to wonder if Jane Austen would have found it amusing.

Vic arrived about half an hour late—quite promptly, by his standards. He'd certainly been playing tennis; he showed up still wearing the white shorts and shirt, with a white cotton sweater tied jauntily around his neck. He rapped cheerfully on the front door; Deb could see him through the open bow windows, and he was so handsome her heart skipped a beat—at least, half a beat. But she was still determined to go through with the plan.

"How are you, babe?" Vic asked, draping his sweater and snappy Tilley Endurable hat over the hat rack.

"I'm feeling lots better."

"Oh, yeah?" he answered, not much interested. "Well—good."

He had stepped into the kitchen; over his shoulder, he added, "Anything to drink?"

"Help yourself!" she called ahead, not quite hurrying to join him as he pulled open the fridge.

The one can of Quick 'n Skinni diet drink looked back at him like a dead mouse.

"What the heck?" Vic asked, roughly as annoyed as he was curious. He didn't turn as she reached him: he was too busy staring into the refrigerator.

"It's pretty good, honey," Deborah said, putting a hand on his back. "Tastes kind of like flat beer with saccharin in it."

"Yeah," he said, still mesmerized by the empty larder. "I mean, what's with the no food?"

Deb looked embarrassed. "I, uh . . . I've kind of been watching it."

He shot a glance at her waistline, shrugged, and shut the refrigerator. "Okay. Well, maybe I can't stay too long. Lotta errands to run."

She put a hand on his chest. "Don't you want to come sit in the living room? We can"—she raised her eyebrows—"you know. Snuggle?"

He shrugged thirstily, glanced at the water tap and changed his mind, and then followed her into the living room—where his suspicions were at last aroused. A brontosaurus would have noticed something had changed.

"Hey! What's with the furniture?"

Deb waved a hand airily. "Oh, *that*. Don't you remember? I told you I was getting new stuff—"

Relief swept into Vic's eyes.

"Only, after I got rid of the old stuff, I started thinking this might not be the best time to go throwing my money around."

Worry and suspicion had clouded Vic's eyes again.

She sat on the torn old couch and patted the cushion beside her. Vic dropped down on the worn cushions. He had picked his spot carefully: the distance between them was noticeable but not vast. She scooted, then leaned toward him, slipped an arm around his shoulders, and said, "Listen, honey, I've been thinking about everything you've said about us being such natural partners— about how great it would be for us to do business together."

Vic's eyes began to glow: the pilot light of greed had hit the gas of opportunity. He said ardently, "Absolutely! You and me, through thick and thin. For better or worse." This last, when he thought about it, made him a little nervous; it sounded somehow like a proposal. But he steadied his smile. He even tried to beam, until Deb answered eagerly—

"I'm really glad to hear you say that. In fact, this could be the perfect time for us to start." She tousled his hair. "I could really use a small loan, just to . . ."

Instantly Vic shot to the far end of the sofa. It was an involuntary, full-body twitch, which carried him a good two and a half feet. His back was against the sofa's shredded armrest. He was now a solid three feet away from Deborah, and there hadn't been even a groan of protest from the tired springs. It was amazing how well he moved.

But Deborah had a few moves of her own. She began to edge slowly toward him. She seemed to pull herself forward by the arm she'd draped across the top of the sofa back, even as her other hand dragged carelessly across the coffee table.

It was that dragging arm which ever so artlessly knocked over the stack of magazines on the coffee table, to reveal, just beneath the latest *Business Week,* the document Krista and I had prepared for her the day before.

It was a hard document to miss—mostly because of the heading. In eighty-point black-letter typeface (the style nineteenth-century Germans used to write stuff like "*Achtung!*") it read, *Petition for Bankruptcy.* This, for Vic, was a major *Achtung!* all by itself, and he was quick to jump on it. Even as Deb was trying to hide it back in the stack of magazines, he asked sharply, "What's that?"

"Oh, babe—you weren't supposed to see that." She brought it back out of the stack reluctantly, held it toward him in a supplicating manner while saying rapidly, "It's not definite. Sophia said it's just a precaution, in case . . ."

Her voice trailed off; and then, after a moment's silence, she asked plaintively, "It doesn't change anything, does it, babe?"

Actually it seemed to have changed everything—beginning with Vic's complexion, which had turned two shades paler than his tennis togs. He had always been tan; now he looked like the belly of a flounder wearing pancake makeup.

He didn't rush to answer—he took his time to open and shut his mouth several times before speaking. Presumably he wanted his jaw good and limber when he started.

"Of course it doesn't!" he cried, bounding to his feet. Suddenly he was an upright man. Like all orators, presumably, he spoke better on his feet, and if he was going to profess his undying love before vanishing forever, he wanted to do it like Patrick Henry.

Actually I doubt if Patrick Henry ever gave a speech while sprinting for the door.

Victor, on the other hand, set a new record for the land back-stroke out of the room.

"Of course it doesn't!" he half shouted, to make sure she could hear him from the hallway.

Deborah took ten or fifteen seconds to feel absolutely miserable and abandoned, then got to her feet to follow him one last time.

"You have no idea how much I care about you!" he cried, edging away and making a behind-the-back reach for his sweater on the peg, like an NBA star in slo-mo. "I'm *dying* with concern. If I could, I'd loan you every penny I have—but, honey, I'm barely holding on, myself . . ."

Not even slowing down, he found the doorknob with his other hand, turned it, and pulled open the door. In an instant he was standing on the front porch, the hot air blowing all around him.

"Listen, babe," he proclaimed in tones suitable for "give me liberty, or give me death," "You were the best—absolutely the best!"

He brought his hand up in a rhetorical flourish, and it was no doubt only bad luck that he used the hand resting on the doorknob, so that the door itself flew sharply closed, cutting the two true lovers off from each other. Oh, cruel door!

The Houdini of love had made almost a perfect escape; except, Deb noticed, he had forgotten his cap on the hook. That might have cost him a tenth of a point from the Italian judge; but still, it was a standing-ovation performance in the compulsory set of the romantic freestyle bailout.

From the open front window Deborah watched Vic go. Her eyes were a little moist, but as he moved away they began to narrow, as if she were back on the target range. It's not exactly Jane Austen when you watch your ex-lover cross a lawn, and you think only of windage and elevation.

Deborah opened the window and sailed his cap out after him, like a life preserver to a dying man. For such a marksman, her aim wasn't much, and it landed on the lawn, in a big, muddy puddle made by a malfunctioning Rainbird.

Deborah spent about five minutes on her bed, first expecting to cry, then wondering, dry-eyed, why she couldn't. Wasn't she crushed? She asked the question of the universe; but as the silence grew in response, she finally answered it herself. A little grudgingly she admitted she wasn't crushed. Yes, a sharp ache of loneliness had settled in her stomach. It felt uncomfortable, about like the pain she'd felt lying in her bunk the first night in boot camp.

But other feelings were overwhelmingly stronger. For one thing, she felt relieved. For another, she was growing angrier by the minute.

She shut her eyes and drew a pillow over her face. Suddenly every rotten stunt Vic had ever pulled returned to her in a montage, as if he were getting a Lifetime Achievement Award in hell.

She stayed for the whole show, and the highlights recap, and then she sat up in bed, surprised. That pain in her stomach had changed its nature.

She realized she was hungry.

She'd nearly reached the kitchen before remembering she'd emptied the fridge as part of Vic's test. The prospect of having to hit the store for a simple sandwich made her *really* furious with the ex-love of her life. Until then, reconciliation might have been possible; but as she stared at the empty wire racks of the Frigidaire, she knew there could be no forgiveness.

With hunger gnawing at her, Deb checked her watch. It was only eleven-fifteen. If she left immediately, she could still make the last half hour of the club meeting.

She grabbed her purse and headed out the door. As she neared her car, she broke into a jog.

If she hurried she could swing by McDonald's on her way.

CHAPTER TWENTY-EIGHT

The Debriefing

Deb reached Martha's house about a quarter to twelve. Leaving the empty McDonald's bag in the car and popping a couple of Breathsavers in her mouth, she ran up the long walkway, past a slightly drooping summer garden, and knocked at the door.

The meeting's business had already been concluded, and we were in that genial, standing-around-the-snack-table-chatting stage preparatory to breaking up. When the doorbell rang, I ran to get it: I'd been halfway expecting Deb's arrival all morning.

"How'd it go?" I asked in hushed tones.

She whispered back fiercely, "The test came back positive."

Deb's whisper was just a little too loud; and Skye, who happened to be nearby (and who had grown vastly more outgoing in the last year), immediately wanted to know what test exactly was being discussed.

A moment later the topic had become general; and Deborah, who wasn't shy about much, was perfectly willing to fill them in, in her usual blunt fashion.

She concluded the summary some two minutes later. "The creep silked—you know, hit the silk—strapped on a parachute and jumped out the first open door."

By this time I had drifted to a dark corner of the room. Whenever the discussion of personal matters turned public, I turned shy. But the discussion didn't suffer from my absence.

The meeting was soon back in order; at least, the ladies returned to their seats to give the topic a better airing.

They tried to console Deborah, to urge her to move on, to cheer her up. It was all kindly meant, and all in their best modern blend of pop psychology and old-fashioned religion—but Deb was just too tough to need that kind of advice. She listened politely and even smiled when Gladys muttered wistfully, "I wish a gigolo would take an interest in *me*."

But it was getting late. They needed some closing words to start them homeward.

"You know," Martha offered helpfully, "a lot of people would say that living well was the best revenge."

At that, Deborah's eyes lit up. She had a fine, old ex-jarhead view of life which said that living well was the second-best revenge. Kicking somebody's ass finished first every time.

Deborah had great respect for Martha as a person. So, very politely, she answered, "I'll think it over."

But she had already decided to settle the score.

CHAPTER TWENTY-NINE

Frankie and Debbie

Deborah needed more than a month to find the plan—or rather, three weeks to find the plan, and a week to gather the nerve—to settle the score once and for all.

The week after the breakup had been like coming out of an anesthetic. She'd thought Vic was dumb but lovable—but he wasn't dumb and he wasn't lovable. Now she imagined three dozen ways of getting even, from the gothic to a sort of Indiana Jones modern. But she didn't figure out the truly just revenge until she realized that Vic had also been a lying rat toward all his gay friends.

Deb knew it was bigotry to say gay men ran the hairdressing industry; beyond that, she didn't care one way or another. She was an equal-opportunity competitor: she wanted to beat everyone, regardless of race, creed, color, or anything else. Still, she realized a truly elegant revenge would involve showing Vic up in front of the other people he'd tricked.

As soon as she realized that, inspiration struck like a Mack truck driven by Mario Andretti.

She decided to carry out her plan without anyone else's prior knowledge. Afterward she could explain and apologize if anyone was offended.

. . .

$\mathcal{C}$aballo was probably Minneapolis's swankest gay bar. It was also, Deb discovered, the main place Vic used to network, recruit stylists, and sometimes raise money.

Deborah, arriving just after nine o'clock, saw Vic, dressed with his usual casual elegance, standing talking at the bar. She took a table across the smallish room and sat so that, half-masked in shadow, she could easily watch him. Fortunately he was using his charm on the bartender—probably to get him to pour a double for the price of a single. It gave Deborah time to practice, until she could summon up a stare like a hawk waiting to take down a sparrow.

The stare took a while to begin working its mojo. During the first ten minutes Victor looked over at her only once, then turned back to his conversation with two buff young guys wearing fashionable tank tops.

Then, exactly at the ten-minute mark, Vic glanced over again—and saw her giving him exactly the same hawklike stare. Vic's handsome face began to lose some of its salon-tanned, well-scrubbed, pore-reduced sheen. In fact, as he began to glance her way with ever-increasing frequency, he started to look a bit ashen and a bit moist about the temples. For a short time his head stopped turning toward her, but his eyes kept shifting in her direction, then darting away. He seemed to be having trouble keeping up the usual smooth flow of his conversation. His smile was growing trembly.

Deb, who read much more than she watched movies, began to think of the few gangster films she'd seen. She began wishing she'd worn a double-breasted coat so she could reach her hand in under her armpit, as if going for her shoulder holster. Ah, well; nobody could think of everything. She dropped the temperature of her stare another ten degrees and ostentatiously slipped her hand into her purse, as if fishing around for something small—say, about .38 caliber.

Victor now began looking remarkably like a guy who knew there was a contract out on him.

After all, Deborah was ex-military. And Victor—who'd taken up swimming because nobody ever got hit swimming—was not exactly heroic.

Sometimes—not often—the universe backs our play. Just then, over the club's sound system came a great blues rendition of the cheatin' man's anthem, "Frankie and Johnnie." As Deborah stared harder, a dim understanding flickered in Vic's skull. It was *just* possible, his twisty little brain realized, that she might imagine he was her man, and he'd done her wrong. Now he pressed back harder against the bar, and his neck began twisting about, as he desperately sought a back exit through the smoky darkness.

Deborah decided it was time to move—and for an ex-marine, she could do a pretty fair imitation of an Apache dancer. Rising, eyes smoldering, she kicked back her chair—sent it skidding ten feet across the room—and darted toward him. She had him in the crosshairs.

Victor staggered back as if he'd already been shot; with his arms spread wide, he exposed that manly chest, and Deborah went straight for it, throwing her arms around him, and crying, "Oh, *honey*!" Deborah had a fine, clear voice, and she put plenty behind it. It dripped passion—but somewhere between lust and a blood-curdling rebel yell.

Vic still looked nautical—now more or less like a baby whale, harpooned in the moonlight an hour or two before. Done flopping, but still twitching.

Deborah was on him—or at least against him. The two tank-topped young men, meanwhile, had stepped back, torn between equally natural feelings that they ought to come to Vic's aid and that something was decidedly fishy.

"Oh, baby! Come on. We don't have to wait. I've got a car. It's got a backseat. Oh, *yes*!"

By this time the bar of Caballo was the quietest social-gathering place in the entire Midwest. You could have heard an innuendo drop at fifty paces.

Deb took official notice of the two other men for the first time. "What?"

She paused until she pretended to have caught an elusive thought. "You don't mean he was playing his old pretending-to-be-gay gag, do you?"

They looked at her aghast, then began eyeing Vic with swelling suspicion.

Deb turned back to Vic. "Honey!" she said reproachfully. "You promised!"

So it ended, about three minutes later. In the process of acting love-distraught, Deborah made it clear to all surrounding that Vic was a duplicitous, prejudiced swine. Even as she nominally struggled to excuse his behavior, she buried him so deep they'd never find the body.

Vic barely tried to defend himself. When Deb backed away briefly, he stammered, "I'm . . . I'm . . . I'm . . ."

Then he got stuck. He didn't know what he was, and nobody else cared.

By the time he fled into the night, Deb had blown his cover forever.

Actually he did stop at the back door and seem for an instant about to speak. But no words came.

He was a lie-powered machine and he'd just run out of fuel.

That was the end of the ballad of Debbie and Victor. Vic closed Vic's #3 a month later, and before spring, he'd sold off #1 and #2 at a huge loss and moved to a city out west. Deborah doubted it was San Francisco.

She wasn't sorry.

He was her man, and he done her wrong.

CHAPTER THIRTY

A New Office— and Heidi

The success of Combat! could not have come at a better time for me. After a couple of years in private practice, I'd discovered the big-firm life was not my style.

Not that I had it worse than any other young associate trying to make it in a big firm without rich or famous parents, or a major client in her back pocket. All of us were worked, without discrimination, like unwanted dogs. The joke at Senior, Winters & Willow was, "If you don't come in on Saturday, don't *bother* coming in on Sunday." The fact that they rated that as a joke ought to give you a sense of the high spirits, the jollity of life at Senior, Winters. Each year summer associates were brought in for ten weeks of light work, lake parties, Twins tickets, and plays at the Guthrie—and as soon as they signed onto the ship, out came the leg irons and the cat-o'-nine-tails.

How do you tell a junior lawyer from a really depressed mortician?

The mortician's wearing the black tie.

Of course, every year thousands of junior lawyers, from San Diego up to Maine, endured exactly the same treatment. They settled for those few little compensations—like making roughly four times what a schoolteacher or policeman made—and hung on for partnership.

It just wasn't for me. I didn't mind the work. I did mind the feeling that we were expected to maximize profits—and since we were lawyers, that meant maximizing the amount of conflict in the world.

Above all—let's face it—I was lonely. My friend Marcy said her lawyering job paid "eighty grand a year and twice-daily visitation rights with a BMW." That was, once at six A.M. while driving in to work, and once at nine P.M. while driving home.

The difference between Marcy and me was that I lacked even the BMW. Especially after Krista, my secretary, quit to have a baby, I realized how fragile my attachments were to my work colleagues. I liked Krista as well as anyone there; but when she left, I threw her a going-away party/baby shower, and we both promised to keep in touch and both knew we wouldn't.

So Combat!'s success came at a perfect time. For one thing, it meant I finally had a client the firm cared about. In fact, the day I opened Combat!'s incorporation file was the day my supervising partner stopped calling me Peters and started calling me Sophia.

It also meant the Ladies could now afford roughly the half-time services of an attorney. At least, they could so long as they didn't have to pay the big-firm markup, which took two-thirds of my hourly billing rate. Since they had lately bought a second, larger office building in Larksdale—this one on Main Street—and since the lousy shape of the local economy kept it half-empty, they decided they could give me space as a bonus.

My plan was simple. My old firm would keep me on as a contract attorney to handle their overflow work on smallish cases, for vacationing attorneys, and so on. (They agreed to this quite amicably after the firm's top rainmaker called Deborah Cohen, to see if they'd keep her business after I left; and she told him if they didn't make me happy, they'd get her business back the same day hell got a pro ice-hockey franchise.)

That meant half-time work, a lower pay rate, and no chance of partnership—what people were calling the "mommy track"—but I didn't mind. With my Larksdale money as shares in the investment partnership, there'd be no BMW for Sophia; but if I worked hard, and the Ladies kept up their amazing streak, in about five years I'd be able to move to Tahiti and write a novel—or at least read one. Or at least maybe get a date.

It was a brilliant plan—or at least satisfactory to nearly everyone. Of course *Veronica* had to object, both because that was her nature and because the more the Ladies made, the more it galled her that I was getting an investment share and she wasn't. I heard there was a short, nasty debate, with Veronica arguing they couldn't afford me. But I won in a landslide: since Veronica didn't have voting rights, the decision was unanimous—a tribute more to my mom's importance than to mine.

I started on a warm July day in 1987. It was warm even before sunrise, which was when I arrived at my new office to begin painting it: in the best Midwestern tradition of frugality, I was doing the redecorating on my own.

Or not entirely on my own.

It turned out the Ladies had arranged for me to have secretarial help, in the form of a young woman named Heidi Langland.

Somebody once described Minnesota at Thanksgiving as a place where "out in the backyards, blond giants play football—while in the kitchen, the men cook dinner." Heidi was one of *those* Minnesotans. But it got worse from there.

Heidi was probably the most beautiful woman I'd ever seen. She was like some weird Scandinavian experiment to prove all men are idiots. She was six-foot-one, golden blond, with the body of a goddess and the face of a sexy Nordic Madonna. When she sashayed down the street, men didn't honk or whistle. Their bodies locked up in some strange tetanuslike seizure, and they drove into the sides of buses. In the background, some vague, basso chorus of voices always seemed to be chanting, "We're not worthy"—a sound intermingled with moaning and drooling. She was the love goddess of Minnesota; I was the schlub in the Armani skirt.

The particular Saturday morning when we met, as the sun rose over the summer mosquitoes, the difference between us was not quite so apparent. Heidi, in paint-daubed blue jeans and a Duluth Women's Rugby sweater which looked loose-fitting until she stood, rose from the sidewalk where she'd been sitting with her back against the building's front wall.

"Sophia?"

"Yes?"

She put out her hand. "I'm Heidi. Your new secretary."

"It's six-thirty in the morning. On Saturday." I said it a little blearily. My three morning cups of coffee were inside a thermos inside my canvas carryall, instead of being inside of me, where they belonged. As a result, the thermos had more brainpower than I did.

I looked down at her paint-spattered jeans.

"How'd you know I'd be here to paint?"

"It's what I would have done."

Despite the lack of coffee, I was waking up—at least to the extent of deciding I liked her. I started fumbling for the building key; she lifted the carryall bag off my arm. I liked her better and better.

Trying to work the sticky lock, I asked, "Want to tell me about yourself?"

"Not much to tell. I'm twenty-one. One year of college, then paralegal school. I want to take night-school courses to get as far as I can for not much money, then finish at the U, and go to law school."

From anyone else who looked like Heidi, this might have sounded like a dramatic reading of a *Playboy* centerfold's career ambitions. From Heidi, it sounded like a stone-solid plan.

"Do you know much about our workload?" The lock was still sticking, and I was on the verge of getting frustrated.

"Not much. I know it's part corporate transactional, and part for a group of lady investors."

"The Ladies are most of it. They're characters, but I like them. I think you will, too. Mostly we just watch their investments and handle any personal issues." I shook the door with frustration. "Make sure nobody gets rough with them."

Heidi eased me aside and fiddled with the lock. In a second it opened: she pushed the door wide and gestured for me to enter.

"Okey-doke," she said as I walked past her. "If anybody gets rough, you knock 'em down, and I'll stomp them."

$\mathcal{B}$y the time we finished painting, near six that evening, Heidi and I were friends.

CHAPTER THIRTY-ONE

The Ladies Are Rich

Meeting Heidi was about my only fun that summer. Unlike Marcy, who seemed to blow through the mid-eighties just shifting into fifth, I never seemed quite able to get things in gear.

I won't bore you with the details of my sex life. In fact, I couldn't bore you. Only long stories, with too many incidents, are boring. Despite an occasional flurry of dates—some arranged by MMC members, some spontaneous—my love life was a disaster.

The men with the right education and jobs all looked down on me when they found out what I did for a living—which was tainted with the yuppie equivalent of botulism: lack of ambition. The nice, ordinary guys were scared off by my education and work.

Things seemed to be going much better for the Ladies.

Quite aside from bringing Vic onto the scene, Combat! played a key role in the evolution of their outlook.

Before Combat!, I don't think any of them really thought of the money as real. An abstract good, yes—but still an abstraction. But Combat! was throwing off so much cash, it became impossible to ignore.

At first the Ladies were too timid to do anything with their newfound prosperity. Or perhaps too *stunned:* the day Veronica (with a style I must admit was gracious, even likable) rose to begin her monthly report by saying that the Club had $1,000,000 in the bank, they looked collectively like a herd of does trapped in the headlights of an onrushing Brinks truck.

Except for modest monthly stipends, the Ladies voted to keep reinvesting every penny. The Club's success, by freeing them from the need to save out of their family paychecks, gave them most of the scant extra spending money they desired.

Still, even without extravagance, the money was becoming real in different ways for each of us. For me, it was mostly just having Heidi—my own, honest-to-goodness secretary—in my own office.

For the Ladies, it was Combat!, and the bank balances, and discovering they owned real estate on Larksdale's best, prettiest, and shadiest business street. That was a thrill for them. Every now and then, on those summer evenings, you could find one or more of them standing out in front of the building looking up at it admiringly, as if they were tourists and it was the Arc de Triomphe.

But I was just driving the tour bus, and not enjoying it as much as I'd expected.

CHAPTER THIRTY-TWO

I Come Out Swinging

That's not to say I spent all my time quietly bemoaning my fate.

Sometimes I found noisy ways to bemoan it.

Like a lot of shy people, I've spent much of my life shadow-boxing at life's villains. While Deb was suffering Vic's abuses, I spent time imagining what I'd do to him, if only I were bigger, tougher, and, "Well, take that, you dog."

Which was perhaps why I finally gave in to yet another of Marcy's importunities and agreed to join her at her thrice-weekly martial-arts class.

I had previously taken one of Mike's weekend YWCA self-defense courses for women and can say in all modesty that I was the first person there for each session and always had my pen and notebook. I liked the class, both because Mike was a careful, patient, and gentle instructor, and because the cornerstone of his advice was to stay out of dangerous places. Not being in places is one of my favorite strategies, anyway—so I was widely viewed as being a natural at self-defense.

Marcy's school was different.

The main area was a single large room, brightly lit, with mirrors covering one long and one short wall. A polished wooden floor, like a slightly elevated platform, covered all but a small bordering strip, the only area on which people were allowed to wear shoes. Side bins bulged with pads, boxing gloves, shin guards, and the like; and on one wall hung a genuinely terrifying display of Asian weaponry: swords, spears, and throwing stars. The place could have been a set for *Aerobics Studio of the Living Dead*.

As we walked in, a one-hundred-fifteen-pound woman with a black belt was choking about a two-hundred-pound man. His face was growing purple, and I didn't think he was doing it to be polite.

I said, "Thanks, Marcy, but my old self-defense instructor said the first step to self-preservation was to stay out of dangerous places, so—bye."

She caught my shoulder before I could turn all the way back to the door.

"Relax. Nobody here will hurt you."

Against my better judgment, I went into the dressing room. The women there were surprisingly pleasant and talking—oh, how reassuring!—about work. I unpackaged my brand-new *gi*—a deluxe model of the standard karate uniform. Marcy had told me it was the very best grade, but it was remarkably unlike Armani's idea of good fabric. In fact, it fit like a particularly stiff grade of cheap cardboard. I also found that I had neglected to bring anything appropriate to wear *under* the *gi* jacket, which kept slipping open. I was a scandal. A small scandal, but a scandal.

It turned out—lucky me—that I was there for judo-and-jujitsu night, which meant that a guest instructor ("from the world-famous U.S. Marine Corps Force Recon!") was going to show us how to throw each other from one end of the room to the other and to engineer the most painful landing possible.

The universe treats me like I'm a big bug, overdue for squashing.

"Just remember," the house-sized guest instructor concluded, "if you know you're going down, be sure to look at your belt. That will make you tuck in your chin and reduce the chances of a broken neck."

I looked over to Marcy in a panic; she mouthed back, "You'll be fine." It was either that or, "So long, sucker."

It certainly started well enough. My partner was a fairly grim-looking, somewhat unshaven fellow built more or less like a refrigerator, but he had what I took to be a pleasant half smile. We bowed at each other. Then we grasped each other's uniform, one hand on collar, the other on sleeve, and began dancing around each other in what looked to me like a slowed-down version of West Coast swing. If the band had just started playing "Blow, Gabriel, Blow," it might have been quite nice.

I was on the verge of telling my partner how much fun this was.

Then he dropped from sight, and an instant later, while pulling me toward him, he planted his foot in my stomach with a sharp upward thrust. This would have been mean enough for most people—but, no. His foot continued upward, taking me skyward with it.

That was merely uncomfortable. The event became perverse when he simultaneously yanked down on my arm and collar, flipping me in midair like a large, blond pancake. A very unhappy pancake.

It was at this point—as the room around me appeared quite normal except for being upside down—that I devised a plan. I would panic.

In my half second of remaining lucidity, I tried to do as instructed and look down at my belt. It would have been a lot easier to do if my belt had not been flying in about six directions at once. So I decided instead to look around for someone to complain to.

I can think very fast when flying upside down toward a thin canvas mat. Unfortunately not quite fast enough.

I very likely would have broken every bone in my body, except that I managed to cushion the blow by landing flat on my back and letting the impact push every bit of air out of my lungs, after which I made a noise like a mouse being strangled, and passed out.

When the room came back in view, Marcy was pulling my partner off me and saying something a bit less printable than, "Get off her, you idiot."

Not moving, I asked, "Ow! How come nobody hits *you*?"

"Did you tell them you're a lawyer?" She was pulling me to my feet.

"No. Let go of my arm. Don't you believe in death with dignity?"

She had me up.

"Silly Sophia. Tell them you're a lawyer, and they'll be afraid you'll sue them."

*A*n hour later—and roughly seventy-five years older—I lowered myself gingerly into the passenger seat of Marcy's BMW. Definitely a young person's car, I decided. Still, I'd discovered that if I leaned to the right, looked to the left, and held my breath, it didn't hurt too much. Marcy, whistling a Cole Porter medley, fired up the engine and started us out of the lot.

"You know what I've noticed?" I asked as she braked gently for the first light and the seat belt pressed excruciatingly against my bruised right hip.

Still watching the road, she shook her head slightly.

"These days my life seems to divide into things that are no fun and things that have no point."

Now she *did* glance over.

"That's just post-whack-in-the-snoot syndrome."

"I don't think so."

She took her time before answering. Then she sighed, and said, "Yeah, well—welcome to the eighties, Sophia." She paused. "In fact, welcome to real life." She paused again. Rain was starting to splat against the windshield, and she leaned forward to peer through it. "So, anyway, Thursday is straight kickboxing. You coming?"

I reached over and switched on the wipers. "Yeah. I guess so. With any luck, I'll break my neck, and my heirs will get to file a huge lawsuit against them all."

CHAPTER THIRTY-THREE

The Roof Falls In

*P*sychiatrists say cases of depression drop dramatically during wartime. Give people something real to worry about, and they get over their vague existential miseries real quick.

I don't know whether that's always true; but some variation of it certainly hit home for me a couple of months after my great kung fu adventure.

I'd spent those months in a growing funk. I had too much time to dwell on my own disappointments, in part because things were going so smoothly for my main clients.

Yes, Deb had some fence-mending to do with her gay friends; but both because they really were her friends, and because Vic's character was not nearly so successful a fraud as he'd imagined, soon everything returned to normal. In fact, the whole ballad of Deb and Vic endured as a running joke for months thereafter and could still raise smiles when a year had passed. And, of course, it was not an issue that required my assistance in any important way.

The Ladies, meanwhile, spent all of September in a mood of pleasant late-summer languor. Indeed, except for my own gloom, I remember it as a very pleasant season, the sort I imagined I'd enjoyed in elementary-school days. Everything seemed suspended; even my parents had stopped fighting in a kind of summer truce.

On the first Sunday of October, I sat on the porch of my parents' house thinking that autumn was late and summer might linger another month.

I wasn't exactly happy; but an autumn sunset without a hint of cold made me feel, almost pleasantly, like a little girl on an endless summer holiday.

The very next Thursday was October 7, 1987—and autumn swept in like an arctic blizzard.

I was at my desk writing a blunt letter to Agnes's landlord, when Heidi, who sometimes listened to the radio on a Walkman, rushed into my office and straight up to my chair.

She pulled off the earphones, and said, "I think we'd better turn on the TV."

I followed her to the snack-and-storage room, where we kept a small TV for following important events—like old Cary Grant movies—when we were working late. It had cable, and Heidi switched on CNN, where, with almost theatrical precision, the very first words we heard were, ". . . where the panic selling continues unabated."

When your primary task in life is to look after the investments of your family and best friends, a phrase like "panic selling continues unabated" is probably the last thing you want to hear. It ranks right up there with "we found something on your X ray," and "President Limbaugh said today . . ."

And yet, I can say honestly I didn't panic.

I later heard that in some of the New York brokerages, people just sat back with their fingers laced behind their heads and watched, too stunned to act. I understand that completely. There was a notable sense of unreality about it all—panic wasn't the question; more like a half-bored, half-nauseated, slightly confused lethargy.

It had been fifty-eight years since the Crash of '29; nobody on the floor really had an idea what a market crash looked like. But we were quickly getting the picture.

I did a rough calculation in my head, just based on the Dow Jones average numbers the reporter was citing, plus the ticker streaming past on the bottom of the screen. It looked like we were losing about $3,000 a minute. Probably more.

I asked Heidi to call all the Ladies and ask them to come into my office immediately. "Don't panic them—but make sure they know it's urgent."

"Got it," she said, and started away. Any job given to Heidi could be treated as done.

I called Axel Langsgaard, our broker—who deserves more credit than I have given him so far—to ask how he saw things. He came on the line quickly but calmly.

"You've been watching the TV coverage?"

"Oh, yeah. How bad is it?"

"Well, it might be a real crash, but I don't think so."

"When will you know?"

"In about two months. If stocks are still going down—"

That sounded unhelpful. I interrupted, "Hold on?"

"I would. If your Ladies can stand it."

"How much are we down?"

I heard the click of keyboard keys.

"A little over seven hundred thousand."

"Jesus Christ."

"Sophia!" He said it jokingly, pretending to be scandalized by my language. It helped.

"One of those days. Okay. For now, we're holding. But you might get the band on deck and see if they know 'Nearer My God to Thee.' "

"Right. Call me when you know more."

If I was feeling lethargic, the Ladies certainly were as energetic as ever. Heidi started calling them at nine-thirty-five; at eleven-fifteen, when Deborah, smelling of that clean salon blend of perfumes and soaps, came through the door, she was the last to arrive.

It's hard to remember today how clumsy the technology was

just back in '87. We had no on-line trading, no videoconferencing with our broker—nothing like that. Just CNN, the phone, and the frightened looks on each other's faces.

What was happening, of course, was that we were suddenly realizing that the money we were losing—which had seemed so abstract while we were making it—was absolutely real. Those numbers on the statements Veronica prepared each month weren't just ink on paper; they were comfortable retirements, new cars, and European vacations. They were as much security as this world offers.

The market was crumbling. Moreover, because we were heavily invested in aggressive-growth stocks, our losses were proportionately greater: by ten-thirty, when I called Axel back, the Dow Jones average was down 12 percent, and we were down nearly 22. Float like a butterfly, sink like a stone—that was us.

The Ladies, when they arrived, were universally flustered—with good cause. I figured their average loss at roughly $140,000 so far that morning. For a fund manager in Boston, that's just a number. For them, it was a disaster.

By the time they arrived—first Martha, with just the tightening around her eyes showing how worried she was; then Dolly, in a sweet-tempered panic, which grew more evident with each new report from CNN; and then the others—we much better understood what was happening.

The sell-off had started quite ordinarily, with professional managers trimming their positions in a large number of stocks they considered overpriced. Nothing odd about that.

Unfortunately, during the previous six years, quite unnoticed, the "rocket scientists"—physicists and mathematicians hired by the big Wall Street firms—had been designing computer systems to control their buying and selling, based upon complex formulae. Those programs were meant to track interest rates, options prices, money supplies—dozens of factors in all. Unfortunately one of the factors they watched was what the other big program traders were doing. If the other big players were selling too much, the computers were supposed to begin dumping their firms' holdings, too.

Now the computers were running the trading, and they were performing about as well as the automatic bulkheads on S.S. *Titanic*. In fact, a reported $200 million worth of mainframes and top-secret software had just created the world's first computer simulation of the hysterical panic on *Titanic*'s "A" deck. They were doing the electronic equivalent of pushing each other into the freezing North Atlantic in a desperate scramble to be first in the lifeboats.

This, of course, would have been absolutely hilarious to contemplate, had I been reading about it in a comic story by, say, P. G. Wodehouse. But that morning, listening to the Ladies try to figure out what it all meant to them, was anything but funny.

I won't stick names on every opinion voiced in that next hour. To the Ladies' undying credit, though, they kept strictly away from blaming each other. They debated avidly enough, but they pointed no fingers. Still, the alarm in their voices was frightening enough— as was the perception (which I may have invented whole cloth) that they were expecting me to fix everything.

The problem was that we had built our success upon our solid knowledge of individual companies, and this was a collapse based upon market-wide issues we didn't even vaguely understand.

Lacking the hard facts, or even the right language, we began arguing in unhelpful metaphors. Thus, when Agnes offered timidly that the drop had to stop sometime, Dolly answered rather tartly, "Even a 747 falling out of the air with all four engines ablaze will stop falling eventually—usually when it hits the ground."

Maybe she ended her remark more sarcastically than she intended. In any case, with each passing minute, the debate was growing sharper, largely because of Dolly. Wringing her hands, and seeming the only one of us close to panic, she began pushing for us to sell out and cut our losses.

Things only grew more heated when Veronica (who showed up

late and uninvited) took the floor to second the case for selling. As calm and persuasive as she appeared, I couldn't escape the feeling that she took a secret delight in the thought of the Ladies' losing a bunch of money. Of course, that made no sense—they were certainly her most valuable clients—but it was a feeling I couldn't shake.

We'd been arguing about forty minutes—roughly $120,000's worth of additional losses, with the TV on in the background and a certain panic creeping into our voices. The more we debated, the further apart we drifted—and the longer we debated, the more money we lost. Everyone understood the situation, with the result that, while still trying to be civil, they began talking faster and faster, until we sounded like one of those FedEx world's-fastest-talker commercials—played at double speed.

By then it was noon, and the market was down nearly four hundred points, and clearly unable to rally.

Running my own guess poll, I made the situation pretty much as follows:

For holding on: Skye, Deb, and I, with Martha a possibility

For selling out: Dolly and Veronica

Undecided, but rapidly leaning toward selling: Gladys, Mom, Mary, and Agnes

Perhaps Dolly had reached the same conclusions. She took the floor again and said anxiously, "That's enough talking. I say it's time to vote. Do we dump our stock or not?"

That was when Agnes—in probably the only active part she ever took in one of the debates—amazed us all by raising her hand for attention. When Martha recognized her, she stood not quite straight and asked, "Are you sure we've thought of everything?"

A question, of course, is a shy person's way of steering a conversation. This time it worked.

Martha asked, "What do you mean?"

"Well, maybe this is dumb; but isn't it true that . . . well, that the time to go shopping is when prices are down? I mean, when was the last time you said, 'Hey! Dillard's just raised prices—I think I'll run down to the store'?"

While the Ladies contemplated that, an obscure fact fluttered into my mind: in 1814, one of the English Rothschilds had made a vast fortune in a single day by a simple device. He had a courier system set up to bring him the first news of the Battle of Waterloo. When the messenger reached him on the floor of the stock exchange, he read the message carefully, shook his head sadly, and began selling all his stocks.

Everyone knew Rothschild had inside information and assumed that England must have lost at Waterloo. They panicked, and the stock market crumbled. Then, suddenly, with prices at a fraction of what they had been, Rothschild jumped back in and bought all the shares he could afford—in fact, bought control of the entire market. Minutes later a second messenger arrived, announcing the same news Rothschild had earlier received privately: Napoleon had been trounced.

Rothschild had started a panic by shaking his head, and in one day became the richest man in the world.

The lesson—aside from the obvious one that inside info is always useful—is that if your nerves are good enough, you should always buy into a panic.

In the instant I'd needed to think of this, the discussion had come to its crisis. Veronica, not very effectively hiding her contempt for Agnes's economic theories, asked her sharply, "Just what are you saying?"

Agnes didn't flinch. "I'm saying, we've got the List." This was the list we kept, updated biweekly, of the six to ten stocks we most wanted to buy. "And we should use it. Half an hour, say, before the market closes, we should figure out which four or five stocks on the list have dropped the most, and we should buy all of them we can afford."

"But that's everything! That's all the money we have." I'm not sure who said that; but I know all of us were thinking it.

Skye, who had lately declared her intention to get her MBA after graduation, and who had been the most aggressive in favoring sitting tight, now seconded Agnes loudly. Speaking even as she jumped to her feet, she demanded, "Think about it. Can you see any reason why the economy should fall apart all of a sudden?"

They sat looking at each other for a full minute—searching, I guess, for economic reasons in each other's faces. Dolly, I could see, was ashen. I couldn't imagine why she was even more worried than the rest of us—but clearly she was.

Then, one by one, they began nodding their heads.

Martha called for a vote, and except for Dolly, they decided unanimously to throw every penny they had into the market.

If nothing else, they were going down with guns blazing.

CHAPTER THIRTY-FOUR

The Consequences of Success

*W*e followed Agnes's unexpected advice. Or rather, we followed a slightly modified version of it. At Axel's suggestion, I sold out some of our most volatile stocks around noon—and bought them back, two hours later, at about a 20 percent discount. It was the big Day After Christmas Sale at the New York Stock Exchange.

Of course, the market recovered its losses within a few months—and then began a steady upward climb from 2,500 to well over 10,000 (as I write this). It didn't take any brains at all to make money in the market for the eleven years after the '87 Crash: you just threw your money on the waters, and it came back increased by 15 or 20 or 40 percent every year.

But it had taken guts to stay with the market that one cool day in October, and the Ladies had guts. In fact, after the first vote, Dolly had changed hers to make it unanimous—and I wouldn't realize until much later how much guts that had really taken.

A great deal changed after the market crash—or rather, after the market's recovery. It wasn't just that from then on we knew the money was real; it was that we began to have too much money simply to tuck away in a portfolio. We had to start deciding what to do with our success.

Ultimately, despite their best intentions, the Ladies began leaking money and information. It's possible, after all, to pretend you found an extra fifty dollars tucked away in the cookie jar; but when all of a sudden you have the cash for a new car or a new tractor . . . or a minority interest in an NFL franchise, well, explanations are in order.

For some of the Ladies, though, the situation was even more complicated. Not everything that comes with success is easy or even pleasant.

One of my favorite poets put it this way: "Even victors are by victory undone." By growing rich, we had distanced ourselves from our friends and neighbors. We had to start taking steps to bridge that gap.

Now, in small towns and rural counties, at least in the Midwest, there have always been monied families who hide their money. The farmer with the worst-looking truck may well be the one with $5 million in land and another couple of million in the bank.

In other times, that same style might well have worked for us. Unfortunately the eighties were tough on farmers, and tougher on the industrial Midwest. For years we'd watched footage on TV about the "rust belt"—watched Detroit, especially, turned into a weird cross between a Western ghost town and the world of *Road Warrior*.

In the midst of all that trouble, all that worry, the Larksdale Ladies had sat secure, making their investments and piling up their returns. They were essentially a handful of grannies who'd figured out that the old Midwestern way of working harder the harder it snowed wasn't working anymore. They'd discovered a way of working smarter, so much smarter it almost wasn't like working at all. For them, the eighties were just great.

I hadn't realized, even vaguely, how different we'd become from the majority of our friends and neighbors, until the end of that

Black Thursday collapse. The other Ladies went home around four-thirty—as Dolly put it, "Market crash or no market crash, Buzz is going to want his dinner." Heidi and I stayed another two hours, sorting papers and watching the news. By seven o'clock, a succession of pundits had convinced us the world economy wasn't doomed. In fact, that the Ladies might have made yet another smart play.

So we closed up and went home. Or rather, I went to the Circle K convenience store down the street from my apartment, to see whether it was possible to put together a balanced meal from a combination of potato-chip brands.

The Circle K was never empty; when I arrived, it was almost crowded. Ahead of me in line were four middle-aged, broad-shouldered but paunchy men who looked like truck drivers or old-line factory workers. (They all wore Cat baseball caps; but in the Midwest, that means nothing.)

Already at the counter, they were taking their time picking out chewing gum and beef jerky, and paying: they were using their location as a stage for their comments.

"See what happened to the market?"

"Yeah. Ain't it great? Maybe all those rich bastards'll get a feeling for what it's like to worry about something more than what color Mercedes to buy."

"Damn straight. I hope they lose their asses. Gimme a pack of the Marlboros, too."

The boy behind the counter smiled noncommittally at all this, took their money, and gave them their change.

And they went on their way. But they left me something to think about.

CHAPTER THIRTY-FIVE

About Prairie Machine

I was still thinking about the conversation in the Circle K a week later, when the bombshell dropped on Larksdale.

Larksdale had stayed lucky until '87. Our one big employer, Prairie Machine Tool, had hung on fairly well—mostly because the Halvorsens, the family who controlled its stock, had been willing to take big losses to keep the town together. Indeed, old Jakob Halvorsen had even taken the unusual step of putting his own money back into the company. Much of that money went to fund the very bright R&D group, the Hog Farm, run by Mary's husband, Mike. The Hog Farmers developed computerized versions of the cash machines and credit-card terminals that were PMT's main business. PMT never led the pack, but (thanks largely to Mike's team) they never fell out of the race entirely—and in an age when American midsized manufacturers were getting pulled down by the hundreds like the sickest gazelles in the herd, old Jakob's achievement was worthy of respect.

But in August of '87, Jakob Halvorsen, the last surviving son of the company's founder, had keeled over on the eighteenth hole of the Rice Creek Municipal Golf Course. The immediate cause of death was a heart attack brought on by a backfiring car—which makes sense only when you realize that Rice Creek Course is half a mile from the huge U.S. Army Twin Cities Ammunition Plant, and that old Jakob was eighty-seven years old and of a nervous disposition.

The moment old Jakob hit the green for the last time, his two daughters, Lucy Halvorsen and Anita Halvorsen Evans Linsdale Lane, became the sole owners of Prairie Machine Tool. Exactly twelve days later those two issued a short statement: they had agreed to sell the company to a New York City–based conglomerate called Arcturis Holdings. We heard the sweet girls had opened negotiations by cell phone from the old man's gravesite the day of the funeral; but that may have been mere spiteful gossip.

Certainly neither of Jakob's daughters would ever have to play on a municipal golf course the way their old man had: with the dough and stock they collected from the sale, they could fly straight to Edinburgh, hire the best caddies in Scotland, and for all we cared, go drop dead on the fourteenth green of St. Andrew's.

That was late September of 1987, and it was as if the last of summer had been suddenly frosted over. Immediately the sole topic of conversation became the future of Prairie Machine.

Arcturis was one of those newly minted names corporate raiders used to slap on acquired companies—in this case, Buffalo Specialty Steel—the way car thieves change the plates on a hot car. Run by a former IBM executive and fueled by seven hundred million in junk bonds raised by a Manhattan investment bank, Arcturis was snapping up troubled but technically savvy manufacturers all over the Midwest.

Their general plan seemed to be to fire about 20 percent of the workforce right off the bat, then to give the acquired company eighteen months to show a major jump in profits. Overwise, everything in sight was shut down, sold off, or moved overseas.

By the standards of the time—or of, say, the Imperial Japanese Army, circa 1934—they were downright generous.

But even five hundred job cuts can be significant when they fall among your friends and family.

And it was the week after the Great Crash of '87 that Arcturis announced that effective immediately, they were laying off five hundred of Prairie Machine's twenty-five hundred workers.

That seemed bad enough; but it was only the beginning.

CHAPTER THIRTY-SIX

A Cold Christmas

*A*s layoffs went in the mid-eighties, five hundred people was small potatoes. Indeed, after years of rust-belt stories, we were, at first, a little startled at how modest the numbers sounded.

That was before they went from numbers to people. With four weeks' notice factored in, the five hundred PMT workers really lost their jobs the day before Thanksgiving—leaving those without a strong taste for irony somewhat less than usually thankful. The Ladies did their bit to help, making considerable anonymous donations to the town's main relief groups, but that was mostly a gesture.

It was still too early for the effects of the layoffs: most people in town—except for the glum five hundred and their families—had perfectly nice, if subdued, Thanksgiving dinners. Still, it bode ill: the theme for most Christmas planning was "things we can do without."

For me, as the weather turned cold, nothing was stronger than the sense of living in two worlds. In Minneapolis, my friends (well, Marcy and *her* friends) were buying everything that wasn't nailed down, mostly as Christmas gifts for themselves. In Larksdale, a certain gloomy shabbiness had set in: not quite Dickensian, but with an aura of last year's tinsel. Prices in shop windows were marked down two weeks before Christmas; people were studying themselves in mirrors and wondering just how far they could tighten their belts.

My parents by that time had found a focus for all their sundry fights in the surrounding economic mess. My father brandished the tough job market to assert his privileges—the more keeping his job seemed difficult and humbling, the more credit he wanted. My mother, whose investments were recovering, resisted the temptation to tell him what he could do with his getting up every morning and going to work—or even to say they could retire anytime they liked. Sometimes, I guess, she showed a superior air that would have irritated anyone; but even her calm angered him.

The holidays brought my brothers home for dinners and open houses, church services and present opening on Christmas morning. The family was both nervous and sad, like a losing team playing out the season. My parents did their best. They even stopped their fighting; but that just made the pressure build up between them. It was a cold, snowless Christmas, and we held our breath until we could open our presents, eat our last supper together, then rush Arthur, Daniel, and William to the airport so they could get the hell out of town.

My best present that frugal year was an on-line service membership from Milt, my law-school pal and favorite correspondent. Instead of long weekly letters, we could now exchange short, snappy notes at our every slight literary urge.

Milt's first urge was to invite me to visit him in New York, where he (though too modest to say it) was burning up the Skadden, Arps M&A department and—unbeknownst to them—preparing to jump to McKinsey for enough money to blow the hinges off the vault of the Swiss Federal Bank.

I left Milt's generous urge unanswered. New York sounded exciting, but I was way ahead of the curve on cyber-romance. I'd already decided that Milt on-line was the perfect man: witty, considerate, and invisible.

At least, that's what I told myself. Perhaps I mostly disliked the prospect of actually seeing a classmate doing so much with the same education I'd gotten.

While Milt, thick glasses, frizzy hair, and all, stood atop the Empire State Building knocking biplanes out of the air with one hand and closing deals with the other, I was trying to aid the most namby-pamby of the Ladies. He was helping GE snag NBC; I was trying to save the Christmas party at the Larksdale Public Library's Children's Room.

Of course, I told myself, the secret was to bloom where I was planted—but if anything is more annoying than trying to live by a saying cross-stitched on a cheesy sampler, I don't know what it is.

It was a dirty job—and I had to do it.

CHAPTER THIRTY-SEVEN

Poor Agnes

*A*nd getting darned little help from the woman behind it. No one in my circle lived smaller than Agnes.

If, in retelling this story, I've ignored the group's second librarian, Gladys's friend and junior colleague at the Larksdale Public Library, it's because she liked it that way. If emotional camouflage exists, Agnes wore it. Her bold stance in urging us to buy during the market collapse aside, she was most eloquent in her endless silence. I liked her: she didn't have a mean bone in her body.

She could have used a couple.

Agnes was almost too much the old stereotype of the librarian—the children's librarian, at that. She'd had cancer at twenty; survived it handily but come out shy and tentative as a small bird. Now, in her thirties, she was diffident, opaque, and able to be content with almost nothing. The news of a sequel to *The Wind in the Willows* was enough to keep her happy for a week.

The one great joy in Agnes's life was the children's reading room of the Larksdale Public Library. It was her classroom and studio, her social club and sanctuary. She was fond of, and loved by, all her coworkers. She could even draw smiles from Wally, the library's sullen, up-country gardener-handyman. Wally, who routinely ignored everyone, annually made Agnes several dozen handcrafted kites, which she lent out to the children to fly on the courthouse lawn across the street on breezy spring days. But her friendships all had that same subtle element of childishness.

In fact, it's hard not to tell Agnes's story as a fairly grim fairy tale, beginning, "Once upon a time . . ." and ending . . . well, you'll see.

The ogre haunting the castle in Agnes's life was named Inigo Stout.

Inigo Stout, you may recall, was the head of the Larksdale Public Library and to do him justice, he was competent at his job. In fifteen years, he had steadily built the library, until it was a genuine civic treasure. He raised money brilliantly, spent it wisely, and never stole a penny.

His success was only slightly marred by his being a small-minded, mean-spirited, rule-bound, woman-hating bully.

He ran a tight ship—modeled as closely as possible, it seemed, on a Roman slave galley. The library's thirty or so employees universally feared and disliked him, although they rarely said so. He was aided, of course, by the natural gentleness of most library workers: few of them, of course, choose librarianship after narrowing it down to that or the Navy SEALs.

And of all the employees, Agnes was the most timid.

So when Inigo Stout called her into his office the first week in December to announce that her pride and joy, the annual Children's Holiday Party, had been canceled, he surely expected instant surrender.

He even went so far as to explain:

"Prairie Machine just called. They're canceling their annual donation—which means we're dropping all noncore activities. That includes your party."

"But—" Agnes exclaimed. This faint protest was forced out of her: the party was her annual labor of love. Yet still it was a mistake.

Inigo Stout shot out of his chair. He stood no more than five-foot-eight and, despite his name, was slight and round-shouldered, but he had a trick of flushing a mottled red when angered, like some weird South American lizard.

"Listen!" he commanded. "This is the time we should all be pulling together, not making trouble for each other. The last thing I need is a whiny complainer. Can I count on you or not?"

Agnes, shaking in a way that made it seem she was nodding in agreement, simply turned and left. She was still shaking when she reached her desk; but after a few minutes there, a small, tight smile appeared on her face.

She'd come up with a plan.

$\mathcal{T}$he plan was to underwrite the party herself—or rather, to ask me to arrange for her to do it anonymously. I told her I thought the Ladies would be glad to do it collectively—but she said she wanted it done on her nickel and absolutely anonymously.

The minute she left, I picked up the phone and called Inigo Stout.

I took my usual line in these matters: I represented a donor who wished to remain anonymous, but who wanted to replace the lost funds for the Children's Holiday Party. If that went well, there was a virtual certainty of funding for future projects.

Then I sat back and waited for his grateful reply. What he said, in a very tense voice, was, "Thank you—but no."

"Excuse me?"

"I said no. The plans—the orders for food, entertainment, and everything else—have been canceled. There's no chance of being ready."

He sounded as if they'd scheduled Madonna to perform privately at a Caesars Palace banquet. My understanding was that entertainment actually was a guy in a reindeer suit handing out small presents. As for food, the Ladies would have buried the place a foot deep in homemade cakes in forty-eight hours. "My clients are prepared," I answered mildly, "to provide all that. Eager to, in fact."

"There's something else," he said, obviously stalling and thinking desperately.

"Yes?"

"It's an insurance issue." He'd thought of it on the fly.

"We'll self-insure." I was bluffing: I had no authority to take on unlimited liability for the Ladies. On the other hand, it was hard to imagine a kiddie party turning into a drunken brawl with gunfire. That was several years ago, of course.

It didn't matter. Inigo Stout had his countermove ready. "Who's 'we'?"

He had me. I couldn't name the Ladies. Game, Inigo Stout; but I still had to play to the end.

"I'd rather not say. But our bank will post a bond in any reasonable amount." Again, I had no authority to offer this—but I knew he'd never take it, so what the hell.

He let me off the hook while trying to be sarcastic:

"The library carries one million dollars in liability—and that's *under* the city's umbrella policy. You'll post a million dollars?"

He had a genius for being annoying. I bit my tongue to keep from blurting, "We'll post *five,* you bastard." When my tongue was more annoyed with my teeth than with Inigo Stout, I let up the pressure and, sounding slightly choked, answered, "This is important to my client. I'd like to make the case to your governing—"

"I'm sorry," he interrupted, sounding anything but, "the issue's closed. Our governing board doesn't meet again until January." He paused, then added gleefully, "Merry Christmas."

He hung up before I could wish the same to him and the horse he rode in on.

That was the end, I thought. We couldn't publicize another location, or take legal action, fast enough to save the party—and

Agnes would just have to live with it. I was sorry to have let her down; but after all, it was still just a kids' party.

The next day Inigo Stout took his revenge for what he saw as a challenge to his authority.

The details probably seem small: he simply stood up at that afternoon's weekly staff meeting and, while staring angrily at Agnes, announced that *someone* had betrayed the library's secrets, broken its bonds of solidarity, and exposed him, Inigo Stout, to shame and humiliation. He added that in his estimation, people of such cowardly instincts had no place in the family of the Larksdale Public Library.

Never mind that the family of the Larksdale Public Library was the most dysfunctional since Henry the VIII's, or that there was a hint of Stalinist show trial in the announcement which ought to have made it laughable. To Agnes, who lived so fearfully, it was a nightmare, and she left in tears.

It was that last, great insult which finally brought Agnes to my office. After telling me the whole story, interrupting herself only occasionally by sniffling, she summarized, "He's a really bad man, and I want him to stop treating me this way. I'm really fed up."

I felt an extraordinary satisfaction—mostly, probably, because I saw the chance to avenge my own insulted feelings. I sat up straight, grabbed pen and pad, and said in my best legal-pit-bull voice, "Now you're talking! Let's sue his pants off. We'll start with maintaining a hostile work envir—"

"No lawsuits," Agnes interrupted, quietly but firmly.

This was a blow. I sank back, dropping the pen, but still slugging.

"Not even a little one?" I asked, as if offering a plate of cookies.

"None."

I must have stared at her while I collected my thoughts. My job was serving my client, not pleasing myself.

"Okay. Here are some options." I ticked them off on my index finger. "One, you can take leave until he realizes he needs you. You've got plenty of money, and—"

Agnes shook her head.

"Okay," I went on, tapping a second finger. "If you want to keep working, you can always get a better job at another—"

"We've got the best children's room in Minnesota," Agnes interrupted.

I shrugged. "Okay. Three, you can quit and just enjoy life. Travel. Buy a yacht and sail Lake Larksdale—or the Mediterranean. See 'plenty of money' above. You—"

Once again, she interrupted by shaking her head. I'd been waiting to be interrupted by applause, but merely asked politely, "No?"

"I don't believe in retirement, as long as a person's able to work."

Highly moral, but unwilling to kick butts. Not exactly a lawyer's dream client. My fingers weren't the only thing getting ticked off. "What about a whole new career? You could go back to school and—"

"I'm a librarian."

"You couldn't *write* children's books, I suppose?"

Amazingly enough, she actually paused to consider this. *Then* she shook her head. "Maybe someday, when I know more. What else?"

I came *that* close to asking, "How much do you have to know to write a kids' story? You want to write about Mojo the Red Dog? He's red—he's a dog—write the damn story!" But then, what did I know about children's books?

Suddenly I understood the utter frustration with which my mother had uttered such remarks as, "Sophia Peters, you can have the red dress or the blue dress, or we're going home right now." I wasn't cut out to handle an eight-year-old client.

I put my elbows down on the desk.

"Agnes, you can quit, you can take legal action, or you can just go out and sit in the car until we're ready to leave."

"Huh?"

"I mean, you have to choose. Fish or cut bait. If the good Lord helps those as helps themselves, you can't expect me to do any better." I leaned farther forward. "So, which do you want?"

"Can you do anything short of suing him?" she asked faintly.

I slapped the desk. "Now we're talking! Fee, fi, foe, fum, let's go out and whack the bum!" Sophia Peters, kiddie lawyer.

As I was picking up pen and pad again, Agnes said quietly, "Sophia, I never know what you're talking about."

I sent Agnes home so I could craft the letter—which basically said that out of the kindness of Agnes's heart, we *weren't* suing Mr. Inigo Stout, as long as he straightened out immediately. If, on the other hand, he continued his evil ways—

I told him we would seek not only administrative relief, but civil remedies in accordance with state and federal employment and sexual discrimination laws, including but not limited to . . . well, you get the idea.

Heidi printed out the letter on my "Law Office of . . ." stationery and arranged to have it hand-delivered by a process server. That was not, strictly speaking, correct procedure; but Agnes wanted to shake him up without really raising a legal stink.

The next morning Agnes made a point of arriving at the library before sunrise. Wally, the kite-flying gardener, had a key to the back door and was happy to let her in. Agnes went straight to her desk. In her own way she was preparing for battle: she made sure she was up-to-date on everything from supply inventories to the health of Mad Max, the library's live pet bunny.

Inigo Stout would find nothing to attack in the way she ran the children's room.

At two minutes after nine—holiday hours—the first children rushed into the room, paid their respects to Max by yanking his ears, and began pulling books from the shelves. Already the bright cold sun was shining through the tall windows; Agnes, who ought to have been in her glory, instead sat rigidly at her desk, while children came up to ask every few minutes if she was all right.

Lunchtime finally arrived, and she took her meal in its brown paper bag from the bottom drawer of her desk and went to find Gladys in the lunchroom.

Gladys wanted to eat on the comfortable padded benches of the reading nook some clever architect had designed into the corridor leading to the executive offices. The prospect of being anywhere near the executive offices made Agnes particularly nervous—but being Agnes, she reluctantly agreed.

Almost as soon as they sat, a vague rumbling came from the office of the head librarian. Agnes, who'd recently seen *The Ten Commandments* with Charlton Heston on TV, tried to ignore the idea that it resembled the cloud of angry red smoke which kept rising out of Mt. Sinai while Moses dithered in the desert.

Thus, while Gladys chatted cheerfully and munched her egg-salad sandwich, Agnes felt the world and all its sandwiches had lost their savor. Her own peanut-butter sandwich stuck—well, like peanut butter, in her mouth. She could scarcely swallow.

She had almost gathered the nerve to ask for Gladys's help when a banging came from inside the head librarian's office, and an instant later Mildred, Inigo Stout's assistant, flew out the door, looked both ways like a messenger in a really bad stage play, and spotting Agnes, hurried toward her.

"He wants to see you *right now*."

Agnes knew he had gotten the letter. She felt as if her whole body had turned suddenly to peanut butter.

*I*nigo Stout's office furniture was strictly civil-service standard issue: pale wood desk and chairs, and a set of dark olive file cabinets. The overhead fluorescent lights seemed to dim the winter sunlight edging around the venetian blinds and paradoxically to cast all into bureaucratic gloom.

But the room's decorations were pure Inigo Stout, from the bronze bald eagle on his desk to the oversized framed black-and-white photos of Douglas MacArthur, George Patton, and other giants of American library administration.

He'd gotten the letter, all right.

He held it up toward her. He was so angry he couldn't speak—until he saw how scared she was, and then he got control of himself. He wanted her shaking, not unconscious. She was going about 5.0 on the Richter scale; she was shaking enough that you could hear the rattling, but not enough to bring the building down.

It was enough to make Inigo Stout smile. Perhaps it wasn't technically a smile—maybe it was more a grimace or a tortured leer—but it certainly involved some sort of movement in the general neighborhood of his mouth.

And then, very slowly, he tore the letter in half, squared the two pieces, and tore them both in half—and repeated the process until he had pinched between his fingers a half-inch-thick stack of tiny pieces of paper.

He threw the pieces straight at her. They flew sharply a foot or two while she shut her eyes tightly; then, as she opened them, they fluttered earthward a few inches from her face.

Inigo Stout had calmed enough to speak a whole sentence. He pointed a finger at Agnes and said thickly, "If you ever try a stunt like this again, you'll regret it as long as you live."

Agnes staggered back a step. She was trembling worse than ever and felt somewhat numb.

But then she did something unexpected. She took a step forward. She looked Inigo Stout directly in the chin and said, almost audibly—

"Oh, no, I won't."

It may not rank with, "Fifty-four forty, or fight"; but from Agnes, it was honorable—even heroic. Had she said it loudly enough for Inigo Stout to hear it, it would have rated as magnificent.

"What was that?" Stout's tone was nasty automatically, not because he had any hint of an idea she'd stood up to him.

"Nothing, sir." The opportunity had passed.

Stout was content with that. He'd reached cruising altitude for anger. Without getting any nastier, he said thickly, "All right. Get out."

Agnes got.

We had one more meeting about the great Christmas-party fiasco. It lasted about twenty seconds.

Agnes, clearly still upset, came into my office and said, without sitting down, "I'm going to do something about Inigo Stout."

Slow learner that I am, I brightened. "It's not exactly the Christmas spirit, but if I work late I think I can file the papers this week."

"I'm not suing him. I'm going to do something, but not that."

"*What,* then?" I'd gone in an instant from enthusiasm to apathy.

"I have to think about it. I'll let you know." She turned and started away. At the door she stopped and looked back. "Sophia? I know I annoy you. But thank you for trying."

I grunted something.

She went through the door, and I assumed, with mixed annoyance and relief, that was the last I'd ever hear of the matter.

Which was fine with me. I felt the Great Library War as yet another rebuke from an annoyed universe. I'd taken the cowardly way out, a hometown job, while all my classmates had gone on to adventure and risk. And this was my reward:

Not only was I spending my time in legal kindergarten, fighting petty tyrants over petty issues; I was losing. It was the graduate course at the School of Humility.

And things were about to get worse.

CHAPTER THIRTY-EIGHT

Meeting the General

*T*he main problem with forgiveness is that, most often, the people you have to forgive are real jerks.

Except for that, I'm sure, forgiveness would be far more popular. *No problem, Mother Teresa. Don't give it a thought. Happens to the best of us—as you'd well know.*

As things stand, most of us find forgiveness hard to muster.

Even Agnes needed four days' hard thinking, and harder feelings—of alternately blaming Inigo Stout for being a villain and herself for being a coward—before she sat down and wrote her most unusual letter:

Dear Mr. Stout:

I seem, by extraordinary (and unearned) good fortune, to have come into enough money to pursue a dream of mine.

I want to sponsor a technology center where children will be able to learn about—to play with—computers as freely as they are currently allowed to play with books.

I have a location in mind and a friend to advise me on the computers, but an experienced administrator, who

*could volunteer to oversee matters of a business nature,
would be a great help.*

*I know you and I have had our differences, but I believe
we could make an ideal team for this. I don't know anyone
who could do a better job than you.*

*Whatever you decide, thank you for having employed
me as a librarian these past nine years.*

Yours very sincerely,
Agnes Brinkley

She sent that in an envelope marked *Personal and Confidential*
and mailed it in the same envelope containing her resignation.
Then she waited over the Christmas holiday, plus an extra day to
make sure, and went down to the library to clean out her desk.

She arrived, as usual, so early the winter sky was still dark
outside. For nine years' occupancy, her niche didn't really contain
much that was personal—an emergency sweater, a couple of photos, and a few posters collected at book fairs. She was nearly done
when, from behind her, someone asked softly, "Agnes?"

She didn't recognize the voice, so she was calm when she turned
and saw Inigo Stout standing beside her. She stayed calm when he
asked, "Will you come with me, please?" His voice and his manner
were altered. She didn't understand it, but she sensed she needn't
fear it.

They walked in silence to his office, which looked as sinister as
ever. A cynic would have feared Inigo Stout was going to conk
Agnes over the head with a copy of *Lord of the Rings*. Instead . . .

When they were seated there, he cleared his throat. He cleared
it several times. Then he said, "I've torn up a number of your
letters. I'd like to tear up one more. Or would you rather do it?"

He handed her a sheet of stationery—and because both her
letters had been about the same length, she felt a moment's un-

certainty about which he had handed her. In that moment, oddly, she wasn't alarmed or even concerned. But she *was* curious.

He'd given her back her resignation.

Agnes wasn't much of a hand at tearing, but she ripped it fairly neatly in half, then dropped it in the nearby trash.

"Thank you," Inigo Stout said. It seemed a very inclusive "thank you."

"You're welcome."

"Were you serious about wanting my help?"

"Yes."

"I think I'd enjoy doing that. When do we start?"

"I was thinking of the week after Christmas."

"That's fine." He stood up and offered his hand. Agnes shook it willingly; but when she let it go, he seemed to have more sentiment to express.

"I'm sorry," he said, "about a lot of things. In fact, will you tell your lawyer—no, never mind. I'll tell her myself."

Agnes nodded.

Inigo wasn't done. He looked around the room frantically for some topic of sociable conversation. Finally his eyes lit on one of the large framed photos. He stepped to it, touched it familiarly, and smiled at Agnes.

"General Patton," he said.

CHAPTER THIRTY-NINE

Dolly and Her Husband

Good old Inigo Stout called me that afternoon. He was so apologetic—in fact, so gracious—that we wound up agreeing that as Agnes's project advanced, he would call me for free legal advice. I hung up ready to kick myself for being such a marshmallow—but a minute later I grudgingly decided I was pleased. I'm what you might call a conditional cynic, the sort who knows that overall you have more fun at Disneyland if you pretend Mickey Mouse is real.

But just as fighting was going out of style in Libraryland, matters heated up back in the real world.

Some of the fighting was quite mild. Skye, who had sped through her computer-science course work, had impressed us by starting work that autumn on her MBA degree. Martha, of course, could hardly contain her enthusiasm, and the other Ladies were decidedly pleased; but Lynne, Skye's girlfriend, shocked Skye with angry accusations that by pursuing business, she was "selling her soul for lousy money." She added a great many other charges along the same lines—all adding up to an ultimatum: Skye could choose Lynne or business.

The Ladies, as usual, proved themselves troopers. By this time they were as well organized as the emotional equivalent of a volunteer fire department. All they needed was a cookie tray with a siren on it. When, this time not crying but still extremely upset, Skye told them about Lynne's ultimatum, they were instant and uncompromising in their support.

"If she's really . . . if she really . . . Oh, hell, if she really loves you she should stand by you. Period, end of story," offered Deb, fumbling over Skye's romantic status, but firm on the rest.

"It they can't take you as you are, say good-bye," Dolly added in categorical summation for them all—after which, Skye sat thinking a few seconds, sighed, and then nodded.

A few days later Skye told Lynne she'd made her choice, and a few days after that her undischarged Soviet paratrooper wardrobe got traded in for the tweeds and silk blouses of an aspiring MBA.

But her hair stayed soft pink. Skye was changing at her own pace, and that was fine with the Ladies.

It would not be long before I'd understand just how bizarre Dolly's last remark was. But that afternoon I was taken as usual with the Ladies. They weren't like some people who endorse "tough love" as a handy slogan just because they love to be tough. Their love was reserved for better things.

*T*hen again, sometimes you just have to be tough.

Arcturis dropped its second shoe on the fourth of January. *Due to rapidly worsening economic conditions,* the press release ran, they were laying off another three hundred workers, effective immediately.

This was both a small disaster and a warning sign of a big one. At least that was how it seemed to me, though when I tried talking about it with my dad (who was, after all, a Prairie Machine executive), all he did was grunt and say, "We'll survive." I didn't exactly believe him; but he settled back in his chair and picked up his paper again, so the discussion ended like most of ours did, with awkward silence.

A couple of days later Dolly appeared in my office.

Dolly, at forty-five, had grown stout—but when in her normal high spirits, she still had a measure of florid blond beauty. As I've said elsewhere, I had known her from church since I was a little girl—and singing in the choir, she had looked to me like some sort of Valkyrie from my *Junior Book of Norse and German Legends*.

But that day her big, blond form seemed both shrunken and paler. She was somehow a little tilted off the even, like a partly deflated soufflé. When she was seated, she mumbled, "I'm going to be needing some money. You think I could get some here?"

She had her hands folded in her lap and her head down, and her voice was so soft I could hardly hear her. Probably still reveling in the fairy-tale atmosphere of Agnes and her library adventure, I waved my arms and demanded, "Hey! What're you doing?"

She looked up and tried to smile.

"Now, when you come in here," I continued, "I want you to start acting like an owner. Hammer on the desk, or—" I stuck two fingers in my mouth, and blew hard. Ever since I was six, I'd had a wolf whistle that would shatter glass. The racket was considerable—Heidi ran in to see why the teakettle had exploded. And Dolly was smiling—albeit a bit wanly.

"Okay," I continued, after Heidi had glared at me reproachfully and left, "how much do you need?"

I had purposely avoided the question of why she needed it; but she answered, "Buzz got fired yesterday. So we'll need as much as his paycheck, until he catches on elsewhere." She paused. "Sixteen hundred a month."

I exhaled and sat back in the chair:

"No problem. The bylaws say you can borrow up to twenty-five thousand from our cash reserves, at pri—at eight percent interest—without reducing your partnership share." I tried to smile encouragingly. "But the rule is, you have to pound on the desk and demand it."

She looked down and shook her head.

"Or not," I added, suddenly ashamed of myself, and switched on my computer to print out a loan form. Then I looked up and added, "This stupid economy is hitting everyone."

$\mathcal{D}$olly had altered my mood more than I had altered hers. I left the office that afternoon solemn and determined to pay attention to fundamental things.

I walked the five blocks of Main Street in bluish late-afternoon light and counted six "Going Out of Business" signs, most plastered over store windows still filled with Christmas displays. Certainly it was a trick of perception, but suddenly the cars seemed rustier, the streets dirtier, than ever before. Snow had finally fallen the previous three days; but not much of it, and already it had become gray-black slush.

Three moving vans, heading for the freeway, passed me just on that short stroll.

The fairy-tale part of the winter had decidedly ended.

CHAPTER FORTY

Dolly's Problem

Dolly had told me only the most sanitized version of her problem. She would never have chosen me to confide in; but she trusted Mary, and through Mary, much later, we were all informed.

Dolly's husband, Buzz, was a big man with a small heart and a worsening drinking problem. That much we all knew, even though he had been a part of our circle only on those rare occasions he had shown up at social functions looking hungover and unshaven—or even, as on the Fourth of July, actually drunk.

What we hadn't known was that Buzz couldn't endure Dolly's success.

Why, exactly, Dolly had told Buzz about the Club, I don't know, although, of course, the obvious guess is that she meant to appease his anger.

Her strategy worked at first. At first he had wanted to spend the money—and she indulged him as far as she could. All through the previous year, she had been turning over to him her monthly stipend checks from the Club, and the quarterly bonuses, and then had signed for as much debt as possible.

Even while accepting these gifts as his due, Buzz had resented them bitterly. They all—even the chocolate-brown Cadillac Seville she leased him for his Christmas present—had the bizarre effect of simultaneously placating and enraging him.

And so, the loss of his job—which might have happened without Arcturis, so bad had his drinking become—only exacerbated problems long building.

The Christmas holidays, and his flood of gifts, had bought her a short cease-fire. Then the loss of his job turned even that sour. Buzz waited his chance (not long) to pick the big fight—which, with remarkable perversity, he cast in pseudoreligious terms. He insisted Dolly stay home from her job as a store buyer so that he might have company in his unemployment. When she refused on the simple grounds that they needed the money, he went on the attack.

"I thought you were a God-fearing woman!"

"I am, honey!"

"Then how in God's name can you run off making money instead of staying home keeping under my authority!"

"Maybe God wants me to be a success?" She said it almost—but not quite enough—as a question.

And he turned furious: "Are you saying God doesn't want *me* to be one?"

"No, honey! No . . . I . . ."

But it was too late; that was as far as she got before he drew back his fist and hit her. He'd meant it as a slap, but it landed much harder, and she staggered backward, putting her hand up to cover her bleeding mouth.

At once he was apologetic, hovering over her, huge, menacing, trying to be gentle.

She was afraid to do what she most wanted to do, which was to pull away. Staying close to him, but turning slightly aside, she said, "It's okay, honey. But I think I'd better get some ice. Okay? Because you broke one of my teeth, I think." As she was leaving the room, with her bloody hand still over her mouth, she added, "Want me to get you anything while I'm there?"

Dolly's misery and Buzz's overdue rush of shame at what he'd done bought her a couple of days' peace after that. But within days Buzz, steadily more violent, stopped apologizing and took to blaming her for making him lose his temper.

CHAPTER FORTY-ONE

The Meeting

Buzz had hit her a couple of times before—and shoved her as well—and bullied her more times than she could count. But that second week in January, when he broke her tooth, the cut in her mouth got badly infected, and she couldn't hide the swelling that puffed out one side of her face. After a week of antibiotics, she was back near enough to normal to appear at the Ladies' Saturday meeting, but not well enough to avoid the obvious questions.

Still, she couldn't bring herself to answer, except with the not-quite-a-lie that she'd been to the dentist with an infection, and yes, it hurt quite a lot.

But since none of the Ladies was stupid, they had strong suspicions that would have been certainties, except for their faith in Dolly's honesty.

And just a week later the charade ended.

It was full winter, and the snows had finally come. We all wore gloves or mittens, of course, but we took them off when we arrived. All except Dolly, who wore a long-sleeved, high-necked dress and moved—I can't say it any better—like a hospital patient.

It was the most completely mystifying meeting. Not one of us was dim enough to lack suspicions—even Veronica, in the midst

of her report, kept glancing at Dolly with a kind of sick concern—
yet we went on with business as usual.

Except that, at the end of the session, while the other Ladies
departed unusually early, and Martha and Skye began removing
the untouched snacks, Mary caught my eye and led me to intercept
Dolly. Even as a member, I never knew how the Ladies decided
some things, but clearly there had been a wordless vote, and Mary
was elected.

Mary, quiet and undemonstrative as always, took Dolly aside,
to that dim nook of Martha's living room which always seemed
preferred for important conversations. There, while Dolly looked
about for an escape, Mary asked her quietly, "Will you do something for me?"

"What?"

"Will you take off your gloves?"

"No." Dolly said it defiantly, but her eyes were almost pleading.
It crossed my mind that she was defying the wrong person, but I
kept my mouth shut. Mary waited for her to say more, then
changed tactics.

"Look, honey. I want you to come home with me."

"I can't." Dolly spoke so flatly, and so categorically, that Mary
was stymied. There was nothing for her to argue with—it was like
Dolly wasn't even there. Mary opened and closed her mouth; finally, trying again, she insisted, "Then I want you to call me every
two hours until bedtime. Just so I'll know you're okay."

Dolly looked at her hopelessly—at least, it looked hopeless to
me—and shrugged weakly.

"You will?" Mary asked.

Dolly nodded vaguely. "I'll keep in touch."

It was a feeble plan, all in all; but the Ladies clung to the idea
that what happened between husband and wife was, if not strictly
sacred, at least untouchable by outsiders.

Mary said, "Okay," and, putting a hand lightly on Dolly's back,
walked her to the door. There Mary and I watched, while Dolly
left, with a fine, jaunty stride suitable for a prisoner on death row.

CHAPTER FORTY-TWO

The Bad News Gets Worse

But by ten o'clock that evening, having heard nothing, Mary decided to act. She called Dolly's number and got no answer; she called the rest of us and found out we hadn't heard from Dolly, either. Then, automatically, not even realizing how agitated she was, she went to the closet and pulled on her coat.

Mike, it turned out, had been watching her closely. Now he came up behind her so silently that when she turned and saw him, she jumped.

It's one of the small glories of a good marriage that a great many things can be said briefly.

"I'm worried about Dolly. Buzz is kind of out of control."

"He's violent?"

Mary nodded.

"And you're going over there?"

She nodded again. Mike reached past her into the closet and took down his jacket.

"I'd feel better if I came along."

"All right."

He was finishing pulling on the jacket by tugging at the zipper edges.

"I need just a minute," he said. "Meet me at the car?"

She nodded. It seemed time to say more, but she wasn't sure what. So she brushed his arm under pretext of straightening the jacket and started for the front door.

With the door open, she looked back and saw Mike, barely visible at the far end of the hall, twisting his neck from side to side, even as he leaned forward in the doorway to stretch his legs as runners do. It seemed, in quick order, first comical, then frightening, and at last reassuring that he was treating this as some sort of athletic event.

She almost walked back to him. Then she thought the better of it and went to wait at the car.

*T*he night was frozen; the few Christmas lights still strung seemed bright as lasers, and no warmer. They drove without talking.

Mike had a genius for silence, Mary decided; and while she often appreciated it, she understood just then why people often said geniuses were hard to live with.

She wished he would drive faster; then she glanced at the speedometer and was startled at how fast they were going.

She felt no better at that.

CHAPTER FORTY-THREE

At Dolly's

Dolly's house looked as battered as the others on the street, but an absence of Christmas lights, and the new Cadillac parked halfway out of the garage, made it easy to spot. Light leaked through small tears in the drawn curtains.

The snow on the walkway was newly fallen, the sort you step through silently, until that faint squeak as your foot turns on the cement.

Mary nodded to Mike, opened the car door as quietly as she could, and started up the path while the still, frozen air stung her face. She hesitated, listening, on the doorstep. Then she knocked softly, and was startled by the rough noise of the door being thrown open.

Buzz was tall and broad, thick-armed and with a thicker gut swelling well out over his belt. For a dark moment he didn't speak. His eyes were glassy, and he breathed heavily, unconsciously, like a diesel truck idling. The smell of whiskey blew off him in waves. If Dolly in happier days had seemed like a Valkyrie, he was a Viking—but from the motorcycle gang, not the ancient warriors.

"What do you want?" He didn't seem to recognize her.

"I'd like to see Dolly."

"She's busy." The voice was fat with menace.

Still, Mary felt unaccountably fearless. She tried to step past him; when he wouldn't move, she said, as if to a child, "You're hurting her. You have to stop."

"Get the hell out of here."

"No! She's coming home with me."

There was a three-second silence.

Then Dolly's voice came, very softly. "Mary?" *That* was the child's voice.

Buzz turned to look—and that was enough: Mary squeezed past him and saw Dolly cowering in the kitchen doorway. She didn't look ample and powerful anymore; she looked cringing and pathetic.

And the room, with water-stained walls and a broken lamp, said much. It held two expensive things: a plump new leather recliner and a big-screen TV. The recliner was placed with fierce selfishness for watching the big TV alone.

Mary didn't trust herself to speak, so she hurried to Dolly and eased her, quickly but gently, into the kitchen. She did it by pressing a hand softly on Dolly's back. Dolly's arms were covered with red welts and darker patches of black and blue.

In the kitchen, with only the light spilled from the living room, they whispered.

"You got to get out of here, honey. It's not safe."

"Yeah. But I love him."

"Honey, I love dogs. I wouldn't let one bite my leg off."

Maybe they would have argued, but Buzz began a lumbering run from the front room toward the back of the house. The kitchen floor vibrated from it. Dolly, knowing something, turned frantic—and started pulling Mary back into the abandoned front room. "Come on," she whispered urgently.

Buzz had left the front door open; as they reentered the front room, freezing air rushed over them. Dolly fumbled an instant for her coat on a wall peg. She took too long; Buzz, with that crashing, unstable stride, was returning.

Dolly dropped the coat and ran. They were out the door, but at the bottom of the steps he caught them and, grabbing Mary's shoulder from behind, nearly pulled her over when he spun her around.

He stepped closer to her, leaned down till his face was close to hers, and the air stank of alcohol.

"Listen, you bitch. You try to come between my wife and me, and I'll kill you."

His hand was still heavy on her shoulder, pushing hard enough to keep her off balance. Now Mary was scared—suddenly and completely, as if she'd stepped off a cliff in a nightmare. Equally, she felt stupid. Why had she not seen this coming?

Then she heard the Pontiac door open, with the old, rusty squeak. A moment's utter silence—Buzz staring toward the car, but Mary afraid to turn and look. Then footsteps crunched faintly through the snow, growing louder until they stopped just behind her, and she heard Mike saying:

"Everything okay?"

Buzz turned on him angrily. "Oh, shit. Now you're getting involved, too?"

Mary was suddenly angry now that both of them were in danger. Angry with Mike—with Buzz—with everyone.

But Mike, who had cooled off many an upset warrior, kept his look placid and his tone even, and answered, "Just trying to get everybody settled down and safely home."

"Yeah, well, why don't you go fuck yourself?"

It was a half-slurred growl. Buzz was reaching for something tucked into his belt, far over by his hip, and even before Dolly screamed, Mary knew what Buzz had run to get at the back of the house.

Mary froze; she couldn't even yell as the gun came out. Mike lunged toward Buzz. It seemed just the wrong thing for Mike to do.

Yet even as the gun appeared, Mike was pushing it down and

away from him, and taking a pirouetting half-step to Mike's side, blocking Mary's view.

The gun roared.

She had no idea a gun threw flames at night—but there they were, bright orange for an instant, above the snow's bluish white. The gun's roar seemed minor compared with that.

The flame tongue ought to have been horrible, but the fact that it extended all the way to the snow told her Mike wasn't shot—and at that, Mary relaxed. Her pulse still raced, but like that of an athlete running on after the finish line. Whatever had held her paralyzed released her.

Yet before Mary could move, Mike brought his knee up hard on Buzz's wrist. Bone cracked, and the gun dropped. Mike swiveled again and slammed his fist deep into Buzz's stomach. It sounded unlike a movie punch—she barely heard it as a muffled slap—but she saw pain and surprise flash across Buzz's face.

Buzz's head jerked forward with the pain; as it did, Mike caught him by the throat and, stepping past him, shoved and tripped him. As they fell, Mike somehow turned the bigger man, and in an instant Buzz, his arm pinned behind him, was facedown in the snow. He was groaning as if about to be sick, and struggling weakly. Mary watched in unbelieving, repelled fascination.

Dolly whimpered and started toward him—and at last Mary moved. She threw her arms around Dolly. Dolly, much bigger, tried to shrug her off, but, slipping on the snow, went down to her knees. Mary went with her and held on, and that was the end of the struggle: Dolly, looking momentarily infinitely sad, shrugged, exhaled, and was still. Mary, who had better balance, helped her to her feet.

Mike's face was pale in the moonlight. He made a swift overhand gesture, like throwing a ball, but ending pointing at the front door. Mary somehow knew—from old war movies or some army TV ad—it was an infantry officer's gesture. She felt at the same instant that at last she understood about Vietnam—and that he was an utter stranger to her. Confusion made her almost cry.

But Dolly still wavered, so Mary gripped her arm and told her very firmly, "Come on, honey. Let's get your bag. You're staying with us tonight."

As they started for the house, Buzz cursed incoherently, and Mike was saying, in his slow, pleasant way, "Brother Suckling, I'm concerned about you."

Mary wanted to stay with Mike, but she knew her duty. She took Dolly's arm and began tugging her toward the house.

But at the doorstep, Dolly, in a kind of daze, stopped and said, echoing the story Mike and Mary had let circulate long ago, "I thought Mike was a clerk in the army."

In the midst of all this, it suddenly annoyed Mary deeply to have her own privacy invaded. Reconciled to the idea that humiliation should be general, she shook her head and whispered, "No, honey. He was a jungle fighter, a captain in the Green Berets— but we don't talk about it. Now hurry, *please*."

Stepping into Dolly's bedroom was the last bad part. Not the clutter, the beaten furniture, or the closet stuffed with Buzz's clothes; what upset Mary was the absence of any sign that her friend—a good woman, tall, solid, and blond, of means and substance—even existed. Here she seemed less than a ghost.

But Dolly, quite real, needed under a minute to throw a few things into a giveaway Reebok bag; then they were back out the door. Mike still held Buzz on the ground, his arm bent sharply back. Mike had fished the gun out of the snow. As they approached, he did something to it, and the cylinder swiveled out. He tipped it, and the cartridges spilled onto the snow; then he flung it across the yard.

By then, sirens wailed loud and close. Across the street, neighbors were coming out of their houses or standing on their snowy front yards, with vapor clouds puffing from their nostrils, and watching curiously.

.   .   .

$\mathcal{T}$he police—three men and a woman—treated Mike like a comrade-in-arms. Mary was annoyed at that, then proud of him when he told Dolly he was pressing charges, whether she did or not. Dolly hesitated while the woman cop stared at her. But finally she nodded—and in that instant seemed to grow younger.

Buzz, subdued, in pain, and still drunk, was loaded into the squad car; but they said Mike and Mary could drive Dolly to the police station to do the paperwork.

As the three of them walked back to the old Pontiac, Mary again had the frightening sense that her soldier-husband was a stranger to her.

But it was all right. As he helped Dolly into the car, Mary heard him say, "It's nice you're coming to visit us. Tomorrow's Saturday. I hope you like pancakes."

CHAPTER FORTY-FOUR

Tough Times Everywhere

With Buzz, forgiveness was never an issue. He made some noises about being sorry, but could scarcely finish a sentence before he began blaming Dolly for his failings. She stepped aside and let the legal system do its pathetic best.

Buzz's public defender proved a clever young fellow. Buzz became the unlucky victim of the economic downturn. Beating his wife and trying to shoot a neighbor were bargained down to a guilty plea on discharging a firearm within the township limits. I figured we were lucky Mike wasn't charged with disrupting a sporting event.

Buzz served ninety days, then moved to Tulsa, where he had a brother.

Dolly, bruises healed, still seemed a lost soul. But the Ladies, by this time, were old hands at intervention. They sat her down and gave her a series of lectures on self-esteem, of which Deborah's was the most blunt: "What are you, chopped liver? I know chopped liver, and you're not it. Remember when you found Earth&Nature—our first big moneymaker? Of course, that was before you decided you were chopped liver. Treat yourself better. Buy a big house or go to Europe. Don't just sit there. You're an embarrassment." Only Deborah could make that sound compassionate.

Dolly compromised by renting a cabin up north and taking a trip to Chicago, which we all felt was a fair start.

Some of the Ladies' domestic problems I did not have to hear about secondhand. Some I got to see.

My mother and my father had stayed together, I imagine, from habit, from fading-but-still-real affection, and for the children. Each of those reasons had weakened steadily over the years.

My father had always been a successful, honorable, and inaccessible giant of a man: his friends call him "Mack" both because it's short for MacKenzie and, I suspect, because he reminds them of a Mack truck. He went to the U on a football scholarship (All-Conference tackle his senior year, and still got his degree in electrical engineering); went to work for Prairie Machine straight out of college; picked up an MBA by going to school nights; and rose about as far as anyone whose last name was not Halvorsen possibly could at Prairie Machine.

By 1990 my brothers were all long out of the house—and though I was there more often than I liked (my thrilling social life, again), it was fair to say my parents were empty-nesters.

Of my brothers, the nearest, Arthur, was a junior banker in Chicago—once a month he'd call home, and Dad would always end the call, "You keep kickin' butts, son!" Daniel was in San Francisco, where he kept most of his life a secret from us; and William, the nice one, was a schoolteacher in Dallas and happily married. He didn't keep in touch with me, but it wasn't personal—he wanted as little to do with the family as possible. All three tried to make the pilgrimage home to Minnesota for Christmas at least every other year.

That still left my dad an awfully lonely man. All his energy and hopes had been concentrated on the boys. He had been fiercely rough on them—once, when Daniel was fourteen and William was twelve, he drove them nearly to the Canadian border, ostensibly to go fishing, and then kicked them out and told them to make their own way home. It was his idea of teaching them self-reliance. They made it and got new bikes for their efforts—but I doubt they ever turned their backs on him again.

Dad never treated me that way. In fact, he rarely had much of anything to do with me—mostly, I think, because he felt girls should be treated gently, and gentle was not in his repertoire. He was generous and tried to be genial, but that was about it.

He did try (as I reached thirty) to become my friend; but it just didn't seem right to him to punch me on the arm, on some crisp autumn day, and ask, "What say we drive up near the border and shoot some ducks?"

That was much of a pity, since I might have liked him to try it.

The curious thing was that, over the years, my mother's investments had made her rich, at the same time my father's devotion to Prairie Machine had made him almost unemployable anywhere else: she had won by breaking the rules and he had lost by following them. Her opportunities were growing daily, even as his were shrinking. That meant their staying together required a different kind of sacrifice from each of them: he had to abandon his ideal of self-reliance, and she had to hide all her opportunities for independence. They made a good game of it for a long while; but day by day, especially as the news about Prairie Machine got worse and worse, the game became harder to play.

So we blundered on into summer—which, with life's usual perversity, proved one of the prettiest any of us remembered.

CHAPTER FORTY-FIVE

Go East, Young Sophia

By the summer of 1991, the stress was telling on all of Larksdale.

Rumors of PMT's closing were sounding daily less like rumors. At the Arcturis annual meeting, the directors announced they were "reviewing with an eye to reducing" all noncore operations. PMT was about as noncore as an operation got.

Late in June, the *Larksdale Herald* reported as virtually certain that Arcturis would be closing at least PMT's research operation, the "Hog Farm" where Mike worked, before year's end. Mary said if that happened, she and Mike would leave immediately for California's Silicon Valley, where jobs for people like Mike were going begging. Certainly they would have been begging for Mike. In his usual quiet way, a couple of years earlier he had begun to enjoy Mary's new prosperity by taking graduate computer-science courses part-time at the U, and so now had up-to-date, red-hot academic credentials to go with his business experience.

Even among those of us who were doing well, something had changed. The eighties, America's own personal Mauve Decade, were over in spirit as in fact.

My first hint of that came when Marcy, my hard-charging, party-crazed best friend, began talking up Eastern philosophy. One

June night, instead of dragging me to some singles bar, she met me at a vegetarian restaurant in St. Paul and began praising a lecture series on the religions of India.

I didn't pay much attention. Marcy's an intellectual omnivore: she wants to know everything. She might just as well have chosen to talk about Balkan politics or Chinese archaeology. It's one of many reasons I like her.

To be polite, I asked, "What was your favorite part?"

"The best stuff was on Buddhist ethics. Especially nonopposition to aggression. It's brilliant—way better than the fighting in Western law."

"So you could practice Buddhist, nonoppositional law? Chain yourself to the witness stand instead of making a summation? Or—better!—stand up in court and yell things like, 'Objection, Your Honor! Lacks harmony with the universe!' And she bangs the gavel and yells back, 'Sus-tained!' and tells opposing counsel to go meditate?"

"Why are you making fun of me?"

"I'm just startled to see you interested in religion again."

"It's not religion exactly. More metaphysics."

"Can you explain the difference?"

She thought, then admitted, "Well, no."

"Then I'll pass. I've already got a religion. I'm a Methodist, remember? I practice Meth-a-physics."

"Very funny, Sophia."

"Best I can do on short notice." Truth was, I was anxious about so many things by that point, that adding doubts about a religion I scarcely still practiced—and which seemed my last tie with my family—was more than I wanted to face.

But Marcy, as always, was pure energy.

"Listen," she said, leaning toward me, "I designed my own Eastern culture immersion this weekend. Join me!"

With "Danger—Enthusiasm!" warning bells ringing in my ears, I shook my head.

"It'll be really great, Sophia. *Come on!*"

Suddenly I saw something different in Marcy. Always before, her invitations had been either pure fun or else her doing me a favor. Now—I didn't know why—her eyes said it was my turn to help her.

"Sure. Sounds like fun."

"I'll pick you up Saturday morning at six-thirty."

"Oh," I said, sighing internally, "that's perfect."

*M*arcy—who never did things by half measures—had planned a full day of enough peacefulness to kill a Marine.

We started at six forty-five, with three laps around Lake Larksdale. A two-hour karate class followed, even though Marcy said she was thinking of quitting it as too violent and confrontational, and I hadn't been to a class for months. Fifteen exhausting minutes into the warm-ups, I remembered why I'd dropped it.

After that, we rested—sucking dry two bottles of imported water each, while the temperatures started up toward the mid-nineties—then took the two-hour aikido class. Marcy was right about aikido—which I think is Japanese for Flowing Water, or Call a Doctor, or something. It's the world's most philosophical way to beat someone senseless.

When it was over, Marcy drove us to a tiny vegetarian restaurant atop a grassy slope leading down to Lake Carlyle. After she'd pulled onto the dirt parking lot, I needed a moment to rally my energy and stumble from the car. Overall, though, I felt oddly happy, grateful to Marcy for her initiative, and in gentle harmony with nature.

Then a mosquito bit me on the nose.

Despite that, the setting was lovely, and a certain drowsy peacefulness hung over the hot day. We found a window table, with the lake a pale blue glow stretching softly into the distance. The restaurant was about half-filled with slightly puzzled-looking

Minnesotans. The service was slow, in keeping with the day's lazy heat; when the food arrived, it was prettily arrayed, like a Japanese watercolor, but not exactly plentiful.

As we were finishing, Marcy asked, "How was your eggplant?"

"Tasty. But if I don't get some more calories, I'm going to bite one of the customers."

"Sophia!"

"I'm a human mosquito. That baby over there in the corner looks plump."

"You really need to get centered, Sophia."

"I'll get centered. Give me a *Wall Street Journal* and a double Starbucks mocha latte, and I'll be the center of the universe. In fact, I think I'll launch a mission to deliver the *Journal* and mocha grandes to all the ashrams of India. In six months they'll be exporting—"

"Time for yoga," Marcy interrupted, serenely, putting money down atop the check. She stood, and started for the door.

I wobbled to my feet and followed. On the way out, I grinned at the baby. She grinned back.

*M*arcy had discovered an entire underground world of countercultural, Eastern-style activities. And, being Marcy, she went after tranquillity as if it were Pork Chop Hill.

Our next stop, the Asawani Golden Rainbow Yoga Center, was a storefront on a very peaceful, very pricey street in one of St. Paul's best neighborhoods: on either side of the yoga center were a high-end antique shop and a larger store which, as nearly as I could tell, sold arrangements of candles and citrus fruits starting at about $300.

I went through the door first—and jumped back as a blast of baking air hit me.

"Oh, my God! The place is on fire. Call the—"

Marcy shoved me back through. "Don't be ridiculous. They keep it at one hundred fifteen degrees."

We were in a small anteroom, dimly lit with reddish-orange bulbs. Indian music played soothingly nearby. I'd been sweating since we left the Bimmer; now, instantly, the sweat evaporated from my forehead. An early sign of heatstroke, according to my Girl Scout training.

"We're training for the Afrika Korps?"

"Silly Sophia! It helps your muscles relax."

"If mine relax any more, you're going to have to roll me to the car."

*B*ut it seemed my muscles could relax. In fact, I was suddenly the Jim Thorpe of relaxing, a triple threat: offensive, defensive, and unconscious relaxing. Twenty minutes of the spice-scented heat, and I'd mastered them all.

And then we started the class.

It turns out that yoga is remarkably like being stretched out on a medieval rack, only they do it without the rack and make you stretch yourself. It's also a lot like being a demented mime trying to imitate various industrial products and machines: Look, I'm a pretzel; no, wait—I'm a fiberglass hunting bow. An accordion. A dead lawyer.

I shook off the pain and made it back to the car under my own power. By this time, actually, it was all rather pleasant. In fact, I was seeing a bright, white light at the end of a . . .

As we drove away, Marcy looked as fresh as ever—indeed, positively radiant. She was turning into an earth mother; I was turning into, well, earth. I was curling into a fetal position on the seat of the car when she asked, "Now what do you say, Sophia?"

"Huh?"

"Was that great, or what?"

"Huh?"

"Are you okay?"

"Huh?"

She shook my shoulder. "Sophia! Very funny."

"Did you know there are tiny holes punched in the upholstery? I think they're vents." It was easy to notice such things. I was flopped over in the seat, with my right eye about an eighth of an inch from the elegant dark green leather.

"*W*ake up, Sophia. We're at meditation class."

"No need. I reached nirvana half an hour ago. It's a lot like sleeping." I closed my eyes again to check my research.

Marcy shook my shoulder. "Soph-i-a! *Meditation!*"

I looked at her desperately. "I'll talk, you bastards. All our submarines—"

"Oh, Sophia. You *really* need enlightenment."

That was a concept I really couldn't attack, so I just nodded, and stumbled after her out of the car.

*A*t four in the afternoon—of a very drowsy, hot summer's day, with the insects seeming to buzz unusually loudly—we reached the meditation class, at the Buddhist center near the university. I was feeling like overcooked spaghetti.

The room had an elegant simplicity to it which immediately garnered respect; but what took most of my attention was the instructor.

He was about six-foot-three, with light blond hair and star-tlingly blue eyes. I figured his ancestors had come from somewhere around the ancient Indian city of Copenhagen, and I began to have some suspicions about the depth of Marcy's philosophical convictions. Ideas weren't the only thing she was omnivorous about.

But his speech ended that. Of all the vastness of Buddhism, this was one small bit; but being about refusing anger, it had remarkable pertinence for every lawyer in the audience. Lawyers generate anger like cars generate used tires.

And when I looked closer at Marcy as the lecture began, I was ashamed of my suspicions. I won't say she looked as though she'd achieved spiritual peace; but there was no doubt in my mind she wanted it badly. At that point I began to be ashamed of myself, and resolved to meditate, or die trying.

It would have been a nobler ambition if I hadn't been so stupefied with exhaustion. Even while swearing to fight on for enlightenment, I collapsed, more or less cross-legged, onto my pillow. I was tilting so far over, I was almost on Marcy's shoulder.

"Close your eyes," the handsome instructor commanded.

At last, something I was a natural at. My eyelids met in a soft eyelid embrace. Nothing would part them in this lifetime.

"Clear your mind."

Not a problem. I was empty as the summer sky.

I was *that* close to enlightenment, when I began to hear a most disagreeable buzzing sound. I had the vague, frustrating sense it was undoing all my efforts at enlightenment—especially when, after a long stretch of confusion, I recognized the sound.

Somebody was snoring. Another few minutes, and I recognized the culprit.

It was me.

CHAPTER FORTY-SIX

Gladys Steps Out

That was how the summer went. We had, in some measure, stopped worrying about what we could not control. We concentrated on finding fun, comfort, or enlightenment wherever we could. I never developed Marcy's passion for Eastern ways, but I stopped laughing at her for it.

The Ladies stuck doggedly with their weekly schedule, even though Skye was often too busy to attend, and Dolly, who'd finally bought that small cabin up-country, was often away. Investing was not so exciting by then. Even the biggest excitement was almost antiexcitement: Deborah decided she'd lost interest in selling high-priced haircuts while all her neighbors were struggling, so she sold Combat! to an investment group from Chicago, which paid cash, then promptly overexpanded and ran it into bankruptcy. *Sic transit gloria mousse.*

The Ladies spent more of their time trying to think of ways they could use their money to help the town, but few of their plans seemed to stand scrutiny. They still donated money (and later, office space) to various relief and job-training programs; and they helped underwrite Agnes's work on the Children's Computer Center. But Larksdale was very slowly beginning to dissolve around the edges, like a tablet left in water.

And we were beginning to accept it. Buddhist or Methodist, everything's transitory in this life; so why not enjoy what you can?

Still the universe shows, at surprising moments, a sense of humor.

*W*e were probably foolish to imagine we could keep the Club a secret forever. Still, I can think of *many* more elegant ways it could have reached public notice than the route it actually used.

Not that anyone blamed Gladys. She'd spent nearly all her (let's be polite) sixty-odd years as somebody else's object of pity: from asthmatic child to spinster librarian (a job now much less fun with Agnes gone half-time), she'd relied far too long upon the kindness of strangers. In particular, she'd depended for many years upon the holiday hospitality of her nephew, Jack Nelson, and his very proper wife, Phyllis. Each year that proper couple had her spend a proper week in midsummer and another week around Christmas with them and their two boys in Duluth.

So it was only natural that one spring day Gladys decided she would show her nephew's family a really good time. Gladys thought she was simply expressing her gratitude for all their holiday treats and sundry kindnesses over the years. *You* may think she was showing them they could now stick all their kind gestures in their collective ears. And it's possible, I suppose, that you and Gladys are both right.

*T*he idea, she said, struck her in the boys' clothing department of the Dayton-Hudson store. She was picking out a couple of very nice summer shirts on end-of-season sale, when suddenly she had a vision of herself stepping down out of a limousine in front of Jack and Phyllis's house. She wore an elegant white-and-pale-gold dress, and either it was a *very* sunny day, or she had a diamond tiara in her silvery hair.

Now, Gladys was plenty smart enough to realize this was less a divine revelation than an outtake from Frank Capra's *Pocketful of Miracles* with Glenn Ford and Bette Davis. Still, a good idea is a good idea, old movie plot or not. She set the shirts back on the counter, turned on her heel, and left Dayton-Hudson forever.

All librarians are explorers. Not the mud-on-the-boots, python-in-the-sleeping-bag kind, perhaps; but still, their souls delight in unknown territory. Gladys sat down at the research desk of the Larksdale Public Library, and before she knew it she had booked a limo, an appointment at the snazziest hair salon (after Combat!) in the Twin Cities—and a two o'clock meeting with a private shopper at an extremely upscale boutique called Coat d'Azure.

Perhaps it was Gladys's fresh-from-the-salon look and smell that made the chic salesgirl take her seriously, despite her straight-from-Sears little dress. After barely a minute of cold attitude, she became in equal parts shamelessly flattering and genuinely helpful. And Gladys, meanwhile, fell in love with the setting: the soft Edith Piaf songs in the background; the elegant, uncrowded displays; and above all, the spring colors—now subtle, now bold—and soft fabrics of the clothes themselves. To Gladys, who'd never been east of Detroit, those blouses and skirts were April in Paris, summer in Provence. They were striped café awnings and Perrier umbrellas. The rack holding her selections began to fill almost unnoticed.

The hand that signed the credit-card slip was a little shaky, but still did it. For one instant, looking at the tab, Gladys hesitated— she was spending more on a blouse than she'd ever before spent on a season. It crossed her mind (more precisely, her stomach) that she was being played for a fool. Maybe the salesgirl considered her the kind of hick who thought Moulin Rouge was something you used to redden your cheeks. Then she decided better a happy fool than a dour wise woman. Fools get to wear the best colors.

As she walked her to the door, the salesgirl told Gladys she was made for elegant clothes. For an instant Gladys's doubts returned;

then the salesgirl gave her a sudden, honest, approving grin, as if to say Gladys was one of her own, who had made it to the big time.

Gladys's plans were amended that night on the phone. Jack and Phyllis announced that much as they'd love to join her, they had a nine A.M. golf date, followed by a long lunch, with friends. So Gladys arranged to pick up the boys at nine the next morning and to return them in the late afternoon.

Gladys didn't mind. The boys, Will and Andrew, ten and twelve, were lively and pleasantly uncivilized. Their lives included all the exciting things—camping and hiking and raising hell generally—she'd missed out on, and they retold their adventures enthusiastically. And they were honest: if they were bored or disappointed, they'd let her know—loudly. That was a relief. Gladys needed all the feedback she could get.

Excitement made it hard for Gladys to get to sleep that night. For decades she had traveled to Duluth on the Greyhound bus. It wasn't bad. She always rode in daytime, so rough stations made no difference. Her fellow riders were always civil, often friendly. And a bus trip to Duluth in a December blizzard would always start the blood pulsing.

But Gladys had ridden her last Greyhound.

In fairy tales and old movies, transformations fill everyone with awe and gratitude for life's mystery and the wonders of providence. In real life, they send people looking for the joke, the scam, or the loony. Too many people consider life's good things much too good to be true.

And that's exactly what got Gladys in trouble.

It started well enough. The limo driver, a polite young man named Sal, knocked at Gladys's apartment door at six A.M. He escorted her downstairs to a day of sunshine caressed by hopeful summer breezes. The stretch Lincoln, with an acre of gleaming white paint and chrome, and a soft black leather interior, looked wonderfully out of place in her scruffy neighborhood. Sal, who liked her instantly, found a classical-music station for the drive's first hour, then pulled off the road and showed her how to load her cassette tapes into the player and how to get into the minibar.

She insisted that Sal help himself, too; and sipping 7UP and listening to Mozart (probably not Sal's favorite), they drove to Duluth under blue skies and small, snow-white clouds.

Gladys wanted to sit up front with Sal to keep him company, but he drew the line at that. Still it was a wonderful drive, especially after Sal agreed to roll down the inside glass divider and began telling stories of his hobbies and ambitions. He was a fanatical stock-car racer, working his way up in the rankings. With luck he would land a NASCAR ride in another year or two—"and then look out, world!"

She was so happy, her heart didn't begin fluttering with alarm until the outskirts of Duluth came in sight.

Jack and Phyllis had already left with their friends (actually, clients of Jack's wholesale lumberyard) by the time Gladys arrived; but the two boys were properly dazzled by the limo and real, live chauffeur. They liked everything even better after Gladys suggested they let Sal throw their mountain bikes in the trunk. They liked Sal particularly well—he was burly and wore his long hair back in a ponytail, and looked like a guy who'd roll his cigarettes up in his T-shirt sleeve when he was off duty, so naturally he was better than any aunt.

Yet Gladys came through. She started by promising they would do absolutely nothing educational or healthy, unless by strict accident. Then she gave them fifty bucks apiece in rolls of quarters to spend at the video parlor. Until the change actually hit their grubby palms, the boys might have had a sneaking fear Aunt Gladys was really going to drag them to the natural-history museum—but after that, they relaxed. Gladys relaxed, too. Museums are nice, but who would want to gaze at a giant stuffed iguana or a plaster scale model of Lake Superior if they could play a rousing game of Terminator?

After playing video games until their eyes rolled back, they rode into the country for lunch.

The waiters at the Iron Knife River Lodge knew how to treat an aunt in a limousine. They had a window table, giant hamburgers with extra-crisp shoestring fries instead of boring surf and turf, and finally (after Gladys took one of the waiters aside and whispered to him) a large chocolate cake with *Good Luck, Will and Andrew* on it. Since it was neither boy's birthday, that was the best she could think of. "Because," as Gladys told the boys, "you can never have too much luck."

Next, after the boys had mountain-biked down a trail for half an hour, they decided to try something bolder.

It was the exuberance of being on a roll, combined with having three hours left before the boys were due back, that led Gladys to listen indulgently when Andrew pried out of Sal that he did sometimes race at the Duluth Speedway.

Later Gladys could not quite reconstruct the sequence of events. She had been too excited to be a very accurate witness.

She remembered the outline of it: that Sal had taken them into the track-side garage of one of the best teams, Burt Mahoney Performance, Inc. That a joking and then serious agreement had been struck that for $500 Sal could take the number-two car out for a dozen laps. That Sal had driven her to the cash machine, where she'd drawn out $400 to go with the cash she already had.

And then, suddenly, the helmet was squishing down her expensive silvery hairdo. And then she was climbing into the bare cage interior of the car, with Sal at the wheel, and the engine switching on—only, over the roaring, it felt more as if someone was rapidly and methodically kicking the car with steel boots. And then they were first rolling and then rocketing down the straightaway with the tires billowing blue smoke.

And lastly, while the car drifted sideways through a turn, a voice yelled, "Weeee-*ha*!" over the thunder of the blueprinted V-8 Ford racing engine, and Gladys realized the voice was hers.

In the end she was sorry the twelve laps—four for her, four for each of the boys—ended so quickly; but there was an electric excitement arcing among them all as they climbed back into the limo (while already the day was cold enough for Sal to run the car's heater) and started back to Jack and Phyllis's.

The electricity was still arcing when the limo pulled up in front of the gray two-story home at four-thirty that afternoon. Maybe that's why their arrival struck Jack and Phyllis like a lightning bolt between the eyes.

Jack and Phyllis were out in the driveway lugging golf clubs between their minivan and the garage when the limo screeched to a halt and Sal dashed around it to open the passenger door.

Jack and Phyllis actually jumped back at the sight of the limo, as if a spaceship had settled on their lawn. When the boys rushed out and, yelling, declared Gladys the greatest aunt in the history of Western civilization, they were staggered. And when Gladys, dressed to the nines and carrying a cute little bag that had set her back four hundred bucks, followed them out, high-fived the grinning Sal, and waved at them, their mouths simply fell open.

But never underestimate the human mind.

By the time Gladys, her glorious yellow silk-print dress only slightly wrinkled from the six-point racing harness, made her way up the short walkway, Jack and Phyllis had fit this alien apparition into their own rational view of the universe. They had digested the information and made perfect sense of it.

Gladys was nuts.

They didn't quite say it that directly, of course. They kind of *hinted* at it. Taking her elbows, they led her into the cool of the living room.

"Aunt Gladys, why don't you sit down?" Phyllis half ordered her firmly.

"Are you dizzy?" Jack inquired slowly and rather loudly. Phyllis was already running to the kitchen for a glass of water.

Gladys's first thought was that people with money definitely got nicer treatment than people without it. But just as she was enjoying that pleasant delusion, she realized what was happening.

"Are you taking any medication?" Jack asked.

"Or *not* taking it?" Phyllis asked. She was holding the water glass to Gladys's lips, and tilted it just as Gladys started to answer, "Of course not, you idiots" (or something similar). The water ran down Gladys's chin, which solidified Jack and Phyllis's conviction she was demented, or perhaps having a stroke—and also made Gladys angry for the first time in many years.

But Gladys was a woman of sound religious principles; rather than give in to anger, she closed her eyes and prayed, "Lord, give me strength."

Unfortunately Gladys tended to move her lips when she prayed. Phyllis and Jack decided she was having some kind of fit.

Even more unfortunately, Phyllis and Jack got their medical training from TV dramas; it was a near thing they didn't slap Gladys's face and shout, "Stay with me!"

"Auntie, do you know where you got the money for that limo— and those *clothes*?" Phyllis asked, leaning forward and trying to loosen Gladys's collar. She asked it as if there wasn't a prayer Gladys would know.

Gladys decided to suspend all praying until further notice. She sat up—pulling her collar away from Phyllis's appraising fingers— squared her shoulders, and answered, "Of course I do, silly. From my investment club."

More pitying looks exchanged.

"Investment club? You mean Social Security?"

"Don't be ridiculous. I'm sixty-four. I won't be eligible for Social Security for another four months." In sixty seconds Gladys had sped from surprise, to confusion, straight past severe self-doubt, to a noble struggle between patience and fierce annoyance.

Annoyance won.

This was, with all allowances made, an extremely shabby way to treat a generous and well-meaning aunt, and Gladys was starting to resent it. Some very choice phrases were forming in her extremely well-read brain, and her delicate little hands were forming into decided fists.

Now, there's nothing more satisfying, when you have been a font of civility and kindness and have had it thrown back in your face, than to rise up and smite yourself a handful of Philistines. You might do it verbally—or you might (much more fun) do it physically. Gladys was ready to pull down the temple.

Alas, while Gladys had quite a cutting wit, she wasn't really equipped for banging the table so hard the glass candies in the dessert dish bounced. She had Schwarzenegger's soul trapped in Jane Austen's body. More to the point, she realized that in trying to play Godmother, she had made them all an offer they couldn't understand—and that whatever she tried to say or do to explain, she'd just sink farther in the quicksand.

So, with a yelp they all misinterpreted, she shrugged loose from Phyllis's protecting arm on her shoulder, stood, and headed for the windows.

The living-room sofa was set against the broad windows opening on the front lawn. Gladys stepped to one of the casements, cranked it open, and called outside.

"Sal! Start the car!"

Turning back, she said to Jack and Phyllis with snapping irony, "It's been a lovely day, dears, but I want to get back to Minneapolis. It's Friday, and I want to go out drinking and maybe start a bar fight."

She winked at the boys and started for the door.

.   .   .

*A*s the limo drove away, the whole family stood on the front porch watching, with Jack and Phyllis shaking their heads in pitying alarm and the boys waving with wild enthusiasm.

The boys were also shouting. Of course, it was impossible to hear their words. But Gladys, looking out the limo's back window, decided it was amusing to think they were yelling, "*Shane!* Come back!"

All in all, it was a lot of fun.

"Oh, we had *such* a good time," Gladys told me later, her voice filled with amazement and regret. "And I kept my word. I didn't make them do a single thing I thought would be good for them."

She paused, then added thoughtfully, "It's too bad their parents are idiots."

She had no idea how right she was.

CHAPTER FORTY-SEVEN

The Club Hits the Fan

*T*he LLIC was way ahead of the curve on "Casual Friday" dress policies. In fact, by early 1991, we'd already expanded the program to include casual Tuesdays, Wednesdays, and Thursdays as well. (Mondays I worked at home, so for all I know, Heidi ran the office dressed as the King of Prussia.)

Still, I would have preferred it if I'd been wearing something other than blue jeans and a Grateful Dead T-shirt the morning James Puttersmith, JD, arrived an hour after asking if he could see me immediately on a matter concerning Ms. Gladys Vaniman. His precise words included the phrase "I hope I can save you a lot of trouble." That was a bad sign. Whenever people say that, they mean they intend to *cause* you a lot of trouble.

The minute Puttersmith clicked off, I called Gladys to find out what she knew. She was mystified, but told me to help him out as best I could. Naturally that brought to mind the old joke, "I'd like to help you out. Which way did you come in?" but all I told Gladys was that I'd get back to her shortly.

I knew Puttersmith was trouble when he walked in, straight past Heidi, without dropping to his knees and asking her to marry him.

It meant he was either the living dead or a work-obsessed twit. Instead he strode, short, plump and ruddy, through my open door and up to my desk, thrust out his hand fiercely, and barked, "You're Sophia Peters?"

Now, you've got to understand, this was Minnesota. The police won't stop a bank robbery in progress without wishing everybody a real good day and asking after everybody's health and family. James Puttersmith, JD, wasn't playing by the rules. In fact, he seemed to be going out of his way to be rude.

Still, I figured he might have been from some foreign land, like, say, Chicago, so I nodded and shook his hand.

"And you represent Gladys Vaniman." There wasn't even a hint of a question. He glanced around the office, his expression showing how closely he felt I fit the picture of attorney to a crazy old lady. Now, I was in-house counsel to a private investment trust. If I chose to decorate my office with King Kong models and Errol Flynn posters, what business was that of his?

In fact, his look was so ungracious, I decided to stop handing him freebies.

"No, I don't. I'm general counsel of the Larksdale Ladies Independence Club, and she's a principal investor. I understood you had a financial question."

He nodded. I was doing better with him by acting tougher. "I'm sorry to bother you, and I appreciate your giving me some of your time on short notice."

He sat, then went on in a middling-polite tone: "Miss Vaniman's family is worried about her. She's acting . . . Well, she's acting sort of crazy."

"Crazy, how?"

"Crazy with money mostly."

I gave him my friendly idiot look fixedly, until he had to go on. "She . . . she rented a limousine."

"Uh-huh."

"And took her nephews out to play video games and gave them fifty dollars apiece to spend."

"Yes?" I was tapping my pen on the desk and looking for something to read. I had already relaxed. The boys hadn't spilled the beans about hot-lapping Duluth Motor Speedway.

Little beads of sweat were popping out on his forehead. "And she took them to dinner at the best restaurant in Duluth."

"That's it?"

"So far, yes. But it's a bad sign, you'll agree."

"So she's not wearing aluminum-foil hats?"

"No."

"Not standing in the rain trying to feed caviar to pigeons?"

"No."

"Doesn't think she's the Gladys of Gladys Knight and the Pips?"

"No!"

"Just wanted to get the whole picture." I leaned forward companionably. "Gladys said I could speak frankly, so I will. I can tell you in confidence that Gladys can afford what she's spending. In fact, she could spend like that until America elects a cow president, and still not run short. She's got the dough."

"How much dough is that?"

"That's confidential information. We're a private investment group."

"Ballpark figure."

"Ballpark? Well, over three million, certainly. And that's just where she holds spring training. The big park's a *lot* bigger."

"I don't think that's very funny."

"Good. Then we have similar tastes in humor. I like the Marx Brothers, myself. 'On safari once, I shot an elephant in my pajamas. How it *got* in my pajamas, I'll never . . .' " I do a fair Groucho, if I do say so—if you can go for a blond, thirty-two-year-old Groucho. Apparently Mr. Puttersmith couldn't.

"Then maybe I could trouble you for a straight answer?" he interrupted rather harshly.

"You just had one. It's unaudited, but it's a good minimum figure—although it's certainly low. Gladys can take a limo just about whenever and wherever she wants."

"You can prove that, I suppose?"

"I don't have to prove anything. I *thought* I was doing you a favor and relieving the worries of a couple of concerned relatives. If you want more, ask the court for a sanity hearing and subpoena the records."

I leaned forward in the chair. "Of course, you probably ought to advise your clients that Gladys is revising her will. You know she loves cats, and there are a *lot* of homeless cats in the Twin Cities. She might just decide her money ought to go to endowing a home for homeless cats. Her kind of money could build a feline Four Seasons. A tabby Taj Mahal. A Ritz for cats—we could call it The Ratz. Or—"

He was on his feet and moving. I told his back, "Hey! You have a *real* good day, and come back and see us soon!"

He left without wishing me the same.

Some people just don't understand Minnesota.

Someday—probably not in this life—I'll learn to keep my mouth shut.

A week later we got served papers. Among the principal points argued was that Gladys was planning to leave her vast fortune (which other parts of the papers argued she didn't have) to a bunch of mangy animals.

"Well," I told Heidi, "it's a great day for the cats."

And she looked at me like I was crazy.

CHAPTER FORTY-EIGHT

As Sane As You or Me

I'd like to say I gave the greatest courtroom performance since Perry Mason—but the best I can say is I *would* have given it, had it been necessary. We all have a few delusions, don't we?

As a matter of fact, I just about went crazy walking slowly up the courthouse steps beside Gladys that morning. When I get nervous I need to move fast; and I was so terrified I could have used the Olympic track trials. But Gladys was entirely at peace and full of confidence. She kept stopping on the stairs to inhale the sweet October breezes, and to turn and look back over Larksdale's blooming town square.

Three times on those twenty steps we stopped—she to take a deep, life-affirming breath, and I to stifle a scream.

Somewhere in the course of my two-week preparation for the hearing, I'd forgotten one teeny little detail about my nature as a lawyer; namely, that public appearances have always turned me into a trembling idiot. When I was six I shook all the red craft-paper apples off my tree suit during the first-grade production of *This Is Nutrition!* Twenty-six years later, far bigger and stronger, I could shake the fruit off a real apple tree.

.　　.　　.

*O*f course, I had my tremendous courtroom record to fall back upon. Counting that morning, I'd appeared before a judge exactly once in my career—when I was sworn in as an attorney, and in the company of thirty other neophytes, had raised my hand, and proudly said, "I d-d-d-d-d-d-d—" I was still trying to get the "oooo" out while everybody else was having drinks at the restaurant in the IDS Tower.

I was glad for the table and the lid of my open briefcase, so the judge wouldn't be able to see my knees and hands trembling when he entered.

Not that Judge Naycroft was exactly intimidating.

In fact, he looked like a road-company version of Mark Twain, with the snowy-white hair and bright blue eyes. He viewed us all with such broad, beaming benevolence that I was immediately suspicious—and went from shaking to paralytic.

Gladys did it all herself. First, she was dressed in impeccable good taste, and good taste (anywhere outside the fashion industry) is presumptive evidence of sanity. In the second, she had the alert-but-calm demeanor of an interested citizen eager to see the American legal system in action. Third, she had the benefit of contrast, since her poor lawyer was now so frightened as to be doing an apt imitation of a victim of tertiary lockjaw. In comparison, Gladys looked as calm and capable as the Statue of Liberty.

She only grew calmer when Judge Naycroft smiled benevolently at us all, then looked to Gladys and began: "Now, Miss . . . Vaniman. This isn't a trial; it's just an informal hearing to make sure you're . . . well, qualified to keep managing your own affairs. Do you understand?"

"Certainly, Your Honor." Gladys was looking bright, alert—positively dazzling, in fact. Suddenly she had a sort of unaccountable glow about her. All I could think was that maybe she'd knocked back a few shots of applejack while I wasn't looking.

"Good. Well . . . why don't you tell us how you feel about the whole process—in your own words."

Gladys beamed back at him, and all of a sudden it hit me. Gladys had the hots for Judge Naycroft. The room became suddenly quieter. I'd quit breathing.

"It's quite a novelty to me, frankly, Your Honor. It's a little like one of those classic movies. Like, oh, *Mr. Deeds Goes to Town*."

She said this in the most flattering tones, and then—so help me—she batted her eyelashes at him. Eyelash batting went out with Mae West—but there it was.

This wasn't a trial; it was a memorial service for my legal career. It was also a religious encounter: suddenly, miraculously, I knew all the words to "Hail Mary." In Latin.

But to my amazement, Naycroft stared briefly, then smiled broadly.

"Or *Miracle on 34th Street*!" he replied with evident pleasure.

"Or *Harvey*."

"*That's* not a trial," Judge Naycroft corrected her, with fine judicial insight.

"Not technically—but there's a judge, and basically they conclude Jimmy Stewart's crazy before they commit him," Gladys shot back. "In fact," she added slyly, "it's probably the closest of any to the situation here today." She concluded with a little smile, "*If* you think I'm crazy, that is."

"Mmm . . . true. True. *If . . .*"

Judge Naycroft was looking more and more like the young Mark Twain; but now he pulled himself up, with a quick clearing of his throat and a, "Yes, well . . ." He looked down at his papers awkwardly, then resumed.

"Ms. Vaniman, you've read what your nephew and his wife have claimed about your actions. How would you explain them?"

Gladys kept right with him; he stopped being Mark Twain, and she stopped being Mae West. She straightened herself admirably, looked him squarely in the eye, and said, "I have more trouble accounting for their actions than for mine, Your Honor. In recent years I've earned—or anyway, been blessed with—a lot of money. Because I'm set in my ways, I never spent much, except for a little on some charities.

"But about a month ago it occurred to me there was nothing wrong with having some fun, and that one way to have a *lot* of fun would be to surprise my nephew and his family. I thought that would accomplish three things: it would give them a thrill, and thank them for their many past kindnesses, and it would let me feel like I counted for something in this life.

"Now, they've been kind to me—absolutely—but even the kindest charity wears you down after a while. And maybe I was reacting—a little too vigorously, and without quite realizing it—against that wearing-down. Maybe I really did want people, just for once, to step back and say, 'Wow!' when I went down the street.

"I suppose it was ostentatious of me—and maybe in bad taste. But, well, I'd been everybody's poor spinster aunt for a long time. A little bit of a splurge seemed to be in order—so I went ahead and did it." She paused, then finished, "I guess I believe we're all entitled to make some noise in this world. Even the quiet ones. I don't think that's crazy—do you?"

Judge Naycroft drew a deep breath, then released it as slowly and patiently as if he were seeing it off on a world cruise. Then he shook his head. He turned to Puttersmith, fixed him with a judicial stare, and said levelly, "Counselor, if you've got a rabbit you plan to pull out of a hat, I'd say now's the time."

"No rabbit, Your Honor," Puttersmith said after a long pause and a longer sigh.

As we were leaving, Judge Naycroft asked me to stay behind. I told Gladys I'd see her later and followed the judge into his chambers.

"Puttersmith is an annoying man," he told me after we were both seated in his comfy leather chairs.

I was grinning and nodding.

"But that doesn't mean you should go around threatening to have your clients disown his clients, does it?" The judge went on, looking at me, still kindly but with just a hint of coolness.

I stopped grinning and nodding. In fact, I was trembling a little as I shook my head and answered, "No, Your Honor." I had no idea how big a gaffe I'd made, or how hot the water was going to get. As a lawyer, I'm a pretty good businesswoman.

But he concluded quite nicely, "So, let's not have any more of that in the future, 'kay?"

"Absolutely, Your Honor."

Sometimes paternal's not all that bad.

But that wasn't the whole story. Now, as I calmed down, I realized he was hesitating. The nice blue eyes were a little less paternal and a lot more questioning. Embarrassment was etched on his face, and it took a long hesitation before he asked:

"Ms. Vaniman . . . is she . . . that is, is she seeing anyone?"

I went home feeling on top of the world. *Sophia, my girl,* I told myself, *the legal profession suffered a tragic loss the day you weren't born twins.* I was so delighted with dodging a legal bullet that I even forgot to be depressed about my love life.

Unfortunately this world has not only greedy attorneys and honest judges, but newspaper interns—eager college students desperate to find a story. And some of those interns even have the brains to look beyond the police blotter.

Two days later I got a phone call. A very young man's voice, with the kind of zip you heard only from cub reporters on TV sitcoms, said, "This is Rick Davis from the *Star Tribune*. I'd like to interview you about your millionaire ladies' club."

"I'm sorry," I answered breezily while knowing the game was over, "I'm afraid I don't understand."

"Oh, sure you do. It was all in the court papers. You represent a bunch of housewives who made a gazillion dollars in the stock market. It's really cool. I'm writing a story about them."

A sudden chill passed over me. The Larksdale Ladies had been one heck of a stealth mission. Now we were right over Baghdad, lit up by searchlights, and square in the crosshairs.

CHAPTER FORTY-NINE

Two Short Conversations

As soon as I got off the line with Larksdale's own one-man version of Woodward and Bernstein, I phoned each of the Ladies, to explain that we might be in for some publicity. I asked them to avoid reporters until we could meet and set our policy. Most of them sounded excited, as though this might be a lot of fun. As a last-minute thought, I left the same message on Veronica Harris's answering machine.

I wasn't sure how I felt about the news; but as I was summarizing the situation for Veronica's machine, Heidi stepped into the office. When I'd hung up, she exclaimed, "This is sensational." She was flushed with excitement.

"How do you figure?" I was worried we'd be hounded by every freeloader in the state—and more worried about how our friends and neighbors would take the news. In small towns, having money is viewed with suspicion, and advertising it is unforgivable.

Heidi dropped into a chair. "Are you kidding? Why do you think that kid wants to do a newspaper story about the Ladies? They're *so* cool. I bet somebody even asks them to write a book."

"Oh, come on." I was genuinely surprised. "I mean, who would be interested in a bunch of little old ladies who made ten mi—" I stopped. I may be dim, but I can spot a wall within a minute after walking into it. "Hey!" I added brightly. "You don't suppose . . ."

By the time Heidi stepped back to her desk, I was exuberant. The more I considered our prospects, the more they resembled a Cole Porter overture: they just got better and better. In fact, to enjoy it all, I got up and put on my CD of *Anything Goes*. It was just one of those days.

Just before I jitterbugged out the door to order a Lamborghini, I got the call that changed everything.

It was Veronica Harris responding to my call.

I turned down the music and heard, for the first time, the sounds of a thunderstorm hitting hard outside the office.

The thunderstorm was first-rate, alternately battering the windows with hail and rattling them with concussive bursts. I had to press the phone hard to my ear to hear Veronica.

She wanted to know if she could see me immediately.

"Are you sure you want to come now?" I asked.

"Yes." There was a faint hiss to the word.

Veronica regularly missed meetings on the grounds of bad weather; this was unusual.

"Fine, then. I'll see you anytime in the next hour."

*W*hen Veronica arrived, she was breathing in gasps. Her face was red, and her eyes seemed to bulge a bit. She stood in the doorway of my office, staring as if she'd never been there before, and shaking off Heidi's efforts to help with her raincoat.

"Did you run to get here?" I asked.

She shook her head briefly, then thought the better of it and nodded. "I wanted to get out of the rain."

"Oh. Well, have a seat."

She didn't sit exactly. More like she perched at the edge of the chair. She still had her kerchief tied over her head. Water was running down the front of her face and onto the carpet. Behind her, Heidi was still standing, curious, in the doorway. I waved her off.

Veronica turned to make sure Heidi had gone, then said off-handedly but very softly, "I just had a quick question."

"Coffee? Tea?"

She shook her head. "I only have a minute."

"Okay. Shoot."

She had to moisten her lips with her tongue before speaking. Then she asked, hesitantly, "This publicity you mentioned. Is there any chance, do you think, it will lead to people being curious about our . . . you know, our financial records and such?"

Something tightened in the pit of my stomach.

I asked carefully, "Would that be a problem?"

She laughed, or tried to, and waved her hands weakly, as if shooing a cloud of mayflies. "Not a bit. I just thought I might need to straighten things up a little. Maybe prepare some handouts or a few remarks. I'm not used to the press, you know."

Not liking what I was thinking, I nodded. "Sure." Still nodding, I added, "Makes sense. Go ahead, by all means."

She rose quickly. "Well," she said, clutching tightly to her purse, "sorry I bothered you."

Before she reached the door, I said quietly, "Veronica?"

She turned.

"Is anything wrong?"

She gave rather a sickly smile, answered, "Not a thing," and turned away.

"*Veronica!*"

She turned—and this time her face was angry, almost snarling. "*What!?*"

I hit the buzzer for Heidi, who was both bigger and younger than Veronica. Having her blocking the doorway wouldn't hurt.

"Come back here and sit down," I told Veronica as Heidi's footsteps approached. "We have more to talk about."

She looked at me with a strange blend of hatred and relief, nodded, and came and sat.

CHAPTER FIFTY

The Truth of Our Situation

When Veronica quit talking twenty minutes later, I was the one sweating.

As nearly as I could tell, she had embezzled more than $1.5 million of the Ladies' money in the past year—mostly from the large amount of cash they'd collected for estate-planning purposes. Counting interest we thought we'd earned, the losses totaled about $2 million.

She had an explanation, but I scarcely had patience to hear it. Basically she thought we had treated her like a hack and an outsider and had made her feel ashamed. She had taken the money, not to spend on herself, but to prove that she was as shrewd an investor as any of the Ladies. And her shrewd—even brilliant, she'd no doubt thought—plan was to plunge into penny stocks and commodities futures. The only worse strategies would have been taking the money to Las Vegas, and setting fire to it on her front lawn.

"How much is left? Of what you took, I mean."

"About three hundred thousand. Well, maybe four hundred thousand."

My first thought was that I wanted to shoot myself; but pretty quickly I thought of another target. Especially after she added, "Of course, I owe some outstanding bills, too."

I sat back and closed my eyes. Nero Wolfe, the great fictional detective, used to do this whenever he was about to solve a big case. All that happened to me was that I saw the backs of my eyelids. They had nothing useful to contribute. I opened my eyes again, more annoyed by the second.

"You're sure about these numbers?"

"Oh, yes." She said it snottily. I'd injured her professional pride. *She* was annoyed with *me*.

I looked to Heidi. She's a much better poker player than I'll ever be. But like it or not, it was my deal. I told her, "Get your coat," and as she rose I said to Veronica, "Let's go check the damage."

I didn't really think Veronica would make a break for it; but with Heidi along, it wouldn't even be a possibility.

CHAPTER FIFTY-ONE

Decision Time

*I*f I'd been just a little bit gutsier, the process would have been a lot simpler. I would have told Heidi to keep Veronica in the office—to tie her to a chair if she had to—and then gone and explained everything to the district attorney.

Instead I played sucker to my legal training: all that high-sounding stuff about due process and the right to confront one's accusers affected me. That may explain why I'll never get anywhere as a lawyer. Five minutes later, having locked up the office, Heidi and I escorted Veronica out to my car. Under pouring rain, we set off to her office to review her books.

I was in a blazing mood and searching for fuel to feed my anger. Veronica's office—which I'd never seen—was a two-story wood-pile. A converted home, set back from the street in maple-shaded, white-framed comfort, its exterior spoke of solid Midwestern values. Its interior screamed hot money and cooked books.

The interior ignited me. We walked down a corridor of gray Wilton carpets and dark, expensive wallpapers gracefully highlighted by nineteenth-century English prints. The office, where a gas flame blazed cheerfully in the fireplace, sported furniture suitable for an extremely successful solicitor in, say, Edwardian England. I'd decorated out of Office Depot; Veronica had used the feature pages of *Architectural Digest*.

I would have killed for an office like that—and right now I had a candidate in mind. Turning to Heidi as we entered, I said, only half-jokingly, "Somebody get a rope."

And looking at the gold-framed hunting print hung over the fireplace, I couldn't help wondering which of the beagles in the pack was Veronica's mother.

*B*ut if the place was beautiful, the fraud was extraordinarily ugly.

Yet it wasn't a very *clever* fraud—in fact, it was much less a fraud than a bank robbery with a pen. Veronica had been absolutely certain she was going to make a quick profit in excess of what the Ladies' investments would have earned. All she had done was to plunder our cash reserves—every account she could touch. She'd recorded the transfers as going to individual Ladies' accounts—but in fact, they'd all gone straight into Veronica's.

Or, more precisely, they'd gone *briefly* into Veronica's—just long enough for the deposits to register, so she could mail the money out to a series of penny-stock and other scam artists from Denver to the Cayman Islands. It was as if she were running her own private MacArthur Fellowships for world-class crooks.

I was amazed she could have been so stupid—or so desperate.

Frankly it was pure good luck (for her) that she hadn't been caught sooner. We had accumulated far more cash than normal of late; but if we had decided to make any large investment in, say, real estate, the cash shortage would have been obvious at once. She lacked trading authority on our stock accounts—the cash was all she could touch. And she didn't control the money of any other clients, except a couple of nearly senile retired doctors.

She'd stolen from one of them, too—but only a few thousand dollars, she claimed, and that very quickly repaid from our funds.

Clearly, whether she would admit it or not, this was a personal vendetta against the Ladies. Bits of that anger came out as we sat in her office. At some moments Veronica sat meekly; at others she wanted to snarl at me and fight over every document.

Two hours of reviewing her books, and Heidi and I had most of the story. From a numbers point of view, it made no sense; it made sense only in terms of her absolutely frustrated ambition and her mad desire to show us all up.

Of course, the books also explained why she'd worked so hard against our making further investments in the past year: the minute we'd made any significant call against our "liquid" (more accurately "evaporated") funds, her covers would have been pulled.

At the end of those two hours, it was time either to leave or to call the cops. Or maybe the paramedics. My head felt like it was going to explode.

I closed the last ledger, turned to Heidi (who rolled her eyes in sympathetic frustration), and said, "Let's go."

Heidi let Veronica into the backseat of the car, slammed the door, then turned to me.

"We should drive her straight to the district attorney."

The water was pouring over us in buckets. Heidi's hair was plastered down over her dripping face. She looked like an ad for women's rugby gear. I was starting to shiver. But I shook my head.

"No. She gets to talk to the Ladies."

"You're sure?"

"Yeah."

Actually I had the strong feeling our problem could best be solved by two guys named Louie wearing double-breasted pin-stripe suits and driving a bulletproof '26 Stutz.

But those guys are never around when you need them.

CHAPTER FIFTY-TWO

Amazing Veronica

The storm was turning into an epic thing, an almost biblical downpour. Okay, not that—but water was swirling down the streets in thick, fast sheets.

As I stepped out of my car in front of Martha's house, the water skipped merrily up over the low tops of my boots and puddled instantly around my toes. It was extraordinarily unpleasant—and added just the perfect finishing touch to my already foul mood.

The Ladies had all gathered in the living room. Outside, the storm had darkened the late-afternoon sky almost to black; inside, the lamps were on. Summer was over.

The Ladies, democratic to a fault, were offering Veronica not just the chance to face her accusers, but the chance to give them one heck of a lecture.

It started calmly enough, with my summarizing, very briefly, what the day had brought, then Veronica rising and admitting the basic truth of the charges.

Then it got weird.

Three minutes into her talk I realized Veronica was turning it into Sunday-morning testimony.

This, if you've never seen it, is quite special about Methodism. Those of us who are serious about our faith, when feeling bold or bad enough, will attend a special meeting before church on Sundays. There we confess our sins publicly and ask for strength and encouragement from our coreligionists.

As a spiritual form, testimony is wonderful. As a way of running a legal inquiry, it's a tad bonkers.

Veronica may not have known all the words of testimony, but she was shrewd enough to hum the tune. All the toughness she'd shown with me that afternoon was replaced with a truly moving humility. She did everything but begin, "Our text today is from First Corinthians . . ."

She talked about fifteen minutes, her confession gradually becoming spiritual autobiography, full of words like "pride" and "blindness." I was waiting to hear words like "crook" and "scam"—but she kept everything on a very profound and moving level. We were about two minutes away from holding hands in a circle while a soft chorus in the background sang "Amazing Grace."

John Wesley would have loved it.

More to the point, looking around the room, I saw that the Ladies were buying it, too. By the time she finished talking, and they asked her to wait outside, I had a bad feeling about the way things were going.

The feeling wasn't half bad enough.

Of course, they were religious. Dolly, especially, had lately gotten religion in a big way—which often happens, of course, to people left suddenly on their own. She was for forgiving everyone, everywhere, every time.

She rose and said, "I can see she's sorry. I say we give her another chance." She paused and tried to look wise. "Not without controls, of course—and restitution."

I was twisting in my chair. Heidi put a hand on my arm to keep me from rising.

Then my mom stood and added, "That might work, I think."

"You're letting her get away with it!?" I wished my voice had sounded less like someone complaining to her mother.

Mom answered, "We're not letting her get away with it. We're giving her a chance to make something good of her life."

"She robbed you!" I sputtered.

"Maybe we gave her cause. We never really treated her as one of us—especially you, Sophia."

Perfect. Now I was in trouble for being rude to Al Capone.

Agnes spoke up. "I don't see how bad it could be. It couldn't be *too* bad." She swallowed. "Could it?"

I decided it was time for a few quotes from the Book of Get Real, Chapter One. So I slipped free of Heidi, stood, and said, "About two million dollars' worth of bad."

Every face in the room went pale. I cranked up my rhetoric another ten degrees. "She's going to jail. Even if we don't press charges, some of her other clients probably will. She *says* we're the only ones she cheated—but can we believe her?"

A long silence followed. Then Agnes, sounding pathetic for the first time in a long time, asked plaintively, "What are we going to do?"

I jumped on it. "Now you're talking! She's got a million-dollar malpractice policy." I tried not to smirk. Making her buy it, years before, had been my idea. "If we file a claim, we'll get a whack at recovery."

"And what happens to Veronica?" Martha asked.

She wasn't expecting an answer—since we all knew it already.

I was going to sit tight and not say a word until they came to their senses.

Then—bad move—I looked again toward Agnes and remembered her remarkable conversion of nasty Inigo Stout. As far as I was concerned, that was the moral equivalent of trying to win every game on a ninety-foot shot at the buzzer.

On the other hand, what was faith if not that?

And it was—mostly—their money.

I held my breath—and when nobody had answered Agnes after a full thirty seconds, I exhaled, stood up, and said somewhat miserably, "I have an idea."

CHAPTER FIFTY-THREE

I Hire a Consultant

My idea, basically, was that I would work out something. Unfortunately my thinking had gotten no farther than a dual objective: to make sure Veronica never got another crack at the Ladies' money, while at the same time to honor their wish that she somehow get another chance.

I was thinking frantically about this as we left Martha's—even while, glancing sideways at Veronica, I tried to decide whether I really was to blame, even a little, for what she'd done.

Veronica certainly didn't make it easy.

All the humility evaporated from her face the moment we three were alone on the sidewalk.

"All right, genius, what's your idea?" she demanded.

"My idea is that you and your new friend here"—I indicated Heidi—"go off and have a pleasant dinner together and meet me back at my office in two hours."

"That's your idea?"

I nodded.

"It stinks."

Heidi didn't like it any better. She's a gentle soul, for all her size. She couldn't stand Veronica and was afraid that, left alone with her, she would bop her on the nose.

I was in no mood for more debate.

I drove them back to the office, dropped them at Heidi's car, told them to meet there again in two hours, then parked and went inside.

My office was actually quite nice by any standard short of Veronica's version of No. 10 Downing Street. But the heat was off, and the autumn chill went through me. I got hand towels from the bathroom and rubbed some of the rainwater off my face and hair.

I was back in my chair and feeling better when I realized my plan had just a tiny flaw:

It didn't exist.

What I needed was a consultant—and for playing hardball, there was only one to consider.

I had her cell phone number, so I tried that. It rang five times, and then, over the background clatter and shouting of one of those singles bars she loved, I heard, "Hello?"

"Marcy? It's me. Where are you?"

"Gee, Mom, curfew's not for another hour."

"Sorry."

"No, it's *me*. I'm cut off, surrounded by jerks, and running out of ammo. Makes me grumpy."

"I need to tell you something in confidence."

"Like, lawyer to lawyer?"

"*Please.*"

"Girl Scout oath?"

"Better."

"Shoot."

"Somebody embezzled a couple of million bucks from my ladies."

"Holy Christ." More background noise. "Listen, if you're serious, we'd better meet somewhere. Cell phones—"

"I know. How about Matrelli's on Eighth?"

"Thirty minutes." Then, away from phone, "Shut up, Bill." And the line went dead.

I got to Matrelli's in ten, used the balance of the time figuring out what I was going to say, and finally decided, with my usual precision, that I didn't have a clue.

Mostly I was *asking,* asking for Marcy's advice. Not only was she a very good attorney, far more experienced in rough-and-tumble than I, but also she was still the spitwad-firing independent spirit I had always wanted to be. I hoped she would be brilliant, even as I fought down yet again that pointless wish that Veronica had never crossed my threshold. If she had just hopped a jet to Brazil with a suitcase full of money, she'd have saved us all a world of trouble. But she hadn't. Instead, she'd come to see me.

*W*hen she arrived, about ten minutes later, Marcy looked only half the legal pit bull I expected. Her other half looked red-eyed and dog-tired. Eastern religions seemed to have gone by the wayside. Trying to ignore that, I said, "There she is! Super-lawyer by day, party animal by night!"

"Please. I'm so sick of that stuff I can hardly keep food down anymore. However"—she slapped her purse and cell phone down on the table, and plopped herself heavily onto the seat opposite me—"that is a topic for another day. Right now, your problems have the floor."

Marcy had left the Methodist church when she started college. In fact, "left" was a vast understatement. I doubt anybody had left anything with as much wild enthusiasm since the Rough Riders sailed from Florida in 1898. Still, she knew everyone in the Club except Skye. Especially to the point, she knew what they deserved for themselves and what they would tolerate for Veronica.

She listened without interruption; but I could trace a silent discourse in her expressions. She ran quickly from curiosity to re-spect, alarm, close thinking, and—finally—a kind of fierce, fighting alertness.

When I finished, she asked about a detail I'd left out. "What in God's name did she do with all this money?"

"Spent a little. Mostly traded futures and bought penny stocks."

"Jesus. At least in Vegas they give you a floor show."

Of course, I felt a sudden sympathy for Veronica.

"She just wanted to be respected."

"She just wanted to screw you. She's a crook. Fuck her."

Good old Marcy. The subtlety queen of the upper Midwest.

She leaned toward me confidentially. "Let's take a walk."

CHAPTER FIFTY-FOUR

Rough Justice

The rain had stopped, and the glistening streets made a kind of film noir background to our conversation. Since this was Larksdale, it was a *safe* mysteriousness; but still, it spoke of plots and conspiracies.

Marcy walked much faster than I did; I had to tug her raincoat sleeve to slow her. Even then, I was losing my breath as I explained what the Ladies wanted done.

She stopped and snorted. "Are you serious?"

"We can do it, can't we?"

She thought before she answered. "Sure, I guess. You can write a predated letter authorizing her to use the Ladies' money to buy penny stocks. That covers her against the regulators charging her with cheating your Ladies. Of course, *you*'d be certifiable as a lunatic—but she'd be off the hook."

She paused for effect, then added, "Plus, of course, if you don't blow the whistle you'd be responsible—morally and maybe legally—for anybody else she ripped off. And they'd come after you for sure, because you're the deep pockets."

"She claims we're the only ones she stiffed."

"You believe that?"

I shrugged. I really wasn't sure—I'd had just two hours with her books, and I'm no accountant. "Sort of. Almost."

We started moving again so Marcy could think. After half a block we halted by a bench at the edge of the park. The thick-painted green wood was dotted with fat blobs of water.

Marcy flicked at several of them with a fingertip, looked about carefully, then said quietly, "All right—here's the alternative. Veronica hires me as her attorney. I advise her that she's likely to be charged with fraud, conversion, violation of various professional codes, and heaven knows what else. I give her a strong hint that taking off for Mexico is an excellent way to simplify everybody's life—especially hers. Tonight she drives to the airport, and to-morrow morning you wake up and discover—to your utter shock—that your accountant has flown the coop. Of course, you immediately notify the authorities and file a claim against her malpractice insurance. You get your dough—or some of it—and she gets away."

She finished up, sounding extraordinarily glum.

"Are you happy with that?" I was studying her face. Under the harsh orange of the streetlight, she looked more old than anything else.

"Happy? The law's not about happiness."

The law certainly wasn't making *me* happy.

It wasn't even keeping my attention. All I could think about were the times I'd treated Veronica badly—in the course of twenty years, I'd had a lot of chances and I'd rarely wasted one.

Then, suddenly, under that street lamp I finally had an idea. I wasn't sure it made sense, but it was the first one of the night that didn't make me queasy.

I checked my watch. There wasn't time to discuss it. I didn't really want to, anyway.

"We have to go," was all I said.

She nodded and for once let me lead the way.

CHAPTER FIFTY-FIVE

I Cut a Deal

When Heidi and Veronica walked in, I told Heidi she could go home and asked Veronica to take a seat.

They both looked at me accusingly; but I was protecting Heidi from a legal mess and I didn't care what Veronica thought. Heidi seemed to realize that; after a long questioning stare at me, she shrugged and left.

I went on the offensive the minute Veronica sat down.

"Do you have a passport?"

She nodded, not especially mystified. "I go to France every spring."

That figured. The only place I'd ever been was Manhattan Beach for a Young Methodists conference in high school. Manhattan Beach is often called "The French Riviera of L.A. County"—by members of the Manhattan Beach Chamber of Commerce.

"All right. Here's the deal. We're driving together back to your house. I stay with you while you pack one bag and pick up your passport. Then you write out a short letter to me saying you need a vacation and asking me to find a new CPA to take over your accounts while you're away."

Marcy was staring at me. I put up a hand to keep her from

speaking and kept at Veronica. "Marcy and I drive you straight to the airport, and you get on the first outbound international flight. You stay away from Minnesota for ninety days while that other accountant handles all your other clients. If, after ninety days—or let's say, by Monday, the week before Christmas—none of your other clients is accusing you of fraud, theft, or anything else, I'll believe you were just mad at us.

"In that case, you can come back and work out whatever kind of deal with the Ladies that you and they can live with. I'll even help as best I can. But if anybody else files suit or even complains a little bit that you screwed things up, we'll jump into the front of the lawsuit."

I stopped for a breath. I felt like I was suffocating, purely from nerves. Veronica looked like she wanted to slug me.

But I finished.

"One last thing. If, before the ninety days are up, I hear you're back in Minnesota, I go straight to the authorities and offer to give testimony. And I don't mean about God's grace to sinners. Right?"

"Forget it."

"Fine. Then I call the police." My hand, though moving fast, was only halfway to the phone when she said, "All right."

Afraid of more discussion, I jumped to my feet and started for the coatrack. Before I got there, Veronica turned to Marcy.

"Can't I stay until Thanksgiving?"

For some reason she'd decided Marcy would be the more sympathetic listener. Boy, did she have the wrong girl.

"You can have turkey *mole* at some cantina in Guadalajara. Let's move it," Marcy said, just a bit like Humphrey Bogart.

She herded Veronica through Heidi's office and out the door. Then she shut it partway so she could ask me privately, "Sophia? Do you know what you're risking?"

"Yep."

She grinned at me. "Then good for you."

CHAPTER FIFTY-SIX

A Beautiful Friendship

We started for the airport just before midnight, aiming for the Northwest Airlines red-eye to Mexico City at one-fifteen A.M. By the time we got there, with Marcy driving through rain showers, I was exhausted from stress as much as the late hour.

Veronica had partly overcome her fury in the course of that long night. Her mood first began to soften as she sat writing the letter at the fine rosewood desk in her study. I think she realized that with luck, she might actually return there one day.

From then on, silence replaced snarling. Accompanied by Marcy, she went upstairs and packed without protest, and when she returned downstairs a little before eleven-thirty, she actually asked us if we wanted coffee.

Crossing the concourse, I was yawning almost nonstop. I'd long since quit trying to stifle my yawns. Throwing my head back and stretching my jaw as far as it would go, I looked like a silent beagle.

"Northwest Flight twenty-one eighteen is now ready for boarding."

Veronica stepped away from the counter holding a sleek overnight bag and two luggage checks. She was going to sunny Mexico. I was going back to Larksdale in a promised hailstorm to explain to the Ladies.

And yet—perhaps from the fatigue, though I don't think so—I was no longer angry with Veronica.

"Veronica!"

She turned and eyed me without friendliness. She might already have been in Mexico, for all she seemed to notice me.

"If I *was* bad to you . . . I'm sorry." I put out my hand.

First she was going to pretend her arms were too full; but then, just as the line moved, she reached out and brushed my offered hand.

Then she was gone.

It was as close as I ever got to a noble gesture. I rather liked it. But it was nothing I'd make a habit of.

"Well," I said as we started back for the parking garage. "Thank God that's over with." I was feeling, not especially proud of myself, but extremely fond of Marcy. "You know, I'm thinking we'll have a lot of fun this holiday—"

Marcy had been studying the ground as she walked. She was still looking down when she interrupted—

"The thing is, Sophia, I don't think I can. I took a job with a Manhattan firm and I'm supposed to be there by the end of the week."

I stopped in my tracks. I felt as if I'd been slapped. I *felt* like saying what a rat she was for not telling me sooner, or at least something about how much I was going to miss her.

All I *actually* said was, "But that's not right. She got on the plane. In the movies this is where you and I walk off into the fog, and you say, 'Louie, I think this is the beginning of a beautiful friendship.' "

Marcy looked at me with a sympathy so strong I wasn't sure which of us she pitied.

"Yeah, well, Sophia, that's why it's the movies."

We didn't talk again until we said good night when she dropped me at my office.

Two days later Marcy left for New York.

CHAPTER FIFTY-SEVEN

The Roof Falls In

The Ladies didn't object. My mother started to be critical, but I stood my ground. I'd decided overnight that if they didn't like my deal with Veronica, they could just have my resignation. Frankly, given that I hadn't caught Veronica long before, I *should* have resigned.

The great irony, though, was that the incident that brought Veronica to the surface became absolutely moot a few days later. The threatened article about the Ladies was a tempest in a teacup, just before the teacup shattered.

On Friday, November 6, the poor little *Larksdale Herald* managed to reverse (for one day) a decade-long circulation slide with a special afternoon edition.

The special covered that morning's short announcement from Arcturis Corporation: effective in sixty days, Prairie Machine Tools was shutting down and moving all its jobs to Mexico.

Roughly 55 percent of Larksdale's men and 20 percent of its women worked for PMT. The only way to have harmed the town more would have been to atomic-bomb it.

Suddenly nobody cared about a bunch of Ladies buying stock. Not even the Ladies themselves. The *Herald*'s special edition became the sole topic of conversation at their Saturday-morning meeting. Each brought a copy of it to Martha's, and each looked either sick or furious. For the first time I saw them behave aimlessly.

Martha, after letting them in, only returned to her chair and stared blankly at the fireplace flames. Dolly, who in recent months had lost forty pounds by eating right and spending days at her cabin chopping wood and clearing brush, sat by the side table popping Mexican wedding cookies in her mouth with robotic desperation. The rest huddled together, waving copies of the paper and calling the guys from Arcturis names.

I felt like grabbing them and shaking sense into them. Prairie Machine could be shut down, moved to Mexico, or blown off the face of the earth, and none of them would be ruined. Somehow, they'd forgotten that even after Veronica's crimes, they all had money. I was angry because I thought they'd confused themselves with all the helpless Midwesterners they'd seen losing jobs on the evening news over the previous ten years. I expected better sense from them.

Then I realized they weren't worrying about themselves, but about their neighbors. If anything, they were too aware of their own good fortune. It was exactly what bothered them.

I began wondering where, on the standard system of taxonomy, a Sophia fitted—closer to a skunk or a weasel? I'd *thought* I cared about my neighbors—but at crunch time I'd been ready to sit back and smoke cigars.

Just then Martha started the meeting, which became our closest approach ever to an absolute flop. It turned out I wasn't the only one in a foul mood.

We were out of ideas. We'd had an entire year to invent a plan, and the best we'd managed were Band-Aids for gunshot wounds. Now we simply rehashed ideas we'd previously dropped.

Could we sue to preserve the jobs? People had tried that all over the country, without notable success. Hire a PR firm to pressure Arcturis to sweeten their offer with, say, retraining grants? A long shot, at best. Ask the government to help? Hold a press conference? Convert the PMT grounds into an industrial park? Lure foreign companies with tax breaks (to fabulous, sunny Minnesota)?

Other people could do those things at least as well as we could. Indeed, meetings were scheduled all over town and out at the plant to explore them. Nobody needed us.

We couldn't even make any more donations without selling stock. We were out of cash, thanks to our erstwhile accountant.

Of course, we would sell the stock if we thought that would help. The real problem was the Ladies loved to act on some bright idea—and we didn't have one bright idea among us. That made us all by turns grumpy, quarrelsome, and silent.

At eleven o'clock, tired of hearing ourselves complain, and equally tired of the silence, we gave up and went home.

It wasn't until late that afternoon, when Mary Maitland called me, that things got interesting.

CHAPTER FIFTY-EIGHT

Afternoon at the Maitlands'

Mary was just as glad to get home early that morning. Mike had been glum and silent all the previous night. He seemed to be slipping into his old habits of self-contained misery.

Indeed, when Mary returned from our aborted meeting, Mike had pulled a kitchen chair to the window and was staring blankly out at the snow.

"We'll be fine," she said softly, coming up behind him.

He didn't turn to look at her. "Sure." A pause. "It's not that."

"What, then?"

"Just bad luck, I guess." A long silence, then he added reluctantly, "We came up with something at the Hog Farm—something really good. I swear, we could be the next IBM off it."

Mike, who got a lot of mileage out of his complaints, was done. But Mary had heard something extra in his words.

"Wait a minute," she said, not coddling him anymore. "Is this something I could tell the Ladies about? As an investment?"

He twisted in the chair to look back at her.

"I mean, it's not a company secret?" she explained.

Mike thought, then said firmly, "Not if they're shutting us down and moving to Mexico, it isn't." Still, he hesitated an instant before going on, more strongly. "*Heck* no. If they're firing all my guys and throwing away our work, I don't owe them anything."

Now he was excited, too. Pushing the chair forward as he rose, he said, "We figured out—"

But Mary held up a hand. "Wait a minute. Save it. I think you should tell the Ladies."

"Really?" He wanted to go on.

"Absolutely." She was already starting for the phone.

She picked up the receiver. Before dialing, she said, "Oh, and honey? When you tell them, use that line about 'the next IBM.' That'll interest them."

"Oh, yeah?" A certain chipper Minnesota way of saying "yeah" as "ja" was back in his voice.

"Oh, yeah," she answered. Then she got on the line and asked me to help set up a meeting for that night.

CHAPTER FIFTY-NINE

The Damnedest Thing

I got to Martha's about seven-thirty and was the last to arrive. The chairs and sofa had been assembled in a semicircle facing the fireplace.

The Ladies, meanwhile, were crowded around one of Martha's buffet tables. They were looking better—and I was feeling better—without knowing exactly why. Even the room was seeming prettier. I was startled to realize how elegantly, and how quietly, Martha had refurbished it over the past year.

Mike, after his burst of excitement the day before, had decided he still owed something to his bosses. At his request, I'd drawn up a Confidential Disclosure Agreement, a statement promising we'd make no unfair use of anything Mike told us. Since the prospect of Martha's launching a high-tech start-up from her potting shed seemed remote, we all signed without reservations.

The Ladies took their seats. Mike stood beside the fireplace. He was dressed between weekday and weekend: he wore old chino pants but with a good shirt and a tie and an old down jacket over them.

Sounding ill at ease, he began. "Okay. I'm only here because Mary and I were talking this over, and she thought you ought to hear about it." He paused, as if some of us might object. When nobody did, he went on. "I don't know how much you know about this thing called the Internet . . ."

Then he launched into a twenty-minute talk, during which he glanced over at Mary about every thirty seconds—as nearly as I could tell, to see whether she thought he was being too technical.

The essence of his talk was this:

In 1991, three things stood in the way of making the Internet the biggest commercial revolution in human history: security, verification, and transaction processing. In plain English: people had to know their credit-card numbers weren't being stolen; merchants had to know the order received from some computer out in cyberspace really came from the person whose credit card was being charged; and providers needed to get paid—even down to fraction-of-a-cent transactions.

The Hog Farm had solved all three problems.

It was extraordinary, but no miracle. In the early eighties, PMT had invented credit-card-verification systems—the gadgets that link your credit card at the store to your bank—then lost the market to a company called VeriFone, which was a little bit faster to market. But a few years later one of Mike's bright grad students had, in a stroke of genius, foreseen that the Internet (then linking only universities and government labs) was about to explode into a *global* link. No, *the* global link—especially for business. "And we set out to make our software work over that global link and we did it."

For Mike that was a pretty eloquent finale—but now, to our amazement, he outdid himself. I thought he was going to sit down, but he paused and added: "You know, twenty years ago we were first with electronic cash registers, and ten years later with remote credit verification. Those were nothing to this. With the right leadership, this could make us the . . . uh, the next IBM."

Mike looked quickly to Mary, who nodded in approval. He cleared his throat and said, "I don't know how good a job I've done of explaining. So if you've got any questions . . . fire away."

And fire they did. Amid all the questions, here's what struck me most:

The Internet in 1991 was no better known than personal computers had been in 1985. But in '85 the Ladies had been laughably ignorant.

They weren't laughable now.

They knew the score and they asked the right questions—about risks, competitors, and rollout times. (Mike said five years for the Internet to show up everywhere, but pieces of the NetLink software, for company-to-company links, were salable immediately, at shocking profit margins.) And on and on—for better than an hour—with Mike getting calmer and more persuasive the more technical the questions became.

The last questions all came from Skye and were highly technical indeed. Their talk was interesting—not that I understood much of it—but it was entirely off the point.

The one great truth about small-town life was that we knew each other to the bone. In beige chinos, faded pink pin-striped shirt, and dark blue tie, Mike hardly looked like a high-tech wizard. But if he said flat out they could deliver the product, they could deliver the product.

Which was why Martha's question, coming at the end of the hour, was the whole ball game. After Skye was done with the technical issues, Martha asked, "I realize it's hard to guarantee these things—but if we can somehow get hold of this software business, can you make a go of it?"

Mike seemed to be looking off into the distance, but it was just that he was considering carefully. After a second he nodded. "Yeah," he said slowly. "We can."

Nobody spoke after that—if this had been a regular venture-capital pitch, you'd have assumed Mike had flopped. But this was Larksdale, and we knew what Mike's word was worth. He couldn't have been more convincing if he'd delivered Churchill's "We will fight them on the beaches . . ." speech.

But Mike, instead of waiting for applause, just raised a hand and said, "Thank you, ladies"—then added, a little more softly, to Mary, "I'll see you at home, honey," and started for the door.

He hesitated by the snack table, reached for one of the Mexican wedding cookies, but then drew back his hand and continued for the exit.

He wasn't sure he was entitled.

I wanted to run after him, give him the whole plate, and tell him, "Nice job, Don Pedro."

CHAPTER SIXTY

The Ladies Vote

The Ladies knew they had to move fast if they were going to have a chance to make a difference. They took a ten-minute break and settled to decide.

Martha, who meant to go down if she had to with the patrician flag nailed to the mast, started them off.

"Making money isn't the only issue. I think we owe something to the town. If somebody else wanted to save it, I'd gladly say we should step aside. But I don't see anybody else volunteering."

A silence, then Agnes asked nervously, "How do we know that stuff will actually work?" She wasn't always heroic.

"Are you saying you don't believe Mike?" Mary demanded, though she'd promised herself she'd stay neutral.

"Of course I believe him," Agnes answered hastily. "I just wonder why all those big corporate hotshots are throwing his work away."

"They're New Yorkers. They think we're village idiots who can't do anything intelligent." *I* threw that in. I figured it would get the Ladies steamed.

It did.

"Well, they're *wrong*," Agnes declared.

"We're smart enough, I guess," Dolly added.

"You bet on it!" Gladys couldn't help herself. "Why, we could . . ."

In seconds, with pride as the spark, the entrepreneurial fires were blazing; the Ladies were whizzing plans at one another. And very soon those plans coalesced around one dazzling super-idea so grand it scared and excited them at the same time.

They'd have to buy the company.

They might later spin off parts of it, but going in—and on very short notice—they'd have to bid for everything. The company's less glorious parts, the cash registers and such, were going to pay the bills until the software started selling. Besides, if they just closed down those old-line businesses and laid off the workers, how would they be better than Arcturis?

Even for the Ladies this was close to overwhelming. Prairie Machine Tool, after all, was the heart and soul of Larksdale. And it was also something else.

"You realize," Deborah offered tartly, "that a couple of thousand guys are going to have to get used to the idea of women owning the main source of power in this town."

Skye couldn't contain herself. "Oh, yeah. We'll have to sit around and smoke all the cigars and drink all the brandy. Tough job. And tough break for them."

Skye's tone was more amused than harsh. The others picked up on it.

"And do all the hard stuff, like go to Rotarian dinners. And take business trips to Europe."

"And drive company cars."

"And give money to United Way every year."

"Oh, I think we can manage that one."

Skye, who had started this, ended it. "What? Women run things? I'm shocked!"

Still, Deborah, who'd been out in the world more than the others, tried to remind them that men could play rather rough. "Trust me. They'll be yelling that we brought PMS to PMT."

"So let 'em yell," Skye answered firmly. "If we own the place, there'll be just two categories of men in Larksdale. Those who want to help us save the town and those who are *leaving* town."

This sounded a little harsh to some of the others—I could see Dolly, Agnes, and Gladys were uncomfortable with it.

It was Dolly who spoke. Since she had perhaps the least reason to honor the town's tradition of male power, what she said surprised us.

"Look," she began, "I know they've been pretty rotten to us, some of them, but they're our neighbors—our families—and they're in trouble. I don't think this is about trying to beat anybody up. I move we try to help—by buying Prairie Machine, if that's possible. But whatever we do, let's do it with good hearts."

To my amazement, I saw Deborah and Skye were both touched by this. Deborah whispered to Dolly, quite fondly, "You sure know how to take the fun out of stuff, kid." Then, more loudly, she added, "Second the motion. What the hell. If we can't avoid it, let's be heroes—and make a fortune."

The Ladies looked startled—several reddened—then slowly they began relaxing.

A nod went around the room, like a very genteel version of the Wave at a baseball game. A murmur accompanied it, and they had decided to launch their first corporate raid—on a very spiritual plane, of course.

They weren't the same sweet ladies they used to be.

Martha tapped her teacup with her spoon and announced primly, "Motion carried."

Everyone was rising, when Deborah called, over the noise of shifting chairs—

"Hey! I hate to mess everything up, but who're we going to get to *run* it?"

"Run what?" Dolly asked.

"The *company*?" Deborah replied with nearly the inflection everybody uses for the word "duh?"

"I mean," she went on, "I don't know about you, but I might have just a little bit of trouble running the next IBM."

"You'd have trouble running the next Hair Club for Men," Gladys said in a good-natured return of fire for Deb's shot at Dolly.

Deb took it well. "Yeah, two million bald guys—just what I need," she answered genially.

Then, waving her hands in assent (and to draw the Ladies back from the snack table), she went on. "Point is, we've learned a lot about investing over the last eight years—and heck, with enough time we probably *could* learn to run IBM. But right now, no way. True?"

Skye shot me an urgent glance. I could see from her look, like a greyhound straining at a leash, that she wanted to make a bid for the job. But at the same instant I saw it, the look went out of her eyes. She knew she wasn't ready for the post.

I'd taken little part in the discussion. I'd assumed from the moment Mike stopped talking they were going to try to buy the company. They just needed time to convince themselves.

Instead I'd been thinking, without success, about exactly Deborah's question: who would we get to run PMT? Mike was brilliant—he was also a fine human being and the right guy to walk down a dark alley with you. But CEO? Not even in Lake Woebegone.

But just then—

I suddenly had a flash—much like a kick in the stomach—of discovery. I realized I knew the perfect person to run Prairie Machine Tool. For the brief, kicking moment I thought the person was me. Then, with a weird blend of relief, disappointment, and alarm, I realized it was someone else.

The perfect candidate was Milton Green.

CHAPTER SIXTY-ONE

The Perfect Man, Except . . .

Milton Green, as you already know, had been my study partner in law school. That had been my one unqualified piece of academic luck, since Milt had, by common consent, the best mind of anyone in my entire class. He was, as my friend Becky Overton put it, "Order of the Coif—with sideburns."

He was also one of those rare, sweet people who seem incapable of giving offense—even to hard-nosed law students who prided themselves on being p.o.'d by anything less than buccaneer ruthlessness. Partly it was his innate good temper: he was generally about as happy as one of those dancing green flubber people. Partly it was his sense of humor: happy himself, he also had the wit to make other people happy. And partly—eccentric as this was in law school—it was his genuine goodness. Milt would help the biggest jerks in the class whenever they asked.

Besides, even those competitive jerks who hated his brains took solace in knowing that except for studying with me four nights a week, Milt had as much chance of getting a date as I did of playing in the Rose Bowl.

You see, unfortunately, Milt also bore an unsettling resemblance to Bill Gates's homely brother. He was six-feet-two; weighed one hundred and forty-five pounds; and had unkempt curly hair, medium-thick glasses, crooked teeth, and the fashion sense of a minor Balkan bureaucrat under Stalin.

He also had—probably proof that genius and madness are closely connected—an absolutely inexplicable crush on me.

The result, of course, was that I found myself telling him at least once a week what good friends we were—both because it was true and because the last thing I wanted was for him to get the wrong idea. Milton, of course, took it like a gentleman, the way he took everything else. Still, there was always just an instant of hurt on that kind face of his. Only somebody who enjoyed kicking puppies—or little green flubber people—would have enjoyed telling Milton what good friends we were. Even if she meant it.

In fact, I went so far to avoid hurting him that during fall term of our second year, when he was short on money, I invited him to my parents' house for Thanksgiving. This struck me as a brilliant plan for at least three reasons. First, it was kind. Second, it would convince my parents I had at least the rudiments of a social life. Third, by showing him my family, I figured I'd get rid of Milt's unspoken romantic ambitions once and for all.

I was particularly certain that Milt would get a frosty reception from my dad, who doubted the masculinity of any male who'd not gotten his nose broken at least twice before graduating high school.

Except for the slight risk that Dad and my brothers would take Milt out to the backyard and beat him senseless, it seemed like the perfect plan.

Unfortunately things worked out vastly differently.

It started about ten-thirty on Thanksgiving morning. The doorbell rang; my parents opened it, and Milt stood there, holding what looked like a particularly delicious homemade pecan pie.

"Hi! I'm Milt. I made this for you," he said, handing it to my mom.

"You baked a pie?" Dad asked ominously.

I felt no remorse. I'd warned Milt my dad believed a man's role in life began with sports, veered toward work, and returned to sports.

But Milt looked surprised. "What's wrong with baking? Bill Mazerewski used to bake. He made the team a coconut chiffon cake the night before game six of the forty-nine World Series, then hit three-for-four."

I almost started laughing. I was sure Milt was making this up.

But Dad answered, "You mean four-for-five." And my smile dropped a notch. If Milt had ever read a baseball book, I was in trouble. Because if he *had* read one, it was the *Baseball Encyclopedia,* and he remembered every word of it.

Milt shook his head. "He reached first in the fifth on a throwing error by Franzetti."

"Oh, yeah," Dad said after a moment's thought—and I stopped smiling altogether. "You're right."

From the kitchen door, still holding the open pie box, Mom called, "Mack, come smell this pie. It smells delicious. I think it has brandy in it!"

"Be there in a minute, babe. I want Milt, here, to see my football trophies."

Milt was in solid, and I was in trouble. I decided to go into the kitchen and see how vanilla ice cream would taste covered with cooking sherry.

*I*t only got worse from there. By the time we left on Sunday morning to drive back to Chicago, my father had announced that Milt was "a hell of a guy for a pencil-neck," and my mother was trying to decide whether my bridesmaids would look better in turquoise organdy or pink silk. My life had become like a lost episode of *The X-Files.* The one starring Lucy Ricardo.

. . . .

L made sure Milt never returned to Larksdale, but that didn't stop my parents from asking about him every few weeks. Accordingly, it was with great relief that I bid Milt a warm farewell at the end of third year. I drove him to the airport; his new firm was flying him to New York first-class. I even kissed him good-bye. It wasn't as unpleasant as I'd feared. In fact, it was rather nice.

Milton took a job in Manhattan—with Skadden, Arps, as a matter of fact. In those days, Skadden was about as far up the legal ladder as you could start, even if your daddy owned the ladder, which Milton's daddy certainly did not.

From then on, Milton at a distance became ever dearer to me. Part of it was just fond memories, but a bigger part was that the best and the funniest part of Milt came through in his letters and, beginning after a few years, his e-mails. Milt was the first great e-mailist I'd met.

The slightly alarming aspect of these notes was the way they charted his skyrocketing career. Among the many highlights:

—From Milton, two years after graduation: *Congratulate me! Junior partner!*

—From Milton, two years after that: *Don't think I'm crazy, but I'm going for my MBA. If you're in Philadelphia next fall, don't hesitate to drop in!* (Every letter, he made sure I understood it would be okay for me to drop in, if I happened to be in the area—or within, say, a two-thousand-mile radius).

—From Milton, another two years later: *Guess who's Wharton class valedictorian?*

—From Milton, a week after that: *Guess who just got recruited by McKinsey?*

McKinsey, of course, was the Dallas Cowboys of business consulting firms, famous for charging $100 million or so to reengineer a company so it ran just fine with half as many employees, or crushed the foreign competition, or did other phenomenal things. So, six years out of law school, Milt was the fair-haired boy of the world's hottest business consulting group.

I, meanwhile, had skyrocketed all the way from attorney to my mom's investment club to—attorney for my mom's investment club. I felt like a film clip of one of those early American rocket tests, where there's a small puff of smoke, then the missile falls over on the pad.

In short, I had issues—a whole memo pad's worth of them—concerning Milton. Envy was one. Friendship was another—and not the least of them. For years I'd kept a particularly geeky-looking photo of Milt. I thought it would prevent me from romanticizing him in his absence; but in a certain annoying way, I'd grown ever fonder of that picture as the years passed.

Photos are sneaky that way.

*A*ccordingly, I took the proper precautions to make certain I wasn't pushing Milt as a candidate for my own personal reasons. My memory may not be in Milt's class, but it's good, and I dredged up everything I could remember about his grades, his job interviews, his personal life. I really did my own mental background check on him—and couldn't come up with a thing against him. Unless his being so fond of me was a sign of incipient mental illness.

My mind had reported the result out of committee in ten seconds or less. My heart just needed a couple of hours to ratify it. I fished my mittens out of the jacket pocket, donned them, and walked another thirty minutes until my nose was numb. Then I veered into the nearest Starbucks to steady my nerves with a tall, skinny latte and a cranberry-orange scone.

I deserved it. I'd decided to call the Ladies together to propose we offer Milt the job.

Time was so short, we scheduled an extra meeting on Tuesday morning to decide. It was, for all the cozy informality, a most serious meeting—not only because the Ladies had become business professionals, but because we had decided no other candidates were within our reach.

Absolutely determined to treat the proposal as pure business, I wrote out my summary of Milt and read it word for word. I covered very neatly his academic record, career successes, and business philosophy. I spoke for ten minutes precisely.

When I was done I pushed my glasses back up on my nose and said:

"In conclusion, I believe Milton Green's credentials make him a viable candidate, and upon direction of the members, I am prepared to invite him to Minnesota for an interview by the Club."

At which point my mom leaned over to Martha and said quite primly and quite loudly, "He was Sophia's old boyfriend in law school."

I was mortally determined never to end a business presentation by yelling, *"Mom!"* in an aggrieved voice. So I gathered my papers and walked directly from the room, staring at the floor and afraid my cheeks were about to burst into flames.

I got back to the office about one, and shortly after I arrived, Gladys called. She said they'd taken a vote and wanted to offer the job to my boyfriend. I clenched my teeth and muttered, "Okay." Then I hung up and put my head down on the desk with my hands pressed over my ears.

After that, I asked Heidi for Milton's number and dialed it.

I shifted the receiver to my left hand so I could wipe the sweat off my right one.

"Milton Green's office."

She had an English-public-school accent. English executive secretaries were all the rage that year. She also sounded about twenty-five and extremely sexy. I hated her.

But I managed to choke out my name and was confounded to hear her ask at once, "Milt's old law-school chum?" in a tone I took to be snidely condescending. I wondered how on earth she could have heard from my mother. After a second's silence she added, "He's in a meeting"—I decided I was being blown off—"but I know he'll want to talk with you. Can you hold?"

I said I could, and then she put me on hold. Two minutes later she was back.

"Sophia?"

"Yes?"

"He'll be with you in two minutes."

"So I guess he was in a meeting with, like, the Coke machine?"

Her voice got very low and confidential. "Not exactly. It's Jack Welsh, CEO of General Electric?"

"Sorry."

"Not at all. You're just the way Milt described you. Charming."

That's me: a size-sixteen mouth in a size-seven face. I said, "Oh," and fell silent.

It actually took about five minutes before Milt's voice said, "Hey, there!"

Having meanwhile decided I was going to be as tough as "Neutron Jack" Welsh, I imagined myself smoking a foot-long Havana cigar. Then I imagined myself coughing uncontrollably. Then I said gruffly, "You still interested in running your own show?"

And he answered, "Prairie Machine?"

So much for getting a jump on Milt.

"How'd you know?"

"I'm not dumb, Sophia. But that company's in a lot of trouble."

"Is that a no?"

"It's a yes, for you."

Sophia has the ball at the top of the key. She moves to shoot.

"There's something about it you don't know—that nobody knows."

"Don't tell me now. I'll have to call Legal and see if I'm conflicted out."

The shot's blocked. Milt meant he couldn't be involved in any activity that conflicted with the interests of any McKinsey client—in this case, he needed to see if they represented Arcturis or any of its divisions. He was right, of course; but I was disappointed.

"So you want to bail out?"

"No, I want to call Legal, then get on a plane. I can't come today. How about tomorrow morning?"

"Call my office. I'll pick you up at the airport. Remember what I look like?"

"I remember everything about you."

"You remember everything about Bobo Kysmatsky's one at-bat with the thirty-six Brooklyn Dodgers," I replied, and hung up.

CHAPTER SIXTY-TWO

The Storm
Blows In

As if we needed anything else to complicate our lives, that December was the prelude to the worst Minnesota winter in sixty-some years—and when you're talking Minnesota winters, you're talking the World Series of ice and snow.

The first two weeks of the month had been a real Whitman's Sampler of frozen water: we had (in no particular order) hail, sleet, frost, snow, and slush. Mother Nature was behaving like a fussy baby.

But that morning when I went to pick up Milt, the Old Lady pulled out all the stops: the forecast on my clock radio was, roughly, for blizzards with a 50 percent chance of the end of the world.

For safety's sake, I had borrowed Heidi's Jeep. It sure wasn't one of those luxo-mobiles so common today. It was a flat-black, web-seated, roll-barred antique. I had a feeling that if I'd rummaged around long enough under the backseat, I'd've found one of General Patton's old K rations.

We were sure going to impress the hell out of McKinsey's fair-haired boy.

It took me fifteen minutes, with the defroster on full, to chip all the ice off the front windshield, and by then it had started snowing again. I knocked as much accumulation as I could off the pebbly black vinyl top, then wrestled open the balky door and dove inside. The interior was no more than five or ten degrees colder than the outside.

Just before a really big storm, the clouds get a certain glassiness, like mirrors; they had that now. The front wasn't all the way in; but as far as it had advanced, the sky was inky black. The engine had been warming for a good quarter hour and was still stuttering. The last thing I wanted to hear was another weather report, so I rummaged between the seats for audiotapes. Heidi's taste was, well, eclectic: two Beatles albums, one Charlie Musselwhite, and three classical albums. I plugged in *The Best of Richard Wagner,* and "The Ride of the Valkyries"—perfect for Heidi, but ridiculous for me—boomed out of the speakers.

For no particular reason, I yelled, "I give it a nine, Dick. Great melody, but you can't dance to it." I cranked up the volume, turned the wheel, and punched the gas—and found out four-wheel-drive is nearly as great as they say it is.

Except for one pretty interesting encounter when I decided to downshift and zip around a jackknifing truck, the ride was dull as dishwater.

I was at the airport twenty minutes early. It seemed odd; my heart was beating hard. But the snowplows were rumbling across the runways, and planes were circling. The arrival time for Flight 818 was suddenly pushed back an hour—which in Minneapolis in winter means a 90 percent chance it was going to be diverted to another airport.

Despite my gloomy expectations, the good-looking boy in the mock pilot's uniform behind the Northwest counter said he was more like 90 percent sure the snow was going to quit, and the plane really would land in an hour. So I sat in one of the chilly black plastic chairs to wait out the time.

I was calm by then, and even a little bored when the door to the passenger tunnel opened, and a minute later the first passengers began straggling out.

I was looking for my geeky best pal, when this gorgeous guy, strong and lean like a tennis pro, with curly brown hair and soft brown eyes, stopped in front of me and eyed me curiously. He was handsome enough to rate attention—but he was blocking my view of the other passengers, who were rushing by.

As I stepped around him, he asked rather plaintively, "Sophia?"

I looked—and blinked—and looked again. It was like *The Exorcist:* Milt's voice was coming out of this Adonis's mouth.

"Milt?"

He was laughing—not at me, really, but with a bubbling personal satisfaction. It ought to have been deeply annoying, but—

"Yeah. Weird, huh?" He said it with so obvious a plea for approval that I forgave him instantly.

"But you're . . ." I was looking up at his curly locks.

"Hairstylist," he said.

My gaze dropped. "And you're . . ."

"Contact lenses, and braces for two years."

My eyes had drifted down a little farther.

"And *you're* . . ."

"Weights and running, alternate days, and tae kwon do. I'll test for black belt in the spring." He started laughing again. "And we still finish each other's sentences, and I'll thank you to go no lower with your questions—for one thing, you don't have any baseline info for a comparison. And besides, it's *my* turn to tell *you* how beautiful you look and to say how much I've missed you. Which was a lot."

He looked at me until I got embarrassed—which was about four seconds, probably. Then I realized *he* was embarrassed. "I mean," he finished up, "why do you think I went through all this? 'Milt, the ugly yuppling'?"

Suddenly blushing, he straightened the shoulder strap of his flight bag, then held out his hand. "Come on. Let's go over the proposal. Then I've got a proposal of my own I want you to hear."

CHAPTER SIXTY-THREE

Working Again

Maybe Milt had used up his stocks of boldness, or maybe it was just force of habit for him to treat me like his best friend. In either case, long before we'd reached the chill of the parking garage, we were talking as if we were back in law school, without a hint of romance.

In one way, the change was disappointing, as if we'd retreated from what was most important. In another, it created a great rush of nostalgia. When, pulling the Jeep's door shut beside him, Milt suddenly yelled, "Snack run!", I had a sudden flash of pleasant panic, an irrational reminder of the days when I wondered whether I'd survive the contracts final.

Actually Milt had something else in mind before we hit the 7-Eleven. He was eager that—blizzard or no blizzard—we drive straight out to Prairie Machine's main plant. That meant a detour, but I was game.

The long drive went pleasantly enough, but as we sped along the security fence behind the company's air strip, the weather turned nasty, with snow flurrying in the gusty winds.

I stopped the Jeep behind a small power station, just outside the perimeter's barbed-wire-topped Cyclone fence. The station blocked us from view, but not from the wind, which was roaring.

Feeling uneasy, and with the winds buffeting the Jeep, I asked, "Can't we do our industrial espionage over coffee from my office? With computers, these days—"

"Shush," he answered. He'd donned some $2,000 Armani fur-lined parka and, with a Huck Finn gleam of enthusiasm on his face, looked like Nanook of Rockefeller Center. Fishing binoculars from the side pocket of his soft luggage, he stepped outside and around the corner of the power station.

He was focusing the glasses on the back of the main plant, a couple of hundred yards away. The snow was blowing up pretty hard, and following him, I was getting annoyed.

"Oh, honey," I said, "our own little manufacturing plant. With a white picket fence and roses in front, it'll be just perfect."

He handed me the glasses and said, "My eyes aren't that good. Are those guys on the loading docks using clipboards or laptop computers?"

I squinted through the binoculars.

"Clipboards."

"Fuckin' great!" he said, and slapped mittened fist into mittened palm.

Now that I'd figured out what he was doing, it was easy enough to help: after all, I'd been hearing snippets about the company's obsolete technology and outdated methods from my friends and family for years.

I handed him back the glasses and said coolly, "It's worse than that. They're running five separate computer systems: inventory, manufacturing, personnel, general accounting, and billing—and none of them can talk to the others."

Milt's face began glowing. "God, you're good. We'll rip 'em all out and switch over to SAP R/3 on HP—save six hundred grand the first year!"

"Hell, yes!" I answered stoutly, and made a mental note to ask

Skye what the hell "SAP R/3 on HP" was. It sounded like a line from an engineering rap song.

"Come on," I added. "I'll buy you lunch."

"Great! I saw a little diner about three miles back, off the freeway. I can try native Minnesota cuisine."

"Native Minnesota cuisine," I said, "is lutefisk in dill butter sauce. It would kill a goat."

I drove us eight miles back to the Black Angus.

CHAPTER SIXTY-FOUR

We Sprint for the Finish

The next seventy-two hours may make dull telling, but they were, in some ways, the best of my life—lack of sleep and acute indigestion notwithstanding.

We reached my office about one. Heidi jumped up when we arrived and, seeing me walk in with a gorgeous stranger, blurted out, "Sophia! What happened to your funny-looking friend!?"

Looking closer and realizing her mistake, Heidi blushed bright red. Realizing why she'd made it, I blushed a brighter red. An instant later Milt figured out what was going on, and *he* turned crimson. The place looked like the sunburn clinic at St. Tropez.

Heidi tried to redeem herself by taking my elbow and pulling me into the next room, where she leaned close to me, and whispered, "You are a very dishonest woman and you ought to be ashamed of yourself. And incidentally, your mother's right: if you don't marry him, you're crazy."

"Don't be silly. And who invited you to—"

"Crazy," she repeated, and stepped past me, back into the reception area. From there I heard her say in her best professional voice, "If you'll step over here, Mr. Green, I have the nondisclosure agreements you need to sign."

*H*eidi had been organizing the documents sent over by Harvey Dettermeier, the temporary head of PMT. Technically I couldn't let Milt see any of them until he signed the nondisclosure agreement, promising that he would keep what he read to himself. He signed it; Heidi witnessed it; and then I had her fax a copy to Harvey and put the original in an overnight envelope to be FedEx'd to him.

The paperwork filled sixteen legal-size banker's boxes. That formed merely a fraction of the documentation; but complete due diligence would be done only after we had a deal.

Milt opened his trial case and pulled out yellow legal pads and pens. Handing me one of each, he grinned and said, "My share of costs."

"Snookered again," I answered.

"I figure I'll do the numbers, you do the legal side. Anything we have questions about, we tag—then go over the tags together later. Okay?"

I pulled two of the boxes toward me. "Okay. Talk to you later."

*H*eidi left at midnight, with Milt walking her to her car for safety. When he returned, I was yawning.

"It's getting late. Where are you staying? I'll drop you—"

I stopped. He was blinking at me in a way I recognized.

"Where am I staying? Same as you—right here." He looked around quickly. "In fact, dibs on the couch."

I tried to laugh; but the best I managed was a sort of open-mouthed gurgle. Only Meg Ryan could make a noise that way and not sound like an idiot—and I'm not Meg Ryan. So I hurried. "You're kidding, right?"

"Not unless you got old and soft when I wasn't looking." He sat down on the couch and patted it for me to join him. I was about to remind him he was my best friend when I saw that the look in his eye was entirely businesslike.

When I sat, he gave me a look that was equal parts excitement, affection, and forced seriousness. He almost took my hand, stopped himself, and said, "You know very well your call gave me a shot at the three things I want in life: to be near you, to run my own business, and—well, yeah—to do some good for pretty nice people.

"But precisely *because* I want it, I intend to be realistic about our chances." He sat up very straight, then leaned a little bit toward me. "We've got three major strikes against us: we've got no time, no credibility, and probably not enough money. The way we're going to overcome those are, in order, nonstop work, a drop-dead-great presentation, and the smartest deal structure that you, I, and those brilliant ladies of yours can invent."

"You think we don't have a chance."

"I think we have *a* chance. One shot. This is December eighteenth. If we have our pitch ready in seventy-two hours—and it's good enough—we'll sell it to your ladies on the twenty-first. If the Ladies sign on, we send the offer letter to Arcturis by same-day air courier. We give Arcturis three days to decide. That makes it the twenty-fourth, which is the last possible day this year we'll get them out here for a meeting—and also convenient because the plant closes on the twenty-third for the Christmas holiday, which means we can meet out there without drawing a lot of attention. And I can tell you right now that if we don't get them out here before year's end, we can forget it. The machinery to crate up Prairie Tool and ship it out will be in gear, and no way will they stop.

"So that's the short form—which is all we have time for. I'm talking about starting right now and going until we have a deal outline or get carried out feet first, and if that's not how you see it, then thanks for the tour of Larksdale, and let's have dinner in the next millennium. Because you won't be the Sophia I came to see."

"So what do you say?"

"They can't possibly close a deal before year's end."

"Doesn't matter. It's an instinct to nail deals before year's end. Trust me. All we need is their John Hancocks on a deal memo." He grinned. "Heck, at least it's a short season. Christmas Eve night we go home in a Cadillac, or we're out of the game." He paused—and, being Milt, smiled, leaned back, and flipped a loose-wristed hand, as if it didn't matter.

"So what do you say?"

It was the oddest moment of my life. My heart was beating wildly.

"God, you know how to turn me on. Let's go get 'em."

He looked at me and grinned, and in most Shakespearean tones misquoted from *Henry V:* "Lawyers now abed in England will think themselves accursed, and hold their pinstripes cheap, while any speak who fought with us upon St. Nicholas's Day."

"I saw that play," I answered, "and that's not how the line goes."

"You want a writer or a takeover artist?" he said while he rose and started again for the boxes of documents.

*N*ot much more need be said about those three days. We were by turns serious, giddy, angry with each other, and too tired to see straight. We slept in short naps—and by the end of the second night, we were generally cuddled up against each other in various sprawls reminiscent of sheep on a cold meadow. By day three, when we began drafting the proposal, we were bleary and rumpled, and Milt had the unshaved look of the hero in a French detective movie. One more Big Mac, and I was going to start wearing a sesame-seed bun for a hat.

It wasn't exactly moonlight and roses, but it was perfect for us. And our report was even better.

CHAPTER SIXTY-FIVE

The Best Meeting Ever

I knew Milt was smart, but that morning I found out he was brilliant.

We met with the Ladies at Martha's at seven A.M. on the twenty-first. The courier was scheduled to pick up the proposal at my office at eleven, which gave us roughly three hours to sell it to the Ladies and get their signatures.

Milt's first idea was that I should give the presentation, but I vetoed that. "They're betting on you to run the company, not me. Besides, those ladies know everything about me, starting with how I look in a diaper and going forward from there. If they don't trust me by now, it's hopeless."

His second, better idea was to treat the Ladies with absolute respect. Milt had spent his previous seven years hobnobbing with everybody from Supreme Court justices to CEOs of Fortune 100 companies. If he had talked down to the Ladies, it would have been understandable but disastrous. As it was, he charmed them by treating them with absolute seriousness—and then by letting them in on the biggest joke of all.

Of course, the Ladies had come a huge distance since their first business meeting, those years ago. But they still *looked* like pretty ordinary Midwestern housewives—and Milt had brains enough to see beyond that.

He was in high spirits, cleaned up and confident. He'd found just what he wanted in the PMT financial documents: the right blend of superficial problems and underlying strengths that made a quick turnaround possible. I'd found no legal land mines—and frankly it hadn't been until day two that he'd actually grasped that the Ladies' total holdings, including stocks and real estate, were just at $14.5 million, with Dell and Microsoft (thank you, Skye) our key holdings.

*H*e started just right. While handing out the proposal copies, he told them: "Ladies, I don't want you to think I'm slighting your decision-making process. But speed matters, so please keep that in mind.

"I'm going to hand out copies of the proposal; I'm going to go over it carefully; and then I'm going to ask for questions—but as few of them as possible."

He nodded to me. "Sophia's told you our situation. So stop me if you need to; but remember: we're cutting this so close that minutes count."

When they had the copies, he gave them the inevitable minute of flipping through, then said, "We believe one great factor's running in our favor: Arcturis bought PMT from the heirs at a fire-sale price: we can cut them a deal we can afford that will let them turn a hundred percent profit in under eighteen months, get a problem off their books, *and* look like sensitive corporate citizens.

"Now, they may not give a da—darn about Larksdale, but they've got to love the numbers part of it. *That*'s why we have a shot."

That said, he cleared his throat, picked up his copy of the proposal, and started reading.

It took more than an hour to go through the document. Where

we had doubts, he admitted them. He moved fast, but the impression was of purposefulness, not some used-car hustle. I was so anxious I could scarcely sit still. But I wasn't worried any longer about Milt.

I'd picked the right guy.

When Milt finished, Skye asked the question that counted: "If I understand what you've put in writing—and what you've told us—we're probably committed for every cent we've got."

Milt raised his eyebrows at me approvingly, then answered her. "I'd go farther. On the best deal Sophia and I have been able to put together, the odds are it will take every penny you've got, every penny I've got, and probably every penny we can collectively borrow."

He took just the right pause, then said, "But it'll be worth it." And then, to my amazement, Milt grinned, and added, "And even though I can't explain just yet, I can promise you this will be the most fun you've ever had in business."

He'd hit just the right note of conspiratorial fun—just the sort of thing the Ladies liked best. I thought he was absolutely charming.

Still, if the Ladies were going to fold up and go home, that was the moment.

The room grew awfully quiet.

Milt waited a moment, then added softly, "You're betting a lot on Sophia and me, I know; and of course there's risk."

I wasn't sure that was the right line.

But they exchanged glances, in the manner I'd come to know so well, and then Martha said, "I think you missed the point. We're investors. In this case, we're investing in you and Sophia, to help us invest in Prairie Machine. We don't expect to avoid risk; we expect you to do your best."

That was the whole debate. I'd been holding the air-courier envelope. Now I opened it, took out the last two copies, flipped to the last page of each, and signed. Then I handed the pen to Martha, and she signed as managing partner.

I took one copy from her and slipped it back into the envelope.

That small ceremony was a formality, I suppose, but they deserved it.

Milt said, "Thank you, Ladies."

I thought, *God have mercy on us now.*

We shook hands all around, and then Milt and I dashed for the door.

It was eight-twenty; we'd met for eighty minutes, and I don't think any two minutes had gone by in a row without Milt's checking the clock on Martha's mantel. I was going to have to talk with him about that.

As we hit the sidewalk, we were running.

*O*f course, there was a hitch.

Normally these deals move forward one of two ways: either you are a major corporation with a huge business-development group to make the first contact, or else you hire some big powerful organization—a major law or investment-banking firm to represent you.

We certainly weren't a major corporation, and the fees for a top law firm or investment bank easily run into the millions of dollars.

We didn't have credibility ourselves and we couldn't afford to hire it. Given the time pressure, there was only one hope.

We needed someone *very* important to call ahead and make sure the president of Arcturis would read our proposal the minute he got it, instead of kicking it over to some subordinate, or (most likely alternative) heaving it into the nearest trash can.

Our solution wasn't elegant, but it *was* the best we could contrive.

Milt was going to call in his IOUs. He was also going to beg every favor he could from every important person he'd ever helped, impressed, or even fought against successfully in his career.

We had one day to establish our bona fides, and that was our only shot.

Milt had waited this long because of a character quirk—until he absolutely believed we had a real deal to offer, he couldn't have sounded convincing.

Now, the minute we dashed back into my office, he turned to me and said, "I can't do it with you watching. Come back in sixty minutes."

It was, of course, my office; but this was no time to stand on principle. I nodded, straightened my hat and coat, and left.

When I returned, the first thing I asked was, "Who'd you call?"

"Friends."

"*Who?*"

"You wouldn't believe me if I told you."

"Don't pull that."

"Okay," he said after a pause. And told me.

And you wouldn't believe me if I told you. But I was sure of one thing:

The proposal would be read.

CHAPTER SIXTY-SIX

The Longest Day

Waiting, for people like Milt and me, is the hardest thing in the world. Unfortunately Milt and I had set ourselves up to do nothing else: we'd handed off our fate (at least, as much of it as we could see that day) to a bunch of New York executives. Now the only way we could help our cause was to make sure we were there to answer the phone, in case they decided to call.

The courier picked up the proposal twenty minutes after I returned to the office. We had debated hand-carrying it to New York, but finally decided, on nothing but instinct, that this was wiser: a courier was better theater and made us seem less desperate.

The downside was it left us drumming our fingers and suffering our doubts. We had calculated the package couldn't reach Manhattan in under four and a half hours. We were free until then; but afterward we felt obliged to be available at the phone every minute until we heard back.

How to fill the next four hours? And how to occupy ourselves while stuck in the office over the following days? Those questions were all we had to distract us while we tried not to go nuts waiting for the phone to ring.

Driving into the Cities for holiday shopping sounded repulsive;

none of the six movies playing at the Larksdale Multiplex held the slightest appeal; and we wanted to be back in four hours, on the remote chance New York might answer sooner than we imagined.

We decided to walk downtown to stock up on supplies—especially reading material and snacks.

A year before, Larksdale's main street at Christmas had seemed battered, under siege—but still hopeful. The people of Larksdale had endured uncertainty; but now ruin was at hand. They were good folks, but not that good. Now, as Milt and I pushed forward against an icy, raging wind, I saw a kind of meanness had entered some eyes, a giving-up gone over to anger. Hopes had been dashed too many times: it was like repetitive emotion injury. Something evil and cruel was in the air. Call it, if the phrase isn't too melodramatic, the stench of rotting dreams.

We spent a few minutes in the town's last bookstore, where Milt thoughtlessly brought out too large a wad of folded bills and drew stares of dislike. He quickly realized his mistake and thrust the money back in his pocket, but it was too late. I was upset to see him not fitting in; and wondering why I should care so much.

We returned to my office with books and sandwiches from Maggie's diner, sent Heidi home, made coffee, and sat eating and reading.

I also spent a bit of time watching Milt. I liked everything about him—even his choosing a copy of *Persuasion* after he saw me pick *Mansfield Park,* but I was annoyed at how often I looked up at him.

Very likely, other people would have seen it as a time for romance. Not us, not then. The deal was looming too large. We were full-time, type A work obsessives.

Still, when we finally gave up at midnight—one A.M. in New York—and I was driving Milt to his hotel, I had the strongest desire to invite him to come home with me.

But I still had just barely enough sense to know a really bad idea, and I dropped him at the Holiday Inn a little before midnight, while the wind howled bitterly.

*T*he night was a sleepless nightmare. I couldn't even keep straight in my mind all the things that seemed to be riding on some phone call that might or might not come in the next two days. I thought about the town; the tight grouping of the Ladies, my admired friends; my parents' marriage; and uncountable other marriages that would not survive more blows; and, of course, Milt's unaccountably, suddenly welcome presence in the town.

The next morning we met at my office at six. Heidi, with great sweetness, had brought us breakfast rolls and volunteered to make coffee. We all sat around my desk and ate, discussed the news listlessly, and then settled into an aching anxiety of waiting I'd not approached even the day before the bar exams.

Finally, a little after three in the afternoon, the phone rang; Heidi dashed to the reception area, and perhaps ten seconds later her voice came over my phone's speaker. "New York on line one."

Milt, in a pathetic attempt at detached calm, leaned forward with his chin resting on the back of his hand. He looked like Rodin's *Thinker* getting the electric chair. As I picked up the receiver, he seemed to be biting the fleshy part of his hand just above his thumb.

A woman's voice said, "I have Bancroft Hemmings for Sophia Peters. Will you take the call?" I wished I could tap "yes" on the phone, like the trapped survivor of a capsized ship; but I managed to croak the word instead. Bancroft Hemmings was president of Arcturis.

His voice sounded neither friendly nor RoboCop cold, but merely curt. It spoke a total of two sentences. When it was finished, I replied, "Absolutely. I understand completely. Thank you very much."

I pressed the button to end the call and get another line; but before dialing Martha to relay the news, I looked up at Milt.

"Well," I said, "don't plan to go elk hunting Friday. We're busy."

CHAPTER SIXTY-SEVEN

The Worst Night Ever

Somewhere between wild excitement and absolute panic, we split the preparation work still to be done.

Milt dropped me at my parents' house, then drove my car out to the plant to meet with Harvey Dettermeier. Harvey, longtime number two to Prairie Machine's late owner, Jakob Halvorsen, was a perfect administrator, but no leader. The question was whether he and Milt would make the right team to run the company.

I, meanwhile, was joining my mother to cook a special dinner for my dad.

Of course, I knew only bits of what had transpired between my parents over the years. I knew they had tensions, which had lately been growing worse—as they had been for nearly every Larksdale family.

But only as we stood at the sink peeling potatoes did I finally realize that Mom had told Dad almost nothing about what the Ladies had accumulated over the past seven years.

I had asked, idly, what Dad had done to rate prime rib and potatoes lyonnaise, his favorites, when a certain embarrassed look swept over Mom's features. Suddenly fascinated by the broccoli she was rinsing, she answered without looking up, "I just want him in a good mood when we talk about the big plan."

Suddenly lawyerlike, I asked sharply, "Mom? How much does Dad know about the Ladies?"

"He knows that . . . well, not very much, I guess."

"Mom, how smart was that?"

"I'm going to fix it—tonight."

"And I'm going to help?"

She looked at me guiltily and nodded.

It was hardly the ideal time for us to try it. My dad's life had been crumbling at least since Arcturis bought PMT, and his marriage to Mom with it. Now he was a fifty-seven-year-old middling executive whose only employer was about to vanish: in those years, such graying, discouraged men filled unemployment offices and retraining seminars all across the country.

The difference between them had grown vast, and they had tried to ignore it. Dad was a manager who had just lost his job; Mom was a self-made millionaire and the only one who could save their future. Sure, she'd been lucky, and he hadn't. Yet he refused to acknowledge it—appeared never to follow even the obvious clues of change—and she, for her part, had let him stay ignorant.

They'd invented a whole new way to be dysfunctional.

All through December, with the plant scheduled to close in days and his own job dead, he still came home, dropped his briefcase by the little table in the entranceway, and yelled, "Honey! What's for dinner!?" in a tone you'd never use for a waitress.

I understood he was scared and confused. The old social compact whereby men went to work, uncomplaining, five days a week, and provided security in return for lifetime domestic service, was unraveling around him. It was as if there were, somewhere, a *Mobil Guide to Wives*, and only guys could buy it and only guys could contribute to it—and all the American women were in it, with zero to five stars by their names. Now, it seemed, Mom wasn't living up to her ratings, and he watched, not with a violent fury, but like an unhappy traveler mentally composing a really nasty letter to the editors.

Mom had a better grasp of the problems. But events had moved too fast—and her skills were too slight—for her to manage them better. By the time the plan was in place to bid for PMT, the time was gone for edging Dad into it. She had to act quickly and directly.

Mom hoped she could set the marriage right—upon a better basis—by bringing Dad into the takeover discussions. For her, the practical and enjoyable courses were the same. Milt, who planned to focus on the software side long-term, would need a manufacturing expert to run PMT's electronic-cash-register business for the next few years. After that, it would either grow into a different product line—perhaps computers designed specifically to run our Internet software—or else would be spun off. Dad (who really was a good engineer and manager) would either run an important division, or else have a chance to head the spin-off.

To do that, though, he would have to learn a little new technology and a lot of new values.

Women have been smoothing the delivery of bad news with good food since the beginning of time. "Look, Oog: mastodon stew. Oh, by the way, honey, an ice slide just crushed the north edge of the village." Food was the original gelcap coating of ten thousand years' worth of bad news and unpleasant medicine.

Mom's plan was to warm Dad up with prime rib and lyonnaise potatoes before mentioning casually that the world had been turned upside down. My job was to keep the conversation pleasant during the transition.

I did my best. It was hardly cheery—cheery conversations had been rare in that house for a long while—but we talked about the Vikings, world affairs, and the evils of modern business sufficiently to fill the time of soup and salad and main course.

Not until I was clearing away the dishes, and Mom was bringing in the dark chocolate cake, did I mention that Milt was in town.

Dad brightened. "Milt, huh? What brings him here?"

"Oh," I said, feeling vaguely treacherous, "Mom can tell you about that. I need to look over some papers." I took my slice of chocolate cake, which bore a strange resemblance to thirty pieces of silver, and headed for the living room.

For the first time in my life I left a piece of chocolate cake uneaten. My appetite had been swept away by a tidal wave of nervousness.

I also felt an irritating desire to call Milt. It was getting to be like some strange internal itch. I was wishing drinking calamine lotion would help.

I knew in general what Mom intended to say, and later I heard the details. But just then I was guessing at the conversation's course from overheard words and faint noises.

The plan was simply to invite Dad to help save the company. He had brains; he knew PMT; he could contribute.

Alas, times were no longer simple. Instead of scratching her pretty little head and telling Dad how smart he was, Mom started peppering him with questions about market research, time-to-production, projected margins, and the like. She wanted his help; she didn't want him running things.

Their talk was a disaster: Dad, who'd grown tougher and moodier as PMT's fortunes declined, dug in his heels, first moodily on the general principle that Prairie Machine was his business, and then more ferociously when he at last began to believe the Ladies were serious about buying the company.

It was all of a piece: he could give but not take. Of course, he had a right to feel tricked when all this was sprung upon him. But the real problem was different. The idea that Mom and her lady friends might be in a position to save his career was like the last

insult, as if the entire universe had reared up to laugh in his face—
a particularly brittle, high-pitched, and feminine laugh. It was
more than he could take.

He retreated steadily into monosyllables and then silence. And
as Dad got quieter, Mom got louder. Issues and emotions became
hopelessly confused. She believed she was treating him with the
ultimate regard, respect for his knowledge; but he saw it as her
usurping his rightful and only place.

Finally, with the fury that comes of baffled goodness, she heard
herself loudly giving him two choices. He could cooperate and help
the Ladies save the town—"Or you can divorce me, if you're that
much of a jackass."

I heard her moving through the swinging door to the kitchen,
then a silence, and Dad's footsteps approaching.

When he stormed into the living room alone, I didn't know
whether he wanted sympathy, information, or a mediator. His
style was not to yell or threaten; rather, he showed a kind of hurt
indignation, then stayed silent until noticed.

Mom and I knew the same basic truth: at this stage Dad's feelings, or ours, didn't really matter.

Still, I'd tried to prepare myself to be as kindly as I could.

But what I felt was a rush of bitterness. At this one most important juncture, when we wanted his support so much, he was
obsessed with his own disappointments and demands. He, who
was always there for the boys (with sports, with outings, with
encouragement), but never there for me. He was a good man,
honest and hardworking. But always good on his terms. He'd
work late to get me the money for ballet lessons. But if I said I'd
rather play baseball with him, he'd somehow never, ever hear it.
A weird, uncomprehending deafness came over him, no matter
how loudly I spoke.

Which was why I couldn't help him now. He just didn't have
the habit of hearing me.

He dropped into his oversized chair and, leaning toward the

couch where I sat, demanded, "What on earth has gotten into your mother?"

"What do you mean?"

"She has some crazy plan about buying Prairie Machine."

"I don't think it's crazy. Anyway, it's the best plan we've got. If you've got a better one, she wants to hear it. If not, she wants you to support hers. So do I."

"So you're both working against me."

"*Against you?*"

"You aren't saying you're *helping* me?"

"I'm saying what you should already see. This isn't about *you*. It's . . ." I was so frustrated, I stole a line. "It's like in *The God-father*. 'It was never personal; it was always business.' "

I should have been ashamed to use the same words as that skunk Vic Carter. But I was so upset, imagination had failed me. I wanted my father to listen.

We'd always avoided fighting, except in those brief exchanges that made me feel petulant and left me apologizing. But not now. If he wanted a fight, he was going to get it.

And he knew it.

He rose halfway up out of the chair. He was my father; he'd never been violent with me. But he was still six-foot-five, broad, and scary.

"What the hell do you want from me? You wanted to play soccer; I let you. You wanted to go to college; I let you. You wanted to go to law school; I let you."

I stood up, too.

"What do I *want*, Daddy? We're trying to save your ass. At least, I want you to say 'thank you.' And at most, I want you to help us."

He didn't say anything. Instead, he spun on his heel and left the room. I heard his heavy footsteps on the stairs, then some banging around upstairs, and a few minutes later he came back down the stairs, still hurrying but quieter, even though he was carrying a suitcase.

The loudest noise was the slam of the door as he left.

*I*n the silence, with all we had facing us, I could think only that there was no tree up yet in the living room. The missing of it, as I stared at the corner where it had stood shimmering each year, was much more anger than nostalgia, but painful nonetheless. Of all the stupid worries.

Mom slipped into the room beside me; and easily enough from where I was staring, she knew what I was thinking.

"Never mind that," she said slowly. "We've still got the meeting. Get your coat. And, well . . . keep your faith."

I put my arm briefly around her shoulder, just for a moment, then went to do as I was told. When I got back, she was waiting by the front door.

Her eyes were puffy, and her hands were shaking, but otherwise she looked all right.

CHAPTER SIXTY-EIGHT

We Bring the House Down

I ought to have felt much worse when we reached Martha's, but gloom about my parents was overshadowed by the excitement of events. I was jumpy, nervous; but I wanted to ride this horse all the way to the finish.

Instead, I nearly trampled the crowd.

The Ladies were worried. Our sole real business was to ready them for the negotiations; yet from the moment I entered, their faces clearly said they craved reassurance. They'd landed their match with the champ, but there still remained the small matter of the fight.

Even worse, Milt hadn't arrived, which put them still more on edge. He finally rushed in twenty minutes late, took me aside, and said hurriedly, "Sorry. Harvey kept me talking."

"I should have warned you. Harvey's great, but he loves to yak." I was already stepping toward the fireplace, where speakers stood to address the Ladies, when Milt caught my arm.

"Sophia—I thought of something the Ladies should do. I think—"

I interrupted him. "We've got to start. Just wing it. It'll be fine."

Famous last words.

Being a little short on reassurance myself just then, I closed my eyes—hoping I made it look like I was merely tired—and uttered a brief prayer that I wouldn't blunder.

Then I opened them and commenced blundering.

I started vigorously, handing out cards Milt and I had prepared with sample remarks for the Ladies to make, to dazzle the Arcturis guys with their business expertise. Our goofy thought had been that the Ladies would enjoy the charade. Instead, of course, they saw it (quite rightly) as a vote of no confidence.

I should have apologized at once, recalled the cards, and let them design their own tactics. Instead, like a silent comedian re-treating after brushing a goblet off the table only to knock over the whole china shelf behind him, I tried to explain my mistake.

"It's just that Arcturis is one of the country's toughest deal mak-ers," I stumbled. "They've grown from almost nothing to ten bil-lion a year in sales, in just four years. They're notorious for hard-nosed . . ."

The longer I talked, the more they panicked. Big surprise.

Or, let's be honest, *we* panicked. I was the worst of all. As I built the Arcturis executives into supermen, I began to share the Ladies' doubts about themselves, myself, our whole plan. What had seemed a lark now looked more like a vulture. Out of our league? We were playing the wrong game entirely.

Our confidence crumbled, then collapsed. The Ladies began whispering among themselves dispiritedly. Their own accountant had conned them blind. What hope did they have against a high-powered corporation?

Then Milt jumped in.

As he spoke, I realized he'd grabbed the chance to play the hero, but I couldn't blame him. He'd offered to share it with me before we started. Now I was just relieved to see the cavalry arriving.

"Ladies," he said firmly, stepping up to join me, "I kind of left Sophia in the lurch by arriving late. She's only given you half the plan."

That helped. Once they brightened, he continued.

"You Ladies have a tough role to play. You're first-rate businesswomen, no doubt—and naturally you want to be treated with respect.

"But here's the kicker. If the Arcturis guys figure you're *that* smart, they'll wonder why you're buying PMT. If they get suspicious enough, they'll call a halt and run their own review to find out what's *really* inside PMT—and if they do that, we're sunk."

He paused, eyed them closely, and asked, "Agreed so far?"

When they'd each nodded, he exhaled with relief, and went on.

"Okay. So I'm—we're—asking"—he flashed a slightly wicked, conspiratorial grin—"if you can fool these big-city hotshots into thinking you're just a bunch of small-town housewives who got lucky."

He had them hooked and concluded energetically, "In fact, the real trick is going to be for you to seem rich enough to buy Prairie Machine, but also gullible enough—and crazy enough about Larksdale—that they don't get suspicious."

I had a bad feeling about this. Sure, Milt had promised the Ladies fun—but he was playing with fire and didn't know it. The Ladies, however, were well ahead of him.

"You mean we need to put on a show," Agnes responded at once—with scarcely a question on it. "Set them up to expect a bunch of hicks, and then dazzle them with our style," she elaborated, her usually subdued, soft brown eyes suddenly aglow.

The idea of the Ladies dazzling anyone with their style ought to have been universally hilarious—but before I could get even a good chuckle going, I realized Agnes was serious.

In fact, her eyes held exactly the blaze of faintly amused, fiercely determined creativity I'd seen in the Ladies so often before. Milt had promised them the most fun ever. They were taking him at his word.

Even worse, they were whispering among themselves; and that strange light of enthusiasm was spreading. Did I say "fire"? Milt was playing with dynamite.

I began quaking inwardly. It was going to be Gladys and the limo all over again. Only a hundred times worse.

And then, unexpectedly, Dolly called out to Milt, "Hold on! They might figure *we're* doofuses—but they know *you're* not. How will we explain *your* moving to Larksdale and trying to save PMT?"

"That's easy," Mom interjected with loud confidence, "he's in love with Sophia."

"Oh, yeah," everybody responded, as if they'd momentarily forgotten the most obvious thing—except for Milt and me, who looked as if we wanted to link arms and disappear through the floorboards.

Nobody noticed. The Ladies, sold on the plan, were already neglecting us to plot among themselves.

Desperately I signaled my mother to step aside with me.

"Mom!"

"Let us handle this one, dear . . ."

I turned to Milt; but before I could speak, he said coolly, "Your mom's right, Sophia."

So much for loyalty. The big rat.

It was a hell of a way to run a business, but I just worked there. I nodded, and headed to Martha's kitchen for a glass of water.

As I left, Gladys was explaining how she'd rented the limo to Duluth.

*L*ater, when we were driving back to my parents' house, Mom seemed to have lost the brief optimism the meeting had brought. As she sat slumped in the passenger's seat, I asked, "Want me to stay with you tonight?"

"No, dear. I'll be fine. Drop me off, then take the car. You want to be getting home to call Milt."

That last bit stung me. I replied very curtly, "We already said everything we needed to this morning."

"Of course you did," she answered with a faint, annoying smile, and fell silent.

For about ten seconds.

Then she burst out, "Let's see, dear: you're thirty-two years old. You're lonely as a barn owl—your idea of a big night is to come over on Fridays and watch movies on tape with your dad and me. Or it was when your dad was here," she added awkwardly, then resumed with vigor. "And now you're afraid because a man might want you? A lawyer, an MBA, a big success and your intellectual equal, who respects you and loves you madly? My God; no wonder you can't stand him."

She took a quick breath, before—

"Are you crazy?" she concluded. "I mean—and I say this as your loving mother—you're not exactly Heidi in the looks department, you know."

My ears were more than burning; it was a good thing I didn't run the car off the road.

"Mother! Will you—" I said, then stopped. If she wanted to pick that lonely moment to reinforce some bond with me, I wished I could be gracious enough to go along. For moms, it's always the Advice Hour.

But I wasn't noble enough to want her cheered up at the expense of my private feelings—at least not then. Just then, work had to come first.

Of course, I'd been putting work ahead of feeling all my life; but that was another matter.

I clamped my jaw shut to keep from saying anything snooty, nodded rather convulsively, and kept the car on the road.

In front of her house, we settled for three, not unkind, words:

"Sure you're okay?"

"Yes."

I stayed in the car and watched her walk up the path and open the door of the dark house. Just briefly, oddly, I wanted to cry for us all.

But odder still, when I returned to my apartment, my only concern was to call and talk with Milt.

We talked for an hour. He and Harvey Dettermeier had cooked up some sort of scheme they weren't yet ready to share. I could hear the glee in his voice, so intense I lacked the heart to tell him the Ladies were out of control.

Of course, our talk was mostly business; but even I knew it was more than that. For one thing, it beat the heck out of e-mail.

We still weren't quite ready to join our lives together.

But we were close.

*A*t eleven the next morning—the day before the big meeting—the Ladies took the train to Chicago. Mom called from the hip and ritzy Sutton Place Hotel to say they were all fine, and she'd see me the following morning. *Her* voice was gleeful, too.

So there you had it. I planned to surprise Milt; he planned to surprise me; and the Ladies planned to surprise everyone.

Right at the payoff, we were turning a corporate raid into the last reel of *Steamboat Bill Jr.,* with everybody playing Buster Keaton.

CHAPTER SIXTY-NINE

Milt's Idea of Fun

The twenty-fourth of December dawned brilliantly clear and absolutely freezing: with windchill, the temperature was a nippy thirty-four below zero. Of course, the forecast was for warming later in the day. Temperatures always rise a few degrees when a blizzard blows in.

Larksdale, with the Ladies gone, had been painfully quiet. Milt, suddenly shy, declined the use of my apartment or my parents' house and insisted on staying at his hotel. I showered and dressed that morning with the sky still black outside.

I reached the Holiday Inn at seven exactly—and no sooner had I pulled up out front than Milt ran out from the lobby to tug open the Chevy's door.

He looked pale, almost tortured.

"Are you okay?" I asked.

"Yes, except for trembling hands, profuse sweating, and a slight desire to throw up all over your dashboard."

"Good. I really go for the strong, silent, nauseous type."

We didn't say anything else for about ten minutes. The heater and the road rumble were loud.

Then Milt began by saying, "Look, Sophia, Harvey and I decided something last night." He stopped, embarrassed.

"Yeah?"

"We figured Arcturis might be less excited about keeping Prairie Tool if they thought Minnesota was . . . well, a . . . less desirable place to spend much time."

"Cool!" I said. "Let's take 'em out behind the woodshed and beat the stuffing out of 'em the second they arrive."

His sense of humor wasn't awake yet. He stared straight ahead into the predawn and muttered, "Let's save that for last."

*B*y the time we reached Prairie Tool, Milt had recovered his *joie de vivre*. In fact, the more nervous I got, the jollier he became.

The sun was just rising, gold in an ice-blue sky—and the only sign of activity was the gray silhouette of a corporate jet out on the landing strip. As we got closer, I could see it was the Arcturis Industries Learjet parked on the center of the runway.

Nearer to us, Harvey Dettermeier and his young assistant, Mike McKay, huddled by the airstrip control shack. They wore heavy parkas over their business suits, and judging from their blue lips, I knew they'd been standing there awhile.

"Where are the Arcturis guys?" I asked, leaving the car.

Harvey grinned. "In the executive dining room, having coffee with Irish."

Mike added, without a hint of a smile, "They're gonna need it. Somebody accidentally broke a couple of windows in there last night. It must be about thirty below. And all we could find to feed 'em this morning was a coupla dozen day-old greasy doughnuts."

"What about the Ladies?" I asked with more concern.

Mike shrugged uneasily and looked to Harvey, who scanned the road beyond the gate, where they'd drive in after they reached Minneapolis.

"I don't know. Chicago weather's pretty rotten. United may be grounded."

"Then let's fall back on plan B," Milt offered with mock seriousness.

"What's plan B?" I asked. It was my day to play straight man—straight woman. I wasn't really enjoying it. All of a sudden it seemed Milt was treating this all like too much of a joke. He answered with relish.

"Take all the executives out and get them blitzed. Then drive them to the middle of nowhere and tell 'em the plant just burned down. Offer 'em ten grand for the scorched earth. They're New Yorkers—they can't tell one patch of Minnesota from another."

"Too late!" Harvey said happily, and pointed back toward the buildings. A station wagon with magnetic "Prairie Machine Tool" signs stuck to its front doors was fishtailing, engine gunning, up the ice-covered road from the headquarters building. At the wheel sat Bunky Hanson, a slight youngster with thick horn-rim glasses, who'd been profiled in the company newsletter because of the winter weekends he spent racing old SAABs in ice slaloms up near Duluth. Beside him and in back were the well-dressed and absolutely terrified Arcturis negotiators. As the wagon, swerving and throwing slush higher than its roof, spun to a backward halt about twenty yards beyond us, they looked as if all they wanted to negotiate was their surrender.

"We should've sent them ice fishing for sixteen hours first!" Harvey yelled happily.

"Oh, sure, *now* you think of it!" Milt answered, and they both laughed. For about two seconds I continued to feel deeply scandalized by these adolescent high jinks—then the humor of it hit me, and I started laughing, too.

We strode up to help them from the car. The combination of bad doughnuts, Irish whiskey, and the Ice Fields Grand Prix had done its work: except for the tall, distinguished guy who resembled Charlton Heston and was sitting up front, they all exited looking wobbly and faintly green.

"Welcome to Minnesota, gentlemen. You sure picked a nice day for it!" Harvey cried.

"Yeah," Milt added solemnly, kicking ice off his boots. "If this heat wave holds, we'll have a right pleasant Christmas."

Actually the Arcturis guys weren't bad. I was trying to dislike them, but they just wouldn't cooperate. The best I could manage was a mild suspicion of their CEO, Bancroft Hemmings. His looks matched his name: he was the handsome guy sitting up front who looked like Charlton Heston.

Leaving the car, he squinted, as though he was trying to see through the powder smoke but didn't have to—he understood the battlefield intuitively. He was tall and fit and, with prematurely white hair and piercing blue eyes, too good-looking to be an actor. Actually Milt said his reputation was solid, and he'd made some brilliant moves both at IBM and then later at Arcturis. It's just not in my nature to take people like that too seriously. Look like Charlton Heston, get treated like Charlton Heston—that's my motto.

But old Charlton and his colleagues showed gumption. Shaking off their rough treatment, they waited patiently another twenty minutes in the freezing cold, searching the distant highway for some sign of the approach of the Ladies.

The minutes stretched like old rubber bands; the road stayed empty, and our nerves began to fray. Harvey caught my eye; I could see he was thinking it was time to call the meeting off.

That was when the nice young man from engineering ran, puffing white clouds of breath, all the way from the engineering building out to the yard where we stood. He wasn't exactly a prime physical specimen. He bent over, hands on knees, and took a full twenty seconds to catch his breath.

"Word from the Ladies' Club," he whispered.

"They're not coming," said Hemmings, making a guess sound like an announcement. He didn't say it meanly, so I gave him points. I was still trying to dislike him, but he still wasn't cooperating.

But the young man shook his head, gasped for more air, and pointed to the sky in the general direction of Chicago. He straightened, not talking, just shaking his head and sucking in spasmodic breaths.

"What, then?" Hemmings asked.

The young man, having caught his breath, lifted his head.

"Their jet is two minutes out, and they'd be obliged if you'd get your crate off the field."

We walked as quickly as we could out to the landing strip, where the Arcturis plane was already being pushed onto the frozen tundra. Flecks of snow blew in the air, like cold stinging gnats against the skin, and far off to the east, angling in, shone the smallish green-and-white needle of the Ladies' jet.

Even during landing a jet travels over a hundred miles an hour. By the time I realized they were lined up not to land, but to buzz us, they were already closing at a blazing pace. A second later they flashed overhead with a deafening roar, augmented by Milt and Harvey yelling, "Yee-*hah*!"

By the time we were calmed down, the field had been cleared, and the Ladies' jet had circled and started back toward us.

It banked and settled lower, growing bigger all the while, and then it touched down.

"Just like John-flockin'-Wayne," said Harvey Dettermeier reverently.

It was showtime.

CHAPTER SEVENTY

Wheeling and Dealing

The Arcturis team never really recovered from the arrival of the Ladies' jet.

And neither, nearly, did I.

I'd expected improvement, but what I saw was transformation. The Ladies who stepped off that jet were the fashion equivalent of a Jack Dempsey uppercut.

Eight small-town ladies dressed to the high-fashion nines might easily have been absurd. But that day, as they stepped from the white Citation in the pristine clarity of a winter morning's light, I didn't think they looked silly.

I thought they looked terrific—and they took the Arcturis guys to yet a higher level of confusion.

First out, after the stewardess, was a young woman who seemed molded into her Armani Black Label business suit. Her fine blond hair stylishly coiffed, she carried herself with striking authority.

I did a pure double take when I recognized her, because every time I'd seen her before, her hair had been pink.

Whoever had advised the Ladies deserved a prize. With hair and makeup perfect, they wore the most expensive, fashionable designs, chosen to highlight both their individual characters and their role as a team. It took me a second to figure out it was a shade of dark blue, used mostly in accessories, which linked them. Very clever, but—

It worked because of the way they acted. They behaved like powerful women—because that was what they'd become. Led by Skye, they were smoothly handing out business cards and shaking hands while I hung back, slightly dazed.

Last off was Deborah. As she passed, she answered my unspoken question by whispering, "Slice about forty thousand off our net worth, kiddo."

The Arcturis guys, who'd expected a clutch of small-town ladies, stood with mouths agape—a posture that only grew more pronounced a minute later, when the two stretch limos arrived from St. Paul to chauffeur the Ladies about.

During the ride to the main plant, Team Arcturis fought back manfully to decorum, but they were on the ropes. They'd been blinded by money and sucker punched by fashion. It was "mission accomplished" for phase one of the Ladies' game plan.

We ran the rest of the day like an atomic clock with a Mickey Mouse dial. Old Charlton Heston might have caught up with them in time, but no sooner did we make it back to the headquarters building, where Mike Maitland met us in the executive conference room, than the Ladies reversed field.

The Ladies had brought an extra passenger: a scholarly-looking professor of information science from the University of Chicago. At their request, he and Mike headed off to review the Hog Farm's patents and trade secrets.

Checking the patent portfolio was good business; but more importantly, it gave the Ladies the chance to run an end reverse.

The moment Mike and the professor left the room, Gladys undid the string on a large brown paper box she'd been carrying, set the box on the table, and opening it, asked the Arcturis guys in her best little-old-lady tones, "How about some nice Christmas cookies?"

For the next two hours the Ladies made small—no, *micro-*

scopic—talk with the Arcturis guys. While Milt concentrated (rather hammily, I thought) on staring at me with love-struck eyes, the Ladies outdid themselves at playing good-natured hicks. It was like a ten-year sentence in Mayberry R.F.D. They raised boring chat to an art form, until the Arcturis guys were rolling their eyes, squirming, and wondering whether it would be less painful to hang themselves in the men's room or hear any more about the Larksdale Civic Theater's production of *Brigadoon*. Finally the door opened, and the U. of C. professor entered from the next room. He shook his head sadly, as if to say he'd never seen a sadder display of technological incompetence. This seemed bleak, but . . .

I had the best angle on the door and could see Mike in the hallway beyond the professor. He flashed a brief grin and a thumbs-up sign. Just for that moment, even as I realized the professor's gloom had been still more of the psychological warfare, I imagined Mike as he must have been, the prank-playing high-school student my mom had known.

Then Mike stepped into the room so the others could see him, and told the professor dispiritedly, "If we hustle, I might get you back to civilization before the blizzard hits, Doc."

"Thank God," the professor answered, shivering, and I realized the room temperature must have been about fifty-five.

As the two of them left, Martha took the cue. Looking as though the prof's shrug had sapped most of her enthusiasm for the deal, she told the executives, laying her hands palms down on the table, "Well, this may be hopeless, but we're here to try to save jobs. What do you say we order lunch in and get down to it?"

As if Martha had called an audible from the huddle, the Ladies switched styles, from bubbleheads to dead serious. The chat about their pets and favorite recipes ended instantly.

And I, done playing Snow White to their Seven Dwarfs (Whacky, Silly, Vacuous, and the others), had to make the change to General Counsel.

"Perhaps," I said, straightening the papers in front of me, "we could ask Mr. Green to flesh out the bullet points on the offer letter."

$\mathcal{M}$ ilt spoke for an hour, and he seemed to have factored in everything. By the time he finished, I, and everyone else, knew absolutely that Arcturis could make far more money selling to us than by moving the plant to Mexico.

Just as Milt finished, the campaign to show that Larksdale ranked three steps above Sarajevo on the "I'd rather burn in hell than work there" scale went into overdrive.

The storm blew in with a vengeance. At midday, with the winds howling and snow swirling outside, and the room temperature plunging, the sky suddenly turned so black we needed to switch on the overhead lights.

Oddly, half the fluorescent bulbs were missing.

Just then, lunch arrived. The delivery boys from the commissary, ice chips in their sideburns, pushed in the serving carts. The first two carts carried nothing but lifeless sandwiches and lukewarm potato soup.

But the third delivery cart looked more promising, since it held a large, elegant, covered silver dish. The third server set it in the center of the conference table and lifted the silver lid. The Arcturis guys leaned forward hopefully.

They recoiled instantly, as a stench like an exploded sewer line spread through the room.

"Thought you gentlemen might like to sample our local cuisine," Milt offered with the thin smile of a riverboat gambler. "Lutefisk in dill sauce, anyone?"

All lutefisk smells bad; this stuff looked like something the evil witch would stir in a Conan the Barbarian movie. You kept waiting for the eyeballs to pop to the surface. Milt reached for a ladle, and as he pushed it into the pot, he told the Arcturis guys cheerfully, "Every Wednesday and Friday in the executive dining room. Minnesota doesn't get any better than this."

It was all I could do not to jump onto the table and belt out a chorus of "You're the Tops."

Of course, the showy stuff wasn't going to carry the day.

Neither would goodwill. Arcturis really did want to be "The Big Company with the Big Heart." But only as long as it didn't cost them anything.

So the deal wasn't easy. The Arcturis guys might have been a little rattled, but they were pros.

We knew our first offer was close, or they would never have come out to see us. The question, as the talks got hot, was whether Arcturis's demands would push us beyond our small negotiating reserve.

We argued hard all afternoon and perilously close to Christmas Eve. We settled small issues about warranties, indemnifications, real estate, taxes, and the like—dull, lawyerly things, but the Ladies made not a single misstep. Skye in particular showed she wasn't just another pretty MBA. We made good progress, but always with the Godzilla issue, the final selling price, looming above us. Arcturis wanted more than we could pay.

At day's end, we threw in our big sweetener: a royalty for three years on every unit of software we sold. The Arcturis execs may have been the Guys with the Big Hearts—but their brains weren't exactly tiny. They wanted to unload Prairie Machine, but they also wanted a guaranteed taste of the upside, in the unlikely event that we were smarter than we looked and really made a go of it.

After another two hours' hard arguing, we'd reduced it all to the royalty question—but were far apart on it. Arcturis wanted 5 percent for four years. That fourth year was the deal breaker. Based on our confidential sales projections, 5 percent of sales in year four would cost us $15 million. Neither side had budged for the last hour, and positions had hardened.

That was when Milt called the intermission.

At ten minutes to four our team adjourned to the coffee room down the hall.

As we walked down the corridor, Milt was looking frayed around the edges but wildly excited. That was exactly how I felt. Now I knew why he loved deal making. It was like downhill skiing—on money.

The second we had the door closed behind us, Deborah asked, "What do you think they'll take?"

Milt swallowed hard and answered, "I think they'll take two-point-five for four."

"Can we afford it?"

He thought, then nodded. "Yeah."

Deborah looked at the other Ladies. This time, no mystic polling. She waited for them to nod in turn, before she looked back to Milt, and said, "Okay. Let's do it."

We had gone about halfway back up the dim corridor. Milt, walking fast, was in the lead, and I was running to catch him.

He slowed to let me reach him. When I did I was almost sorry.

He took my arm and drew me into a doorway, to let the Ladies continue past us. Then he bent down toward me and said, "You're up, kid."

"What!?" I asked—but I already knew the answer.

"You pitch it any way you want. You know the plan: the Ladies want the deal; I think they're overpaying."

I would have refused, but the Ladies had already reached the conference-room door. So, trying not to let my panic show, I nodded.

Milt took my arm. "Great. Let's go get 'em."

As we walked into the room, everyone looked to Milt—and Milt looked to me, which guaranteed their eyes would follow. I thought I was going to start shaking, and then, strangely, was positive I wouldn't. Milt was giving me the expected disapproving glare; but all of a sudden it didn't matter. I was going to do it my way.

When all their eyes were on me, I said, "Gentlemen, two-point-five for four. This is all there is in the cookie jar. Our last offer."

I'd expected a lot more back-and-forth haggling, but Hemmings's glance, very sharp, went from me to Milt, and then back to his colleagues. They must have seen something in his eyes, because their response looked exactly like a football sideline when the last field goal's tried. Instantly two of his team members jumped and grinned with relief, and the third—the tough one—grimaced and swiveled away, as if he'd just lost the big game.

But Hemmings, looking back to me, grinned, stepped forward, and held out his hand for me to shake.

"Merry Christmas. You just bought yourself a company."

CHAPTER SEVENTY-ONE

The Short Good-bye

So, at four-thirty in the afternoon, Christmas Eve, we sat down together and signed the deal memo.

The process was extraordinarily jolly, in part because, while the memo was being printed, Mary slipped away and, about fifteen minutes later, returned with a huge and steaming pewter bowl filled with a dark reddish liquid. Thin orange slices and slivers of almonds floated atop it; raisins and cloves bobbed just under the surface.

At once the room filled with the scents, not only of clove and orange, but of brandy and cinnamon and lemon zest.

Wafting lushly all about us, in other words, was that old Swedish holiday treat called glögg, a cheery Christmas blend of wine, brandy, whiskey, and (just in case somebody has a working brain cell left) vodka or gin. All the spices and bits of fruits and nuts, in short, were merely decorative—like daisy stickers on a cruise missile.

Glögg is one negotiating tactic the Larksdale Ladies could teach to Donald Trump and Bill Gates.

Nor was this any less calculated than the dealings of those legendary deal makers: as she ladled me out a cup, Mary whispered, "Mike left the ingredients in his office. Skoal, dear."

．　．　．

$\mathcal{T}$echnically only the officers of Arcturis and of the LLIC had to sign; but in the spirit of the season, we made room for everyone's mark. Did the glögg influence our behavior? Let's just say that one more round, and we would have had the plant guard dogs in to add their paw prints.

The airfield was dark, except for the red marker lights on the two jets and the stars in the clearing sky; but as we limo'd out there, the landing lights were switched on, and the sequence of their flashing seemed, in a funny way, like robotic Christmas lights. I decided someday I was going to write a children's book called *Sophia's Corporate Christmas*. This is why one cup of glögg is my annual consumption of alcohol.

That one cup, plus the natural high of closing the deal, probably explains why I missed what was being set up around me. That's how Neville Chamberlain got into trouble after Munich. Walking away with a signed deal in hand, you feel great even if you've just tossed Czechoslovakia to the Nazis.

Of course, there were plenty of other distractions.

The Arcturis guys were hitting the limo minibar for something to dilute the glögg and were talking loudly (and, I thought, sincerely) about their eagerness to get home to their families. The car skidded once, sharply, over some patch of ice, and momentum threw us cheerfully into one another.

Still, I couldn't help thinking at least some of us were acting too cheerful to keep melancholy at bay.

$\mathcal{A}$s we arrived, the snowplow was just finishing its clattering, diesel-thumping clearing of the strip, and the stars shone bright.

We kept our good-byes to the Arcturis guys friendly but brief, then returned to the limos to avoid the noise of their takeoff, and to keep warm while the Ladies' plane was moved into place.

We were out of the cars again and waiting for the cabin door to open, when Harvey Dettermeier pulled a disposable Kodak camera from somewhere and called cheerfully, "Hey! Team picture!"

It seemed at first almost too much festivity; then somehow at once we all decided the day should be memorialized and stopped protesting.

We lined up beside the plane, under the purplish glow of the fluorescent lights, while Harry fiddled with the camera. My nose was numb, whether from the cold or the glögg, I didn't know.

Milt hovered at the edge of the group, uncertain, until Deborah grabbed his arm and yanked him into the shot.

The glances we exchanged just before the flash went off were what I remember.

The one I looked to was Gladys. Why she and I understood each other so well, I'll never know. But she took my hand and looked at me silently just a moment—and I realized absolutely that we both had the same thought.

The great and wild part of the adventure—the only part we had cared about—was over. Whatever followed, however prosperous or worthwhile, would be dull and tame and formal in comparison.

The camera clicked and flashed.

After that, we got quieter. The wind flapped, as lifeless as the noise of the stars, and we prepared to say good-bye.

The Ladies, still jolly but preoccupied, were splitting into groups. Those with homes—Mike and Mary, Martha and Skye—were taking the limos back to Larksdale. All the others were flying to Chicago to spend Christmas together.

The limos left. The jet's cabin door opened, and the steps were lowered. Our remaining group traded just hugs and hasty "Merry Christmases," except that Deborah shook Milt's hand and said, "O-kay, kiddo"—which, from her, was high and elaborate praise.

Mom was last to board. Only then, with a shock nearly physical, did I realize she had placed herself among the homeless ones. We hugged more tightly than we usually did.

Then she stepped back—almost bumping the hanging cabin steps—to take us both in and said in a tone of benediction, "Goodbye, dears. Happy holidays. Enjoy your company, and make us lots of money."

She climbed the steps and in; but just before they pulled the door closed behind her, she looked back and gave Milt what seemed a most meaningful smile.

As I say, the glögg explains why I never saw what was coming.

CHAPTER SEVENTY-TWO

A Funny Time for a Chat

*I*nviting Milt to my parents' house felt inevitable.

We drove down streets bright with Christmas displays: most of our neighbors had clearly decided at the last minute that Larksdale's farewell was going to be with lights blazing.

My parents' street was dimmer, mostly because their house was dark. Walking up the black path to their house seemed surpassingly strange.

At the door I stopped to look back at the quiet street, with its small brightness of glowing reindeer and holiday lights. With all that had happened, my feelings were a confused rush of loneliness, good cheer, nostalgia, and a *very* strange excitement.

But I said only, "Gosh, it's quiet," which was likely what one of General Custer's privates said at Little Bighorn, just before company arrived.

Milt eyed me solemnly, then replied, stammering a bit, "With the rush and everything, I picked this out in a hurry." From inside his coat, he pulled out a tiny box, very carefully wrapped. He glanced down at it, then thrust it toward me.

The rush of feelings had just gone supersonic. Being me, however, I took it wordlessly, then stood like a stuffed toy on the doorstep.

"Open it!" Milt sounded strangely pleading.

I obliged, took out a hinged box covered in light blue velvet, and raised its lid. When I saw what was inside, I said, "It's awfully small for a napkin ring."

"Sophia! I'm proposing."

"Proposing what?"

"Sophia!" He sounded genuinely shocked.

"Come on. Lawyers like clarity. Besides, I've been negotiating all day. I'm on a roll."

Milt decided to relax and humor me.

"Call it a promise to love, honor, and protect—with an option to buy."

"Just what kind of a girl do you think I am?"

"Exactly the kind I want."

So that was how I came to marry my best friend—who, oddly enough, has stayed my best friend ever since. Any further details I shall, like one of those eighteenth-century romance-novel Sophias, leave to the reader's imagination.

It was very romantic.

But not as romantic as what followed.

*D*espite the big news, Christmas was just a little grim—since, as it turned out, my father had decided to drive to Milwaukee to see his side of the family, and my brothers had gone with him.

But the next day, Saturday, was much better. Mom called to say she was fine, and we'd have the house to ourselves until midday Sunday.

All Saturday morning we were like a nineties revival of a fifties family show. *Ozzie and Sophiet* or something.

It was like heaven. Or at least a suburb of heaven.

That lasted all the way until two-fifteen in the afternoon. By then, we'd listened to two discsful of Handel's concertos; eaten popcorn and drunk hot chocolate; and gone to the last tile in an epic game of Scrabble which Milt lost on my proving that "Skonk-works," while technically a word, had been trademarked by the cartoonist Al Capp, and so was ineligible—see *Capp* v. *Lockheed Aircraft,* 1959. Milt took it like a gentleman and a lawyer, arguing until I started throwing the tiles at him.

After that we just sat cozily on the carpet in front of the couch and, with our arms around each other, stared into the cheery fire.

"Boy, this is the life."

"You said it."

About five minutes passed in comfortable silence. Then I asked, "Are you thinking what I'm thinking?"

He turned, studied me for a long minute, and then, jumping up, cried joyfully, "I'll get some notepads."

I reached under the couch. "Right here." I handed him one and kept the other. They had pens attached. Milt pulled the cap off his pen with his teeth, then blew it somewhere we'd never find it again.

"So," he asked, "how do you see us structuring the software division?"

It was a match made in heaven.

CHAPTER SEVENTY-THREE

We Go Public

We used the long weekend to prepare our public announcement. We assumed rumors would be circulating, but still figured we could keep the facts of the sale secret for seventy-two hours. Mike—who was desperately afraid his Hog Farmers would start taking job offers elsewhere—wanted permission to tell them the whole story, but finally agreed to wait.

Harvey Dettermeier's team took charge of plant publicity so Milt and I could work on the zillion details needed to turn the deal memo into a final set of contracts. Normally this would have been handled by a team of high-priced outside lawyers, but since the Ladies were pioneering the bargain-basement corporate raid, we drafted nearly all the papers ourselves. That left Harvey's team to prepare to break the news to the two thousand or so people who did the real work at PMT.

Harvey's folks were up to the job.

By the time those two thousand people returned to work on Monday morning, posters and flyers everywhere announced a company-wide meeting "of the greatest possible importance" for that evening.

· · ·

$\mathcal{T}$wo hours before the meeting, as we sat down to decide what we'd say, Milt startled me by announcing he expected me to give part of the presentation.

Fighting down panic, I told him the story of my second-grade role as a fruit tree.

"I'm not kidding. The apples were falling off me like leaves. Never mind gravity. If Isaac Newton had been under me, he'd've discovered quantum mechanics—or suffered a concussion."

"If Isaac Newton had been under you, he'd've had to answer to *me*," Milt answered gallantly. Macho humor isn't his favorite style, but I gave him points for trying. Especially under the circumstances.

I said I'd do my best—a remark vague enough for any purpose.

$\mathcal{T}$he company auditorium was designed to hold fourteen hundred people, and the aisles were full, but some of those were spouses. I figured we had about two-thirds of the workforce there.

Certainly they were rocking the house, especially after the clock swept past the start time with Mr. Dettermeier still backstage writing his opening remarks on the back of an empty Publishers Clearing House envelope, like the Abraham Lincoln of Larksdale, Minnesota.

Harvey might have been slightly negligent in the speechmaking area, but otherwise he'd done well, even to rounding up the erstwhile Prairie Machine Marching Band. They'd been a big item under old Jakob Halvorsen, then disbanded under Arcturis, so they were a little rusty. But there they were, assembled down in front of the stage, and around eight-oh-two—two minutes after start time, as the crowd was getting restless—they restored partial order by launching into the U. of Minnesota fight song, a little ragged but with spirit.

Finally, at ten after eight, as it began to sound like the third try at getting a mass foot stomping going would be the charm, Harvey straightened his tie, pushed his glasses back on his nose, and stepped out through the curtains.

We watched from the wings as he walked to the podium, smoothed out the envelope, and began. "We called this meeting, even though we knew a lot of folks would be out of town, because we didn't want to keep the news from you any longer."

He paused dramatically—a little longer than I would have, but he had them leaning forward in their seats. Then he gave them the facts in three beats.

"I got some good news for *you*."

A loud murmur swelled from the crowd.

"Prairie Machine *isn't* going to Mexico."

The murmur began turning into a cheer. Over it, Mr. Dettermeier leaned forward and yelled into the microphone, "Prairie Machine is staying right here in Larksdale!"

The cheer became an outright roar. People were on their feet, stomping and applauding.

Mr. Dettermeier, fists thrust into the air, let it go on for a full minute before opening his hands and waving them forward in a call for quiet.

They paid him absolutely no attention. At first I thought they were being silly; but then, looking at the nearest faces, I realized that in their estimation we really had saved them.

Mr. Dettermeier was getting frustrated—comically red-faced and annoyed. He began pounding on the podium, as close to the microphone as he could, with his fat little hand.

Fortunately his voice was bigger than his hand, or we would have been there until New Year's.

He boomed out, "Friends—friends!" They subsided. "Friends, I don't have to tell you this has been a tough year for us all. Things have been going from bad to worse for months and months; and when we shut down last Thursday, I guess most of us figured the party was about over—that it was time to put out the fire and call in the dogs."

He paused to let this hit home. Then he must have flashed them his biggest grin. Even from the wings, I could see his cheeks puffing out.

"But I'm serious: those of you who've been studying Spanish and planning to follow the machinery down to Ensenada had better call the airline and cancel your tickets. Prairie Machine is *staying in Minnesota*!

"And now, friends, I'd like you to give a big Larksdale welcome to . . ." He paused for effect and, pointing at the curtain behind him, punched out the words, "Prairie . . . Machine's . . . New . . . Owners!"

The band, apparently weary of the Gophers fight song, switched energetically to "On, Wisconsin!"—not exactly appropriate, but a much better tune.

And then, just on cue, the curtain rose to reveal the Larksdale Ladies lined up on the stage like some high-school basketball team.

The auditorium gradually became as silent as the forest after a snowstorm. The music and the cheering fell away together.

I didn't blame them. The silence was, in fact, one giant, unvocalized "huh?" There on the stage, the masters (or mistresses) of their destiny, were four housewives, two librarians, a grad student, and a hairdresser.

We could have inspired less confidence or more confusion only by putting Bozo the Clown at one end of the line and Barney the Dinosaur at the other.

Mr. Dettermeier, at the podium, just stood there stunned. He'd obviously expected a far different reaction and didn't know what to do next.

Which was when my mom saved the day.

She stepped to the microphone—raised it up to her height (she was about four inches taller than Mr. Dettermeier), and said into the silence, "I guess we surprised you. Um, we didn't mean to—but we planned this pretty quickly." She paused to see how they took it, then went on calmly, while sweeping her arm back to indicate the other Ladies.

"We had some good luck in investments over the past few years, and we decided that we couldn't make a better investment than Prairie Machine."

Well spoken, Mother! They were still mystified, but now they were flattered—and a little hopeful, too.

She went on: "But don't worry."

I recognized that voice. It was the "don't worry, sweetie, nobody ever died of a bee sting" voice. I'd been hearing it all my life.

"But don't worry—we won't be trying to run things. We found someone quite marvelous to do that." She smiled at them and smiled again toward the wings where Milt and I stood.

Then she faced them levelly and said, just a little more grandly, "He holds a law degree with highest honors from the University of Chicago—was the class valedictorian at the Wharton School of Business of the University of Pennsylvania—was the third-youngest partner in the history of McKinsey and Company." She paused and added with a little smile, "And as some of you know, he's also my daughter Sophia's old boyfriend."

I saw the color drain out of Milt's face.

Poor Milt. About thirty years from now, some spellbinding orator is going to stand before thirty thousand delegates to a Democratic National Convention and conclude a nominating speech, "Mistuh Chairman! I give you a statesman—a leader—the only Grand Slam winner of the Nobel Prize—the next President of the United States . . . and Sophia Peters's old boyfriend . . . Milton Daniel Gu-*reen*!"

Just then, as I shoved him out onto the stage, Milt Gu-reen looked ghostly pale.

He made it to the podium, but as he tried to raise the microphone, his hands were shaking. The noisy crowd quieted. He swallowed hard. In the quiet he got the microphone adjusted. By then he was back in control. He turned to Mom.

"Thank you, Mrs. Peters, for all those kind words."

Then, back to the workers.

"Those words should tell you I don't act on sentiment. I'm here because I've looked at the hard facts and figures and I think our potential is tremendous. I think we're going to do things together that will dazzle American business. I believe in Prairie Machine and I believe in *you*."

It was going over well. They were hardheaded, and they'd been kicked around, but they believed him.

He looked back out over the audience. "Now, Elizabeth, here"—he pointed to Mom—"mentioned Sophia." A glance toward me in the wings. "She's certainly my best friend. And she's one hundred percent Larksdale—and that's what I hope to be, too."

He leaned toward the microphone and said very clearly, "You see, yesterday Sophia made a very rare error in judgment. She—well, she agreed to marry me."

The place went nuts.

We had managed to restage a high-end leveraged buyout as a PTA meeting. But it was working—and that was everything.

It just couldn't get any cornier.

And then it got cornier.

Milt leaned still closer to the mike and, over the clapping and cheering, almost shouted, "So let's bring her out here right now. Ladies and gentlemen, how about a big Larksdale welcome for Prairie Machine's new Executive Vice-President and General Counsel—and my fiancée—Sophia . . . *Peters*!"

I was thinking I'd get him back for this if it took me twenty years.

But anything to make the deal. Head slightly bowed with embarrassment, blushing the color of a ripe plum, I'm sure, I stepped out from the wings and started for the podium. The stage lights made everything a glare.

Milt leaned toward me and whispered levelly, "Thank you."

I didn't really mind. It was my farewell to the American Theater, ending a career that had covered twenty-four years and (counting playing an apple tree) exactly two performances.

The crowd broke up, exiting to the Prairie Machine Band's zippy rendition of "New York, New York." At first I'd thought that was a cheap shot at Arcturis, which didn't deserve it; but I decided they really only had about three songs in their repertoire. Minnesotans don't take cheap shots.

Milt and Mr. Dettermeier had to chat for several minutes with several anxious middle managers, so Mom, Milt, and I were the last ones to leave the building. Mr. Dettermeier walked us to a back door, then closed it behind us, and suddenly we were alone, and the excitement was over.

The outside air was cold and still, and a very light snow, the kind you notice only when it brushes your lips or eyes, was falling. We had about a fifty-yard walk to the parking lot. We walked together, quite close, but silent.

We had covered perhaps half the distance, when I saw that a big figure—a looming shadow, really—lay under one of the aspens by the side of the path. I had scarcely cringed when it moved from the direct path of the overhead parking-lot light, and I saw it was my dad.

He took one step toward us as we took ten or more toward him. Milt and I were hanging back a little, so that Mom was nearest when he asked humbly, "Can I talk to you?"

Mom turned to me. "Honey?"

I looked to Milt, who nodded. "We'll get home okay."

We turned back for the building to call for a cab. At the last second I looked over my shoulder and saw Mom and Dad standing quietly talking out by her car. They were standing close together, and I couldn't hear their voices. From that, or from something, I knew everything was going to be okay.

It was just the PMT parking lot, with a handful of old small cars, but somehow it looked romantic. Like snow falling on Civics.

Happily Ever After

*T*hat was, in one way, the end of the Larksdale Ladies Independence Club.

The deal we finally structured was one for the record books. Arcturis loaned us almost half our down payment, and most of the rest came from State of Minnesota Economic Development Fund bonds. The Ladies put up only about $3 million.

When people ask about my part in the negotiations, I just say I drove the getaway car.

Prairie Machine earned $800,000 the first year we ran it; the next year, with the first NetLink systems shipping, it cleared $3 million after heavy expenses for software patents and marketing. Pretty soon it was making the Club so much money that scouting the countryside for promising little companies began to seem kind of pointless. We had more money than any of us needed—and besides, we now get fifteen or twenty business plans a day from entrepreneurs with proven records. Deborah thinks we should organize our own venture-capital company, and I'm looking into it.

*T*he Ladies, meanwhile, are finding themselves famous, with book deals, TV appearances, and all the golden rush of success.

It's stately, stylish Martha Crittenden who's caught the media's fancy: "She's like Martha Stewart on Medicare" as a local TV-talk-show host elegantly put it offscreen before one of her appearances. But the only Lady with any notable interest in, and talent for, producing business text is Deborah. With typical good sense, she's agreed to write the books and to let all the Ladies' names appear on them. As she told me—

"Fact is, kiddo, the only thing you get from getting older is getting practical. They want Martha to get most of the press? Okay, then Martha gets most of the press. They want everybody's names on the books? Fine by me. And ditto for anything else we can get out of this. Behind the scenes is just perfect."

Indeed, Deborah surprised us all. When a very bright and good-looking young editor from a big New York publisher took charge of the Larksdale Ladies projects, and Deborah had to make several trips to Manhattan to see to the details, we all got the strong impression the two of them were hitting it off. Of course, being Deb, she has her own special way of showing affection. One day I walked into her office just in time to hear her roar, "If you knew how to read, I might listen! As it is—how can you edit, if you can't fuckin' *read*!?" Then she slammed down the phone, turned to me, and sighed. "I'm in love." Only Deborah. She may not be the happily-ever-after type; but neither is she likely ever to die of boredom.

Deb's not alone in her literary—or romantic—pursuits. She's trying to persuade Mary to write *The Religious Woman's Guide to Wild Sex* and claims she could land her an agent in no time. But Mary takes teasing cheerfully these days: she just smiles and makes her same small joke about "why write it, when you can live it?"

Speaking of living, even Agnes has begun. No one will ever mistake her for Amelia Earhart; but with the help of her pal Inigo Stout, she's running her Children's Computer Center like a cross between Disneyland and a Microsoft demo lab. And last month she bought a rottweiler to keep her cat company. You've got to start somewhere.

Some just *might* mistake Gladys for Amelia Earhart. She made up with her family, and her nephews will have college money—but most of her fortune is headed elsewhere. Even the cats of Minneapolis will likewise have to survive on their own; after Judge Naycroft retires next month, he and she are taking off for an "Adventurer's" world tour.

Martha Crittenden had a hip replaced last year, and while the new one works just fine, she's become more stately than ever. She gave a million dollars to the St. Paul Chamber Orchestra, and they put her on the board. She spent another million or so to bring her fine old home up to snuff, including buying the house next door and leveling it for expanded gardens. She likes me to come to tea once a month or so, and I always go. She still scares the hell out of me.

Dolly's engaged to marry Harry Stensrup, a fine fellow she met at a Gophers Boosters club picnic. He was a lumberjack as a young man, then made a midsized fortune in construction. He's six-foot-three, probably weighs two-eighty (not much of it fat), and generally looks like a retired Viking warrior, except that he wears string ties and flannel shirts and sometimes great north hats with fur earflaps. He always holds the chair for Dolly when she sits, and stands when she leaves the table, and in between gazes at her like she's some rare, delicate flower—which, in her heart, I guess she is.

Skye bought a black Corvette and took off last week for Silicon Valley. She plans to start a software company that makes fun educational software for girls. She wants it to help them develop "scientific imaginations." Her burly friend Carter Armstrong is in as an investor, but Skye will run the show. I doubt she's wasted a day of her life since she spent those lonely evenings upstairs in Martha's house teaching herself Basic and C++ and a bunch of other software languages.

When Skye left, Martha stood on the curb near Skye's apartment and waved good-bye. Martha never cries, so I assume the hay-fever season started early this year.

Oh, and Skye didn't travel alone. Heidi went with her, bumming a ride to Stanford, where she starts law school in September.

We'll miss Heidi but we won't lack legal support. A certain huge software company is trying to knock off NetLink, so I've hired back my old pal Marcy to make them see reason. If they don't, I hope their legal department is good at the duck-and-cover. As for Marcy, nothing's wrong with her that a couple of years in Larksdale won't cure. Besides, she'll be working mostly for stock options, which is the way to get rich.

I ought to know.

Well, that's the story of the Larksdale Ladies Independence Club. It isn't often that everybody gets everything they want in this life; but it happens sometimes. Even Veronica Harris survived her ninety-day suspension and reclaimed her job (properly supervised) working for the Ladies. She'll probably never repay all the money but she's trying. Because I'm generally at Prairie Machine, she and I rarely see each other, but at Christmas we exchange cards—the really good ones.

As for me, Milt and I were married two years in June, and we've been making up for lost time. He runs behind the baby carriage in minus-ten-degree weather, and when I ask him if he minds the cold, he says, "I grew up in Brooklyn. Minnesota has winter? Please. It has cold snaps."

It never occurs to either of us to worry about the baby: she's probably the healthiest, cheeriest baby there ever was—and she has more surrogate grandmas than the average baby kibbutznik. We named her Elizabeth Stocks Green, first after her grandmother and then after what made her family rich. Our second is due in December, and we're likely to name him Reginald Options. Reggie O. sounds like a baseball player, which is fine with me.

Is this a great country, or what?